Explore the labyrinths of the illicit world
of mystery with writers of unparalleled skill

CRIMINAL ELEMENTS

Delve into a whirlwind of corruption and
double-dealing. . . .

Other Mystery Anthologies
Edited by Bill Pronzini and Martin H. Greenberg:

POLICE PROCEDURALS

WOMEN SLEUTHS

THE ETHNIC DETECTIVES

GREAT MODERN POLICE STORIES

PRIME SUSPECTS*

SUSPICIOUS CHARACTERS*

*Published by Ivy Books

CRIMINAL ELEMENTS

EDITED BY BILL PRONZINI AND MARTIN H. GREENBERG

IVY BOOKS • NEW YORK

Ivy Books
Published by Ballantine Books
Copyright © 1988 by Bill Pronzini & Martin H. Greenberg

ISBN-0-8041-0127-2

Manufactured in the United States of America

First Edition: March 1988

Acknowledgments

"Sadie When She Died," by Ed McBain. Copyright © 1972 by H.S.D. Publications, Inc. First published in *Alfred Hitchcock's Mystery Magazine*. Reprinted by permission of John Farquharson, Ltd.

"A Man With a Fortune," by Peter Lovesey. Copyright © 1980 by Bookclub Associates. First published as "How Mr. Smith Traced His Ancestors." Reprinted by permission of John Farquharson Ltd.

"She Didn't Come Home," by Sue Grafton. Copyright © 1985 by Sue Grafton. First published in *Redbook*. Reprinted by permission of the author.

"The Cross of Lorraine," by Isaac Asimov. Copyright © 1976 by Isaac Asimov. First published in *Ellery Queen's Mystery Magazine*. Reprinted by permission of the author.

"A Very Desirable Residence," by P. D. James. Copyright © 1976 by P. D. James. First published in *Winter's Crimes 8*. Reprinted by permission of Roberta Pryor Inc. and Elaine Greene Ltd. (England).

"The Witch, Yazzie, and the Nine of Clubs," by Tony Hillerman. Copyright © 1981 by the Swedish Academy of Detection. Reprinted by permission of the author.

"The Double Take," by Richard S. Prather. Copyright © 1953 by Flying Eagle Publications, Inc. First published in *Manhunt*. Reprinted by permission of the author and Richard Curtis Associates, Inc.

"Dust to Dust," by Marcia Muller. Copyright © 1982 by Marcia Muller. First published in *Specter!* Reprinted by permission of the author.

Acknowledgments

Contents

Introduction

The crime story has undergone numerous refinements and updatings during this century. It reflects its times perhaps better than any other form of popular writing, and therefore has not only flourished but has taken its rightful place as a major facet of world literature. Today its popularity is at an all-time high, owing in no small part to the growing number of innovative writers working to stretch the once-confining limits of the genre.

Prime Suspects is an anthology series designed to bring you some of the most unusual, finely crafted, and entertaining stories by these major crime-fiction specialists, and by important figures in other areas of popular literature. The first two volumes contain the work of such luminaries as Stephen King, Ruth Rendell, Loren D. Estleman, Donald E. Westlake, John Jakes, P. D. James, John D. MacDonald, Lawrence Block, Ed McBain, Isaac Asimov, Robert Bloch, Marcia Muller, Brian Garfield, Jonathan Gash, Simon Brett, Edward D. Hoch, Sara Paretsky, and John Lutz. In this third volume you'll find wholly different stories by McBain, James, Westlake, Asimov, and Muller, as well as first-rate tales by Peter Lovesey, Sue Grafton, Tony Hillerman, Richard S. Prather, Francis M. Nevins, Jr., Edward Gorman, Susan Dunlap, and Joseph Hansen.

Many of the authors listed above will appear in future entries in the series. As will Ellis Peters, Stephen Greenleaf, Stuart M. Kaminsky, Reginald Hill, Stanley Ellin, Harry Kemelman, Robert J. Randisi, and numerous others—most if not all of the very best practitioners of mystery and suspense fiction working today. Prime suspects, indeed!

Good reading.

—Bill Pronzini and
Martin H. Greenberg

Sadie When She Died

·

Ed McBain

Ed McBain has been one of the most versatile, popular, and critically celebrated writers of mainstream (under his real name, Evan Hunter) and crime fiction for more than thirty years. As McBain, he has published five mystery novels about Florida lawyer Matthew Hope, and several other criminous works under such pseudonyms as Richard Marsten, Hunt Collins, Ezra Hannon, and Curt Cannon. But it is for his some forty novels and one collection featuring the men (and, recently, women) of the 87th Precinct that he is best known in the mystery field. "Sadie When She Died" is just one good reason why the 87th Precinct stories have been so well received, and why they have been called the finest series of police procedurals ever written.

"I'm very glad she's dead," the man said.

He wore a homburg, muffler, overcoat, and gloves. He stood near the night table, a tall man with a narrow face, and a well-groomed gray mustache that matched the graying hair at his temples. His eyes were clear and blue and distinctly free of pain or grief.

Detective Steve Carella wasn't sure he had heard the man correctly. "Sir," Carella said, "I'm sure I don't have to tell you—"

"That's right," the man said, "you don't have to tell me. It happens I'm a criminal lawyer and am well aware of my

3

rights. My wife was no good, and I'm delighted someone killed her.''

Carella opened his pad. This was not what a bereaved husband was supposed to say when his wife lay disemboweled on the bedroom floor in a pool of her own blood.

''Your name is Gerald Fletcher.''

''That's correct.''

''Your wife's name, Mr. Fletcher?''

''Sarah. Sarah Fletcher.''

''Want to tell me what happened?''

''I got home about fifteen minutes ago. I called to my wife from the front door, and got no answer. I came into the bedroom and found her dead on the floor. I immediately called the police.''

''Was the room in this condition when you came in?''

''It was.''

''Touch anything?''

''Nothing. I haven't moved from this spot since I placed the call.''

''Anybody in here when you came in?''

''Not a soul. Except my wife, of course.''

''Is that your suitcase in the entrance hallway?''

''It is. I was on the coast for three days. An associate of mine needed advice on a brief he was preparing. What's your name?''

''Carella. Detective Steve Carella.''

''I'll remember that.''

While the police photographer was doing his macabre little jig around the body to make sure the lady looked good in the rushes, or as good as any lady *can* look in her condition, a laboratory assistant named Marshall Davies was in the kitchen of the apartment, waiting for the medical examiner to pronounce the lady dead, at which time Davies would go into the bedroom and with delicate care remove the knife protruding from the blood and slime of the lady, in an attempt to salvage some good latent prints from the handle of the murder weapon.

Davies was a new technician, but an observant one, and he noticed that the kitchen window was wide open, not exactly usual on a December night when the temperature outside hovered at twelve degrees. Leaning over the sink, he further noticed that the window opened onto a fire escape on the rear of the building. He could not resist speculating that perhaps someone had climbed up the fire escape and then into the kitchen.

Since there was a big muddy footprint in the kitchen sink, another one on the floor near the sink, and several others fading as they traveled across the waxed kitchen floor to the living room, Davies surmised that he was onto something hot. Wasn't it possible that an intruder *had* climbed over the window sill, into the sink, and walked across the room, bearing the switchblade knife that had later been pulled viciously across the lady's abdomen from left to right? If the M.E. ever got through with the damn body, the boys of the 87th would be halfway home, thanks to Marshall Davies. He felt pretty good.

The three points of the triangle were Detective-Lieutenant Byrnes, and Detectives Meyer Meyer and Steve Carella. Fletcher sat in a chair, still wearing homburg, muffler, overcoat, and gloves as if he expected to be called outdoors at any moment. The interrogation was being conducted in a windowless cubicle labeled Interrogation Room.

The cops standing in their loose triangle around Gerald Fletcher were amazed but not too terribly amused by his brutal frankness.

"I hated her guts," he said.

"Mr. Fletcher," Lieutenant Byrnes said, "I *still* feel I must warn you that a woman has been murdered—"

"Yes. My dear, wonderful wife," Fletcher said sarcastically.

". . . which is a serious crime . . ." Byrnes felt tongue-tied in Fletcher's presence. Bullet-headed, hair turning from iron-gray to ice-white, blue-eyed, built like a compact linebacker, Byrnes looked to his colleagues for support. Both Meyer and Carella were watching their shoelaces.

"You have warned me repeatedly," Fletcher said. "I can't imagine why. My wife is dead—someone killed her—but it was not I."

"Well, it's nice to have your assurance of that, Mr. Fletcher, but this alone doesn't necessarily still our doubts," Carella said, hearing the words and wondering where the hell they were coming from. He was, he realized, trying to impress Fletcher. He continued, "How do we know it *wasn't* you who stabbed her?"

"To begin with," Fletcher said, "there were signs of forcible entry in the kitchen and hasty departure in the bedroom; witness the wide-open window in the aforementioned room and the shattered window in the latter. The drawers in the dining-room sideboard were open—"

"You're very observant," Meyer said suddenly. "Did you notice all this in the four minutes it took you to enter the apartment and call the police?"

"It's my *job* to be observant," Fletcher said. "But to answer your question, no. I noticed all this *after* I had spoken to Detective Carella here."

Wearily, Byrnes dismissed Fletcher who then left the room.

"What do you think?" Byrnes said.

"I think he did it," Carella said.

"Even with all those signs of a burglary?"

"*Especially* with those signs. He could have come home, found his wife stabbed—but not fatally—and finished her off

6

by yanking the knife across her belly. Fletcher had four minutes, when all he needed was maybe four seconds."

"It's possible," Meyer said.

"Or maybe I just don't like the guy," Carella said.

"Let's see what the lab comes up with," Byrnes said.

The laboratory came up with good fingerprints on the kitchen window sash and on the silver drawer of the dining-room sideboard. There were good prints on some of the pieces of silver scattered on the floor near the smashed bedroom window. Most important, there were good prints on the handle of the switchblade knife. The prints matched; they had all been left by the same person.

Gerald Fletcher graciously allowed the police to take *his* fingerprints, which were then compared with those Marshall Davies had sent over from the police laboratory. The fingerprints on the window sash, the drawer, the silverware, and the knife did not match Gerald Fletcher's.

Which didn't mean a damn thing if he had been wearing his gloves when he'd finished her off.

On Monday morning, in the second-floor rear apartment of 721 Silvermine Oval, a chalked outline on the bedroom floor was the only evidence that a woman had lain there in death the night before. Carella sidestepped the outline and looked out the shattered window at the narrow alleyway below. There was a distance of perhaps twelve feet between this building and the one across from it.

Conceivably, the intruder could have leaped across the shaftway, but this would have required premeditation and calculation. The more probable likelihood was that the intruder had fallen to the pavement below.

"That's quite a long drop," Detective Bert Kling said, peering over Carella's shoulder.

"How far do you figure?" Carella asked.

"Thirty feet. At least."

"Got to break a leg taking a fall like that. You think he went through the window headfirst?"

"How else?"

"He might have broken the glass out first, then gone through," Carella suggested.

"If he was about to go to all that trouble, why didn't he just *open* the damn thing?"

"Well, let's take a look," Carella said.

They examined the latch and the sash. Kling grabbed both handles on the window frame and pulled up on them. "Stuck."

"Probably painted shut," Carella said.

"Maybe he *did* try to open it. Maybe he smashed it only when he realized it was stuck."

"Yeah," Carella said. "And in a big hurry, too. Fletcher was opening the front door, maybe already in the apartment by then."

"The guy probably had a bag or something with him, to put the loot in. He must have taken a wild swing with the bag when he realized the window was stuck, and maybe some of the stuff fell out, which would explain the silverware on the floor. Then he probably climbed through the hole and dropped down feet first. In fact, what he could've done, Steve, was drop the bag down first, and *then* climbed out and hung from the sill before he jumped, to make it a shorter distance."

"I don't know if he had all that much time, Bert. He must have heard that front door opening, and Fletcher coming in and calling to his wife. Otherwise, he'd have taken his good, sweet time and gone out the kitchen window and down the fire escape, the way he'd come in."

Kling nodded reflectively. "Let's take a look at that alley," Carella said.

In the alleyway outside, Carella and Kling studied the concrete pavement, and then looked up at the shattered second-floor window of the Fletcher apartment.

"Where do you suppose he'd have landed?" Kling said.

"Right about where we're standing." Carella looked at the ground. "I don't know, Bert. A guy drops twenty feet to a concrete pavement, doesn't break anything, gets up, dusts himself off, and runs the fifty-yard dash, right?" Carella shook his head. "My guess is he stayed right where he was to catch his breath, giving Fletcher time to look out the window, which would be the natural thing to do, but which Fletcher didn't."

"He was anxious to call the police."

"I still think he did it."

"Steve, be reasonable. If a guy's fingerprints are on the handle of a knife, and the knife is still in the victim—"

"*And* if the victim's husband realizes what a sweet setup he's stumbled into, wife lying on the floor with a knife in her, place broken into and burglarized, why *not* finish the job and hope the burglar will be blamed?"

"Sure," Kling said. "Prove it."

"I can't," Carella said. "Not until we catch the burglar."

While Carella and Kling went through the tedious routine of retracing the burglar's footsteps, Marshall Davies called the 87th Precinct and got Detective Meyer.

"I think I've got some fairly interesting information about the suspect," Davies said. "He left latent fingerprints all over the apartment and footprints in the kitchen. A very good one in the sink, when he climbed in through the window, and some middling-fair ones tracking across the kitchen floor to the dining room. I got some excellent pictures and some good blowups of the heel."

"Good," Meyer said.

"But more important," Davies went on, "I got a good walking picture from the footprints on the floor. If a man is walking slowly, the distance between his footprints is usually about twenty-seven inches. Forty for running, thirty-five for fast walking. These were thirty-two inches. So we have a man's usual gait, moving quickly, but not in a desperate hurry, with the walking line normal and not broken.''

''What does that mean?''

''Well, a walking line should normally run along the inner edge of a man's heel prints. Incidentally, the size and type of shoe and angle of the foot clearly indicate that this *was* a man.''

''O.K., fine,'' Meyer said. He did not thus far consider Davies' information valuable nor even terribly important.

''Anyway, none of this is valuable nor even terribly important,'' Davies said, ''until we consider the rest of the data. The bedroom window was smashed, and the Homicide men were speculating that the suspect had jumped through the window into the alley below. I went down to get some meaningful pictures, and got some pictures of where he must have landed—on both feet, incidentally—and I got another walking picture and direction line. He moved toward the basement door and into the basement. But the important thing is that our man is injured, and I think badly.''

''How do you know?'' Meyer asked.

''The walking picture downstairs is entirely different from the one in the kitchen. When he got downstairs he was leaning heavily on the left leg and dragging the right. I would suggest that whoever's handling the case put out a physicians' bulletin. If this guy hasn't got a broken leg, I'll eat the pictures I took.''

A girl in a green coat was waiting in the apartment lobby when Carella and Kling came back in, still retracing footsteps, or trying to. The girl said, ''Excuse me, are you the detectives?''

''Yes,'' Carella said.

10

"The super told me you were in the building," the girl said. "You're investigating the Fletcher murder, aren't you?" She was quite soft spoken.

"How can we help you, miss?" Carella asked.

"I saw somebody in the basement last night, with blood on his clothes."

Carella glanced at Kling and immediately said, "What time was this?"

"About a quarter to eleven," the girl said.

"What were you doing in the basement?"

The girl looked surprised.

"That's where the washing machines are. I'm sorry, my name is Selma Bernstein. I live here in the building."

"Tell us what happened, will you?" Carella said.

"I was sitting by the machine, watching the clothes tumble, which is simply *fascinating*, you know, when the door leading to the backyard opened—the door to the alley. This man came down the stairs, and I don't even think he saw me. He went straight for the stairs at the other end, the ones that go up into the street. I never saw him before last night."

"Can you describe him?" Carella asked.

"Sure. He was about twenty-one or twenty-two, your height and weight, well, maybe a little bit shorter, five ten or eleven, brown hair."

Kling was already writing. The man was white, wore dark trousers, high-topped sneakers, and a poplin jacket with blood on the right sleeve and on the front. He carried a small red bag, "like one of those bags the airlines give you."

Selma didn't know if he had any scars. "He went by in pretty much of a hurry, considering he was dragging his right leg. I think he was hurt pretty badly."

What they had in mind, of course, was identification from a mug shot, but the I.S. reported that none of the fingerprints in their file matched the ones found in the apartment. So the detectives figured it was going to be a tough one, and they sent out a bulletin to all of the city's doctors just to prove it.

Just to prove that cops can be as wrong as anyone else, it turned out to be a nice easy one after all.

The call came from a physician in Riverhead at 4:37 that afternoon, just as Carella was ready to go home.

"This is Dr. Mendelsohn," he said. "I have your bulletin here, and I want to report treating a man early this morning who fits your description—a Ralph Corwin of 894 Woodside in Riverhead. He had a bad ankle sprain."

"Thank you, Dr. Mendelsohn," Carella said.

Carella pulled the Riverhead directory from the top drawer of his desk and quickly flipped to the C's. He did not expect to find a listing for Ralph Corwin. A man would have to be a rank amateur to burglarize an apartment without wearing gloves, then stab a woman to death, and then give his name when seeking treatment for an injury sustained in escaping from the murder apartment.

Ralph Corwin was apparently a rank amateur. His name was in the phone book, and he'd given the doctor his correct address.

Carella and Kling kicked in the door without warning, fanning into the room, guns drawn. The man on the bed was wearing only undershorts. His right ankle was taped.

"Are you Ralph Corwin?" Carella asked.

"Yes," the man said. His face was drawn, the eyes in pain.

"Get dressed, Corwin. We want to ask you some questions."

"There's nothing to ask," he said and turned his head into the pillow. "I killed her."

Ralph Corwin made his confession in the presence of two detectives of the 87th, a police stenographer, an assistant district attorney, and a lawyer appointed by the Legal Aid Society.

Corwin was the burglar. He'd entered 721 Silvermine Oval on Sunday night, December twelfth, down the steps from the street where the garbage cans were. He went through the basement, up the steps at the other end, into the backyard, and climbed the fire escape, all at about ten o'clock in the evening. Corwin entered the Fletcher apartment because it was the first one he saw without lights. He figured there was nobody home. The kitchen window was open a tiny crack; Corwin squeezed his fingers under the bottom and opened it all the way. He was pretty desperate at the time because he was a junkie in need of cash. He swore that he'd never done anything like this before.

The man from the D.A.'s office was conducting the Q. and A. and asked Corwin if he hadn't been afraid of fingerprints, not wearing gloves. Corwin figured that was done only in the movies, and anyway, he said, he didn't own gloves.

Corwin used a tiny flashlight to guide him as he stepped into the sink and down to the floor. He made his way to the dining room, emptied the drawer of silverware into his airline bag. Then he looked for the bedroom, scouting for watches and rings, whatever he could take in the way of jewelry. "I'm not a pro," he said. "I was just hung up real bad and needed some bread to tide me over."

Now came the important part. The D.A.'s assistant asked Corwin what happened in the bedroom.

A. There was a lady in bed. This was only like close to ten-thirty, you don't expect nobody to be asleep so early.

Q. But there was a woman in bed.

A. Yeah. She turned on the light the minute I stepped in the room.

Q. What did you do?

A. I had a knife in my pocket. I pulled it out to scare her.

13

It was almost comical. She looks at me and says, "What are you doing here?"

Q. Did you say anything to her?

A. I told her to keep quiet, that I wasn't going to hurt her. But she got out of bed and I saw she was reaching for the phone. That's got to be crazy, right? A guy is standing there in your bedroom with a knife in his hand, so she reaches for the phone.

Q. What did you do?

A. I grabbed her hand before she could get it. I pulled her off the bed, away from the phone, you know? And I told her again that nobody was going to hurt her, that I was getting out of there right away, to just please calm down.

Q. What happened next?

A. She started to scream. I told her to stop. I was beginning to panic. I mean she was really yelling.

Q. Did she stop?

A. No.

Q. What did you do?

A. I stabbed her.

Q. Where did you stab her?

A. I don't know. It was a reflex. She was yelling. I was afraid the whole building would come down. I just . . . I just stuck the knife in her. I was very scared. I stabbed her in the belly. Someplace in the belly.

Q. How many times did you stab her?

A. Once. She . . . she backed away from me. I'll never forget the look on her face. And she . . . she fell on the floor.

Q. Would you look at this photograph, please?

A. Oh, no . . .

Q. Is that the woman you stabbed?

A. Oh, no . . . I didn't think . . . Oh, no!

A moment after he stabbed Sarah Fletcher, Corwin heard the door opening and someone coming in. The man yelled, "Sarah, it's me, I'm home." Corwin ran past Sarah's body on the floor and tried to open the window, but it was stuck. He smashed it with his airline bag, threw the bag out first to save the swag because, no matter what, he knew he'd need another fix, and he climbed through the broken window, cutting his hand on a piece of glass. He hung from the sill, and finally let go, dropping to the ground. He tried to get up, and fell down again. His ankle was killing him, his hand bleeding. He stayed in the alley nearly fifteen minutes, then finally escaped via the route Selma Bernstein had described to Carella and Kling. He took the train to Riverhead and got to Dr. Mendelsohn at about nine in the morning. He read of Sarah Fletcher's murder in the newspaper on the way back from the doctor.

On Tuesday, December 14, which was the first of Carella's two days off that week, he received a call at home from Gerald Fletcher. Fletcher told the puzzled Carella that he'd gotten his number from a friend in the D.A.'s office, complimented Carella and the boys of the 87th on their snappy detective work, and invited Carella to lunch at the Golden Lion at one o'clock. Carella wasn't happy about interrupting his Christmas shopping, but this was an unusual opportunity, and he accepted.

Most policemen in the city for which Carella worked did not eat very often in restaurants like the Golden Lion. Carella had never been inside. A look at the menu posted on the window outside would have frightened him out of six month's pay. The place was a faithful replica of the dining room of an English coach house, circa 1627: huge oaken beams, immaculate white cloths, heavy silver.

Gerald Fletcher's table was in a secluded corner of the restaurant. He rose as Carella approached, extended his hand, and said, "Glad you could make it. Sit down, won't you?"

Carella shook Fletcher's hand, and then sat. He felt extremely uncomfortable, but he couldn't tell whether his discomfort was caused by the room or by the man with whom he was dining.

"Would you care for a drink?" Fletcher asked.

"Well, are you having one?" Carella asked.

"Yes, I am."

"I'll have a scotch and soda," Carella said. He was not used to drinking at lunch.

Fletcher signaled the waiter and ordered the drinks, making his another whiskey sour.

When the drinks came, Fletcher raised his glass. "Here's to a conviction," he said.

Carella lifted his own glass. "I don't expect there'll be any trouble," he said. "It looks airtight to me."

Both men drank. Fletcher dabbed his lips with a napkin and said, "You never can tell these days. I hope you're right, though." He sipped at the drink. "I must admit I feel a certain amount of sympathy for him."

"Do you?"

"Yes. If he's an addict, he's automatically entitled to pity. And when one considers that the woman he murdered was nothing but a—"

"Mr. Fletcher . . ."

"Gerry, please. And I know: it isn't very kind of me to malign the dead. I'm afraid you didn't know my wife, though, Mr. Carella. May I call you Steve?"

"Sure."

"My enmity might be a bit more understandable if you had. Still, I shall take your advice. She's dead, and no longer capable of hurting me, so why be bitter. Shall we order, Steve?"

Fletcher suggested that Carella try either the trout *au meuniere* or the beef and kidney pie, both of which were excellent. Carella ordered prime ribs, medium rare, and a mug of beer.

As the men ate and talked, something began happening,

or at least Carella *thought* something was happening; he might never be quite sure. The conversation with Fletcher seemed on the surface to be routine chatter, but rushing through this inane, polite discussion was an undercurrent that caused excitement, fear, and apprehension. As they spoke, Carella knew with renewed certainty that Gerald Fletcher had killed his wife. Without ever being told so, he knew it. *This* was why Fletcher had called this morning; *this* was why Fletcher had invited him to lunch; *this* was why he prattled on endlessly while every contradictory move of his body signaled on an almost extrasensory level that he *knew* Carella suspected him of murder, and was here to *tell* Carella (*without* telling him) that, "Yes, you stupid cop, I killed my wife. However much the evidence may point to another man, however many confessions you get, I killed her and I'm glad I killed her. And there isn't a damn thing you can do about it."

Ralph Corwin was being held before trial in the city's oldest prison, known to law enforcers and lawbreakers alike as Calcutta. Neither Corwin's lawyer nor the district attorney's office felt that allowing Carella to talk to the prisoner would be harmful to the case.

Corwin was expecting him. "What did you want to see me about?"

"I wanted to ask you some questions."

"My lawyer says I'm not supposed to add anything to what I already said. I don't even *like* that guy."

"Why don't you ask for another lawyer? Ask one of the officers here to call the Legal Aid Society. Or simply tell him. I'm sure he'd have no objection to dropping out."

Corwin shrugged. "I don't want to hurt his feelings. He's a little cockroach, but what the hell."

"You've got a lot at stake here, Corwin."

"But I killed her, so what does it matter *who* the lawyer is? You got it all in black and white."

"You feel like answering some questions?" Carella said.

"I feel like dropping dead, is what I feel like. Cold turkey's never good, and it's worse when you can't yell."

"If you'd rather I came back another time . . ."

"No, no, go ahead. What do you want to know?"

"I want to know exactly how you stabbed Sarah Fletcher."

"How do you *think* you stab somebody? You stick a knife in her."

"Where?"

"In the belly."

"Left-hand side of the body?"

"Yeah. I guess so."

"Where was the knife when she fell?"

"I don't know what you mean."

"Was the knife on the *right*-hand side of her body or the *left*?"

"I don't know. That was when I heard the front door opening and all I could think of was getting out of there."

"When you stabbed her, did she *twist* away from you?"

"No, she backed away, straight back, as if she couldn't believe what I done, and . . . and just wanted to get *away* from me."

"And then she fell?"

"Yes. She . . . her knees sort of gave way and she grabbed for her belly, and her hands sort of—it was terrible—they just . . . they were grabbing *air*, you know? And she fell."

"In what position?"

"On her side."

"*Which* side?"

"I could still see the knife, so it must've been the opposite side. The side opposite from where I stabbed her."

"One last question, Ralph. Was she dead when you went through that window?"

"I don't know. She was bleeding and . . . she was very quiet. I . . . guess she was dead. I don't know. I guess so."

Among Sarah Fletcher's personal effects that were considered of interest to the police before they arrested Ralph Corwin was an address book found in the dead woman's handbag on the bedroom dresser. In the Thursday afternoon stillness of the squad room, Carella examined the book.

There was nothing terribly fascinating about the alphabetical listings. Sarah Fletcher had possessed a good handwriting, and most of the listings were obviously married couples (Chuck and Nancy Benton, Harold and Marie Spander, and so on), some were girlfriends, local merchants, hairdresser, dentist, doctors, restaurants in town or across the river. A thoroughly uninspiring address book—until Carella came to a page at the end of the book, with the printed word MEMORANDA at its top.

Under the word, there were five names, addresses, and telephone numbers written in Sarah's meticulous hand. They were all men's names, obviously entered at different times because some were in pencil and others in ink. The parenthetical initials following each entry were all noted in felt marking pens of various colors:

Andrew Hart, 1120 Hall Avenue, 622-8400 (PB&G) (TG)
Michael Thornton, 371 South Lindner, 881-9371 (TS)
Lou Kantor, 434 North 16 Street, FR 7-2346 (TPC) (TG)
Sal Decotto, 831 Grover Avenue, FR 5-3287 (F) (TG)
Richard Fenner, 110 Henderson, 593-6648 (QR) (TG)

If there was one thing Carella loved, it was a code. He loved a code almost as much as he loved German measles. He flipped through the phone book, and the address for Andrew Hart matched the one in Sarah's handwriting. He found an address for Michael Thornton. It, too, was identical to the one in her book. He kept turning pages in the directory, checking names and addresses. He verified all five.

At a little past eight the next morning, Carella got going on them. He called Andrew Hart at the number listed in Sarah's address book. Hart answered, and was not happy. "I'm in the middle of shaving," he said. "I've got to leave for the office in a little while. What's this about?"

"We're investigating a homicide, Mr. Hart."

"A *what*? A homicide? Who's been killed?"

"A woman named Sarah Fletcher."

"I don't know anyone named Sarah Fletcher," he said.

"S..e seems to have known you, Mr. Hart."

"Sarah *who*? Fletcher, did you say?" Hart's annoyance increased.

"That's right."

"I don't know anybody by that name. Who says she knew me? I never heard of her in my life."

"Your name's in her address book."

"*My* name? That's impossible."

Nevertheless, Hart agreed to see Carella and Meyer at the office of Hart and Widderman, 480 Reed Street, sixth floor, at ten o'clock that morning.

At ten, Meyer and Carella parked the car and went into the building at 480 Reed, and up the elevator to the sixth floor. Hart and Widderman manufactured watchbands. A huge advertising display near the receptionist's desk in the lobby proudly proclaimed "H&W Beats the Band!" and then backed the slogan with more discreet copy that explained how Hart and Widderman had solved the difficult engineering problems of the expansion watch bracelet.

"Mr. Hart, please," Carella said.

"Who's calling?" the receptionist asked. She sounded as if she were chewing gum, even though she was not.

"Detectives Carella and Meyer."

"Just a minute, please," she said, and lifted her phone,

pushing a button in the base. "Mr. Hart," she said, "there are some cops here to see you." She listened for a moment and then said, "Yes, sir." She replaced the receiver on its cradle, gestured toward the inside corridor with a nod of her golden tresses, said, "Go right in, please. Door at the end of the hall," and then went back to her magazine.

The gray skies had apparently infected Andrew Hart. "You didn't have to broadcast to the world that the police department was here," he said immediately.

"We merely announced ourselves," Carella said.

"Well, O.K., now you're here," Hart said, "let's get it over with." He was a big man in his middle fifties, with iron-gray hair and black-rimmed eyeglasses. "I told you I don't know Sarah Fletcher and I don't."

"Here's her book, Mr. Hart," Carella said. "That's your name, isn't it?"

"Yeah," Hart said, and shook his head. "But how it got there is beyond me."

"Is it possible she's someone you met at a party, someone you exchanged numbers with?"

"No."

"Are you married, Mr. Hart?"

"No."

"We've got a picture of Mrs. Fletcher. I wonder—"

"Don't go showing me any pictures of a corpse," Hart said.

"This was taken when she was still very much alive, Mr. Hart."

Meyer handed Carella a manila envelope. He opened the flap and removed from the envelope a framed picture of Sarah Fletcher, which he handed to Hart. Hart looked at the photograph, and then immediately looked up at Carella.

"What is this?" he said. He looked at the photograph again, shook his head, and said, "Somebody killed her, huh?"

"Yes, somebody did," Carella answered. "Did you know her?"

"I knew her."

"I thought you said you didn't."

"I didn't know Sarah Fletcher, if that's who you think she was. But I knew *this* broad, all right."

"Who'd *you* think she was?" Meyer asked.

"Just who she told me she was. Sadie Collins. She introduced herself as Sadie Collins, and that's who I knew her as. Sadie Collins."

"Where was this, Mr. Hart? Where'd you meet her?"

"A singles bar. The city's full of them."

"Would you remember when?"

"At least a year ago."

"Ever go out with her?"

"I used to see her once or twice a week."

"When did you stop seeing her?"

"Last summer."

"Did you know she was married?"

"Who, Sadie? You're kidding."

"She never told you she was married?"

"Never."

Meyer asked, "When you were going out, where'd you pick her up? At her apartment?"

"No. She used to come to my place."

"Where'd you call her when you wanted to reach her?"

"I didn't. She used to call me."

"Where'd you go, Mr. Hart? When you went out?"

"We didn't go out too much."

"What *did* you do?"

"She used to come to my place. The truth is, we never went out. She didn't want to go out much."

"Didn't you think that was strange?"

"No," Hart shrugged. "I figured she liked to stay home."

"Why'd you stop seeing her, Mr. Hart?"

"I met somebody else. A nice girl. I'm very serious about her."

"Was there something wrong with Sadie?"

"No, no. She was a beautiful woman, beautiful."

"Then why would you be ashamed—"

"Ashamed? Who said anything about being ashamed?"

"I gathered you wouldn't want your girl friend—"

"Listen, what *is* this? I stopped seeing Sadie six months ago. I wouldn't even talk to her on the phone after that. If the crazy babe got herself killed—"

"Crazy?"

Hart suddenly wiped his hand over his face, wet his lips and walked behind his desk. "I don't think I have anything more to say to you gentlemen."

"What did you mean by crazy?" Carella asked.

"Good day, gentlemen," Hart said.

Carella went to see Lieutenant Byrnes. In the lieutenant's corner office, Byrnes and Carella sat down over coffee. Byrnes frowned at Carella's request.

"Oh, come on, Pete!" Carella said. "If Fletcher *did* it—"

"That's only *your* allegation. Suppose he *didn't* do it, and suppose *you* do something to screw up the D.A.'s case?"

"Like what?"

"I don't know like what. The way things are going these days, if you spit on the sidewalk, that's enough to get a case thrown out of court."

"Fletcher hated his wife," Carella said calmly.

"Lots of men hate their wives. Half the men in this city hate their wives."

"But her little fling gives Fletcher a good reason for . . . Look, Pete, he had a motive; he had the opportunity, a golden one, in fact; and he had the means—another man's knife sticking in Sarah's belly. What more do you want?"

"Proof. There's a funny little system we've got here—it

requires proof before we can arrest a man and charge him with murder.''

"Right. And all I'm asking is the opportunity to *try* for it.''

"Sure, by putting a tail on Fletcher. Suppose he sues the city?''

"Yes or no, Pete? I want permission to conduct a round-the-clock surveillance of Gerald Fletcher, starting Sunday morning. Yes or no?''

"I must be out of my mind,'' Byrnes said, and sighed.

Michael Thornton lived in an apartment building several blocks from the Quarter, close enough to absorb some of its artistic flavor, distant enough to escape its high rents. A blond man in his apartment, Paul Wendling, told Kling and Meyer that Mike was in his jewelry shop.

In the shop, Thornton was wearing a blue work smock, but the contours of the garment did nothing to hide his powerful build. His eyes were blue, his hair black. A small scar showed white in the thick eyebrow over his left eye.

"We understand you're working,'' Meyer said. "Sorry to break in on you this way.''

"That's O.K.,'' Thornton said. "What's up?''

"You know a woman named Sarah Fletcher?''

"No,'' Thornton said.

"You know a woman named Sadie Collins?''

Thornton hesitated. "Yes,'' he said.

"What was your relationship with her?'' Kling asked.

Thornton shrugged. "Why? Is she in trouble?''

"When's the last time you saw her?''

"You didn't answer my question,'' Thornton said.

"Well, you didn't answer ours either,'' Meyer said, and smiled. "What was your relationship with her, and when did you see her last?''

"I met her in July, in a joint called The Saloon, right

around the corner. It's a bar, but they also serve sandwiches and soup. It gets a big crowd on weekends, singles, a couple of odd ones for spice—but not a gay bar. I saw her last in August, a brief, hot thing, and then goodbye.''

"Did you realize she was married?" Kling said.

"No. Is she?"

"Yes," Meyer said. Neither of the detectives had yet informed Thornton that the lady in question was now unfortunately deceased. They were saving that for last, like dessert.

"Gee, I didn't know she was married." Thornton seemed truly surprised. "Otherwise, nothing would've happened."

"What *did* happen?"

"I bought her a few drinks and then I took her home with me. Later, I put her in a cab."

"When did you see her next?"

"The following day. It was goofy. She called me in the morning, said she was on her way downtown. I was still in bed. I said, 'So come on down, baby.' And she did. *Believe* me, she did."

"Did you see her again after that?" Kling asked.

"Two or three times a week."

"Where'd you go?"

"To my pad on South Lindner."

"Never went anyplace but there?"

"Never."

"Why'd you quit seeing her?"

"I went out of town for a while. When I got back, I just didn't hear from her again. She never gave me her number, and she wasn't in the directory, so I couldn't reach her."

"What do you make of this?" Kling asked, handing Thornton the address book.

Thornton studied it and said, "Yes, what about it? She wrote this down the night we met—we were in bed, and she asked my address."

"Did she write those initials at the same time, the ones in parentheses under your phone number?"

"I didn't actually see the page itself, I only saw her writing in the book."

"Got any idea what the initials mean?"

"None at all." Suddenly he looked thoughtful. "She *was* kind of special, I have to admit it." He grinned. "She'll call again, I'm sure of it."

"I wouldn't count on it," Meyer said. "She's dead."

His face did not crumble or express grief or shock. The only thing it expressed was sudden anger. "The stupid . . ." Thornton said. "That's all she ever was, a stupid, crazy . . ."

On Sunday morning, Carella was ready to become a surveillant, but Gerald Fletcher was nowhere in sight. A call to his apartment from a nearby phone booth revealed that he was not in his digs. He parked in front of Fletcher's apartment building until five P.M. when he was relieved by Detective Arthur Brown. Carella went home to read his son's latest note to Santa Claus, had dinner with his family, and was settling down in the living room with a novel he had bought a week ago and not yet cracked, when the telephone rang.

"Hello?" Carella said into the mouthpiece.

"Hello, Steve? This is Gerry. Gerry Fletcher."

Carella almost dropped the receiver. "How are you?"

"Fine, thanks. I was away for the weekend, just got back a little while ago, in fact. Frankly I find this apartment depressing as hell. I was wondering if you'd like to join me for a drink."

"Well," Carella said. "It's Sunday night, and it's late . . ."

"Nonsense, it's only eight o'clock. We'll do a little old-fashioned pub crawling."

It suddenly occurred to Carella that Gerald Fletcher had already had a few drinks before placing his call. It further

26

occurred to him that if he played this *too* cozily, Fletcher might rescind his generous offer.

"Okay. I'll see you at eight-thirty, provided I can square it with my wife."

"Good," Fletcher said. "See you."

Paddy's Bar and Grill was on the Stem, adjacent to the city's theater district. Carella and Fletcher got there at about nine o'clock while the place was still relatively quiet. The action began a little later, Fletcher explained.

Fletcher lifted his glass in a silent toast. "What kind of person would you say comes to a place like this?"

"I would say we've got a nice lower-middle-class clientele bent on making contact with members of the opposite sex."

"What would you say if I told you the blonde in the clinging jersey is a working prostitute?"

Carella looked at the woman. "I don't think I'd believe you. She's a bit old for the young competition, and she's not *selling* anything. She's waiting for one of those two or three older guys to make their move. Hookers don't wait, Gerry. *Is* she a working prostitute?"

"I haven't the faintest idea," Fletcher said. "I was merely trying to indicate that appearances can sometimes be misleading. Drink up, there are a few more places I'd like to show you."

He knew Fletcher well enough by now to realize that the man was trying to tell him something. At lunch last Tuesday, Fletcher had transmitted a message and a challenge: *I killed my wife, what can you do about it?* Tonight, in a similar manner, he was attempting to indicate something else, but Carella could not fathom exactly what.

Fanny's was only twenty blocks away from Paddy's Bar and Grill, but as far removed from it as the moon. Whereas the first bar seemed to cater to a quiet crowd peacefully pursuing its romantic inclinations, Fanny's was noisy and rau-

27

cous, jammed to the rafters with men and women of all ages wearing plastic hippie gear purchased in head shops up and down Jackson Avenue.

Fletcher lifted his glass. "I hope you don't mind if I drink myself into a stupor," he said. "Merely pour me into the car at the end of the night." Fletcher drank. "I don't usually consume this much alcohol, but I'm very troubled about that boy."

"What boy?" Carella asked.

"Ralph Corwin," Fletcher said. "I understand he's having some difficulty with his lawyer and, well, I'd like to help him somehow."

"*Help* him?"

"Yes. Do you think the D.A.'s office would consider it strange if I suggested a good defense lawyer for the boy?"

"I think they might consider it passing strange, yes."

"Do I detect a note of sarcasm in your voice?"

"Not at all."

Fletcher squired Carella from Fanny's to, in geographical order, The Purple Chairs and Quigley's Rest. Each place was rougher, in its way, than the last. The Purple Chairs catered to a brazenly gay crowd, and Quigley's Rest was a dive, where Fletcher's liquor caught up with him, and the evening ended suddenly in a brawl. Carella was shaken by the experience, and still couldn't piece out Fletcher's reasons.

Carella received a further shock when he continued to pursue Sarah Fletcher's address book. Lou Kantor was simply the third name in a now wearying list of Sarah's bedmates, until she turned out to be a tough and striking woman. She confirmed Carella's suspicions immediately.

"I only knew her a short while," she said. "I met her in September, I believe. Saw her three or four times after that."

"Where'd you meet her?"

"In a bar called The Purple Chairs. That's right," she added quickly. "That's what I am."

"Nobody asked," Carella said. "What about Sadie Collins?"

"Spell it out, Officer, I'm not going to help you. I don't like being hassled."

"Nobody's hassling you, Miss Kantor. You practice your religion and I'll practice mine. We're here to talk about a dead woman."

"Then talk about her, spit it out. What do you want to know? Was she straight? Everybody's straight until they're *not* straight anymore, isn't that right? She was willing to learn. I taught her."

"Did you know she was married?"

"She told me. So what? Broke down in tears one night, and spent the rest of the night crying. I knew she was married."

"What'd she say about her husband?"

"Nothing that surprised me. She said he had another woman. Said he ran off to see her every weekend, told little Sadie he had out-of-town business. *Every* weekend, can you imagine that?"

"What do you make of this?" Carella said, and handed her Sarah's address book, opened to the MEMORANDA page.

"I don't know any of these people," Lou said.

"The initials under your name," Carella said. "TPC and then TG. Got any ideas?"

"Well, the TPC is obvious, isn't it? I met her at The Purple Chairs. What else could it mean?"

Carella suddenly felt very stupid. "Of course. What else could it mean?" He took back the book. "I'm finished," he said. "Thank you very much,"

"I miss her," Lou said suddenly. "She was a wild one."

Cracking a code is like learning to roller-skate; once you know how to do it, it's easy. With a little help from Gerald

Fletcher, who had provided a guided tour the night before, and a lot of help from Lou Kantor, who had generously provided the key, Carella was able to crack the code wide open— well, almost. Last night, he'd gone with Fletcher to Paddy's Bar and Grill, or PB&G under Andrew Hart's name; Fanny's, F under Sal Decotto; The Purple Chairs, Lou Kantor's TPC; and Quigley's Rest, QR for Richard Fenner on the list. Probably because of the fight, he hadn't taken Carella to The Saloon, TS under Michael Thornton's name—the place where Thornton had admitted first meeting Sarah.

Except, what the hell did TG mean, under all the names but Thornton's?''

By Carella's own modest estimate, he had been in more bars in the past twenty-four hours than he had in the past twenty-four years. He decided, nevertheless, to hit The Saloon that night.

The Saloon was just that. A cigarette-scarred bar behind which ran a mottled, flaking mirror; wooden booths with patched, fake leather seat cushions; bowls of pretzels and potato chips; jukebox gurgling; steamy bodies.

''They come in here,'' the bartender said, ''at all hours of the night. Take yourself. You're here to meet a girl, am I right?''

''There *was* someone I was hoping to see. A girl named Sadie Collins. Do you know her?''

''Yeah. She used to come in a lot, but I ain't seen her in months. What do you want to fool around with her for?''

''Why? What's the matter with her?''

''You want to know something?'' the bartender said. ''I thought she was a hooker at first. Aggressive. You know what that word means? Aggressive? She used to come dressed down to here and up to there, ready for action, selling everything she had, you understand? She'd come in here, pick out a guy she wanted, and go after him like the world was gonna end at midnight. And always the same type. Big guys. You

30

wouldn't stand a chance with her, not that you ain't big, don't misunderstand me. But Sadie liked them gigantic, and mean. You know something?''

"What?"

"I'm glad she don't come in here anymore. There was something about her—like she was compulsive. You know what that word means, compulsive?''

Tuesday afternoon, Arthur Brown handed in his surveillance report on Gerald Fletcher. Much of it was not at all illuminating. From 4:55 P.M. to 8:45 P.M. Fletcher had driven home, and then to 812 North Crane and parked. The report *did* become somewhat illuminating when, at 8:46 P.M., Fletcher emerged from the building with a redheaded woman wearing a black fur coat over a green dress. They went to Rudolph's restaurant, ate, and drove back to 812 Crane, arrived at 10:35 P.M. and went inside. Arthur Brown had checked the lobby mailboxes, which showed eight apartments on the eleventh floor, which was where the elevator indicator had stopped. Brown went outside to wait again, and Fletcher emerged alone at 11:40 P.M. and drove home. Detective O'Brien relieved Detective Brown at 12:15 A.M.

Byrnes said, "This woman could be important."

"That's just what I think," Brown answered.

Carella had not yet spoken to either Sal Decotto or Richard Fenner, the two remaining people listed in Sarah's book, but saw no reason to pursue that trail any further. If the place listings in her book had been chronological, she'd gone from bad to worse in her search for partners.

Why? To give it back to her husband in spades? Carella tossed Sarah's little black book into the manila folder bearing the various reports on the case, and turned his attention to the information Artie Brown had brought in last night. The redheaded woman's presence might be important, but Carella was still puzzling over Fletcher's behavior. Sarah's blatant infidelity provided Fletcher with a strong motive, so why take Carella to his wife's unhappy haunts, why *show* Carella that he had good and sufficient reason to kill her? Furthermore, why the offer to get a good defense attorney for the boy who had already been indicted for the slaying?

Sometimes Carella wondered who was doing what to whom.

At five o'clock that evening, Carella relieved Detective Hal Willis outside Fletcher's office building downtown, and then followed Fletcher to a department store in midtown Isola. Carella was wearing a false mustache stuck to his upper lip, a wig with hair longer than his own and of a different color, and a pair of sunglasses.

In the department store, he tracked Fletcher to the Intimate Apparel department. Carella walked into the next aisle, pausing to look at women's robes and kimonos, keeping one eye on Fletcher, who was in conversation with the lingerie salesgirl.

"May I help you, sir?" a voice said, and Carella turned to find a stocky woman at his elbow, with gray hair, black-rimmed spectacles, wearing army shoes and a black dress. Her suspicious smile accused him of being a junkie shoplifter or worse.

"Thank you, no," Carella said. "I'm just looking."

Fletcher made his selections from the gossamer undergarments that the salesgirl had spread out on the counter, pointing first to one garment, then to another. The salesgirl wrote up the order and Fletcher reached into his wallet to give her either cash or a credit card; it was difficult to tell from an aisle away. He chatted with the girl a moment longer, and then walked off toward the elevator bank.

"Are you *sure* I can't assist you?" the woman in the army shoes said, and Carella answered, "I'm positive," and moved swiftly toward the lingerie counter. Fletcher had left

32

the counter without a package in his arms, which meant he was *sending* his purchases. The salesgirl was gathering up Fletcher's selections and looked up when Carella reached the counter.

"Yes, sir," she said. "May I help you?"

Carella opened his wallet and produced his shield. "Police officer," he said. "I'm interested in the order you just wrote up."

The girl was perhaps nineteen years old, a college girl working in the store during the Christmas rush. Speechlessly, she studied the shield, eyes bugging.

"Are these items being sent?" Carella asked.

"Yes, *sir*," the girl said. Her eyes were still wide. She wet her lips and stood up a little straighter, prepared to be a perfect witness.

"Can you tell me where?" Carella asked.

"Yes, *sir*," she said, and turned the sales slip toward him. "He wanted them wrapped separately, but they're all going to the same address. Miss Arlene Orton, 812 North Crane Street, right here in the city, and I'd guess it's a swell—"

"Thank you very much," Carella said.

It felt like Christmas Day already.

The man who picked the lock on Arlene Orton's front door, ten minutes after she left her apartment on Wednesday morning, was better at it than any burglar in the city, and he happened to work for the Police Department. It took the technician longer to set up his equipment, but the telephone was the easiest of his jobs. The tap would become operative when the telephone company supplied the police with a list of so-called bridging points that located the pairs and cables for Arlene Orton's phone. The monitoring equipment would be hooked into these and whenever a call went out of or came into the apartment, a recorder would automatically tape both ends of the conversation. In addition, whenever a call was made from the apartment, a dial indicator would ink out a series of dots that signified the number being called.

The technician placed his bug in the bookcase on the opposite side of the room. The bug was a small FM transmitter with a battery-powered mike that needed to be changed every twenty-four hours. The technician would have preferred running his own wires, but he dared not ask the building superintendent for an empty closet or workroom in which to hide his listener. A blabbermouth superintendent can kill an investigation more quickly than a squad of gangland goons.

In the rear of a panel truck parked at the curb some twelve feet south of the entrance to 812 North Crane, Steve Carella sat behind the recording equipment that was locked into the frequency of the bug. He sat hopefully, with a tuna sandwich and a bottle of beer, prepared to hear and record any sounds that emanated from Arlene's apartment.

At the bridging point seven blocks away and thirty minutes later, Arthur Brown sat behind equipment that was hooked into the telephone mike, and waited for Arlene Orton's phone to ring. He was in radio contact with Carella.

The first call came at 12:17 P.M. The equipment tripped in automatically and the spools of tape began recording the conversation, while Brown simultaneously monitored it through his headphone.

"Hello?"

"Hello, Arlene?"

"Yes, who's this?"

"Nan."

"Nan? You sound so different. Do you have a cold or something?"

"Every year at this time. Just before the holidays. Arlene, I'm terribly rushed, I'll make this short. Do you know Beth's dress size?"

The conversation went on in that vein, and Arlene Orton spoke to three more girl friends in succession. She then called the local supermarket to order the week's groceries. She had a fine voice, deep and forceful, punctuated every so often (when she was talking to her girl friends) with a delightful giggle.

At four P.M., the telephone in Arlene's apartment rang again.

"Hello?"

"Arlene, this is Gerry."

"Hello, darling."

"I'm leaving here a little early. I thought I'd come right over."

"Good."

"I'll be there in, oh, half an hour, forty minutes."

"Hurry."

Brown radioed Carella at once. Carella thanked him, and sat back to wait.

On Thursday morning, two days before Christmas, Carella sat at his desk in the squad room and looked over the transcripts of the five reels from the night before. The reel that interested him most was the second one. The conversation on that reel had at one point changed abruptly in tone and content. Carella thought he knew why, but he wanted to confirm his suspicion.

Fletcher: I meant after the *holidays*, not the trial.

Miss Orton: I may be able to get away, I'm not sure. I'll have to check with my shrink.

Fletcher: What's he got to do with it?

Miss Orton: Well, I have to pay whether I'm there or not, you know.

Fletcher: Is he taking a vacation?

Miss Orton: I'll ask him.

Fletcher: Yes, ask him. Because I'd really like to get away.

Miss Orton: Ummm. When do you think the case (inaudible).

Fletcher: In March sometime. No sooner than that. He's got a new lawyer, you know.

Miss Orton: What does that mean, a new lawyer?

Fletcher: Nothing. He'll be convicted anyway.

Miss Orton: (Inaudible).

Fletcher: Because the trial's going to take a lot out of me.

Miss Orton: How soon after the trial . . .

Fletcher: I don't know.

Miss Orton: She's dead, Gerry, I don't see . . .

Fletcher: Yes, but . . .

Miss Orton: I don't see why we have to wait, do you?

Fletcher: Have you read this?

Miss Orton: No, not yet. Gerry, I think we ought to set a date now. A provisional date, depending on when the trial is. Gerry?

Fletcher: Mmmm?

Miss Orton: Do you think it'll be a terribly long, drawn-out trial?

Fletcher: What?

Miss Orton: Gerry?

Fletcher: Yes?

Miss Orton: Where are you?

Fletcher: I was just looking over some of these books.

Miss Orton: Do you think you can tear yourself away?

Fletcher: Forgive me, darling.

Miss Orton: If the trial starts in March, and we planned on April for it . . .

Fletcher: Unless they come up with something unexpected, of course.

Miss Orton: Like what?

Fletcher: Oh, I don't know. They've got some pretty sharp people investigating this case.

Miss Orton: What's there to investigate?

Fletcher: There's always the possibility he didn't do it.

Miss Orton: (Inaudible) a signed confession?

Fletcher: One of the cops thinks I killed her.

Miss Orton: You're not serious. Who?

Fletcher: A detective named Carella. He probably knows about us by now. He's a very thorough cop. I have a great deal of admiration for him. I wonder if he realizes that.

Miss Orton: Where'd he even get such an idea?

Fletcher: Well, I told him I hated her.

Miss Orton: What? Gerry, why the hell did you do that?

Fletcher: He'd have found out anyway. He probably knows by now that Sarah was sleeping around with half the men in this city. And he probably knows I knew it, too.

Miss Orton: Who cares what he found out? Corwin's already confessed.

Fletcher: I can understand his reasoning. I'm just not sure he can understand mine.

Miss Orton: Some reasoning. If you were going to kill her, you'd have done it ages ago, when she refused to sign the separation papers. So let him investigate, who cares? Wishing your wife dead isn't the same thing as killing her. Tell that to Detective Copolla.

Fletcher: Carella. (Laughs). I'll tell him, darling.

According to the technician who had wired the Orton apartment, the living room bug was in the bookcase on the wall opposite the bar. Carella was interested in the tape from the time Fletcher had asked Arlene about a book—"Have you read this?"—and then seemed preoccupied. It was Carella's guess that Fletcher had discovered the bookcase bug. What interested Carella more, however, was what Fletcher had said *after* he knew the place was wired. Certain of an audience now, Fletcher had:

(1) Suggested the possibility that Corwin was not guilty.

(2) Flatly stated that a cop named Carella suspected him.

(3) Expressed admiration for Carella, while wondering if Carella was aware of it.

(4) Speculated that Carella had already doped out the purpose of the bar-crawling last Sunday night, was cognizant of Sarah's promiscuity, and knew Fletcher was aware of it.

(5) Made a little joke about "telling" Carella.

Carella felt as eerie as he had when lunching with Fletcher and later when drinking with him. Now he'd spoken, through the bug, directly to Carella. But what was he trying to say? And why?

Carella wanted very much to hear what Fletcher would say when he *didn't* know he was being overheard. He asked Lieutenant Byrnes for permission to request a court order to put a bug in Fletcher's automobile. Byrnes granted permission, and the court issued the order.

Fletcher made a date with Arlene Orton to go to The Chandeliers across the river, and the bug was installed in Fletcher's 1972 car. If Fletcher left the city, the effective range of the transmitter on the open road would be about a quarter of a mile. The listener-pursuer had his work cut out for him.

By ten minutes to ten that night, Carella was drowsy and discouraged. On the way out to The Chandeliers, Fletcher and Arlene had not once mentioned Sarah nor the plans for their impending marriage. Carella was anxious to put them both to bed and get home to his family. When they finally came out of the restaurant and began walking toward Fletcher's automobile, Carella actually uttered an audible, "At *last*," and started his car.

They proceeded east on Route 701, heading for the bridge, and said nothing. Carella thought at first that something was wrong with the equipment, then finally Arlene spoke and Carella knew just what had happened. The pair had argued in the restaurant, and Arlene had been smoldering until this moment.

"Maybe you don't want to marry me at all," she shouted.

"That's ridiculous," Fletcher said.

"Then why won't you set a date?"

"I have set a date."

"You haven't set a date. All you've done is say after the trial. *When*, after the trial? Maybe this whole damn thing has been a stall. Maybe you *never* planned to marry me."

"You know that isn't true, Arlene."

"How do I know there really *were* separation papers?"

"There were. I told you there were."

"Then why wouldn't she sign them?"

"Because she loved me."

"If she loved you, then why did she do those horrible things?"

"To make me pay, I think."

"Is that why she showed you her little black book?"

"Yes, to make me pay."

"No. Because she was a slut."

"I guess. I guess that's what she became."

"Putting a little TG in her book every time she told you about a new one. *Told Gerry*, and marked a little TG in her book."

"Yes, to make me pay."

"A slut. You should have gone after her with detectives. Gotten pictures, threatened her, forced her to sign—"

"No, I couldn't have done that. It would have ruined me, Arl."

"Your precious career."

"Yes, my precious career."

They both fell silent again. They were approaching the bridge now. Carella tried to stay close behind them, but on occasion the distance between the two cars lengthened and he lost some words in the conversation.

"She wouldn't sign the papers and I (   ) adultery because (   ) have come out."

"And I thought (   )."

"I did everything I possibly could."

39

"Yes, Gerry, but now she's dead. So what's your excuse now?"

"I'm suspected of having *killed* her, damn it!"

Fletcher was making a left turn, off the highway. Carella stepped on the accelerator, not wanting to lose voice contact now.

"What difference does that make?" Arlene asked.

"None at all, I'm sure," Fletcher said. "I'm sure you wouldn't mind at all being married to a convicted murderer."

"What are you talking about?"

"I'm talking about the possibility . . . Never mind."

"Let me hear it."

"All right, Arlene. I'm talking about the possibility of someone accusing me of the murder. And of my having to stand trial for it."

"That's the most paranoid—"

"It's not paranoid."

"Then what is it? They've caught the murderer, they—"

"I'm only saying suppose. How could we get married if I killed her, if someone says I killed her ?"

"No one has said that, Gerry."

"Well, *if* someone should."

Silence. Carella was dangerously close to Fletcher's car now, and risking discovery.

Carella held his breath and stayed glued to the car ahead.

"Gerry, I don't understand this," Arlene said, her voice low.

"Someone could make a good case for it."

"Why would anyone do that? They know that Corwin—"

"They could say I came into the apartment and . . . They could say she was still alive when I came into the apartment.

40

They could say the knife was still in her and I . . . I came in and found her that way and . . . finished her off.''

"Why would you do that?"

"To end it."

"You wouldn't kill anyone, Gerry."

"No."

"Then why are you even suggesting such a terrible thing?"

"If she wanted it . . . If someone accused me . . . If someone said I'd done it . . . that I'd finished the job, pulled the knife across her belly, they could claim she *asked* me to do it.''

"What are you saying, Gerry?"

"I'm trying to explain that Sarah might have—"

"Gerry, I don't think I want to know."

"I'm only trying to tell you—"

"No, I don't want to know. Please, Gerry, you're frightening me.''

"*Listen* to me, damn it! I'm trying to explain what *might* have happened. Is that so hard to accept? That she might have *asked* me to kill her?"

"Gerry, please, I—"

"I *wanted* to call the hospital, I was *ready* to call the hospital, don't you think I could *see* she wasn't fatally stabbed?"

"Gerry, please."

"She begged me to kill her, Arlene, she begged me to end it for her, she . . . Damn it, can't *either* of you understand that? I tried to show him, I took him to all the places, I thought he was a man who'd understand. Is that so difficult?"

"Oh, my God, *did* you kill her? *Did* you kill Sarah?"

"No. Not Sarah. Only the woman she'd become, the slut I'd forced her to become. She was Sadie, you see, when I killed her—when she died.''

"Oh, my God," Arlene said, and Carella nodded in weary acceptance.

Carella felt neither elated nor triumphant. As he followed Fletcher's car into the curb in front of Arlene's building, he experienced only a familiar nagging sense of repetition and despair. Fletcher was coming out of his car now, walking around to the curb side, opening the door for Arlene, who took his hand and stepped onto the sidewalk, weeping. Carella intercepted them before they reached the front door of the building.

Quietly, he charged Fletcher with the murder of his wife, and made the arrest without resistance.

Fletcher did not seem at all surprised.

So it was finished, or at least Carella thought it was.

In the silence of his living room, the telephone rang at a quarter past one.

He caught the phone on the third ring.

"Hello?"

"Steve," Lieutenant Byrnes said. "I just got a call from Calcutta. Ralph Corwin hanged himself in his cell, just after midnight. Must have done it while we were still taking Fletcher's confession in the squad room."

Carella was silent.

"Steve?" Byrnes said.

"Yeah, Pete."

"Nothing," Byrnes said, and hung up.

Carella stood with the dead phone in his hands for several seconds and then replaced it on the hook. He looked into the living room, where the lights of the tree glowed warmly, and thought of a despairing junkie in a prison cell, who had taken his own life without ever having known he had not taken the life of another.

It was Christmas day.

Sometimes none of it made any sense at all.

A Man with a Fortune

•

Peter Lovesey

*Peter Lovesey's series of Victorian detective novels featuring
Sergeant Cribb and Constable Thackeray (Wobble to Death,
The Detective Wore Silk Drawers, A Case of Spirits) won
him a wide audience both here and abroad and were made
into a number of TV plays aired by the Public Broadcasting
System as part of its "Mystery" series. In recent years,
Lovesey has turned to nonseries historical suspense novels
with a variety of intriguing backgrounds: The False Inspec-
tor Dew (the stately ocean liner Mauretania in the twenties), Keystone (Mack Sennett's Hollywood). He turns to
the contemporary scene in "A Man with a Fortune," and
provides a frisson or two in his tale of a rich man in search
of his ancestors.*

Most of the passengers were looking to the right, treating themselves to the breath-catching view of San Francisco Bay the captain of the 747 had invited them to enjoy.
Not Eva. Her eyes were locked on the lighted NO SMOKING
sign and the order to fasten seatbelts. Until that was
switched off she could not think of relaxing. She knew the
takeoff was the most dangerous part of the flight, and it
was a delusion to think you were safe the moment the
plane was airborne. She refused to be distracted. She
would wait for the proof that the takeoff had been safely
accomplished: the switching off of that small, lighted sign.

"Your first time?" The man on her left spoke with a

West Coast accent. She had sensed that he had been waiting to speak since they took their seats, darting glances her way. Probably he was just friendly like most San Franciscans she had met on the trip, but she couldn't possibly start a conversation now.

Without turning, she mouthed a negative.

"I mean your first time to England," he went on. "Anyone can see you've flown before, the way you put your hand luggage under the seat before they even asked us, and fixed your belt. I just wondered if this is your first trip to England."

She didn't want to seem ungracious. He was obviously trying to put her at ease. She smiled at the NO SMOKING sign and nodded. It was, after all, her first flight in this direction. The fact that she was English and had just been on a business trip to California was too much to explain.

"Mine, too," he said. "I've promised myself this for years. My people came from England, you see, forty, fifty years back. All dead now, the old folk. I'm the only one of my family left, and I ain't so fit myself." He planted his hand on his chest. "Heart condition."

Eva gave a slight start as an electronic signal sounded, and the light went off on the panel she was watching. A stewardess's voice announced that seatbelts could be unfastened and it was now permissible to smoke in the seats reserved for smoking, to the right of the cabin. Eva closed her eyes a moment and felt the tension ease.

"The doctor says I could go any time," her companion continued. "I could have six months or six years. You know how old I am? Forty-two. When you hear something like that at my age it kind of changes your priorities. I figured I should do what I always promised myself—go to England and see if I had any people left over there. So here I am, and I feel like a kid again. Terrific."

She smiled, mainly from the sense of release from her anxiety at the takeoff, but also at the discovery that the man she was seated beside was as generous and open in expression as he was in conversation. In no way was he a predatory male. She warmed to him—his shining blue eyes in a round, tanned face topped with a patch of hair like cropped corn, his small hands holding tight to the armrests, his Levi shirt bulging over the seatbelt he had not troubled to unclasp. "Are you on a vacation too?" he asked.

She felt able to respond now. "Actually I live in England."

"You're English? How about that!" He made it sound like one of the more momentous discoveries of his life, oblivious that there must have been at least a hundred Britons on the flight. "You've been on vacation to California, and now you're traveling home?"

There was a ten-hour flight ahead of them, and Eva's innately shy personality flinched at the prospect of an extended conversation, but the man's candor deserved an honest reply. "Not exactly a vacation. I work in the electronics industry. My company wants to make a big push in the production of microcomputers. They sent me to see the latest developments in your country."

"Around Santa Clara?"

"That's right," said Eva, surprised that he should know. "Are you by any chance in electronics?"

He laughed. "No, I'm just one of the locals. The place is known as Silicon Valley, did you know that? I'm in farming, and I take an interest in the way the land is used. Excuse me for saying this: You're pretty young to be representing your company on a trip like this."

"Not so young really. I'm twenty-eight." But she understood his reaction. She herself had been amazed when the Director of Research had called her into his office and asked her to make the trip. Some of her colleagues were equally astonished. The most incredulous was her flatmate, Janet—suave, sophisticated Janet, who was on the editorial side at the *Sunday Telegraph*, and had been on assignments to Dublin, Paris, and Geneva, and was always telling Eva how deadly dull it was to be confined to an electronics lab.

"I wish I were twenty-eight," said her fellow traveler. "That was the year I was married. Patty was a wonderful wife to me. We had some great times."

He paused in a way that begged Eva's next question. "Something went wrong?"

"She went missing three years back. Just disappeared. No note, nothing. I came home one night and she was gone."

"That's terrible."

"It broke me up. There was no accounting for it. We were very happily married."

"Did you tell the police?"

"Yes, but they have hundreds of missing persons in their files. They got nowhere. I have to presume she's dead. Patty was happy with me. We had a beautiful home and more money than we could spend. I own two vineyards— big ones. We had grapes in California before silicon chips, you know."

She smiled, and as it seemed that he didn't want to speak anymore about his wife she said, "People try to grow grapes in England, but you wouldn't think much of them. When I left London the temperature was in the low fifties, and that's our so-called summer.

"I'm not interested in the weather. I just want to find the place where all the records of births, marriages, and deaths are stored, so I can find if I have any family left."

Eva understood now. This was not just the trip to England to acquire a few generations of ancestors and a family coat of arms. Here was a desperately lonely man. He had lost his wife and abandoned hope of finding her. But he was still searching for someone he could call his own

"Would that be Somerset House?"

His question broke through her thoughts.

"Yes. That is to say, I think the records are kept now in a building in Kingsway, just a few minutes' walk from there. If you asked at Somerset House, they'd tell you."

"And is it easy to look someone up?"

"It should be, if you have names and dates."

"I figured I'd start with my grandfather. He was born in a village called Edgecombe in Dorset in 1868, and he had three older brothers. Their names were Matthew, Mark, and Luke, and I'm offering no prize for guessing what Grandfather was called. My pa was given the same name and so was I. Each of us was an only child. I'd like to find out if any of Grandfather's brothers got married and had families. If they did, it's possible that I have some second cousins alive somewhere. Do you think I could get that information?"

"Well, it should all be there somewhere," said Eva.

"Does it take long?"

"That's up to you. You have to find the names in the index first. That can take some time, depending how common the name is. Unfortunately, they're not computerized. You just have to work through the lists."

"You're serious?"

"Absolutely, There are hundreds of enormous bound books full of names."

For the first time in the flight, his brow creased into a frown.

"Is something wrong?" asked Eva.

"Just that my name happens to be Smith."

* * *

Janet thought it was hilarious when Eva told her. "All those Smiths! How long has he got, for heaven's sake?"

"Here in England? Three weeks, I think."

"He could spend the whole time working through the index and still get nowhere. Darling, have you ever been there? The scale of the thing beggars description. I bet he gives up on the first day."

"Oh, I don't think he will. This is very important to him."

"Whatever for? Does he hope to get a title out of it? Lord Smith of San Francisco?"

"I told you. He's alone in the world. His wife disappeared. And he has a weak heart. He expects to die soon."

"Probably when he tries to lift one of those index volumes off the shelf," said Janet. "He must be out of his mind." She could never fathom why other people didn't conform to her ideas of the way life should be conducted.

"He's no fool," said Eva. "He owns two vineyards, and in California that's big business."

"A rich man?" There was a note of respect in Janet's voice.

"Very."

"That begins to make sense. He wants his fortune to stay in the family—if he has one."

"He didn't say that, exactly."

"Darling, it's obvious. He's over here to find his people and see if he likes them enough to make them his beneficiaries." Her lower lip pouted in a way that was meant to be amusing, but might have been involuntary.

"Two vineyards in California! Someone stands to inherit all that and doesn't know a thing about it!"

"If he finds them," said Eva. "From what you say, the chance is quite remote."

"Just about impossible, the way he's going about it. You say he's starting with the grandfather and his three brothers, and hoping to draw up a family tree. It sounds beautiful in theory, but it's a lost cause. I happen to know a little about this sort of thing. When I was at Oxford I got involved in organizing an exhibition to commemorate Thomas Hughes—*Tom Brown's Schooldays*, right? I volunteered to try to find his descendants, just to see if they had any unpublished correspondence or photographs in the family. It seemed a marvelous idea at the time, but it was hopeless. I did the General Register Office bit, just like your American, and discovered you simply cannot trace people that way. You can work backward if you know the names and ages of the present generation, but it's practically impossible to do it in reverse. That was with a name like Hughes. Imagine the problems with the name Smith!''

Eva could see Janet was right. She pictured John Smith III at his impossible task and was touched with pity. ''There must be some other way he could do it.''

Janet grinned, ''Like working through the phonebook, ringing up all the Smiths?''

''I feel really bad about this. I encouraged him.''

''Darling, you couldn't have done anything else. If this was the guy's only reason for making the trip, you couldn't tell him to abandon it before the plane touched down at Heathrow. Who knows—he might have incredible luck and actually chance on the right name.''

''That *would* be incredible.''

Janet took a sip of the California wine Eva had brought back as duty free. ''Actually, there is another way.''

''What's that?''

''Through parish records. He told you his grandfather was born somewhere in Dorset?''

''Edgecombe.''

''And the four brothers were named after the gospel

writers, so it's a good bet they were Church of England. Did all the brothers live in Edgecombe?''

"I think so."

"Then it's easy! Start with the baptisms. When was the grandfather born?''

"1868."

"Right. Look up the Edgecombe baptisms for 1868. There can't be so many John Smiths in a small Dorset village. You'll get the father's name in the register—he signs it, you see—and then you can start looking through other years for the brothers' entries. That's only the beginning. There are the marriage registers and the banns. If the Edgecombe register doesn't have them, they could be in an adjoining parish.''

"Hold on, Janet. You're talking as if I'm going off to Dorset myself.''

Janet's eyes shone. "Eva, you don't need to go there. The Society of Genealogists in Kensington has copies of thousands of parish registers. Anyone can go there and pay a fee for a few hours in the library. I've got the address somewhere.'' She got up and went to her bookshelf.

"Don't bother," said Eva. "It's John Smith who needs the information, not me, and I wouldn't know how to find him now. He didn't tell me where he's staying. Even if I knew, I'd feel embarrassed getting in contact again. It was just a conversation on a plane.''

"Eva, I despair of you. When it comes to the point, you're so deplorably shy. I can tell you exactly where to find him: in the General Register Office in Kingsway, working through the Smiths. He'll be there for the next three weeks if someone doesn't help him out.''

"Meaning me?"

"No, I can see it's not your scene. Let's handle this another way. Tomorrow I'll take a long lunch break and pop along to the Society of Genealogists to see if they

50

have a copy of the parish registers for Edgecombe. If they haven't, or there's no mention of the Smith family, we'll forget the whole thing."

"And if you *do* find something?"

"Then we'll consider what to do next." Casually, Janet added, "You know, I wouldn't mind telling him myself."

"But you don't know him."

"You could tell me what he looks like."

"How would you introduce yourself?"

"Eva, you're so stuffy! It's easy in a place like that where everyone is shoulder to shoulder at the indexes."

"You make it sound like a cocktail bar."

"Better."

Eva couldn't help smiling.

"Besides," said Janet. "I do have something in common with him. My mother's maiden name was Smith."

The search rooms of the General Register Office were filled with the steady sound of index volumes being lifted from the shelves, deposited on the reading tables, and then returned. There was an intense air of industry as the searchers worked up and down the columns of names, stopping only to note some discovery that usually was marked by a moment of reflection, followed by redoubled activity.

Janet had no trouble recognizing John Smith. He was where she expected to find him: at the indexes of births for 1868. He was the reader with one volume open in front of him that he had not exchanged in ten minutes. Probably not all morning. His stumpy right hand, wearing three gold rings, checked the rows of Victorian copperplate at a rate appropriate to a marathon effort. But when he turned a page he shook his head and sighed.

Eva had described him accurately enough without really conveying the total impression he made on Janet. Yes, he was short and slightly overweight, and his hair was cut to within a half inch of his scalp; yet he had a teddy-bear quality that would definitely help Janet to be warm toward him. Her worry had been that he would be too pitiable.

She waited for the person next to him to return a volume then moved to his side, put down the notebook she had brought, and asked him, "Would you be so kind as to keep my place while I look for a missing volume? I think someone must have put it back in the wrong place."

He looked up, quite startled to be addressed. "Why, sure."

Janet thanked him and walked round to the next row of shelves.

In a few minutes she was back. "I can't find it, I must have spent twenty minutes looking for it, and my lunch hour will be over soon."

He kept his finger against the place of birth he had reached and said, "Maybe I could help. Which one are you looking for, miss?"

"Could you? It's P-to-S for the second quarter of 1868."

"*Really?* I happen to have it right here."

"Oh, I didn't realize—" Janet managed to blush a little.

"Please." He slid the book in front of her. "Go, ahead—I have all day for this. Your time is more valuable than mine."

"Well, thank you." She turned a couple of pages. "Oh dear, this is going to be much more difficult than I imagined. Why did my mother have to be born with a name as common as Smith?"

"Your name is Smith?" He beamed at the discovery, then nodded. "I guess it's not such a coincidence."

"My mother's name actually. I'm Janet Murdoch."

"John Smith." He held out his hand. "I'm a stranger here myself, but if I can help in any way—"

Janet said, "I'm interested in tracing my ancestors, but

52

looking at this I think I'd better give up. My great-grandfather's name was Matthew Smith, and there are pages and
pages of them. I'm not even sure of the year he was born.
It was either 1868 or 1869.''

"Do you know the place he was born?"

"Somewhere in Dorset. Wait, I've got it written here."
She opened the notebook to the page where she had made
her notes at the Society of Genealogists. "Edgecombe."

"May I see that?" John Smith held it and his hand
shook. "Janet, I'm going to tell you something that you'll
find hard to believe."

He took her to lunch at the Wig and Pen. It tested her
nerve as he questioned her about Matthew Smith of Edgecombe, but she was well prepared. She said she knew
there had been four brothers, but she was deliberately
vague about their names. Two, she said, had married, and
she was the solitary survivor of Matthew's line.

John Smith ate very little lunch. Most of the time, he
sat staring at Janet and grinning. He was very like a teddy
bear. She found it pleasing at first, because it seemed to
show he was a little light-headed at the surprise she had
served him, but as the meal went on it made her feel
slightly uneasy, as if he had something in mind that she
hadn't foreseen.

"I have an idea," he said just before they got up to
leave, "only I hope you won't get me wrong, Janet. What
I would like is to go out to Dorset at the weekend and find
Edgecombe, and have you come with me. Maybe we could
locate the church and see if they still have a record of our
people. *Would* you come with me?"

It suited her perfectly. The parish registers would confirm everything she had copied at the Society of Genealogists. Any doubts John Smith might have of her integrity
would be removed. And if her information on the Smiths

of Edgecombe was shown to be correct, no suspicion need arise that she was not related to them at all. John Smith would accept her as his sole surviving relative. He would return to California in three weeks with his quest accomplished. And sooner or later Janet would inherit two vineyards and a fortune.

"It's a wonderful idea!" she said, "I'll be delighted to come."

Nearly a fortnight passed before Eva started to be anxious about Janet's absence. Once or twice before she had gone away on assignments for the newspaper without saying she was going. Eva suspected she did it to make her work seem more glamorous—the sudden flight to an undisclosed destination on a mission so delicate it could not be whispered to a friend—but this time the *Sunday Telegraph* called to ask why Janet had not been seen at the office for over a week.

When they called again a day or two later, and Eva still had no news, she decided she had no choice but to make a search of Janet's room for some clue as to her whereabouts. At least she'd see which clothes Janet had taken— whether she had packed for a fortnight's absence. With luck she might find a note of the flight number.

The room was in its usual disorder, as if Janet had just gone for a shower and would sweep in at any moment in her white Dior bathrobe. By the phone, Eva found the calendar Janet used to jot down appointments. There was no entry for the last fortnight. On the dressing table was her passport. The suitcase she always took on trips of a week or more was still on the top of the wardrobe.

Janet was not the sort of person you worried over, but this was becoming a worry. Eva systematically searched the room and found no clue. She phoned the *Sunday Telegraph* and told them she was sorry she couldn't help. As she put down the phone, her attention was taken by the letters beside it. She had put them there herself, the dozen or so items of mail that had arrived for Janet.

Opening someone else's private correspondence was a step on from searching her room, and she hesitated. What right had she to do such a thing? She could tell by the envelopes that two were from the Inland Revenue and she put them back by the phone. Then she noticed one addressed by hand. It was postmarked Edgecombe, Dorset.

Her meeting with the friendly Californian named John Smith had been pushed to the edge of her memory by more immediate matters, and it took a few moments' thought to recall the significance of Edgecombe. Even then, she was baffled. Janet had told her that Edgecombe was a dead end. She had checked it at the Society of Genealogists. It had no parish register because there was no church there. They had agreed to drop their plan to help John Smith trace his ancestors.

But why should Janet receive a letter from Edgecombe? Eva decided to open it.

The address on the headed notepaper was The Vicarage, Edgecombe, Dorset.

Dear Miss Murdoch,
I must apologize for the delay in replying to your letter. I fear that this may arrive after you have left for Dorset. However, it is only to confirm that I shall be pleased to show you the entries in our register pertaining to your family, although I doubt if we have anything you have not seen at the Society of Genealogists.

Yours sincerely,
Denis Harcourt, Vicar

A dead end? No church in Edgecombe?
Eva decided to go there herself.

* * *

The vicar of Edgecombe had no difficulty in remembering Janet's visit. "Yes, Miss Murdoch called on a Saturday afternoon. At the time I was conducting a baptism, but they waited until it was over and I took them to the vicarage for a cup of tea."

"She had someone with her?"

"Her cousin."

"Cousin?"

"Well, I gather he was not a first cousin, but they were related in some way. He was from America, and his name was John Smith. He was very appreciative of everything I showed him. You see, his father and his grandfather were born here, so I was able to look up their baptisms and their marriages in the register. It goes back to the sixteenth century. We're very proud of our register."

"I'm sure you must be. Tell me, did Janet—Miss Murdoch—claim to be related to the Smiths of Edgecombe?"

"Certainly. Her great-grandfather, Matthew Smith, is buried in the churchyard. He was the brother of the American gentleman's grandfather, if I have it right."

Eva felt the anger like a kick in the stomach. Not only had Janet Murdoch deceived her, she had committed an appalling fraud on a sweet-natured man. And Eva herself had passed on the information that enabled her to do it. She would never forgive her for this.

"That's the only Smith grave we have in the churchyard," the vicar continued. "When I first got Miss Murdoch's letter, I had hopes of locating the stones of the two John Smiths, the father and grandfather of our American visitor, but it was not to be. They were buried elsewhere."

Something in the vicar's tone made Eva ask, "Do you know where they were buried?"

"Yes, indeed. I got it from Mr. Harper, the sexton. He's been here much longer than I."

There was a pause.

"Is it confidential?" Eva asked.

"Not really." The vicar eased a finger round his collar, as if it were uncomfortable. "It was information that I decided in the circumstances not to volunteer to Miss Murdoch and Mr. Smith. You are not one of the family yourself?"

"Absolutely not."

"Then I might as well tell you. It appears that the first John Smith developed some form of insanity. He was given to fits of violence and became quite dangerous. He was committed to a private asylum in London and died there a year or two later. His only son, the second John Smith, also ended his life in distressing circumstances. He was convicted of murdering two local girls by strangulation, and there was believed to have been a third, but the charge was never brought. He was found guilty but insane and sent to Broadmoor. To compound the tragedy, he had a wife and baby son. They went to America after the trial." The vicar gave a shrug. "Who knows whether the child was ever told the truth about his father—or his grandfather, for that matter? Perhaps you can understand why I was silent on the matter when Mr. Smith and Miss Murdoch were here. I may be old-fashioned, but I think the psychiatrists make too much of heredity, don't you? If you took it seriously, you'd think no woman was safe with Mr. Smith."

From the vicarage, Eva went straight to the house of the Edgecombe police constable and told her story.

The officer listened patiently. When Eva had finished, he said, "Right, miss. I'll certainly look into it. Just for the record, this American—what did he say his name was?"

She Didn't Come Home
•
Sue Grafton

*Kinsey Millhone, Sue Grafton's acclaimed private investigator
operating out of Santa Teresa (Santa Barbara), has starred in
four excellent novels to date: "A" Is for Alibi, "B" Is for
Burglar (which won a PWA Shamus as the best private eye
novel of 1985), "C" Is for Corpse, and "D" Is for Deadbeat.
Kinsey also appears in a number of short stories, of which one
of the most compelling is "She Didn't Come Home." Grafton,
who is a successful Hollywood television writer as well as a
novelist, has also published two nonmysteries,* Keziah Dane
and The Lolly Madonna War.

September in Santa Teresa. I've never known anyone yet
who doesn't suffer a certain restlessness when autumn
rolls around. It's the season of new school clothes, fresh
notebooks, and finely sharpened pencils without any teeth
marks in the wood. We're all eight years old again and
anything is possible. The new year should never begin
on January 1. It begins in the fall and continues as long
as our saddle oxfords remain unscuffed and our lunch
boxes have no dents.

My name is Kinsey Millhone. I'm female, thirty-two,
twice divorced, "doing business" as Kinsey Millhone Investigations in a little town ninety-five miles north of Los
Angeles. Mine isn't a walk-in trade like a beauty salon. Most
of my clients find themselves in a bind and then seek my
services, hoping I can offer a solution for a mere thirty bucks

58

an hour, plus expenses. Robert Ackerman's message was waiting on my answering machine that Monday morning at nine when I got in.

"Hello. My name is Robert Ackerman and I wonder if you could give me a call. My wife is missing and I'm worried sick. I was hoping you could help me out." In the background, I could hear whiney children, my favorite kind. He repeated his name and gave me a telephone number. I made a pot of coffee before I called him back.

A little person answered the phone. There was a murmured child-size hello and then I heard a lot of heavy breathing close to the mouthpiece.

"Hi," I said, "can I speak to your daddy?"

"Yes." Long silence.

"Today?" I asked.

The receiver was clunked down on a tabletop and I could hear the clatter of footsteps in a room that sounded as if it didn't have any carpeting. In due course, Robert Ackerman picked up the phone.

"Lucy?"

"It's Kinsey Millhone, Mr. Ackerman. I just got your message on my answering machine. Can you tell me what's going on?"

"Oh wow, yeah . . ."

He was interrupted by a piercing shriek that sounded like one of those policeman's whistles you use to discourage obscene phone callers. I didn't jerk back quite in time. "Shit, that hurt."

I listened patiently while he dealt with the errant child.

"Sorry," he said when he came back on the line. "Look, is there any way you could come out to the house? I've got my hands full and I just can't get away."

I took his address and brief directions, then headed out to my car.

* * *

Robert and the missing Mrs. Ackerman lived in a housing tract that looked like it was built in the forties before anyone ever dreamed up the notion of family rooms, country kitchens, and his 'n' hers solar spas. What we had here was a basic drywall box; cramped living room with a dining L, a kitchen and one bathroom sandwiched between two nine-by-twelve-foot bedrooms. When Robert answered the door I could just about see the whole place at a glance. The only thing the builders had been lavish with was the hardwood floors, which, in this case, was unfortunate. Little children had banged and scraped these floors and had brought in some kind of foot grit that I sensed before I was even asked to step inside.

Robert, though harried, had a boyish appeal; a man in his early thirties perhaps, lean and handsome, with dark eyes and dark hair that came to a pixie point in the middle of his forehead. He was wearing chinos and a plain white T-shirt. He had a baby, maybe eight months old, propped on his hip like a grocery bag. Another child clung to his right leg, while a third rode his tricycle at various walls and doorways, making quite loud sounds with his mouth.

"Hi, come on in," Robert said. "We can talk out in the backyard while the kids play." His smile was sweet.

I followed him through the tiny disorganized house and out to the backyard, where he set the baby down in a sandpile framed with two-by-fours. The second child held on to Robert's belt loops and stuck a thumb in its mouth, staring at me while the tricycle child tried to ride off the edge of the porch. I'm not fond of children. I'm really not. Especially the kind who wear hard brown shoes. Like dogs, these infants sensed my distaste and kept their distance, eyeing me with a mixture of rancor and disdain.

The backyard was scruffy, fenced in, and littered with the fifty-pound sacks the sand had come in. Robert gave the children homemade-style cookies out of a cardboard box and shooed them away. In fifteen minutes the sugar would probably turn them into lunatics. I gave my watch a quick glance, hoping to be gone by then.

"You want a lawn chair?"

"No, this is fine," I said and settled on the grass. There wasn't a lawn chair in sight, but the offer was nice anyway.

He perched on the edge of the sandbox and ran a distracted hand across his head. "God, I'm sorry everything is such a mess, but Lucy hasn't been here for two days. She didn't come home from work on Friday and I've been a wreck ever since."

"I take it you notified the police."

"Sure. Friday night. She never showed up at the baby-sitter's house to pick the kids up. I finally got a call here at seven asking where she was. I figured she'd just stopped off at the grocery story or something, so I went ahead and picked 'em up and brought 'em home. By ten o'clock when I hadn't heard from her, I knew something was wrong. I called her boss at home and he said as far as he knew she'd left work at five as usual, so that's when I called the police."

"You filed a missing persons report?"

"I can do that today. With an adult, you have to wait seventy-two hours, and even then, there's not much they can do."

"What else did they suggest?"

"The usual stuff, I guess. I mean, I called everyone we know. I talked to her mom in Bakersfield and this friend of hers at work. Nobody has any idea where she is. I'm scared something's happened to her."

"You've checked with hospitals in the area, I take it."

"Sure. That's the first thing I did."

"Did she give you any indication that anything was wrong?"

"Not a word."

"Was she depressed or behaving oddly?"

"Well, she was kind of restless the past couple of months.

She always seemed to get excited around this time of year. She said it reminded her of her old elementary school days.'' He shrugged. "I hated mine."

"But she's never disappeared like this before."

"Oh, heck no. I just mentioned her mood because you asked. I don't think it amounted to anything."

"Does she have any problems with alcohol or drugs?"

"Lucy isn't really like that," he said. "She's petite and kind of quiet. A homebody, I guess you'd say."

"What about your relationship? Do the two of you get along okay?"

"As far as I'm concerned, we do. I mean, once in a while we get into it but never anything serious."

"What are your disagreements about?"

He smiled ruefully. "Money, mostly. With three kids, we never seem to have enough. I mean, I'm crazy about big families, but it's tough financially. I always wanted four or five, but she says three is plenty, especially with the oldest not in school yet. We fight about that some . . . having more kids."

"You both work?"

"We have to. Just to make ends meet. She has a job in an escrow company downtown, and I work for the phone company."

"Doing what?"

"Installer," he said.

"Has there been any hint of someone else in her life?"

He sighed, plucking at the grass between his feet. "In a way, I wish I could say yes. I'd like to think maybe she just got fed up or something and checked into a motel for the weekend. Something like that."

"But you don't think she did."

"Unh-uh and I'm going crazy with anxiety. Somebody's got to find out where she is."

"Mr. Ackerman . . ."

"You can call me Rob," he said.

Clients always say that. I mean, unless their names are something else.

"Rob," I said, "the police are truly your best bet in a situation like this. I'm just one person. They've got a vast machinery they can put to work and it won't cost you a cent."

"You charge a lot, huh?"

"Thirty bucks an hour plus expenses."

He thought about that for a moment, then gave me a searching look. "Could you maybe put in ten hours? I got three hundred bucks we were saving for a trip to the San Diego Zoo."

I pretended to think about it, but the truth was, I knew I couldn't say no to that boyish face. Anyway, the kids were starting to whine and I wanted to get out of there. I waived the retainer and said I'd send him an itemized bill when the ten hours were up. I figured I could put a contract in the mail and reduce my contact with the short persons who were crowding around him now, begging for more sweets. I asked for a recent photograph of Lucy, but all he could come up with was a two-year-old snapshot of her with the two older kids. She looked beleaguered even then, and that was before the third baby came along. I thought about quiet little Lucy Ackerman whose three strapping sons had legs the size of my arms. If I were she, I knew where I'd be. Long gone.

Lucy Ackerman was employed as an escrow officer for a small company on State Street not far from my office. It was a modest establishment of white walls, rust and brown plaid furniture with burnt orange carpeting. There were Gauguin reproductions all around and a live plant on every desk. I introduced myself first to the office manager, a Mrs. Merriman, who was in her sixties, had tall hair, and wore lace-up boots with stiletto heels. She looked like a woman who'd trade all her pension monies for a head-to-toe body tuck.

I said, "Robert Ackerman has asked me to see if I can locate his wife."

"Well, the poor man. I heard about that," she said with her mouth. Her eyes said, "Fat chance!"

"Do you have any idea where she might be?"

"I think you'd better talk to Mr. Sotherland." She had turned all prim and officious, but my guess was she knew something and was dying to be asked. I intended to accommodate her as soon as I'd talked to him. The protocol in small offices, I've found, is ironclad.

Gavin Sotherland got up from his swivel chair and stretched a big hand across the desk to shake mine. The other member of the office force, Barbara Hemdahl, the bookkeeper, got up from her chair simultaneously and excused herself. Mr. Sotherland watched her depart and then motioned me into the same seat. I sank into leather still hot from Barbara Hemdahl's backside, a curiously intimate effect. I made a mental note to find out what she knew, and then I looked, with interest, at the company vice president. I picked up all these names and job titles because his was cast in stand-up bronze letters on his desk, and the two women both had white plastic name tags affixed to their breasts, like nurses. As nearly as I could tell, there were only four of them in the office, including Lucy Ackerman, and I couldn't understand how they could fail to identify each other on sight. Maybe all the badges were for clients who couldn't be trusted to tell one from the other without the proper ID's.

Gavin Sotherland was large, an ex-jock to all appearances, maybe forty-five years old, with a heavy head of blond hair thinning slightly at the crown. He had a slight paunch, a slight stoop to his shoulders, and a grip that was damp with sweat. He had his coat off, and his once-starched white shirt was limp and wrinkled, his beige gabardine pants heavily creased across the lap. Altogether, he looked like a man who'd just crossed a continent by rail. Still, I was forced to credit him with good looks, even if he had let himself go to seed.

"Nice to meet you, Miss Millhone. I'm so glad you're here." His voice was deep and rumbling, with confidence-inspiring undertones. On the other hand, I didn't like the look in his eyes. He could have been a con man, for all I knew. "I understand Mrs. Ackerman never got home Friday night," he said.

"That's what I'm told," I replied. "Can you tell me anything about her day here?"

He studied me briefly. "Well, now I'm going to have to be honest with you. Our bookkeeper has come across some discrepancies in the accounts. It looks like Lucy Ackerman has just walked off with half a million dollars entrusted to us."

"How'd she manage that?"

I was picturing Lucy Ackerman, free of those truck-busting kids, lying on a beach in Rio, slurping some kind of rum drink out of a coconut.

Mr. Sotherland looked pained. "In the most straightforward manner imaginable," he said. "It looks like she opened a new bank account at a branch in Montebello and deposited ten checks that should have gone into other accounts. Last Friday, she withdrew over five hundred thousand dollars in cash, claiming we were closing out a big real estate deal. We found the passbook in her bottom drawer." He tossed the booklet across the desk to me and I picked it up. The word *VOID* had been punched into the pages in a series of holes. A quick glance showed ten deposits at intervals dating back over the past three months and a zero balance as of last Friday's date.

"Didn't anybody else double-check this stuff?"

"We'd just undergone our annual audit in June. Everything was fine. We trusted this woman implicitly and had every reason to."

"You discovered the loss this morning?"

"Yes, ma'am, but I'll admit I was suspicious Friday night when Robert Ackerman called me at home. It was completely unlike that woman to disappear without a word. She's worked here eight years, and she's been punctual and conscientious since the day she walked in."

"Well, punctual at any rate," I said. "Have you notified the police?"

"I was just about to do that. I'll have to alert the Department of Corporations, too. God, I can't believe she did this to us. I'll be fired. They'll probably shut this entire office down."

"Would you mind if I had a quick look around?"

"To what end?"

"There's always a chance we can figure out where she went. If we move fast enough, maybe we can catch her before she gets away with it."

"Well, I doubt that," he said. "The last anybody saw her was Friday afternoon. That's two full days. She could be anywhere by now."

"Mr. Sotherland, her husband has already authorized three hundred dollars' worth of my time. Why not take advantage of it?"

He stared at me. "Won't the police object?"

"Probably. But I don't intend to get in anybody's way, and whatever I find out, I'll turn over to them. They may not be able to get a fraud detective out here until late morning anyway. If I get a line on her, it'll make you look good to the company *and* to the cops."

He gave a sigh of resignation and waved his hand. "Hell, I don't care. Do what you want."

When I left his office, he was putting the call through to the police department.

* * *

I sat briefly at Lucy's desk, which was neat and well organized. Her drawers contained the usual office supplies; no personal items at all. There was a calendar on her desktop, one of those loose-leaf affairs with a page for each day. I checked back through the past couple of months. The only personal notation was for an appointment at the Women's Health Center August 2, and a second visit last Friday afternoon. It must have been a busy day for Lucy, what with a doctor's appointment and ripping off her company for half a million bucks. I made a note of the address she'd penciled in at the time of her first visit. The other two women in the office were keeping an eye on me, I noticed, though both pretended to be occupied with paperwork.

When I finished my search, I got up and crossed the room to Mrs. Merriman's desk. "Is there any way I can make a copy of the passbook for that account Mrs. Ackerman opened?"

"Well, yes, if Mr. Sotherland approves," she said.

"I'm also wondering where she kept her coat and purse during the day."

"In the back. We each have a locker in the storage room."

"I'd like to take a look at that, too."

I waited patiently while she cleared both matters with her boss, and then I accompanied her to the rear. There was a door that opened onto the parking lot. To the left of it was a small rest room and, on the right, there was a storage room that housed four connecting upright metal lockers, the copy machine, and numerous shelves neatly stacked with office supplies. Each shoulder-high locker was marked with a name. Lucy Ackerman's was still securely padlocked. There was something about the blank look of that locker that seemed ominous somehow. I looked at the lock, fairly itching to have a crack at it with my little set of key picks, but I didn't want to push my luck with the cops on the way.

"I'd like for someone to let me know what's in that locker

when it's finally opened," I remarked while Mrs. Merriman ran off the copy of the passbook pages for me.

"This, too," I said, handing her a carbon of the withdrawal slip Lucy'd been required to sign in receipt of the cash. It had been folded and tucked into the back of the booklet. "You have any theories about where she went?"

Mrs. Merriman's mouth pursed piously, as though she were debating with herself about how much she might say.

"I wouldn't want to be accused of talking out of school," she ventured.

"Mrs. Merriman, it does look like a crime's been committed," I suggested. "The police are going to ask you the same thing when they get here."

"Oh. Well, in that case, I suppose it's all right. I mean, I don't have the faintest idea where she is, but I do think she's been acting oddly the past few months."

"Like what?"

"She seemed secretive. Smug. Like she knew something the rest of us didn't know about."

"That certainly turned out to be the case," I said.

"Oh, I didn't mean it was related to that," she said hesitantly. "I think she was having an affair."

That got my attention. "An affair? With whom?"

She paused for a moment, touching at one of the hairpins that supported her ornate hairdo. She allowed her gaze to stray back toward Mr. Sotherland's office. I turned and looked in that direction, too.

"Really?" I said. "No wonder he was in a sweat," I thought.

"I couldn't swear to it," she murmured, "But his marriage has been rocky for years, and I gather she hasn't been that happy herself. She has those beastly little boys, you know, and a husband who seems determined to spawn more. She and Mr. Sotherland . . . Gavie, she calls him . . . have . . . well, I'm sure they've been together. Whether it's connected to this matter of the missing money, I wouldn't presume to guess.'' Having said as much, she was suddenly uneasy. "You won't repeat what I've said to the police, I hope.''

"Absolutely not," I said. "Unless they ask, of course."

"Oh. Of course."

"By the way, is there a company travel agent?"

"Right next door," she replied.

I had a brief chat with the bookkeeper, who added nothing to the general picture of Lucy Ackerman's last few days at work. I retrieved my VW from the parking lot and headed over to the health center eight blocks away, wondering what Lucy had been up to. I was guessing birth control and probably the permanent sort. If she were having an affair (and determined not to get pregnant again in any event), it would seem logical, but I hadn't any idea how to verify the fact. Medical personnel are notoriously stingy with information like that.

I parked in front of the clinic and grabbed my clipboard from the backseat. I have a supply of all-purpose forms for occasions like this. They look like a cross between a job application and an insurance claim. I filled one out now in Lucy's name and forged her signature at the bottom where it said "authorization to release information." As a model, I used the Xerox copy of the withdrawal slip she'd tucked in her passbook. I'll admit my methods would be considered unorthodox, nay illegal, in the eyes of law-enforcement officers everywhere, but I reasoned that the information I was seeking would never actually be used in court, and therefore it couldn't matter *that* much how it was obtained.

I went into the clinic, noting gratefully the near-empty waiting room. I approached the counter and took out my wallet with my California Fidelity ID. I do occasional insurance investigations for CF in exchange for office space. They once made the mistake of issuing me a company identification card with my picture right on it that I've been flashing around quite shamelessly ever since.

I had a choice of three female clerks and, after a brief assessment, I made eye contact with the oldest of them. In places like this, the younger employees usually have no authority at all and are, thus, impossible to con. People without authority will often simply stand there, reciting the rules like mynah birds. Having no power, they also seem to take a vicious satisfaction in forcing others to comply.

The woman approached the counter on her side, looking at me expectantly. I showed her my CF ID and made the form on the clipboard conspicuous, as though I had nothing to hide.

"Hi. My name is Kinsey Millhone," I said. "I wonder if you can give me some help. Your name is what?"

She seemed wary of the request, as though her name had magical powers that might be taken from her by force. "Lillian Vincent," she said reluctantly. "What sort of help did you need?"

"Lucy Ackerman has applied for some insurance benefits and we need verification of the claim. You'll want a copy of the release form for your files, of course."

I passed the forged paper to her and then busied myself with my clipboard as though it were all perfectly matter-of-fact.

She was instantly alert. "What is this?"

I gave her a look. "Oh, sorry. She's applying for maternity leave and we need her due date."

"Maternity leave?"

"Isn't she a patient here?"

Lillian Vincent looked at me. "Just a moment," she said, and moved away from the desk with the form in hand. She went to a file cabinet and extracted a chart, returning to the counter. She pushed it over to me. "The woman has had a tubal ligation," she said, her manner crisp.

I blinked, smiling slightly as though she were making a joke. "There must be some mistake."

"Lucy Ackerman must have made it then if she thinks she can pull this off." She opened the chart and tapped significantly at the August 2 date. "She was just in here Friday for a final checkup and a medical release. She's sterile."

I looked at the chart. Sure enough, that's what it said. I raised my eyebrows and then shook my head slightly. "God. Well. I guess I better have a copy of that."

"I should think so," the woman said and ran one off for me on the desktop dry copier. She placed it on the counter and watched as I tucked it onto my clipboard.

She said, "I don't know how they think they can get away with it."

"People love to cheat," I replied.

It was nearly noon by the time I got back to the travel agency next door to the place where Lucy Ackerman had worked. It didn't take any time at all to unearth the reservations she'd made two weeks before. Buenos Aires, first class on Pan Am. For one. She'd picked up the ticket Friday afternoon just before the agency closed for the weekend.

The travel agent rested his elbows on the counter and looked at me with interest, hoping to hear all the gory details, I'm sure. "I heard about that business next door," he said. He was young, maybe twenty-four, with a pug nose, auburn hair and a gap between his teeth. He'd make the perfect co-star on a wholesome family TV show.

"How'd she pay for the tickets?"

"Cash," he said. "I mean, who'd have thunk?"

"Did she say anything in particular at the time?"

"Not really. She seemed jazzed and we joked some about Montezuma's revenge and stuff like that. I knew she was married, and I was asking her all about who was keeping the kids and what her old man was going to do while she was gone. God, I never in a million *years* guessed she was pulling off a scam like that, you know?''

''Did you ask why she was going to Argentina by herself?''

''Well, yeah, and she said it was a surprise.'' He shrugged. ''It didn't really make sense, but she was laughing like a kid, and I thought I just didn't get the joke.''

I asked for a copy of the itinerary, such as it was. She had paid for a round-trip ticket, but there were no reservations coming back. Maybe she intended to cash in the return ticket once she got down there. I tucked the travel docs onto my clipboard along with the copy of her medical forms. Something about this whole deal had begun to chafe, but I couldn't figure out quite why.

''Thanks for your help,'' I said, heading toward the door.

''No problem. I guess the other guy didn't get it either,'' he remarked.

I paused, midstride, turning back. ''Get what?''

''The joke. I heard 'em next door and they were fighting like cats and dogs. He was pissed.''

''Really?'' I asked. I stared at him. ''What time was this?''

''Five-fifteen. Something like that. They were closed and so were we, but Dad wanted me to stick around for a while until the cleaning crew got here. He owns this place, which is how I got in the business myself. These new guys were starting and he wanted me to make sure they understood what to do.''

''Are you going to be here for a while?''

''Sure.''

''Good. The police may want to hear about this.''

I went back into the escrow office with mental alarm bells clanging away like crazy. Both Barbara Hemdahl and Mrs.

Merriman had opted to eat lunch in. Or maybe the cops had ordered them to stay where they were. The bookkeeper sat at her desk with a sandwich, apple, and a carton of milk neatly arranged in front of her, while Mrs. Merriman picked at something in a plastic container she must have brought in from a fast-food place.

"How's it going?" I asked.

Barbara Hemdahl spoke up from her side of the room. "The detectives went off for a search warrant so they can get in all the lockers back there, collecting evidence."

"Only one of 'em is locked," I pointed out.

She shrugged. "I guess they can't even peek without the paperwork."

Mrs. Merriman spoke up then, her expression tinged with guilt. "Actually, they asked the rest of us if we'd open our lockers voluntarily, so of course we did."

Mrs. Merriman and Barbara Hemdahl exchanged a look. "And?"

Mrs. Merriman colored slightly. "There was an overnight case in Mr. Sotherland's locker, and I guess the things in it were hers."

"Is it still back there?"

"Well, yes, but they left a uniformed officer on guard so nobody'd walk off with it. They've got everything spread out on the copy machine."

I went through the rear of the office, peering into the storage room. I knew the guy on duty and he didn't object to my doing a visual survey of the items, as long as I didn't touch anything. The overnight case had been packed with all the personal belongings women like to keep on hand in case the rest of the luggage gets sent to Mexicali by mistake. I spotted a toothbrush and toothpaste, slippers, a filmy nightie, prescription drugs, hairbrush, extra eyeglasses in a case. Tucked under a change of underwear, I spotted a round plastic container, slightly convex, about the size of a compact.

Gavin Sotherland was still sitting at his desk when I stopped by his office. His skin tone was gray and his shirt was hanging out, big rings of sweat under each arm. He was smoking a cigarette with the air of a man who's quit the habit and has taken it up again under duress. A second uniformed officer was standing just inside the door to my right.

I leaned against the frame, but Gavin scarcely looked up.

I said, "You knew what she was doing, but you thought she'd take you with her when she left."

His smile was bitter. "Life is full of surprises," he said.

I was going to have to tell Robert Ackerman what I'd discovered, and I dreaded it. As a stalling maneuver, just to demonstrate what a good girl I was, I drove over to the police station first and dropped off the data I'd collected, filling them in on the theory I'd come up with. They didn't exactly pin a medal on me, but they weren't as pissed off as I thought they'd be, given the number of civil codes I'd violated in the process. They were even moderately courteous, which is unusual in their treatment of me. Unfortunately, none of it took that long and before I knew it, I was standing at the Ackermans' front door again.

I rang the bell and waited, bad jokes running through my head. Well, there's good news and bad news, Robert. The good news is we've wrapped it up with hours to spare so you won't have to pay me the full three hundred dollars we agreed to. The bad news is your wife's a thief, she's probably dead, and we're just getting out a warrant now, because we think we know where the body's stashed.

The door opened and Robert was standing there with a finger to his lips. "The kids are down for their naps," he whispered.

I nodded elaborately, pantomiming my understanding, as though the silence he'd imposed required this special behavior on my part.

He motioned me in and together we tiptoed through the

house and out to the backyard, where we continued to talk in low tones. I wasn't sure which bedroom the little rugrats slept in, and I didn't want to be responsible for waking them.

Half a day of playing papa to the boys had left Robert looking disheveled and sorely in need of relief.

"I didn't expect you back this soon," he whispered.

I found myself whispering too, feeling anxious at the sense of secrecy. It reminded me of grade school somehow: the smell of autumn hanging in the air, the two of us perched on the edge of the sandbox like little kids, conspiring. I didn't want to break his heart, but what was I to do?

"I think we've got it wrapped up," I said.

He looked at me for a moment, apparently guessing from my expression that the news wasn't good. "Is she okay?"

"We don't think so," I said. And then I told him what I'd learned, starting with the embezzlement and the relationship with Gavin, taking it right through to the quarrel the travel agent had heard. Robert was way ahead of me.

"She's dead, isn't she?"

"We don't know it for a fact, but we suspect as much."

He nodded, tears welling up. He wrapped his arms around his knees and propped his chin on his fists. He looked so young, I wanted to reach out and touch him. "She was really having an affair?" he asked plaintively.

"You must have suspected as much," I said. "You said she was restless and excited for months. Didn't that give you a clue?"

He shrugged one shoulder, using the sleeve of his T-shirt to dash at the tears trickling down his cheeks. "I don't know," he said. "I guess."

"And then you stopped by the office Friday afternoon and found her getting ready to leave the country. That's when you killed her, isn't it?"

He froze, staring at me. At first, I thought he'd deny it,

but maybe he realized there wasn't any point. He nodded mutely.

"And then you hired me to make it look good, right?"

He made a kind of squeaking sound in the back of his throat and sobbed once, his voice reduced to a whisper again. "She shouldn't have done it . . . betrayed us like that. We loved her so much . . ."

"Have you got the money here?"

He nodded, looking miserable. "I wasn't going to pay your fee out of that," he said incongruously. "We really did have a little fund so we could go to San Diego one day."

"I'm sorry things didn't work out," I said.

"I didn't do so bad, though, did I? I mean, I could have gotten away with it, don't you think?"

I'd been talking about the trip to the zoo. He thought I was referring to his murdering his wife. Talk about poor communication. God.

"Well, you nearly pulled it off," I said. Shit, I was sitting there trying to make the guy *feel* good.

He looked at me piteously, eyes red and flooded, his mouth trembling. "But where did I slip up? What did I do wrong?"

"You put her diaphragm in the overnight case you packed. You thought you'd shift suspicion onto Gavin Sotherland, but you didn't realize she'd had her tubes tied."

A momentary rage flashed through his eyes and then flickered out. I suspected that her voluntary sterilization was more insulting to him than the affair with her boss.

"Jesus, I don't know what she saw in him," he breathed. "He was such a pig."

"Well," I said, "if it's any comfort to you, she wasn't going to take *him* with her, either. She just wanted freedom, you know?"

He pulled out a handkerchief and blew his nose, trying to compose himself. He mopped his eyes, shivering with tension. "How can you prove it, though, without a body? Do you know where she is?"

"I think we do," I said softly. "The sandbox, Robert. Right under us."

He seemed to shrink. "Oh, God," he whispered, "Oh, God, don't turn me in. I'll give you the money, I don't give a damn. Just let me stay here with my kids. The little guys need me. I did it for them. I swear I did. You don't have to tell the cops, do you?"

I shook my head and opened my shirt collar, showing him the mike. "I don't have to tell a soul. I'm wired for sound," I said, and then I looked over toward the side yard.

For once, I was glad to see Lieutenant Dolan amble into view.

The Cross of Lorraine

•

Isaac Asimov

*Isaac Asimov's group of armchair detectives known as the
Black Widowers — and the quick-witted waiter, Henry, who
so often outsleuths them at their monthly dinner meetings—
have appeared in scores of short stories to date, most of
which have been collected under such titles as* Tales of the
Black Widowers, More Tales of the Black Widowers, Case-
book of the Black Widowers, *and* Banquets of the Black
Widowers. *The group's guest in "The Cross of Lorraine" is
a stage magician called The Amazing Larri, who proves to
be more than a match for them. Ah, but not for the Amazing Henry. . . .*

Emmanuel Rubin did not, as a general rule, ever permit
a look of relief to cross his face. Had one done so, it
would have argued a prior feeling of uncertainty or apprehension, sensations he might feel but would certainly never
admit to.

This time, however, the relief was unmistakable. It was
monthly banquet time for the Black Widowers. Rubin was
the host and it was he who was supplying the guest. And
here it was twenty minutes after seven and only now—
with but ten minutes left before dinner to start—only now
did his guest arrive.

Rubin bounded toward him, careful, however, not to
spill a drop of his second drink.

"Gentlemen," he said, clutching the arm of the newcomer, "my guest, The Amazing Larri—spelled L-A-R-R-I." And in a lowered voice, over the hum of pleased-to-meet-yous, "Where the hell were you?"

Larri muttered, "The subway train stalled." Then he returned smiles and greetings.

"Pardon me," said Henry, the perennial—and nonpareil—waiter at the Black Widower banquets, "but there is not much time for the guest to have his drink before dinner begins. Would you state your preference, sir?"

"A good notion, that," said Larri gratefully. "Thank you, waiter, and let me have a dry martini, but not too darned dry—a little damp, so to speak."

"Certainly, sir," said Henry.

Rubin said, "I've told you, Larri, that we members all have our *ex officio* doctorates, so now let me introduce them in nauseating detail. This tall gentleman with the neat mustache, black eyebrows, and straight back is Dr. Geoffrey Avalon. He's a lawyer and he never smiles. The last time he tried, he was fined for contempt of court."

Avalon smiled as broadly as he could and said, "You undoubtedly know Manny well enough, sir, not to take him seriously."

"Undoubtedly," said Larri. As he and Rubin stood together, they looked remarkably alike. Both were the same height—about five feet five—both had active, inquisitive faces, both had straggly beards, though Larri's was longer and was accompanied by a fringe of hair down both sides of his face as well.

Rubin said, "And here, dressed fit to kill anyone with a *real* taste for clothing, is our artist-expert, Dr. Mario Gonzalo, who will insist on producing a caricature of you in which he will claim to see a resemblance. —Dr. Roger Halsted inflicts pain on junior high-school students under the guise of teaching them what little he knows of mathematics. —Dr. James Drake is a superannuated chemist who once conned someone into granting him a Ph.D. —And finally, Dr. Thomas Trumbull, who works for the government in an unnamed job as a code expert and who spends most of his time hoping Congress doesn't find out.''

"Manny," said Trumbull wearily, "if it were possible to cast a retroactive blackball, I think you could count on five.''

And Henry said, "Gentlemen, dinner is served.''

It was one of those rare Black Widower occasions when lobster was served, rarer now than ever because of the increase in price.

Rubin, who as host bore the cost, shrugged it off. "I made a good paperback sale last month and we can call this a celebration.''

"We can celebrate," said Avalon, "but lobster tends to kill conversation. The cracking of claws and shells, the extraction of meat, the dipping in melted butter—all that takes one's full concentration.'' And he grimaced with the effort he was putting into the compression of a nutcracker.

"In that case," said the Amazing Larri, "I shall have a monopoly of the conversation," and he grinned with satisfaction as a large platter of prime rib roast was dexterously placed before him by Henry.

"Larri is allergic to seafood," said Rubin.

Conversation was indeed subdued, as Avalon had predicted, until the various lobsters had been clearly worsted in culinary battle, and then, finally, Halsted asked, "What makes you Amazing, Larri?''

"Stage name," said Larri. "I am a prestidigitator, an escapist extraordinary, and the greatest living exposer.''

Trumbull, who was sitting to Larri's right, formed ridges

on his bronzed forehead. "What the devil do you mean by 'exposer'?"

Rubin beat a tattoo on his water glass at this point and said, "No grilling till we've had our coffee."

"For God's sake," said Trumbull, "I'm just asking for the definition of a word."

"Host's decision is final," said Rubin.

Trumbull scowled in Rubin's direction. "Then I'll *guess* the answer. An exposer is one who exposes fakes—people who, using trickery of one sort or another, pretend to produce effects they attribute to supernatural or paranatural forces."

Larri thrust out his lower lip, raised his eyebrows, and nodded. "Very good for a guess. I couldn't have put it better."

Gonzalo said, "You mean that whatever someone did by what he claimed was real magic, you could do by stage magic?"

"Exactly," said Larri. "For instance, suppose that some mystic claimed he had the capacity to bend spoons by means of unknown forces. I can do the same by using natural force, this way." He lifted his spoon and, holding it by its two ends, he bent it half an inch out of shape.

Trumbull said, "That scarcely counts. Anyone can do it that way."

"Ah," said Larri, "but this spoon you saw me bend is not the amazing effect at all. That spoon you were watching merely served to trap and focus the ethereal rays that did the real work. Those rays acted to bend *your* spoon, Dr. Trumbull."

Trumbull looked down and picked up his spoon, which was bent nearly at right angles. "How did you do this?"

Larri shrugged. "Would you believe ethereal forces?"

Drake laughed, and pushing his dismantled lobster toward the center of the table, lit a cigarette. He said, "Larri

81

did it a few minutes ago, with his hands, when you weren't looking.''

Larri seemed unperturbed by exposure. "When Manny banged his glass, Dr. Trumbull, you looked away. I had rather hoped you all would.''

Drake said, ''I know better than to pay attention to Manny.''

"But,'' said Larri, "if no one had seen me do it, would you have accepted the ethereal forces?''

"Not a chance,'' said Trumbull.

"Even if there had been no other way in which you could explain the effect? —Here, let me show you something. Suppose you wanted to flip a coin—''

He fell silent for a moment while Henry passed out the strawberry shortcake, pushed his own serving out of the way, and said, "Suppose you wanted to flip a coin without actually lifting it and turning it—this penny, for instance. There are a number of ways it could be done. The simplest would be merely to touch it quickly, because, as you all know, a finger is always slightly sticky, especially at meal time, so that the coin lifts up slightly as the finger is removed and can easily be made to flip over. It is tails now, you see. Touch it again and it is heads.''

Gonzalo said, "No prestidigitation there, though. We see it flip.''

"Exactly,'' said Larri, "and that's why I won't do it that way. Let's put something over it so that it can't be touched. Suppose we use a—'' He looked around the table for a moment and seized a salt shaker. "Suppose we use this.''

He placed the salt shaker over the coin and said, "Now it is showing heads—''

"Hold on,'' said Gonzalo. "How do we know it's showing heads? It could be tails and then, when you reveal it later, you'll say it flipped, when it was tails all along.''

"You're perfectly right," said Larri, "and I'm glad you raised the point. —Dr. Drake, you have eyes that caught me before. Would you check this on behalf of the assembled company? I'll lift the salt shaker and you tell me what the coin shows."

Drake looked and said, "Heads," in his softly hoarse voice.

"You'll all take Dr. Drake's word, I hope, gentlemen? —Please, watch me place the salt shaker back on the coin and make sure it doesn't flip in the process—"

"It didn't," said Drake.

"Now, to keep my fingers from slipping while performing this trick, I will put this paper napkin over the salt shaker."

Larri folded the paper napkin neatly and carefully around the salt shaker, then said, "But, in manipulating this napkin, I caused you all to divert your attention from the penny and you may think I have flipped it in the process." He lifted the salt shaker with the napkin around it, and said, "Dr. Drake, will you check the coin again?"

Drake leaned toward it. "Still heads," he said.

Very carefully and gently Larri put back the salt shaker, the paper napkin still folded around it, and said, "The coin remained as is?"

"Still heads," said Drake.

"In that case, I now perform the magic." Larri pushed down on the salt shaker and the paper napkin collapsed. There was nothing inside.

There was a moment of shock, and then Gonzalo said, "Where's the salt shaker?"

"In another plane of existence," said Larri airily.

"But you said you were going to flip the coin."

"I lied."

Avalon said, "There's no mystery. He had us all concentrating on the coin as a diversion tactic. When he picked

83

up the salt shaker with the napkin around it to let Jim look at the coin, he just dropped the salt shaker into his hand and placed the empty, folded napkin over the coin."

"Did you see me do that, Dr. Avalon?" asked Larri.

"No. I was looking at the coin, too."

"Then you're just guessing," said Larri.

Rubin, who had not participated in the demonstration at all, but who had eaten his strawberry shortcake instead, said, "The tendency is to argue these things out logically and that's impossible. Scientists and other rationalists are used to dealing with the universe, which fights fair. Faced with a mystic who does not, they find themselves maneuvered into believing nonsense and, in the end, making fools of themselves.

"Magicians, on the other hand," Rubin went on, "know what to watch for, are experienced enough not to be misdirected, and are not impressed by the apparently supernatural. That's why mystics generally won't perform if they know magicians are in the audience."

Coffee had been served and was being sipped, and Henry was quietly preparing the brandy, when Rubin sounded the water glass and said, "Gentlemen, it is time for the official grilling, assuming you idiots have left anything to grill. Jeff, will you do the honors tonight?"

Avalon cleared his throat portentously and frowned down on The Amazing Larri from under his dark and luxuriant eyebrows. Using his voice in the deepest of its naturally deep register, he said, "It is customary to ask our guests to justify their existences, but if today's guest exposes phony mystics even occasionally, I, for one, consider his existence justified and will pass on to another question.

"The temptation is to ask you how you performed your little disappearing trick of a few moments ago, but I quite understand that the ethics of your profession preclude your telling us—even though everything said here is considered under the rose, and though nothing has ever leaked, I will refrain from that question.

"Let me instead ask about your failures. —Sir, you describe yourself as an exposer. Have there been any supposedly mystical demonstrations you have not been able to duplicate in prestidigitous manner and have not been able to account for by natural means?"

Larri said, "I have not attempted to explain all the effects I have ever encountered or heard of, but where I have studied an effect and made an attempt to duplicate it, I have succeeded in every case."

"No failures?"

"None."

Avalon considered that, but as he prepared for the next question, Gonzalo broke in. His head was leaning on one palm, but the fingers of that hand were carefully disposed in such a way as not to disarray his hair.

He said, "Now wait, Larri, would it be right to suggest that you tackled only easy cases? The really puzzling cases you might have made no attempts to explain?"

"You mean," said Larri, "that I shied away from anything that might spoil my perfect record or that might upset my belief in the rational order of the universe? —If so, you're quite wrong, Dr. Gonzalo. Most reports of apparent mystical powers are dull and unimportant, crude and patently false. I ignore those. The cases I do take on are precisely the puzzling ones that have attracted attention because of their unusual nature and their apparent divorce from the rational. So, you see, the ones I take on are precisely those you suspect I avoid."

Gonzalo subsided and Avalon said, "Larri, the mere fact that you can duplicate a trick by prestidigitation doesn't mean that it couldn't also have been performed by a mystic through supernatural means. The fact that human beings can build machines that fly doesn't mean that birds are man-made machines.''

"Quite right," said Larri, "but mystics lay their claims to supernatural powers on the notion, either expressed or implicit, that there is no other way of producing the effect. If I show that the same effect *can* be produced by natural means, the burden of proof then shifts to them to show that the effect can be produced after the natural means are made impossible. I don't know of any mystic who has accepted the conditions set by professional magicians to guard against trickery and who then succeeded.''

"And nothing has ever baffled you? Not even the tricks other magicians have developed?''

"Oh, yes, there are effects produced by some magicians that baffle me in the sense that I don't know quite how they do it. I might duplicate the effect by perhaps using a different method. In any case, that's not the point. As long as an effect is produced by natural means, it doesn't matter whether I can reproduce it or not. I am not the best magician in the world. I am just a better magician than any mystic is.''

Halsted, his high forehead flushed and stuttering slightly in his eagerness to speak, said, "But then nothing would startle you? No disappearance like the one involving the salt shaker?''

"You mean that one?'' asked Larri, pointing. There was a salt shaker in the middle of the table, but no one had seen it placed there.

Halsted, thrown off a moment, recovered and said, "Have you ever been *startled* by any disappearance? I heard once that magicians have made elephants disappear.''

"Actually, making an elephant disappear is childishly simple. I assure you there's nothing puzzling about disappearances performed in a magic act." And then a peculiar look crossed Larri's face, a flash of sadness and frustration. "Not in a magic act. Just—"

"Yes?" said Halsted. "Just what?"

"Just in real life," said Larri, smiling and attempting to toss off the remark lightheartedly.

"Just a minute," said Trumbull, "we can't let that pass. If there has been a disappearance in real life you can't explain, we want to hear about it."

Larri shook his head. "No, no, Dr. Trumbull. It is not a mysterious disappearance or an inexplicable one. Nothing like that at all. I just—well, I lost something and can't find it and it—saddens me."

"The details," said Trumbull.

"It wouldn't be worth your attention," said Larri, embarrassed. "It's a—silly story and somewhat—" He fell into silence.

"Damn it," thundered Trumbull, "we all sit here and voluntarily refrain from asking anything that might result in your being tempted to violate your ethics. Would it violate the ethics of the magician's art for you to tell this story?"

"It's not that at all—"

"Well, then, sir, I repeat what Jeff has told you. Everything said here is in absolute confidence, and the agreement surrounding these monthly dinners is that all questions must be answered. —Manny?"

Rubin shrugged. "That's the way it is, Larri. If you don't want to answer the question we'll have to declare the meeting at an end."

Larri sat back in his chair and looked depressed. "I can't very well allow that to happen, considering the fine hospitality I've been shown. I will tell you the story, but you'll find there's not much to it. I met a woman quite accidentally; I lost touch with her; I can't locate her. That's all there is."

"No," said Trumbull, "that's not all there is. Where and how did you meet her? Where and how did you lose touch with her? Why can't you find her again? We want to know the details."

Gonzalo said, "In fact, if you tell us the details, we may be able to help you."

Larri laughed sardonically. "I think not."

"You'd be surprised," said Gonzalo. "In the past—"

Avalon said, "Quiet, Mario. Don't make promises we might not be able to keep. —Would you give us the details, sir? I assure you we'll do our best to help."

Larri smiled wearily. "I appreciate your offer, but you will see that there is nothing you can do merely by sitting here."

He adjusted himself in his seat and said, "I was done with my performance in an upstate town—I'll give you the details when and if you insist, but for the moment they don't matter, except that this happened about a month ago. I had to get to another small town some hundred and fifty miles away for a morning show and that presented a little transportation problem.

"My magic, unfortunately, is not the kind that can transport me a hundred and fifty miles in a twinkling, or even conjure up a pair of seven-league boots. I did not have my car with me—just as well, for I don't like to travel strange roads at night when I am sleepy—and the net result was that I would have to take a bus that would take nearly four hours. I planned to catch some sleep while on wheels and thus make the trip serve a double purpose.

"But when things go wrong, they go wrong in battalions, so you can guess that I missed my bus and that the next one would not come along for two more hours. There was an enclosed station in which I could wait, one that was as dreary as you could imagine—with no reading matter except some fly-blown posters on the wall—no place to buy a paper or a cup of coffee. I thought grimly that it was fortunate it wasn't raining, and settled down to drowse, when my luck changed.

"A woman walked in. I've never been married, gentlemen, and I've never even had what young people today call a 'meaningful relationship.' Some casual attachments, perhaps, but on the whole, though it seems trite to say so, I am married to my art and find it much more satisfying than women, generally.

"I had no reason to think that this woman was an improvement on the generality, but she had a pleasant appearance. She was something over thirty, and was just plump enough to have a warm, comfortable look about her, and she wasn't too tall.

"She looked about and said, smiling, 'Well, I've missed my bus, I see.'

"I smiled with her. I liked the way she said it. She didn't fret or whine or act annoyed at the universe. It was a good-humored statement of fact, and just hearing it cheered me up tremendously because actually I myself was in the mood to fret and whine and act annoyed. Now I could be as good-natured as she and say, 'Two of us, madam, so you don't even have the satisfaction of being unique.'

" 'So much the better,' she said, 'We can talk and pass the time that much faster.'

"I was astonished. She did not treat me as a potential attacker or as a possible thief. God knows I am not handsome or even particularly respectable in appearance, but it was as though she had casually penetrated to my inmost character and found it satisfactory. You have no idea how flattered I was. If I were ten times as sleepy, I would have stayed up to talk to her.

"And we did talk. Inside of fifteen minutes I knew I was having the pleasantest conversation in my life—in a crummy bus station at midnight. I can't tell you all we talked about, but I can tell you what we *didn't* talk about. We didn't talk about magic.

"I can interest anyone by doing tricks, but then it isn't me they're interested in; it's the flying fingers and the patter they like. And while I'm willing to buy attention that way, you don't know how pleasant it is to get the attention without purchasing it. She apparently just liked to listen to me; I know I liked to listen to her.

"Fortunately, my trip was not an all-out effort, so I didn't have my large trunk with the shoe business advertising all over it, just two rather large valises. I told her nothing personal about myself, and asked nothing about her. I gathered briefly that she was heading for her brother's place, that it was right on the road, that she would have to wake him up because she had carelessly let herself be late—but she only told me that in order to say that she was glad it had happened. She would buy my company at the price of inconveniencing her brother. I liked that.

"We didn't talk politics or world affairs or religion or the theater. We talked people—all the funny and odd and peculiar things we had observed about people. We laughed for two hours, during which not one other person came to join us. I had never had anything like that happen to me, had never felt so alive and happy, and when the bus finally came at 1:50 A.M., it was amazing how sorry I was. I didn't want the night to end.

"When I got onto the bus, of course, it was no longer quite the same thing, even though we found a double seat we could share. After all, we had been alone in the station and there we could talk loudly and laugh. On the bus people were sleeping.

"Of course it wasn't all bad. It was a nice feeling to have her so close to me. Despite the fact that I'm rather an old horse, I felt like a teenager—enough like a teenager, in fact, to be embarrassed at being watched.

Immediately across the way was a woman and her young son. He was eight years old, I should judge, and *he* was awake. He kept watching me with his sharp little eyes. I could see those eyes fixed on us every time a street light shone into the bus and it was very inhibiting. I wished he were asleep but, of course, the excitement of being on a bus, perhaps, was keeping him awake.

"The motion of the bus, the occasional whisper, the feeling of being quite out of reality, the pressure of her body against mine—it was like confusing dream and fact, and the boundary between sleep and wakefulness just vanished. I didn't intend to sleep, and I started awake once or twice, but then finally, when I started awake one more time, it was clear there had been a considerable period of sleep, and the seat next to me was empty."

Halsted said, "I take it she had gotten off."

"I didn't think she had disappeared into thin air," said Larri. "Naturally, I looked about. I couldn't call her name, because I didn't know her name. She wasn't in the rest room, because its door was swinging open.

"The little boy across the aisle spoke in a rapid high treble—in French. I can understand French reasonably well, but I didn't have to make any effort because his mother was now awakened and she translated. She spoke English quite well.

"She said, 'Pardon me, sir, but is it that you are looking for the woman that was with you?'

" 'Yes,' I said. 'Did you see where she got off?'

" 'Not I, sir. I was sleeping. But my son says that she descended at the place of the Cross of Lorraine.'

" 'At the what?'

"She repeated it, and so did the child, in French.

"She said, 'You must excuse my son, sir. He is a great

91

hero worshipper of President Charles de Gaulle, and though he is young he knows that tale of the Free French forces in the war very well. He would not miss a sight like a Cross of Lorraine. If he said he saw it, he did.'

"I thanked them and then went forward to the bus driver and asked him, but at that time of night the bus stops wherever a passenger would like to get off, or get on. He had made numerous stops and let numerous people on and off, and he didn't know for sure where he had stopped and whom he had left off. He was rather churlish, in fact."

Avalon cleared his throat. "He may have thought you were up to no good and was deliberately withholding information to protect the passenger."

"Maybe," said Larri despondently, "but what it amounted to was that I had lost her. When I came back to my seat, I found a little note tucked into the pocket of the jacket I had placed in the rack above. I managed to read it by a streetlight at the next stop, where the French mother and son got off. It said, ''Thank you so much for a delightful time. Gwendolyn.' ''

Gonzalo said, "You have her first name anyway."

Larri said, "I would appreciate having had her last name, her address, her telephone number. Having only a first name is useless."

"You know," said Rubin, "She may deliberately have withheld information because she wasn't interested in continuing the acquaintanceship. A romantic little interlude is one thing; a continuing danger is another. She may be a married woman."

"Have you done anything about trying to find her?" asked Gonzalo.

"Certainly," said Larri sardonically. "If a magician is faced with a disappearing woman he must understand what has happened. I have gone over the bus route twice by car, looking for a Cross of Lorraine. If I had found it, I would have gone in and asked if anyone there knew a woman by the name of Gwendolyn. I'd have described her. I would have gone to the local post office or the local police station."

"But you have not found a Cross of Lorraine, I take it," said Trumbull.

"I have not."

Halsted said, "Mathematically speaking, it's a finite problem. You could try every post office along the whole route."

Larri sighed. "If I get desperate enough, I'll try. But, mathematically speaking, that would be so inelegant. Why can't I find the Cross of Lorraine?"

"The youngster might have made a mistake," said Trumbull.

"Not a chance," said Larri. "An adult, yes, but a child, never. Adults have accumulated enough irrationality to be very unreliable eyewitnesses. A bright eight-year-old is different. Don't try to pull any trick on a bright kid; he'll see through it.

"Just the same," he went on, "nowhere on the route is there a restaurant, a department store, or anything else with the name Cross of Lorraine. I've checked every set of yellow pages along the entire route."

"Now wait a while," said Avalon, "that's wrong. The child wouldn't have seen the words because they would have meant nothing to him. If he spoke and read only French, as I suppose he did, he would know the phrase as 'Croix de Lorraine.' The English would have never caught his eyes. He must have seen the symbol, the cross with the two horizontal bars, like this." He reached out and Henry obligingly handed him a menu.

Avalon turned it over and on the blank back drew the following:

93

"Actually," he said, "it is more properly called the Patriarchal Cross or the Archiepiscopal Cross since it symbolized the high office of patriarchs and archbishops by doubling the bars. You will not be surprised to hear that the Papal Cross has three bars. The Patriarchal Cross was used as a symbol by Godfrey of Bouillon, who was one of the leaders of the First Crusade, and since he was Duke of Lorraine, it came to be called the Cross of Lorraine. As we all know, it was adopted as the emblem of the Free French during the Hitlerian War."

He coughed slightly and tried to look modest.

Larri said, a little impatiently, "I understand about the symbol, Dr. Avalon, and I didn't expect the youngster to note words. I think you'll agree, though, that any establishment calling itself the Cross of Lorraine would surely display the symbol along with the name. I looked for the name in the yellow pages and for the symbol on the road."

"And you didn't find it?" said Gonzalo.

"As I've already said, I didn't. I was desperate enough to consider things I didn't think the kid could possibly have seen at night. I thought, who knows how sharp young eyes are and how readily they may see something that represents an overriding interest? So I looked at signs in windows, at street signs—even at graffiti."

"If it were a graffito," said Trumbull, "which happens to be the singular form of graffiti, by the way, then, of course, it could have been erased between the time the child saw it and the time you came to look for it."

"I'm not sure of that," said Rubin. "It's my experience

that graffiti are never erased. We've got some on the outside of our apartment house—''

''That's New York,'' said Trumbull. ''In smaller towns there's less tolerance for these evidences of anarchy.''

''Hold on,'' said Gonzalo, ''What makes you think graffiti are necessarily signs of anarchy? As a matter of fact—''

''Gentlemen! Gentlemen!'' And as always, when Avalon's voice was raised to its full baritone, a silence fell. ''We are not here to argue the merits and demerits of graffiti. The question is: how can we find this woman who disappeared? Larri has found no restaurant or other establishment with the name of Cross of Lorraine; he has found no evidence of the symbol along the route taken. Can we help him?''

Drake held up his hand and squinted through the curling smoke of his cigarette.

''Hold on, there's no problem. Have you ever seen a Russian Orthodox Church? Do you know what its cross is like?'' He made quick marks on the back of the menu and shoved it toward the center of the table. ''Here—''

He said, ''The kid, being hipped on the Free French, would take a quick look at that and see it as the Cross of Lorraine. So what you have to do, Larri, is look for a Russian Orthodox Church en route. I doubt there would be more than one.''

Larri thought about it, but did not seem overjoyed. ''The cross with that second bar set at an angle would be on the top of the spire, wouldn't it?''

''I imagine so.''

''And it wouldn't be floodlighted, would it? How would

95

the child be able to see it at three or four o'clock in the morning?"

Drake stubbed out his cigarette. "Well, now, churches usually have a bulletin board near the entrance. There could have been a Russian Orthodox cross on the—"

"I would have seen it," said Larri firmly.

"Could it have been a Red Cross?" asked Gonzalo feebly. "You know, there might be a Red Cross headquarters along the route. It's possible."

"The RED Cross," said Rubin, "is a Greek Cross with all four arms equal. I don't see how that could possibly be mistaken for a Cross of Lorraine by a Free French enthusiast. Look at it—"

Halsted said, "The logical thing, I suppose, is that you simply missed it, Larri. If you insist that, as a magician, you're such a trained observer that you *couldn't* have missed it, then maybe it was a symbol on something movable—on a truck in a driveway, for instance—and it moved on after sunrise."

"The boy made it quite clear that it was at the *place* of the Cross of Lorraine," said Larri. "I suppose even an eight-year-old can tell the difference between a place and a movable object."

"He spoke French. Maybe you mistranslated."

"I'm not that bad at the language," said Larri, "and besides, his mother translated and French is her native tongue."

"But English isn't. *She* might have gotten it wrong. The kid might have said something else. He might not even have said the Cross of Lorraine at all."

Avalon raised his hand for silence and said, "One moment, gentlemen. I see Henry, our esteemed waiter, smiling. What is it, Henry?"

Henry, from his place at the sideboard, said, "I'm afraid that I am amused at your doubting the child's evidence. It is quite certain, in my opinion, that he did see the Cross of Lorraine."

There was a moment's silence and Larri said, "How can you tell that, Henry?"

"By not being too subtle, sir."

Avalon's voice boomed out. "I knew it! We're being too complicated. Henry, how is it possible for us to achieve greater simplicity?"

"Why, Mr. Avalon, the incident took place at night. Instead of looking at all signs, all places, all varieties of cross, why not begin by asking ourselves what very few things *can* be easily seen on a highway at night?"

"A Cross of Lorraine?" asked Gonzalo incredulously.

"Certainly," said Henry, "among other things. Especially, if we don't call it a Cross of Lorraine. What the youngster saw as a Cross of Lorraine, out of his special interest, we could see as something else so clearly that its relationship to the Cross of Lorraine would be invisible. What has been happening just now has been precisely what happened earlier with Mr. Larri's trick with the coin and the salt shaker. We concentrated on the coin and didn't watch the salt shaker, and now we concentrate on the Cross of Lorraine and don't look for the alternative."

Trumbull said, "Henry, if you don't stop talking in riddles, you're fired. What the hell is the Cross of Lorraine, if it isn't the Cross of Lorraine?"

Henry said gravely, "What is this?" and carefully he drew on the back of the menu—

Trumbull said, "A Cross of Lorraine—tilted."

"No, sir, you would never have thought so, if we hadn't been talking about the Cross of Lorraine. Those are English letters and a very common symbol on highways if you add something to it—" He wrote quickly and the titled Cross became:

EXXON

"The one thing," said Henry, "that is designed to be seen without trouble, day or night, on any highway, is a gas station sign. The child saw the Cross of Lorraine in this one, but Mr. Larri, retracing the route, sees only a double X, since he reads the entire sign as Exxon. All signs showing this name, whether on the highway, in advertisements, or on credit cards, show the name in this fashion."

Now Larri caught fire. "You mean, Henry, that if I go into the Exxon stations en route and ask for Gwendolyn—"

"The proprietor of one of them is likely to be her brother, and there would not be more than a half dozen or so at most to inquire at."

"Good God, Henry," said Larri, "you're a magician."

"Merely simple-minded," said Henry, "though not, I hope, in the pejorative sense."

A Very Desirable Residence
·
P. D. James

The bestselling novels of P. D. James (A Taste for Death being the most recent) resemble the better works of the Golden Age of Detective Fiction, such as those of Ngaio Marsh, Dorothy Sayers, and Josephine Tey; yet they are also very much in step with current times. James draws her characters in considerable psychological depth; her series detectives—Commander Adam Dalgliesh of Scotland Yard and private investigator Cordelia Gray—grow and change in response to the circumstances to which their jobs subject them. That same combination of the old-fashioned and the modern, and that same psychological depth, can be found in her short stories, of which "A Very Desirable Residence" is among the most satisfying.

During and after Harold Vinson's trial, at which I was a relatively unimportant prosecution witness, there was the usual uninformed, pointless, and repetitive speculation about whether those of us who knew him would ever have guessed that he was a man capable of scheming to murder his wife. I was supposed to have known him better than most of the school staff, and my colleagues found it irritatingly self-righteous of me to be so very reluctant to be drawn into the general gossip about what, after all, was the school's major scandal in twenty years. "You knew them both. You used to visit the house. You saw them together. Didn't you guess?" they insisted, obviously feeling that I had been in some way negligent, that I ought to have seen what was going on and

99

prevented it. No, I never guessed; or, if I did, I guessed wrong. But they were perfectly right. I could have prevented it.

I first met Harold Vinson when I took up a post as junior art master at the comprehensive school where he taught mathematics to the senior forms. It wasn't too discouraging a place as these teaching factories go. The school was centered on the old eighteenth-century grammar school, with some not too hideous modern additions, in a pleasant enough commuter town on the river about twenty miles southeast of London. It was a predominantly middle-class community, a little smug and culturally self-conscious, but hardly intellectually exciting. Still, it suited me well enough for a first post. I don't object to the middle class or their habitats; I'm middle class myself. And I knew that I was lucky to get the job. Mine is the usual story of an artist with sufficient talent but without enough respect for the fashionable idiocies of the contemporary artistic establishment to make a decent living. More dedicated men choose to live in cheap bed-sitting rooms and keep on painting. I'm fussy about where and how I live, so, for me, it was a diploma in the teaching of art and West Fairing Comprehensive.

It only took one evening in Vinson's home for me to realize that he was a sadist. I don't mean that he tormented his pupils. He wouldn't have been allowed to get away with it had he tried. These days the balance of power in the classroom has shifted with a vengeance, and any tormenting is done by the children. No, as a teacher, he was surprisingly patient and conscientious, a man with real enthusiasm for his subject (''discipline'' was the word he preferred to use, being something of an intellectual snob and given to academic jargon) with a surprising talent for communicating that enthusiasm to the children. He was a fairly rigid disciplinarian, but I've never found that children dislike firmness provided a master doesn't indulge in that pedantic sarcasm which, by taking advantage of the children's inability to compete, is resented as particularly unfair. He got them through their examinations, too. Say what you like, that's something middle-class kids and their parents appreciate. I'm sorry to have slipped into using the word "kids," that modern shibboleth with its blend of condescension and sycophancy. Vinson never used it. It was his habit to talk about the alumni of the sixth. At first I thought it was an attempt at mildly pretentious humor, but now I wonder. He wasn't really a humorous man. The rigid muscles of his face seldom cracked into a smile and when they did it was as disconcerting as a painful grimace. With his lean, slightly stooping figure, the grave eyes behind the horn-rimmed spectacles, the querulous lines etched deeply from the nose to the corners of his unyielding mouth, he looked deceptively what we all thought he was—a middle-aged, disagreeable, and not very happy pedant.

No, it wasn't his precious alumni whom he bullied and tyrannized over. It was his wife. The first time I saw Emily Vinson was when I sat next to her at founder's memorial day, an archaic function inherited from the grammar school and regarded with such reverence that even those masters' wives who seldom showed their faces at the school felt obliged to make an appearance. She was, I guessed, almost twenty years younger than her husband, a thin, anxious-looking woman with auburn hair which had faded early and the very pale transparent-looking skin which often goes with that coloring. She was expensively and smartly dressed, too incongruously smartly for such a nondescript woman so that the ill-chosen, too-fashionable suit merely emphasized her frail ordinariness. But her eyes were remarkable, an unusual gray green, huge, and slightly exophthalmic under the arched narrow eyebrows. She seldom turned them on me, but when, from time to time, she gave me a swift elliptical glance, it was as astounding as turning over an amateurish Victorian oil and discovering a Corot.

It was at the end of founder's memorial day that I received my first invitation to visit them at their home. I found that they lived in some style. She had inherited from her father a small but perfectly proportioned Georgian house, which stood alone in some two acres of ground with lawns slanting green down to the river. Apparently her father was a builder who had bought the house cheaply from its impoverished owner with the idea of demolishing it and building a block of flats. The planning authority had slapped on a preservation order just in time, and he had died in weeks, no doubt from chagrin, leaving the house and its contents to his daughter. Neither Harold Vinson nor his wife seemed to appreciate their possession. He grumbled about the expense; she grumbled about the housework. The perfectly proportioned façade, so beautiful that it took the breath, seemed to leave them as unmoved as if they lived in a square brick box. Even the furniture, which had been bought with the house, was regarded by them with as little respect as if it were cheap reproduction. When at the end of my first visit I complimented Vinson on the spaciousness and proportions of the dining-room, he replied, ''A house is only the space between four walls. What does it matter if they are far apart or close together, or what they are made of? You're still in a cage.''

His wife was carrying the plates into the kitchen at the time and didn't hear him. He spoke so low that I scarcely heard him myself. I am not even sure now that I was meant to hear.

Marriage is both the most public and the most secret of institutions, its miseries as irritatingly insistent as a hacking cough, its private malaise less easily diagnosed. And nothing is so destructive as unhappiness to social life. No one wants to sit in embarrassed silence while his host and hostess demonstrate their mutual incompatibility and dislike. She could, it seemed, hardly open her mouth without irritating him. No opinion she expressed was worth listening to. Her small domestic chat—which was, after all, all she had—invariably provoked him by its banality so that he would put down his knife and fork with a look of patient resigned boredom as soon as, with a nervous preparatory glance at him, she would steel herself to speak. If she had been an animal, cringing away with that histrionic essentially false look of piteous entreaty, I can see that the temptation to kick would be irresistible. And, verbally, Vinson kicked.

Not surprisingly, they had few friends. Looking back it would probably be more true to say that they had no real friends. The only colleague of his who visited from the school, apart from myself, was Vera Pelling, the junior science teacher, and she, poor girl, was such an unattractive bore that there weren't many alternatives open to her. Vera Pelling is the living refutation of that theory so beloved, I understand, of beauty and fashion journalists in women's magazines that any woman if she takes the trouble can make something of her appearance. Nothing could be done about Vera's piglike eyes and nonexistent chin and, reasonably enough, she didn't try. I am sorry if I sound harsh. She wasn't a bad sort. And if she thought that making a fourth with me at an occasional free supper with the Vinsons was better than eating alone in her furnished flat, I suppose she had her reasons, as I had mine. I never remember having visited the Vinsons without Vera, although Emily came to my flat on three occasions, with Harold's approval, to sit for her portrait. It wasn't a success. The result looked like a pastiche of an early Stanley Spencer. Whatever it was I was trying to capture, that sense of a secret life conveyed in the rare gray-green flash of those remarkable eyes, I didn't succeed.

When Vinson saw the portrait he said, "You were prudent, my boy, to opt for teaching as a livelihood. Although, looking at this effort, I would say that the choice was hardly voluntary." For once I was tempted to agree with him.

103

Vera Pelling and I became oddly obsessed with the Vinsons. Walking home after one of their supper parties we would mull over the traumas of the evening like an old married couple perennially discussing the inadequacies of a couple of relatives whom we actively disliked but couldn't bear not to see. Vera was a tolerable mimic and would imitate Vinson's dry, pedantic tones.

"My dear, I think that you recounted that not very interesting domestic drama last time we had supper together."

"And what, my dear, have you been doing with yourself today? What fascinating conversation did you have with the estimable Mrs. Wilcox while you cleaned the drawing room together?"

Really, confided Vera, tucking her arm through mine, it had become so embarrassing that it was almost enough to put her off visiting them. But not quite enough apparently. Which was why she, too, was at the Vinsons' on the night when it happened.

On the evening of the crime—the phrase has a stereotyped but dramatic ring, which isn't inappropriate to what, look at it as you will, was no ordinary villainy—Vera and I were due at the school at 7 P.M. to help with the dress rehearsal of the school play. I was responsible for the painted backcloth and some of the props and Vera for the makeup. It was an awkward time, too early for a proper meal beforehand and too late to make it sensible to stay on at school without some thought of supper, and when Emily Vinson issued through her husband an invitation to both Vera and me to have coffee and sandwiches at 6 o'clock, it seemed sensible to accept. Admittedly, Vinson made it plain that the idea was his wife's. He seemed mildly surprised that she should wish to entertain us so briefly—insist on entertaining us was the expression he used. Vinson himself wasn't involved with the play. He never grudged spending his private time to give extra tuition in his own subject but made it a matter of rigid policy never to become involved in what he described as extramural divertissements appealing only to the regressed adolescent. He was, however, a keen chess player and on Wednesday evenings spent the three hours from nine until midnight at the local chess club of which he was secretary. He was a man of meticulous habit, and any school activity on a Wednesday evening would, in any case, have had to manage without him.

Every detail, every word spoken at that brief and unremarkable meal—dry ham sandwiches cut too thick and synthetic coffee—was recounted by Vera and me at the Crown Court so that it has always intrigued me that I can no longer visualize the scene. I know exactly what happened, of course. I can recount every word. It's just that I can no longer shut my eyes and see the supper table, the four of us seated there, imprinted in colors on the mind's eye. Vera and I said at the trial that both Vinsons seemed more than usually ill at ease, that Harold, in particular, gave us the impression that he wished we weren't there. But that could have been hindsight.

The vital incident, if you can call it that, happened toward the end of the meal. It was so very ordinary at the time, so crucial in retrospect. Emily Vinson, as if uneasily aware of her duties as hostess and of the unaccountable silence which had fallen on the table, made a palpable effort. Looking up with a nervous glance at her husband she said: "Two such very nice and polite workmen came this morning—"

Vinson touched his lips with his paper serviette, then crumpled it convulsively. His voice was unusually sharp as he broke in: "Emily my dear, do you think you could spare us the details of your domestic routine this evening? I've had a particularly tiring day. And I am trying to concentrate my mind on this evening's game." And that was all.

The dress rehearsal was over at about nine o'clock, as planned, and I told Vera that I had left a library book at the Vinsons' and was anxious to pick it up on the way home. She made no objection. She gave the impression, poor girl, that she was never particularly anxious to get home. It was only a quarter of an hour's brisk walk to the house and, when we arrived, we saw at once that something was wrong. There were two cars, one with a blue light on the roof, and an ambulance parked unobtrusively but unmistakably at the side of the house. Vera and I glanced briefly at each other, than ran to the front door. It was shut. Without ringing we dashed round to the side. The back door, leading to the kitchen quarters, was open. I had an immediate impression that the house was peopled with large men, two of them were in uniform. There was, I remember, a policewoman bending over the prone figure of Emily Vinson. And their cleaning woman, Mrs. Wilcox, was there, too. I heard Vera explaining to a plainclothes policeman, obviously the senior man present, that we were friends of the Vinsons, that we had been there to supper only that evening. "What's happened?" she kept asking. "What's happened?" Before the police could answer, Mrs. Wilcox was spitting it all out, eyes bright with self-important outrage and excitement. I sensed that the police wanted to get rid of her, but she wasn't so easily dislodged. And, after all, she had been first on the scene. She knew it all. I heard it in a series of disjointed sentences:

"Knocked on the head—terrible bruise—marks all over the parquet flooring where he dragged her—only just coming round now—human fiend—head resting on a cushion in the gas stove—the poor darling—came in just in time at 9:20—always come to watch color TV with her on Wednesday night—back door open as usual—found the note on the kitchen table." The figure writhing on the floor, groaning and crying in a series of harsh grunting moans like an animal in travail, suddenly raised herself and spoke coherently.

"I didn't write it! I didn't write it!"

"You mean Mr. Vinson tried to kill her?" Vera was incredulous, head turning from Mrs. Wilcox to the watchful, inscrutable faces of the police. The senior officer broke in:

"Now, Mrs. Wilcox, I think it's time you went home. The ambulance is here. An officer will come along for your statement later this evening. We'll look after Mrs. Vinson. There's nothing else for you to do."

He turned to Vera and me. "If you two were here earlier this evening. I'd like a word. We're fetching Mr. Vinson now from his chess club. But if you two will just wait in the sitting room please."

Vera said: "But if he knocked her unconscious and put her head in the gas oven, then why isn't she dead?"

It was Mrs. Wilcox who replied, turning triumphantly as she was led out: "The conversion, that's why. We're on natural gas from this morning. That North Sea stuff. It isn't poisonous. The two men from the Gas Board came just after nine o'clock."

They were lifting Emily Vinson onto a stretcher now. Her voice came to us in a high querulous wail.

"I tried to tell him. You remember? You heard him? I tried to tell him."

The suicide note was one of the exhibits at Vinson's trial. A document examiner from the forensic science laboratory testified that it was a forgery, a clever forgery but not Mrs. Vinson's writing. He couldn't give an opinion on whether it was the work of the husband, although it was certainly written on a page taken from a writing pad found in the desk in the sitting room. It bore no resemblance to the accused's normal writing. But, in his view, it hadn't been written by Mrs. Vinson. He gave a number of technical reasons to support his view and the jury listened respectfully. But they weren't surprised. They knew that it hadn't been written by Mrs. Vinson. She had stood in the witness box and told them so. And they were perfectly clear in their own minds who had written it.

There was other forensic evidence. Mrs. Wilcox's "Marks

all over the parquet floor'' were reduced to one long but shallow scrape, just inside the sitting room door. But it was a significant scrape. It had been made by the heels of Emily Vinson's shoes. Traces of the floor polish which she used were found, not on the soles, but on the sides of the scraped heels, and there were minute traces of her shoe polish in the scrape.

The fingerprint officer gave evidence. I hadn't realized until then that fingerprint experts are mostly civilians. It must be a dull job, that constant and meticulous examination of surfaces for the tell-tale composites and whirls. Hard on the eyes I should think. In this case the significance was that he hadn't found any prints. The gas taps had been wiped clean. I could see the jury physically perk up at the news. That was a mistake all right. It didn't need the prosecution to point out that the taps should have shown Mrs. Vinson's prints. She, after all, had cooked their last meal. A cleverer murderer would merely have worn gloves, smudging any existing prints but ensuring that he left none of his own. It had been an overprecaution to wipe the gas taps clean.

Emily Vinson, quiet, distressed but gallant, obviously reluctant to testify against her husband, was remarkably competent in the witness box. I hardly recognized her. No, she hadn't told her husband that she and Mrs. Wilcox had arranged to watch television together shortly after nine o'clock. Mrs. Wilcox, who lived nearby, usually did come across to spend a couple of hours with her on Wednesday nights when Mr. Vinson was at his chess club. No, she hadn't liked to tell Mr. Vinson. Mr. Vinson wasn't very fond of inviting people in. The message came over to the jury as clearly as if she had spelt it out, the picture of a downtrodden, unintellectual wife craving the human companionship which her husband denied her, guiltily watching a popular TV show with her cleaning woman at a time when she would be certain that her husband wouldn't catch them out. I glanced at his proud, unyielding mask, at the hands clutched over the edge of the dock, and imagined what he was thinking, what he would have said.

"Surely you have enough of domestic trivia and Mrs. Wilcox's conversation, hardly exciting I should have thought, without inviting her into your drawing room. The woman should know her place."

The trial didn't take long. Vinson made no defense except to reiterate stubbornly, eyes fixed straight ahead, that he hadn't done it. His counsel did his best, but with the dogged persistence of a man resigned to failure, and the jury had the look of people glad to be faced, for once, with a clear-cut case they could actually understand. The verdict was inevitable. And the subsequent divorce hearing was even shorter. It isn't difficult to persuade a judge that your marriage has irretrievably broken down when your husband is serving a prison sentence for attempted murder.

Two months after the decree absolute we married and I took over the Georgian house, the river view, the regency furniture. With the physical possessions, I knew exactly what I was getting. With my wife, I wasn't so sure. There had been something disturbing, even a little frightening, about the competence with which she had carried out my instructions. It hadn't, of course, been particularly difficult. We had planned it together during those sessions when I was painting her portrait. I had written and handed her the fake suicide note on the paper she had supplied a few days before our plans matured. We knew when the gas was due to be converted. She had, as instructed, placed the note on the kitchen table before scraping the heels of her shoes across the polished floor. She had even managed beautifully the only tricky part, to bang the back of her head sufficiently hard against the kitchen wall to raise an impressive bruise but not sufficiently hard to risk bungling the final preparations; the cushion placed in the bottom of the oven for the head, the gas tap turned on, and then wiped clean with her handkerchief.

And who could have imagined that she was such a consummate actress? Sometimes, remembering that anguished animal cry of "I tried to tell him. I tried to tell him," I wonder again what is going on behind those remarkable eyes. She still acts, of course. I find it remarkably irritating, that habit she has, particularly when we are in company, of turning on me that meek, supplicating, beaten dog expression whenever I talk to her. It provokes unkindness. Perhaps it's intended to. I'm afraid I'm beginning to get rather a reputation for sadism. People don't seem to want to come to the house anymore.

There is one solution, of course, and I can't pretend that I haven't pondered it. A man who has killed another merely to get his house isn't likely to be too fastidious about killing again. And it was murder; I have to accept that.

Vinson only served nine months of his sentence before dying in the prison hospital of what should have been an uncomplicated attack of influenza. Perhaps his job really was his life and without his precious alumni the will to live snapped. Or perhaps he didn't choose to live with the memory of his wife's great betrayal. Beneath the petty tyranny, the impatience, the acerbity, there may have been love of a kind.

But the ultimate solution is barred to me. A month ago Emily explained, meekly, like a child propounding a problem, and with a swift sidelong glance, that she had written a confession and left it with her solicitor.

"Just in case anything happens to me, darling."

She explained that what we did to poor Harold is preying on her mind, but that she feels better now that all the details are written down and she can be sure that, after her death, the truth will at last be known and Harold's memory cleared.

She couldn't have made it more plain to me that it is in my interest to see that I die first.

I killed Harold Vinson to get the house; Emily to get me. On the whole, she made the better bargain. In a few weeks I shall lose the house. Emily is selling it. After all, there's nothing I can do to stop her; the place belongs to her, not me.

After we married I gave up the teaching post, finding it embarrassing to meet my colleagues as Emily's husband. It was not that anyone suspected. Why should they? I had a perfect alibi for the time of the crime. But I had a dream that, living in that perfection, I might become a painter after all. That was the greatest illusion of all.

So now they are taking down from the end of the drive the board which states "This Desirable Residence For Sale." Emily got a very good price for the house and the furniture. More than enough to buy the small but pretentious brick box on an executive estate in North London which will be my cage from now on. Everything is sold. We're taking nothing with us except the gas stove. But, as Emily pointed out when I remonstrated, why not? It's in perfectly good working order.

The Witch, Yazzie, and the Nine of Clubs
·

Tony Hillerman

In his novels, and in such rare short stories as "The Witch, Yazzie, and the Nine of Clubs," Tony Hillerman combines the crime story with in-depth studies of Navajo (and sometimes Hopi and Zuni) culture and folklore, and considerable insight into the Indian mind. His first three novels feature Sergeant Joe Leaphorn of the Navajo Tribal Police; one of these, Dance Hall of the Dead, won an MWA Edgar as best novel in 1973. His second three novels feature a younger and more modernized tribal policeman, Jim Chee, the hero of the story that follows. Leaphorn and Chee combine their talents in Hillerman's seventh and most recent novel, Skinwalkers.

All summer the witch had been at work on the Rainbow Plateau. It began—although Corporal Jimmy Chee would learn of it only now, at the very last—with the mutilation of the corpse. The rest of it fell pretty much into the pattern of witchcraft gossip one expected in this lonely corner of the Navajo Reservation. Adeline Etcitty's mare had foaled a two-headed colt. Rudolph Bisti's boys lost their best ram while driving their flocks into the high country, and when they found the body werewolf tracks were all around it. The old woman they call Kicks-Her-Horse had actually seen the skinwalker. A man walking down Burnt

112

Water Wash in the twilight had disappeared into a grove of cottonwoods and when the old woman got there, he turned himself into an owl and flew away. The daughter of Rosemary Nakai had seen the witch, too. She shot her .22 rifle at a big dog bothering her horses and the dog turned into a man wearing a wolfskin and she'd run away without seeing what he did.

Corporal Chee heard of the witch now and then and remembered it as he remembered almost everything. But Chee heard less than most because Chee had been assigned to the Tuba City subagency and given the Short Mountain territory only six months ago. He came from the Chuska Mountains on the Arizona–New Mexico border three hundred miles away. His born-to clan was the Slow Talking People, and his paternal clan was the Mud Dinee. Here among the barren canyons along the Utah border, the clans were the Standing Rock People, the Many Goats, the Tangle Dinee, the Red Forehead Dinee, the Bitter Waters, and the Monster People. Here Chee was still a stranger. To a stranger, Navajos talk cautiously of witches.

Which is perhaps why Jim Chee had learned only now, at this very moment, of the mutilation. Or perhaps it was because he had a preoccupation of his own—the odd, frustrating question of where Taylor Yazzie had gone, and what Yazzie had done with the loot from the Burnt Water Trading Post. Whatever the reason he was late in learning, it was the Cowboy who finally told him.

"Everybody knew there was a skinwalker working way last spring," the Cowboy said. "As soon as they found out the witch killed that guy."

Chee had been leaning against the Cowboy's pickup truck. He was looking past the Emerson Nez hogan, through the thin blue haze of piñon smoke which came from its smokehole, watching a half-dozen Nez kinfolks stacking wood for the Girl Dance fire. He was asking him-

self for the thousandth time what Taylor Yazzie could have
done with $40,000 worth of pawn—rings, belt buckles,
bracelets, bulky silver concha belts, which must weigh,
altogether, 500 pounds. And what had Taylor Yazzie done
with himself—another 180 pounds or so, with the bland
round face more common among Eastern Navajos than on
the Rainbow Plateau, with his thin moustache, with his
wire-rimmed sunglasses. Chee had seen Taylor Yazzie only
once, the day before he had done the burglary, but since
then he had learned him well. Yazzie's world was small,
and Yazzie had vanished from it, and since he could hardly
speak English there was hardly any place he could go. And
just as thoroughly, the silver pawn had vanished from the
lives of a hundred families who had turned it over to Ed
Yost's trading post to secure their credit until they sold
their wool. Through all these thoughts it took a moment
for the Cowboy's message to penetrate. When it did, Corporal Chee became very attentive.

"Killed what guy?" Chee asked. Taylor Yazzie, you're
dead, he thought. No more mystery.

The Cowboy was sprawled across the front seat of his
truck, fishing a transistor radio out of the glovebox. "You
remember," he said. "Back last April. That guy you collected on Piute Mesa."

"Oh," Chee said. He remembered. It had been a miserable day's work and the smell of death had lingered in
his carryall for weeks. But that had been in May, not April,
and it hadn't looked like a homicide. Just too much booze,
too much high-altitude cold. An old story on the Reservation. And John Doe wasn't Taylor Yazzie. The coroner
had put the death two months before the body was recovered. Taylor Yazzie was alive, and well, and walking out
of Ed Yost's trading post a lot later than that. Chee had
been there and seen him. "You see that son-of-a-bitch,"
Ed Yost had said. "I just fired his ass. Never comes to

work, and I think he's been stealing from me." No, Yost didn't want to file a complaint. Nothing he could prove. But the next morning it had been different. Someone with a key had come in the night, and opened the saferoom where the pawn was kept, and took it. Only Yost and Yazzie had access to the keys, and Yazzie had vanished.

"Why you say a witch killed that guy?" Chee asked.

The Cowboy backed out of the pickup cab. The radio didn't work. He shook it, glancing at Chee. His expression was cautious. The bumper stickers plastering the Ford declared him a member of the Native American Rodeo Cowboys' Assn., and proclaimed that Cowboys Make Better Lovers, and that Cowgirls Have More Fun, and recorded the Cowboy's outdated permit to park on the Arizona State University campus. But Cowboy was still a Many Goats Dinee, and Chee had been his friend for just a few months. Uneasiness warred with modern macho.

"They said all the skin was cut off his hands," the Cowboy said. But he said it in a low voice.

"Ah," Chee said. He needed no more explanation. The ingredients of "anti'l," the "corpse-powder" which skinwalkers make to spread sickness, was known to every Navajo. They use the skin of their victim which bears the unique imprint of the individual human identity—the skin of palm, and finger-pads, and the balls of the feet. Dried and pulverized with proper ritual, it became the dreaded reverse-negative of the pollen used for curing and blessing. Chee remembered the corpse as he had seen it. Predators and scavenger birds had left a ragged sack of bones and bits of desiccated flesh. No identification and nothing to show it was anything but routine. And that's how it had gone into the books. "Unidentified male. About forty. Probable death by exposure."

"If somebody saw his palms had been skinned, then somebody saw him a hell of a long time before anybody

115

called us about him," Chee said. Nothing unusual in that, either.

"Somebody found him fresh," the Cowboy said. "That's what I heard. One of the Pinto outfit." Cowboy removed the battery from the radio. By trade, Cowboy was the assistant county agricultural agent. He inspected the battery, which looked exactly like all other batteries, with great care. The Cowboy did not want to talk about witch business.

"Any of the Pinto outfit here?" Chee asked.

"Sure," Cowboy said. He made a sweeping gesture, including the scores of pickups, wagons, old sedans occupying the sagebrush flats around the Nez hogans, the dozens of cooking fires smoking in the autumn twilight, the people everywhere. "All the kinfolks come to this. Everybody comes to this."

This was an Enemy Way. This particular Enemy Way had been prescribed, as Chee understood it, to cure Emerson Nez of whatever ailed him so he could walk again with beauty all around him as Changing Woman had taught when she formed the first Navajos. Family duty would require all kinsmen, and clansmen, of Nez to be here, as Cowboy had said, to share in the curing and the blessing. Everybody would be here, especially tonight. Tonight was the sixth night of the ceremonial when the ritual called for the Girl Dance to be held. Its original purpose was metaphysical—part of the prescribed re-enactment of the deeds of the Holy People. But it was also social. Cowboy called it the Navajo substitute for the singles bar, and came to see if he could connect with a new girl friend. Anthropologists came to study primitive behavior. Whites and Utes and even haughty Hopis came out of curiosity. Bootleggers came to sell illegal whisky. Jim Chee came, in theory, to catch bootleggers. In fact, the elusive, invisible, missing Yazzie drew him. Yazzie and the loot. Sometime, somewhere some of it would have to surface. And when it did, someone would know it. But now to hell with Yazzie and pawn jewellery. He might have an old homicide on his hands. With an unidentified victim and the whole thing six months cold, it promised to be as frustrating as the burglary. But he would find some Pinto family members and begin the process.

Cowboy's radio squawked into sudden life and produced the voice of Willie Nelson, singing of abandonment and sorrow. Cowboy turned up the volume.

"Specially everyone would come to this one," Cowboy said toward Chee's departing back. "Nez wasn't the only one bothered by that witch. One way or another it bothered just about everybody on the plateau."

Chee stopped and walked back to the pickup. "You mean Nez was witched?"

"That's what they say," Cowboy said. "Got sick. They took him to the clinic in Tuba City and when that didn't do any good they got themselves a Listener to find out what was wrong with the old man, and he found out Nez had the corpse sickness. He said the witch got on the roof—" (Cowboy paused to point with his lips—a peculiarly Navajo gesture—toward the Nez hogan)—"and dropped anti'l down the smokehole."

"Same witch? Same one that did the killing?"

"That's what the Listener said," Cowboy agreed.

Cowboy was full of information tonight, Chee thought. But was it useful? The fire for the Girl Dance had been started now. It cast a red, wavering light which reflected off windshields, faces, and the moving forms of people. The pot drums began a halting pattern of sounds which reflected, like the firelight, off the cliffs of the great mesa which sheltered the Nez place. This was the ritual part of the evening. A shaman named Dillon Keeyani was the signer in charge of curing Nez. Chee could see him, a tall, gaunt man standing beyond the fire, chanting the repetitive poetry of his part of the cure. Nez stood beside him, naked to the waist, his face blackened to make him invisible from the ghosts which haunt the night. Why would the Listener have prescribed an Enemy Way? It puzzled Chee. Usually a witch victim was cured with a Prostitution Way, or the proper chants from the Mountain Way were used. The Enemy Way was ordered for witch cases at times, but it was a broad-spectrum antibiotic—used for that multitude of ills caused by exposure to alien ways and alien cultures. Chee's family had held an Enemy Way for him when he had returned from the University of New Mexico, and in those years when Navajos were coming home from the Viet Nam war it was common every winter. But why use it to cure Emerson Nez of the corpse sickness? There was only one answer. Because the witch was an alien—a Ute, a white, a Hopi perhaps. Chee thought about how the Listener would have worked. Long conversations with Nez and those who knew him, hunting for causes of the malaise, for broken taboos, for causes of depression. And then the Listener would have found a quiet place, and listened to what the silence taught him. How would the Listener have known the witch was alien? There was only one way. Chee was suddenly excited. Someone must have seen the witch. Actually seen the man—not in the doubtful moonlight, or a misty evening when a moving shape could be dog or man—but under circumstances that told the witness that the man was not a Navajo.

The Sway Dance had started now. A double line of figures circled the burning pyre, old men and young—even boys too young to have been initiated into the secrets of the Holy People. Among Chee's clans in the Chuskas ritualism was more orthodox and these youngsters would not be allowed to dance until a Yeibichai was held for them, and their eyes had seen through the masks of Black God and Talking God. The fire flared higher as a burning log collapsed with an explosion of sparks. Chee wove through the spectators, asking for Pintos. He found an elderly woman joking with two younger ones. Yes, she was Anna Pinto. Yes, her son had found the body last spring. His name was Walker Pinto. He'd be somewhere playing stick dice. He was wearing a sweatband. Red.

Chee found the game behind Ed Yost's pickup truck. A lantern on the tailgate provided the light, a saddle blanket spread on the ground was the playing surface. Ed Yost was playing with an elderly round-faced Hopi and four Navajos. Chee recognized Pinto among the watchers by the red sweatband and his mother's description. "Skinny," she'd said. "Bony-faced. Sort of ugly-looking." Although his mother hadn't said it, Walker Pinto was also drunk.

"That's right, man," Pinto said. "I found him. Up there getting the old woman's horses together, and I found him." Wine had slurred Pinto's speech and drowned whatever inhibitions he might have felt about talking of witch business to a man he didn't know. He put his hand on the pickup fender to steady himself and began—Navajo fashion—at the very beginning. He'd married a woman in the Poles Together clan and gone over to Rough Rock to live with her, but she was no good, so this winter he'd come back to his mother's outfit, and his mother had wanted him to go up on Piute Mesa to see about her horses. Pinto described the journey up the mesa with his son, his agile hands acting out the journey. Chee watched the stick-dice game. Yost was good at it. He slammed the four painted wooden pieces down on the base stone in the center of the blanket. They bounced two feet into the air and fell in a neat pattern. He tallied the exposed colors, moved the matchsticks being used as score markers, collected the sticks, and passed them to the Hopi in maybe three seconds. Yost had been a magician once, Chee remembered.

With a carnival, and his customers had called him Three-Hands. "Bets," Yost said. The Hopi looked at the sticks in his hand, smiling slightly. He threw a crumpled dollar on to the blanket. A middle-aged Navajo wearing wire-rimmed glasses put a folded bill beside it. Two more bills hit the blanket. The lantern light reflected off Wire Rims's lenses and off Yost's bald head.

"About then I heard the truck, way back over the ridge," Pinto was saying. His hands created the ridge and the valley beyond it. "Then the truck it hit something, you see. Bang." Pinto's right hand slammed into his left. "You see, that truck it hit against a rock there. It was turning around in the wash, and the wash is narrow there, and it banged up against this rock." Pinto's hands re-created the accident. "I started over there, you see. I walked on over there then to see who it was."

The stick-dice players were listening now; the Hopi's face patient, waiting for the game to resume. The butane lantern made a white light that made Yost's moist eyes sparkle as he looked up at Pinto. There was a pile of bills beside Yost's hand. He took a dollar from it and put it on the blanket without taking his eyes from Pinto.

"But, you see, by the time I got up to the top of the rise, that truck it was driving away. So I went on down there, you see, to find out what had been going on." Pinto's hands re-enacted the journey.

"What kind of truck was it?" Chee asked.

"Already gone," Pinto said. "Bunch of dust hanging in the air, but I didn't see the truck. But when I got down there to the wash, you see, I looked around." Pinto's hand flew here and there, looking around. "There he was, you see, right there shoved under that rabbit brush." The agile hands disposed of the body. The stick-dice game remained in recess. The Hopi still held the sticks, but he watched Pinto. So did the fat man who sat cross-legged beside him.

The lantern light made a point of white in the center of Yost's black pupils. The faces of the Navajo players were rapt, but the Hopi's expression was polite disinterest. The Two-Heart witches of his culture did their evil with more sophistication.

Pinto described what he had seen under the rabbit brush, his voice wavering with the wine but telling a story often repeated. His agile hands were surer. They showed how the flayed hands of the corpse had lain, where the victim's hat had rolled, how Pinto had searched for traces of the witch, how he had studied the tracks. Behind the stick-dice players the chanting chorus of the Sway Dancers rose and fell. The faint night breeze moved the perfume of burning piñon and the aroma of cedar to Chee's nostrils. The lantern light shone through the rear window of Yost's truck, reflecting from the barrels of the rifles in the gun rack across it. A long-barrelled 30.06 and a short saddle carbine, Chee noticed.

"You see, that skinwalker was in a big hurry when he got finished with that body," Pinto was saying. "He backed right over a big chamisa bush and banged that truck all around on the brush and rocks getting it out of there." The hands flew, demonstrating panic.

"But you didn't actually see the truck?" Chee asked.

"Gone," Pinto said. His hands demonstrated the state of goneness.

"Or the witch, either?"

Pinto shook his head. His hands apologized.

On the flat beside the Nez hogan the chanting of the Sway Dance ended with a chorus of shouting. Now the Girl Dance began. Different songs. Different drumbeat. Laughter now, and shouting. The game broke up. Wire Rims folded his blanket. Yost counted his winnings.

"Tell you what I'll do," Yost said to Wire Rims. "I'll show you how I can control your mind."

Wire Rims grinned.

"Yes, I will," Yost said. "I'll plant a thought in your mind and get you to say it."

Wire Rims's grin broadened. "Like what?"

Yost put his hand on the Navajo's shoulder. "Let your mind go blank now," he said. "Don't think about nothing." Yost let ten seconds tick away. He removed the hand. "Now," he said. "It's done. It's in there."

"What?" Wire Rims asked.

"I made you think of a certain card," Yost said. He turned to the spectators, to the Hopi, to Chee. "I always use the same card. Burn it into my mind and keep it there and always use that very same image. That way I can make a stronger impression with it on the other feller's mind." He tapped Wire Rims on the chest with a finger. "He closes his eyes, he sees that certain card."

"Bullshit," Wire Rims said.

"I'll bet you, then," Yost said. "But you got to play fair. You got to name the card you actually see. All right?"

Wire Rims shrugged. "Bullshit. I don't see nothing."

Yost waved his handful of currency. "Yes, you do," Yost insisted. "I got money that says you do. You see that one card I put in your mind. I got $108 here I'll bet you against that belt you're wearing. What's that worth?" It was a belt of heavy conchos hammered out of thick silver. Despite its age and a heavy layer of tarnish it was a beautiful piece of work. Chee guessed it would bring $100 at pawn and sell for maybe $200. But with the skyrocketing price of silver, it might be worth twice that melted down.

"Let's say it would pawn for $300," Yost said. "That gives me three to one odds on the money. But if I'm lying to you, there's just one chance in fifty-two that you'll lose."

"How you going to tell?" Wire Rims asked. "You tell somebody the card in advance?"

122

"Better than that," Yost said. "I got him here in my pocket sealed up in an envelope. I always use that same card so I keep it sealed up and ready."

"Sealed up in an envelope?" Wire Rims asked.

"That's right," Yost said. He tapped his forefinger to the chest of his khaki bush jacket.

Wire Rims unbuckled the belt and handed it to Chee. "You hold the money," he said. Yost handed Chee the currency.

"I get to refresh your memory," Yost said. He put his hand on the Navajo's shoulder. "You see a whole deck of cards face down on the table. Now, I turn this one on the end here over." Yost's right hand turned over an invisible card and slapped it emphatically on an invisible table. "You see it. You got it in your mind. Now play fair. Tell me the name of the card."

Wire Rims hesitated. "I don't see nothing," he said.

"Come on. Play fair," Yost said. "Name it."

"Nine of clubs," Wire Rims said.

"Here is an honest man," Yost said to Chee and the Hopi and the rest of them. "He named the nine of clubs." While he said it, Yost's left hand had dipped into the left pocket of the bush jacket. Now it fished out an envelope and delivered it to Chee. "Read it and weep," Yost said.

Chee handed the envelope to Wire Rims. It was a small envelope, just a bit bigger than a poker card. Wire Rims tore it open and extracted the card. It was the nine of clubs. Wire rims looked from card to Yost, disappointment mixed with admiration. "How you do that?"

"I'm a magician," Yost said. He took the belt and the money from Chee. "Any luck on that burglary?" he asked. "You find that son-of-a-bitch Yazzie yet?"

"Nothing," Chee said.

And then there was a hand on his arm and a pretty face looking up at him. "I've got you," the girl said. She tugged him toward the fire. "You're my partner. Come on, policeman."

"I'd sure like to catch that son-of-a-bitch," Yost said.

The girl danced gracefully. She told Chee she was born to the Standing Rock Dinee and her father was a Bitter Water. With no clan overlap, none of the complex incest taboos of The People prevented their dancing, or whatever else might come to mind. Chee remembered having seen her working behind the registration desk at the Holiday Inn at Shiprock. She was pretty. She was friendly. She was witty. The dance was good. The pot drums tugged at him, and the voices rose in a slightly ribald song about what the old woman and the young man did on the sheepskins away from the firelight. But things nagged at Chee's memory. He wanted to think.

"You don't talk much," the girl said.

"Sorry. Thinking," Chee said.

"But not about me." She frowned at him. "You thinking about arresting somebody?"

"I'm thinking that tomorrow morning when they finish this sing-off with the Scalp Shooting ceremony, they've got to have something to use as the scalp."

The girl shrugged.

"I mean, it has to be something that belonged to the witch. How can they do that unless they know who the witch is? What could it be?"

The girl shrugged again. She was not interested in the subject nor, now, in Jim Chee. "Whyn't you go and ask?" she said. "Big Hat over there is the scalp carrier."

Chee paid his ransom—handing the girl two dollars and then adding two more when the first payment drew a scornful frown. Big Hat was also paying off his partner, with the apparent intention of being immediately recaptured by a plump young woman wearing a wealth of silver necklaces who was waiting at the fringe of the dance. Chee captured him just before the woman did.

"The scalp?" Big Hat asked. "Well, I don't know what you call it. It's a strip of red plastic about this wide," (Big Hat indicated an inch with his fingers) "and maybe half that thick and a foot and a half long."

"What's that got to do with the witch?" Chee asked.

"Broke off the bumper of his truck," Big Hat said. "You know. That strip of rubbery stuff they put on to keep from denting things. It got brittle and some of it broke off."

"At the place where they found the body?"

Big Hat nodded.

"Where you keeping it?" Chee asked. "After you're finished with it tomorrow I'm going to need it." Tomorrow at the final ritual this scalp of the witch would be placed near the Nez hogan. There, after the proper chants were sung, Emerson Nez would attack it with a ceremonial weapon—probably the beak of a raven attached to a stick. Then it would be sprinkled with ashes and shot—probably with a rifle. If all this was properly done, if the minds of all concerned were properly free of lust, anger, avarice—then the witchcraft would be reversed. Emerson Nez would live. The witch would die.

"I got it with my stuff in the tent," Big Hat said. He pointed past the Nez brush arbor. After the ceremony he guessed Chee could have it. Usually anything like that—things touched with witchcraft—would be buried. But he'd ask Dillon Keeyani. Keeyani was the singer. Keeyani was in charge.

And then Jim Chee walked out into the darkness, past the brush arbor and past the little blue nylon tent where Big Hat kept his bedroll and his medicine bundle and what he needed for his role in this seven-day sing. He walked beyond the corral where the Nez outfit kept its horses, out into the sagebrush and the night. He found a rock and sat on it and thought.

While he was dancing he had worked out how Ed Yost had won Wire Rims's belt. A simple matter of illusion and distraction. The easy way it had fooled him made him aware that he must be overlooking other things because of other illusions. But what?

He reviewed what Pinto had told him. Nothing there. He skipped to his own experience with the body. The smell. Checking what was left of the clothing for identification. Moving what was left into the body bag. Hearing the cloth tear. Feeling the bare bone, the rough, dried leather of the boots as he . . .

The boots! Chee slapped both palms against his thighs. The man had his boots on. Why would the witch, the madman, take the skin for corpse powder from the hands and leave the equally essential skin from the feet? He could not, certainly, have replaced the boots. Was the killing not a witch-killing, then? But why the flayed hands? To remove the fingerprints?

Yazzie. Yazzie had a police record. One simple assault. One driving while intoxicated. Printed twice. Identification would have been immediate. But Yazzie was larger than the skinned man, and still alive when the skinned man was dead. John Doe remained John Doe. This only changed John Doe from a random victim to a man whose killer needed to conceal his identity.

The air moved against Chee's face and with the faint breeze came the sound of the pot drums and of laughter. Much closer he heard the fluting cry of a hunting owl. He saw the owl now, a gray shape gliding in the starlight just above the sage, hunting, as Chee's mind hunted, something which eluded it. Something, Chee's instinct told him, as obvious as the nine of clubs.

But what? Chee thought of how adroitly Yost had manipulated Wire Rims into the bet, and into the illusion. Overestimating the value of the man's belt. Causing them all to think of a single specific card, sealed in a single specific envelope, waiting to be specifically named. He smiled slightly, appreciating the cleverness.

The smile lingered, abruptly disappeared, reappeared and suddenly converted itself into an excultant shout of laughter. Jim Chee had found another illusion. In this one, he had been Yost's target. He'd been totally fooled. Yazzie *was* John Doe. Yost had killed him, removed the fingerprints, put the body where it would be found. Then he had performed his magic. Cleverly. Taking advantage of the circumstances—a new policeman who'd never seen Yazzie. Chee re-created the day. The note to call Yost. Yost wanting to see him, suggesting two in the afternoon. Chee had been a few minutes late. The big, round-faced Navajo stalking out of Yost's office. Yost's charade of indignant anger. Who was this ersatz ''Yazzie''? The only requirement would be a Navajo from another part of the reservation, whom Chee wouldn't be likely to see again soon. Clever!

That reminded him that he had no time for this now. He stopped at his own vehicle for his flashlight and then checked Yost's truck. Typical of trucks which live out their lives on the rocky tracks of the reservation, it was battered, scraped and dented. The entire plastic padding strip was missing from the front bumper. From the back one, a piece was missing. About eighteen inches long. What was left fit Big Hat's description of the scalp. His deduction confirmed, Chee stood behind the truck, thinking.

Had Yost disposed of Yazzie to cover up the faked burglary? Or had Yazzie been killed for some unknown motive and the illusion of burglary created to explain his disappearance? Chee decided he preferred the first theory. For months before the crime the price of silver had been skyrocketing, moving from about five dollars an ounce to at least forty dollars. It bothered Yost to know that as soon as they sold their wool, his customers would be paying off their debts and walking away with that sudden wealth.

The Girl Dance had ended now. The drums were quiet. The fire had burned down. People were drifting past him through the darkness on their way back to their bedrolls. Tomorrow at dawn there would be the final sand-painting on the floor of the Nez hogan; Nez would drink the ritual emetic and just as the sun rose would vomit out the sickness. Then the Scalp Shooting would be held. A strip of red plastic molding would be shot and a witch would, eventually, die. Would Yost stay for the finish? And how would he react when he saw the plastic molding?

A split second into that thought, it was followed by another. Yost had heard what Pinto had said. Yost would know this form of the Enemy Way required a ceremonial scalp. Yost wouldn't wait to find out what it was.

Chee snapped on the flashlight. Through the back window of Yost's pickup he saw that the rifle rack now held only the 30.06. The carbine was gone.

Chee ran as fast as the darkness allowed, dodging trucks, wagons, people, and camping paraphernalia, toward the tent of Big Hat. Just past the brush arbor he stopped. A light was visible through the taut blue nylon. It moved.

Chee walked toward the tent, quietly now, bringing his labored breathing under control. Through the opening he could see Big Hat's bedroll and the motionless outflung arm of someone wearing a flannel shirt. Chee moved directly in front of the tent door. He had his pistol cocked now. Yost was squatting against the back wall of the tent, illuminated by a battery lantern, sorting through the contents of a blue cloth zipper bag. Big Hat sprawled face down just inside the tent, his hat beside his shoulder. Yost's carbine was across his legs . . .

"Yost," Chee said. "Drop the carbine and . . ."

Yost turned on his heels, swinging the carbine.

Jim Chee, who had never shot anyone, who thought he would never shoot another human, shot Yost through the chest.

Big Hat was dead, the side of his skull dented. Yost had neither pulse nor any sign of breath. Chee fished in the pockets of his bush jacket and retrieved the concho belt. He'd return it to Wire Rims. In the pocket with it were small sealed envelopes. Thirteen of them. Chee opened the first one. The Ace of Hearts. Had Wire Rims guessed the five of hearts, Yost would have handed him the fifth envelope from his pocket. Chee's bullet had gone through the left breast pocket of Yost's jacket—puncturing diamonds and spades.

Behind him Chee could hear the sounds of shouting, of running feet, people gathering at the tent flap. Cowboy was there, staring in at him. "What happened?" Cowboy said.

And Chee said, "The witch is dead."

The Double Take

·

Richard S. Prather

From 1950 to the early 1970s, Richard S. Prather's virile, white-haired, L.A. private eye, Shell Scott, was enormously popular among readers of softcover originals, who bought more than 40 million copies of such bawdy capers as Bodies in Bedlam, Strip for Murder, Slab Happy, and Dig That Crazy Grave. Prather and Scott retired in the mid 1970s— but not permanently, to the delight of their legion of fans. They reappeared with The Amber Effect (1986), in vintage form, and will continue to be heard from in a series of new adventures. "The Double Take" is one of Shell Scott's early investigations, first published in 1953, and a dandy and typically wacky one it is.

This was a morning for weeping at funerals, for sticking pins in your own wax image, for leaping into empty graves and pulling the sod in after you. Last night I had been at a party with some friends here in Los Angeles, and I had drunk bourbon and Scotch and martinis and maybe even swamp water from highball glasses, and now my brain was a bomb that went off twice a second.

I thought thirstily of Pete's Bar downstairs on Broadway, right next door to this building, the Hamilton, where I have my detective agency, then got out of my chair, left the office, and locked the door behind me. I was Shell Scott, the Bloodshot Eye, and I needed a hair of the horse that bit me.

130

Before I went downstairs I stopped by the PBX switchboard at the end of the hall. Cute little Hazel glanced up.

"You look terrible," she said.

"I know. I think I'm decomposing. Listen, a client just phoned me and I have to rush out to the Hollywood Roosevelt. I'll be back in an hour or so, but for the next five minutes I'll be in Pete's. Hold down the fort, huh?"

"Sure, Shell. Pete's?" She shook her head.

I tried to grin at her, whereupon she shrank back and covered her eyes, and I left. Hazel is a sweet kid, tiny, and curvy, and since mine is a one-man agency with no receptionist or secretary, the good gal tries to keep informed of my whereabouts.

I tottered down the one flight of stairs into bright June sunshine on Broadway, thinking that my client would have to wait an extra five minutes even though he'd been in a hell of a hurry. But he'd been in a hurry the last time, too, and nothing had come of it. This Frank Harrison had first called me on Monday morning, three days ago, and insisted I come right out to his hotel in Hollywood. When I got there he explained that he was having marital troubles and wanted me to tail his wife and see if I could catch her in any indiscretions. When I told him I seldom handled that kind of job, he'd said to forget it, so I had. The deal seemed screwy; he'd not only been vague, but hadn't pressed me much to take the case. It had added up to an hour wasted, and no fee.

But this morning when I'd opened the office at nine sharp the phone had been ringing and it was Harrison again. He wanted me right away this time, too, but he had a real case for me, he said, not like last time, and it wasn't tailing his wife. He was in a sweat to get me out to the Roosevelt's bar, the Cinegrill where we were to meet, and was willing to pay me fifty bucks just to listen to his story. I still didn't know what was up, but it sounded like a big one. I hoped it was bigger than the last "job," and, anyway, it couldn't be as big as my head. I went into Pete's.

Pete knew what I wanted as soon as I perched on a stool and he got a good look at my eyeballs, so he immediately mixed the ghastly concoction he gives me for hangovers. I was halfway through it when his phone rang.

He listened a moment, said, "I'll tell him," then turned to me. "That was Hazel," he said. "Some dame was up there looking for you. A wild woman—"

That was as far as he got. I heard somebody come inside the front door, and high heels clicked rapidly over the floor and stopped alongside me. A woman's voice, tight and angry, said, "There you are, you, you—you crook!" and I turned on my stool to look at the wild woman.

I had never seen her before, but that was obviously one of the most unfortunate omissions of my life, because one look at her and I forgot my hangover. She was an absolutely gorgeous little doll, about five feet two inches tall, and any half-dozen of her sixty-two delightful inches would make any man stare, and all of her at once was enough to knock a man's eyes out through the back of his head.

"Oh!" she said. "You ought to be tarred and feathered."

I kept looking. Coal black hair was fluffed around her oval face, and though she couldn't have been more than twenty-four or twenty-five years old, a thin streak of gray ran back from her forehead through that thick glossy hair. She was dressed in light blue clam-diggers and a man's white shirt which her chest filled out better than any man's ever did, and her eyes were an incredibly light electric blue—shooting sparks at me.

She was angry. She was so hot she looked ready to melt. It seemed, for some strange reason, she was angry with me. This lovely was not one I wanted angry with me;

I wanted her happy, and patting my cheek, or perhaps even chewing on my ear.

She looked me up and down and said, "Yes. Yes, you're Shell Scott."

"That's right. Certainly. But—"

"I want that twenty-four thousand dollars and I'm going to get it if I—if I have to *kill* you! I mean it!"

"Huh?"

"It's just money to you, you crook! But it's all he had, all my father's saved in years and years. Folsom's Market, indeed! I'll kill you, I *will*! So give me that money. I know you're in with them."

My head was in very bad shape to begin with, but now I was beginning to think maybe I had mush up there. She hadn't yet said a single word that made sense.

"Take it easy," I said. "You must have the wrong guy."

If anything, that remark made her angrier. She pressed white teeth together, and made noises in her throat, then she said, "I suppose you're not Shell Scott."

"Sure I am, but I don't know what you're babbling about."

"Babbling! *Babbling!* Ho, that's the way you're going to play it, are you? Going to deny everything, pretend it never happened! I knew you would! Well—"

She backed away from me, fumbling with the clasp of a big handbag. I looked at her thinking that one of us was completely mad. Then she dug into her bag and pulled out a chromed pistol, probably a .22 target pistol, and pointed it at me. She was crying now, her face twisted up and tears running down her cheeks, but she still appeared to be getting angrier every second, and slowly the thought seeped into my brain: this tomato is aiming a real gun at me.

She backed away toward the rear of Pete's, but she was still too close to suit me, and close enough so I could see her eyes squeeze shut and her finger tighten on the trigger. I heard the crack of the little gun and I heard a guy who had just come in the door let out a yelp behind me, and I heard a little tinkle of glass. And then I heard a great clattering and crashing of glass because by this time I was clear over behind the bar with Pete, banging into bottles and glasses on my way down to the floor. I heard the gun crack twice more and then high heels clattered away from me and I peeked over the bar just in time to see the gal disappearing into the ladies' room.

A man on my left yelled, "Janet! *Jan!*" I looked at him just as he got up off the floor, and I remembered the guy who had yelped right after that first shot. He didn't seem to be hurt, though, because he got to his feet and started after the beautiful crazy gal.

He was a husky man, about five-ten, wearing brown slacks and a T-shirt which showed off his impressive chest. Even so, it wasn't as impressive as the last chest I'd seen, and although less than a minute had elapsed since I'd first seen the gal who'd been behind it, I was already understandably curious about her. I vaulted over the bar and yelled at the man, "Hey, you! Hold it!"

He stopped and jerked his head around as I stepped up in front of him. His slightly effeminate face didn't quite go with the masculine build, but many women would probably have called him "handsome" or even "darling." A thick mass of black curly hair came down in a sharp widow's peak on his white forehead. His mouth was full, chin square and dimpled, and large black-lashed brown eyes blinked at me.

"Who the hell was that tomato?" I asked him. "And what's happening?"

"You tell me," he said. And then an odd thing happened. He hadn't yet had time to take a good look at me, but he took it now. He gawked at my white hair, my face, blinked, and his mouth dropped open. "Oh, *Christ*!" he said, and then he took off. Naturally he ran into the ladies' room. It just wouldn't have seemed right at that point if he'd gone anyplace else.

I looked over my shoulder at Pete, whose mouth was hanging completely ajar, then I went to the ladies' room and inside. Nobody was there. A wall window was open and I looked out through it at the empty alley, then looked all around the rest room again, but it was still empty.

I went back to the bar and said, "Pete, what the hell did you put in that drink?"

He stared at me, shaking his head. Finally he said, "I never seen nothing like that in my life. Thirteen years I've run this place, but—" He didn't finish it.

My hand was stinging and so was a spot on my chin. Going over the bar I had broken a few bottles and cut my left hand slightly, and one of those little slugs had apparently come close enough to nick my chin. I had also soaked up a considerable amount of spilled whiskey in my clothes and I didn't smell good at all. My head hadn't been helped, either, by the activity.

Pete nodded when I told him to figure up the damage and I'd pay him later, then I went back into the Hamilton Building. It appeared Frank Harrison would have to wait. Also, the way things were going, I wanted to get the .38 Colt Special and harness out of my desk.

At the top of the stairs I walked down to the PBX again. Hazel, busy at the switchboard, didn't see me come up but when I spoke she swung around. "What's with that gal you called Pete's about?" I asked her.

"She find you? Wasn't she a beautiful little thing?"

"Yeah. And she found me."

Hazel's nose was wrinkling. "You *are* decomposing," she said. "Into bourbon. How many shots did you have?"

"Three, I think. But they all missed me."

"Missed you, ha—"

"Shots that beautiful little thing took at me, I mean. With a gun."

Hazel blinked. "You're kidding." I shook my head and she said, "Well, I—she did seem upset, a little on edge."

"She was clear the hell over the edge. What did she say?"

"She asked for you. As a matter of fact, she said, 'Where's that dirty Shell Scott?' I told her you'd gone to Pete's downstairs"—Hazel smiled sweetly—"for some medicine, and she ran away like mad. She seemed very excited."

"She was."

"And a man came rushing up here a minute or two after the girl and asked about her. I said I'd sent her to Pete's— and *he* ran off." She shook her head. "I don't know. I'm a little confused."

That I could understand. Maybe it was something in the L.A. air this morning. I thanked Hazel and walked down to the office, fishing out my keys, but when I got there I noticed the door was already cracked. I shoved it open and walked inside. For the second or third time this morning my jaw dropped open. A guy was seated behind my desk, fussing with some papers on its top, looking businesslike as all hell. He was a big guy, husky, around thirty years old, with white hair sticking up into the air about an inch.

Without looking up, he said, "Be right with you."

I walked to the desk and sank into one of the leather chairs in front of it, a chair I bought for clients to sit in. If the chair had raised up and floated me out of the window while violins played in the distance, my stunned expression would not have changed one iota. In a not very strong voice I said, "Who are you?"

"I'm Shell Scott," he said briskly, glancing up at me.

Ah, yes. That explained it. He was Shell Scott. Now I knew what was wrong. I had gone crazy. My mind had snapped. For a while there I'd thought *I* was Shell Scott.

But slowly reason filtered into my throbbing head again. I'd had all the mad episodes I cared for this morning, and here was a guy I could get my hands on. He was looking squarely at me now, and if ever a man suddenly appeared scared green, this one did. Except for the short white hair and the fact that he was about my size, he didn't resemble me much, and right now he looked sick. I got up and leaned on the desk and shoved my face at him.

"That's interesting," I said pleasantly. "I, too, am Shell Scott."

He let out a grunt and started to get up fast, but I reached out and grabbed a bunch of shirt and tie and throat in my right fist and I yanked him halfway across the desk.

"O.K., you smart sonofabitch," I said. "Let's have a lot of words. Fast, mister, before I break some bones for you."

He squawked and sputtered and tried to jerk away, so I latched onto him with the other hand and started to haul him over the desk where I could get at him good. I only started to though, because I heard someone behind me. I twisted my head around just in time to see the pretty boy from Pete's, the guy who'd left the ladies' room by the window. Just time to see him, and the leather-wrapped sap in his hand, swinging down at me. Then another bomb, a larger one this time, went off in my head and I could feel myself falling, for miles and miles, through deepening blackness.

I came to in front of my desk, and I stayed there for a couple of minutes, got up, made it to the desk chair, and sat down on it. If I had thought my head hurt before, it was nothing to the way it felt now. It took me about ten seconds to go from angry to mad to furious to raging, then I grabbed the phone and got Hazel.

"Where'd those two guys go?"

"What guys?"

"You see anybody leave my office?"

"No, Shell. What's the matter?"

"Plenty." I glanced at my watch. Nine-twenty. Just twenty minutes since I'd first opened the office door this morning and answered the ringing phone. I couldn't have been sprawled on the floor more than a minute or two, but even so my two pals would be far away by now. Well, Harrison was going to have a long wait because I was taking no cases but my own for a while. What with people shooting at me, impersonating me, and batting me on the head, this was a mess I had to find out about fast.

"Hazel," I said, "get me the Hollywood Roosevelt."

While I waited I calmed down a little and, though the throbbing in my head made it difficult, my thoughts got a little clearer. It seemed a big white-haired ape was passing himself off as me, but I didn't have the faintest idea why. He must have been down below on Broadway somewhere, waited till he saw me leave, then come up. What I couldn't figure was how the hell he'd known I'd be leaving my office. He certainly couldn't have intended hanging around all day just in case I left, and he couldn't have known I'd be at Pete's—

I stopped as a thought hit me. "Hazel," I said. "Forget that call." I hung up, thinking. Whitey couldn't have known I'd show up with a hangover, but he might have known I'd be out of here soon after I arrived. All it takes to get a private detective out of his office is—a phone call. An urgent appointment to meet somebody somewhere, say, maybe somebody like Frank Harrison. Could be I was reaching for that one, but I didn't think so. I'd had only the one call this morning, an urgent call that would get me out of the office—and from the very guy who'd pulled the same deal last Monday. And all I'd done Monday was waste an hour. The more I thought about it the more positive I became.

Harrison might still be waiting in the Cinegrill—and he might not. If Harrison were in whatever this caper was with Whitey and Pretty Boy, they'd almost surely phone him soon to let him know I hadn't followed the script; perhaps were even phoning him right now. He'd know, too, that unless I was pretty stupid, I'd sooner or later figure out his part in this.

Excitement started building in me as I grabbed my gun and holster and strapped them on; I was getting an inkling of what might have been wrong with that black-haired lovely. Maybe I'd lost Whitey and Pretty Boy, but with luck I could still get my hands on Harrison. Around his throat, say. I charged out of the office. My head hurt all the way, but I made it to the lot where I park my convertible Cadillac, leaped in, and roared out onto Broadway. From L.A. to downtown Hollywood I broke hell out of the speed limit, and at the hotel I found a parking spot at the side entrance, hurried through the big lobby and into the Cinegrill.

I remembered Harrison was a very tall diplomat-type with hair graying at the temples and bushy eyebrows over dark eyes. Nobody even remotely like him was in the bar. I asked the bartender, "You know a Frank Harrison?"

"Yes, sir."

"He been in here?"

"Yes, sir. He left just a few minutes ago."

"Left the hotel?"

"No, he went into the lobby."

"Thanks." I hustled back into the lobby and up to the desk. A tall, thin clerk in his middle thirties, wearing rimless glasses, looked at me when I stopped.

"I've got an appointment with Mr. Frank Harrison," I said. "What room is he in?"

"Seven-fourteen, sir." The clerk looked a little bewildered. "But Mr. Harrison just left."

"Where'd he go? How long ago?"

The clerk shook his head. "He was checking out. I got his card, and when I turned around I saw him going out the door. Just now. It hasn't been a minute. I don't—"

I turned around and ran for the door swearing under my breath. The bastard would have been at the desk when I came in through the side entrance and headed for the Cinegrill. He must have seen me, and that had been all; he'd powdered. He was well powdered, too, because there wasn't a trace of him when I got out onto Hollywood Boulevard.

Inside the hotel again I checked some more with the bartender and desk clerk, plus two bellboys and a dining-room waitress. After a lot of questions I knew Harrison had often been seen in the bar and dining room with two other men. One was stocky, with curly black hair, white skin, cleft chin, quite handsome—Pretty Boy; the other was bigger and huskier and almost always wore a hat. A bellhop said he looked a bit like me. I told him it *was* me, and left him looking bewildered. Two bellboys and the bartender also told me that Harrison was seen every day, alomst *all* of every day, with a blond woman a few years under thirty whom they all described as "stacked." The three men and the blonde were often a foursome. From the bartender I learned that Harrison had gotten a phone call in the Cinegrill about five minutes before I showed up. That would have been from the other two guys on my list, and fit with Harrison's checking out fast—or starting to. I went back to the desk and chatted some more with the thin clerk after showing him the photostat of my license. Pretty Boy—Bob Foster—was in room 624;

Whitey—James Flagg—was in 410; Frank Harrison was in 714.

I asked the clerk, "Harrison married to a blonde?"

"I don't believe he is married, sir."

"He's registered alone?" He nodded, and I said, "I understand he's here a lot with a young woman. Right?"

"Yes, sir. That's Miss Willis."

"A blonde?"

"Yes, Quite, ah, curvaceous."

"What room is she in?"

He had to check. He came back with the card in his hand and said, "Isn't this odd? I had never noticed. She's in seven-sixteen."

It wasn't at all odd. I looked behind him to the slots where room keys were kept. There wasn't any key in the slot for 714. Nor was there any key in the 716 slot. I thanked the clerk, took an elevator to the seventh floor, and walked to Harrison's room. There were two things I wanted to do. One was look around inside here to see if maybe my ex-client had left something behind which might help me find him; and the other was to talk with the blonde. As it turned out, I killed two birds with one stone.

The door to 714 was locked, and if I had to I was going to bribe a bellboy to let me in. But, first, I knocked.

It took quite a while, and I had almost decided I'd have to bribe the bellhop, but then there was the sound of movement inside, a muffled voice called something I couldn't understand, and I heard the soft thud of feet coming toward the door. A key clicked in the lock and the door swung open. A girl stood there, yawning, her eyes nearly closed, her head drooping as she stared at approximately the top button of my coat.

She was stark naked. Stark. I had seldom seen *anything* so stark. She had obviously just gotten out of bed, and just as obviously had been sound asleep. She still wasn't awake, because blinking at my chest she mumbled, "Oh, dammit to hell, John."

Then she turned around and walked back into the room. I followed her, as if hypnotized, automatically swinging the door shut behind me. She was about five-six and close to 130 pounds, and she was shaped like what I sometimes muse about after the third highball. Everybody who had described the blonde, and she was a blonde, had been correct: she was not only "stacked" but "ah, curvaceous." There was no mistaking it, either; the one time a man can be positive that a woman's shape is her own is when she is wearing nothing but her shape, and this gal was really in *dandy* shape. She walked away from me toward a bedroom next to this room, like a gal moving in her sleep. She walked to the bed and flopped onto it, pulling a sheet up over her, and I followed her clear to the bed, still coming out of shock, my mind not yet working quite like a well-oiled machine. I managed to figure out that my Frank Harrison was actually named John something. Then she yawned, blinked up at me and said, "Well, dammit to hell, John, stop staring."

And then she stopped suddenly with her mouth stretching wider and wider and her eyes growing enormous as she stared at me. Then she screamed. Man, she screamed like a gal who had just crawled into bed with seventeen tarantulas. I was certainly affecting people in peculiar fashion this morning. She threw off the sheet, leaped to the floor, and lit out for an open door in the far wall, leading into the bathroom, and by now that didn't surprise me a bit.

She didn't make it though. She was only a yard from me at the start, and I took one step toward her, grabbed her wrist and hung on. She stopped screaming and slashed long red fingernails at my face, but I grabbed her hand and shoved her back onto the bed, then said, "Relax, sister. Stop clawing at me and keep your yap closed and I'll let go of you.''

She was tense, jerking her arms and trying to get free, but suddenly she relaxed. Her face didn't relax, though: she still glared at me, a mixture of hate, anger, and maybe fright, staining her face. She didn't have makeup on, but her face had a hard, tough-kid attractiveness.

I let go of her and she grabbed the sheet, pulled it up in front of her body. ''Get the hell out of here,'' she said nastily. There was a phone on a bedside stand and her eyes fell on it. She grabbed it, pulled it off the hook. ''I'm calling the cops.''

I pulled a chair over beside the bed and sat down. Finally she let go of the phone and glared some more at me.

''I didn't think you'd call any cops, sweetheart,'' I said. ''Maybe I will, but you won't. Quite a shock seeing me here, isn't it? I was supposed to meet Frank—I mean, John—in the Cinegrill, not up here. You're in trouble, baby.''

''I don't know what you're talking about.''

''Not much. You know who I am.''

''You're crazy.''

''Shut up, Miss Willis. I got a call from your boy friend at nine sharp this morning. I was supposed to rush out here for an important job; only there isn't any important job. Your John, the guy I know as Frank Harrison, just wanted me out of my office for an hour or so. Right?''

She didn't say anything.

''So another guy could play Shell Scott for a while. Now you tell me why.''

Her lips curled and she swore at me.

I said, ''Something you don't know. You must have guessed the caper's gone sour, but you probably don't know John has powdered. Left you flat, honey.''

She frowned momentarily, then her face smoothed and got blank. It stayed blank.

She was clammed good. Finally I said, "Look, I know enough of it already. There's John, and Bob Foster, and a big white-haired slob named Flagg who probably got his peroxide from you. And don't play innocent because I know you're thick with all of them, especially John. Hell, this is his room. So get smart and—"

The phone rang. She reached for it, then stopped.

I yanked the .38 out from under my coat and said, "Don't get wise; say hello." I took the phone off the hook and held it for her. She said, "Hello," and I put the phone to my ear just in time to hear a man's voice say, "John, baby. I had to blow fast, that bastard was in the hotel. Pack and meet me at Apex." He stopped.

I covered the mouthpiece and told the blonde, "Tell him O.K. Just that, nothing else."

I stuck the phone up in front of her and she said, "The panic's on. Fade out." I got the phone back to my ear just in time to hear the click as he hung up.

The blonde was smiling at me. But she stopped smiling when I stuck my gun back in its holster, then juggled the receiver and said, "Get me the Hollywood Detective Division."

"Hey, wait a minute," the blonde said. "What you calling the cops for?"

"You can't be that stupid. Tehachapi for you, sweetheart. You probably have a lot of friends there. It won't be so bad. Just horrible."

She licked her lips. When the phone was answered I said, "Put Lieutenant Bronson on, will you?"

The gal said, "Wait a minute. Hold off on that call. Let's . . . talk about it."

I grinned. "Now you want to talk. No soap. You can

144

talk to the cops. And don't tell me there isn't enough to hold you on.''

"Please. I—call him later if you have to.'' She let go of the sheet and it fell to her waist. I told myself to be strong and look away, but I was weak.

"You got it all wrong,'' she said softly. "Let's—talk.'' She tried to smile, but it didn't quite come off. I shook my head.

She threw the sheet all the way back on the bed then, stood up, holding her body erect, and stepped close to me. "Please, honey. We can have fun. Don't you like me, honey?''

"What's with that white-haired ape in my office? And what's Apex?''

"I don't know. I told you before. Honest, Honey, look at me.''

That was a pretty silly thing to say, because I sure wasn't looking at the wallpaper. Just then Lieutenant Bronson came on and I said, "Shell Scott here, Bron. Hollywood Roosevelt, room seven-fourteen.''

The blonde stepped closer, almost touching me, then picked up my free hand and passed it around her waist. "Hang up,'' she said. "You won't be sorry.'' Her voice dropped lower, became a husky murmur as she pressed my fingers into the warm flesh. "Forget it, honey. I can be awfully nice.''

Bronson was asking me what was up. I said, "Just a second, Bron,'' then to the girl, "Sounds like a great kick. Just tell me the story, spill your guts—''

She threw my hand away from her, face getting almost ugly, and then she took a wild swing at me. I blocked the blow with my right hand, put my hand flat on her chest and shoved her back against the bed. She sprawled on it, saying some very nasty things.

I said into the phone, "I've got a brassy blonde here for you."

"What's the score?"

"Frankly, I'm not sure. But I'll sign a complaint. Using foul language, maybe."

"That her? I can hear her."

"Or maybe attempted rape." I grinned at the blonde as she yanked the sheet over her and used some more foul language. I said to Bronson, "Actually, it looks like some kind of confidence game—with me a sucker. I don't know the gal, but you guys might make her. Probably she's got a record." I saw the girl's face change as she winced. "Yeah," I added, "she's got a record. Probably as long as her face is right now."

"I'll send a man up."

"Make it fast, will you? I've got to get out of here, and this beautiful blonde hasn't a stitch of clothes on."

"Huh? She—I'll be right there."

It didn't take him long. By ten-forty-five Bronson, who had arrived grinning—and the three husky sergeants who came with him—had taken the blonde away, and I was back in the hotel's lobby. I had given Bronson a rundown on the morning's events, and he's said they'd keep after the blonde. Neither of us expected any chatter from her, though. After that soft, "I can be awfully nice," she hadn't said anything except swear words and: "I want a lawyer, I know my rights, I want a lawyer." She'd get a lawyer. Tomorrow, maybe.

I went into the Cinegrill and had a bourbon and water while I tried to figure my next move. Bron and I had checked the phone book and city directory for an "Apex" and found almost fifty of them, from Apex Diaper Service to an Apex Junk Yard, which was no help at all, though the cops would check. That lead was undoubtedly no good now that the blonde had warned Harrison. I was getting more and more anxious to find out what the score was, because this was sure shaping up like some kind of con, and I wasn't a bit happy about it.

The confidence man is, in many ways, the elite of the criminal world. Usually intelligent, personable, and more persuasive than Svengali, con-men would be the nicest guys in the world except for one thing: they have no conscience at all. I've run up against con-men before, and they're tricky and treacherous. One of my first clients was an Englishman who had been taken on the rag, a stock swindle, for $140,000. He'd tried to find the man, with no luck, then came to me; I didn't have any luck, either. But when he'd finally given up hope of ever seeing his money again, he'd said to me, of the grifter who had taken him, "I shall always remember him as an extrah-dn'rly chahming chap. He was a pleasant bahstahd." Then he'd paused, thought a bit, and added, "But, by God, he *was* a bahstahd!"

The Englishman was right. Confidence men are psychologists with diplomas from sad people: the suckers, the marks, that the con-boys have taken; and there's not a con-man worthy of the name who wouldn't take a starving widow's last penny or a bishop's last C-note, with never a twinge of remorse. They are the pleasant bastards, the con-men, and they thrive because they can make other men believe that opportunity is not only knocking but chopping the door down—and because of men's desire for a fast, even if dishonest, buck, or else the normal greed that's in most of us. They are the spellbinders, and ordinarily don't resort to violence, or go around shooting holes in people.

And it looked as if three of them, or at least two, were up against me. The other one, Pretty Boy Foster, was a bit violent, I remembered, and swung a mean sap. My head still throbbed. All three men, now that the blonde had told Harrison there was big trouble, would probably be making themselves scarce.

But there was still the girl. The gorgeous little gal with black hair and light blue eyes and the chrome-plated pistol. I thought back over what she'd said to me. There'd been a lot of gibberish about $24,000 and my being a crook and—something else. Something about Folsom's Market. It was worth a check. I looked the place up in the phone book, found it listed on Van Ness Avenue, finished my drink, and headed for Folsom's Market.

It was on Van Ness near Washington. I parked, went inside, and looked around. Just an ordinary small store; the usual groceries and a glass-faced meat counter extending the length of the left wall. The place was doing a good business. I walked to the single counter where a young red-haired girl about twenty was ringing up a customer's sales on the cash register, and when she'd finished I told her I wanted to speak with the manager. She smiled, then leaned forward to a small mike and said, "Mr. Gordon. Mr. Gordon, please."

In a few seconds a short man in a business suit, with a fleshy pink face and a slight potbelly walked up to me. I told him my name and business, showed him my credentials, then said, "Actually, Mr. Gordon, I don't know if you can help me or not. This morning I talked briefly with a young lady who seemed quite angry with me. She thought I was some kind of crook and mentioned this place, Folsom's Market. Perhaps you know her." I described the little doll, and she was easy enough to describe, particularly with the odd gray streak in her dark hair. That gal was burned into my memory and I remembered every lovely thing about her, but when I finished the manager shook his head.

"Don't remember anything like her around here," he said.

"She mentioned something about her father, and twenty-four thousand dollars. I don't—"

I stopped, because Mr. Gordon suddenly started chuckling. The cashier said, "Oh, it must be that poor old man."

The manager laughed. "This'll kill you," he said. "Some old foreigner about sixty years old came in here this morning, right at eight when we opened up. Said he just wanted to look his store over. *His* store, get that, Mr. Scott. Claimed he'd bought the place, and—this'll kill you—for twenty-four thousand dollars. Oh, boy, a hundred grand wouldn't half buy this spot."

He was laughing every third word. It had been very funny, he thought. Only it wasn't a bit funny to me, and I felt sick already. The way this deal was starting to figure, I didn't blame the little cutey for taking a few shots at me.

I said slowly, "Exactly what happened? What else did this . . . this foreigner do?"

The manager's potbelly shook a little. "Ah, he gawked around for a while, then I talked to the guy. I guess it must of taken me half an hour to convince him Mr. Borrage owns this place—you know Borrage, maybe, owns a dozen independent places like this, real rich fellow—anyway this stupid old guy swore he'd bought the place. For the money and his little grocery store. You imagine that? Finally I gave him Borrage's address and told him to beat it. Hell, I called Borrage, naturally. He got a chuckle out of it, too, when I told him."

Anger was beginning to flicker in me. "Who was this stupid old man?" I asked him.

He shrugged. "Hell, I don't know. I just told him finally to beat it. I couldn't have him hanging around here."

"No." I said. "Of course not. He was a foreigner, huh? You mean he wasn't an Indian?"

Mr. Gordon blinked at me, said, "Hey?" then described the man as well as he could. He told me he'd never seen the guy before, and walked away.

The cashier said softly, "It wasn't like that at all, Mr. Scott. And he left his name with me."

"Swell, honey. Can you give it to me?"

Her face was sober, unsmiling as she nodded. "I just hate that Mr. Gordon," she said. "The way it was, this little man came in early and just stood around, looking pleased and happy, kind of smiling all the time. I noticed he was watching me for a while, when I checked out the customers, then he came over to me and smiled. 'You're a fast worker,' he said to me. 'Very good worker, I'm watching you.' Then he told me I was going to be working for him, that he'd bought this place and was going to move in tomorrow." She frowned. "I didn't know any better. For all I knew, he might have bought the store. I wish he had." She glanced toward the back of the store where Mr. Gordon had gone. "He was a sweet little man."

"What finally happened?"

"Well, he kept standing around, then Mr. Gordon came up here and I asked him if the store had been sold. He went over and talked to the old man a while, started laughing, and talked some more. The old man got all excited and waved his arms around and started shouting. Finally Mr. Gordon got a little sharp—he's like that—and pointed to the door. In a minute the little guy came over to me and wrote his name and address down. He said there was some kind of mistake, but it would be straightened out. Then he left." She paused. "He looked like he was going to cry."

"I see. You got that name handy?"

"Uh-huh." She opened the cash register and took a slip of paper out of it. "He wanted us to be able to get in touch with him; he acted sort of dazed."

"He would have," I said. She handed me the note. On

it, in a shaky, laboriously scrawled script, was written an address and: *Emil Elmlund, Elmlund's Neighborhood Grocery, Phone WI2-1258.*

"Use your phone?" I asked.

"Sure."

I dialed WI 2-1258. The phone rang several times, then a girl's voice answered, "Hello."

"Hello. Who is this, please?"

"This is Janet Elmlund."

That was what Pretty-Boy had called the girl in Pete's; Janet, and Jan. I said, "Is Mrs. McCurdy there?"

"McCurdy? I—you must have the wrong number."

I told her I wanted WI 2-1259, apologized, and hung up. I didn't want her to know I was coming out there. This time she might have a rifle. Then I thanked the cashier, went out to the Cad, and headed for Elmlund's Neighborhood Grocery.

It was a small store on a tree-lined street, the kind of "Neighborhood Gorcery" you used to see a lot of in the days before supermarkets sprang up on every other corner. A sign on the door said, "Closed Today." A path had been worn in the grass alongside the store's right wall, leading to a small house in the rear. I walked along the path and paused momentarily before the house. It was white, neat, with green trim around the windows, a porch along its front. A man sat on the porch in a wooden chair, leaning forward, elbows on his knees, hands clasped. He was looking right at me as I walked toward him, but he didn't give any sign that he'd noticed me, and his face didn't change expression.

I walked up onto the porch. "Mr. Elmlund?"

He slowly raised his head and looked at me. He was a small man, with a lined brown face and very light blue eyes. Wisps of gray hair still clung to his head. He looked at me and blinked, then said, "Yes."

He looked away from me then, out into the yard again. It was as if I weren't there at all. And, actually, my presence probably didn't mean a thing to him. It was obvious that he had been taken in a confidence game, taken for $24,000 and maybe a dream. I couldn't know all of it yet, but I knew enough about how he must feel now, still shocked, dazed, probably not yet thinking at all.

I squatted beside him and said, "Mr. Elmlund, my name is Shell Scott."

For a minute nothing happened, then his eyebrows twitched, pulled down. Frowning, he looked at me. "What?" he said.

I heard the click of high heels, the front door was pushed open, and a girl stood there, holding a tray before her with two sandwiches on it. It was the same little lovely, black hair pulled back now and tied with a blue ribbon. She still wore the blue clam-diggers and the man's shirt.

I stood up fast. "Hold everything," I said to her. "Get this through your head—there's a guy in town about my size, with hair the same color as mine, and he's pretending to be me. He's taken my name, and he's used my office. But I never heard of you, or Mr. Elmlund, or Folsom's Market until this morning. Now don't throw any sandwiches at me and for Pete's sake don't start shooting."

She had been staring at me open-mouthed ever since she opened the door and spotted me. Finally her mouth came shut with a click and her hands dropped. The tray fell clattering to the porch and the sandwiches rolled almost to my feet. She stared at me for another half-minute without speaking, comprehension growing on her face, then she said, "Oh, no. Oh, no."

"Oh, yes," I said. "Now suppose we all sit down and get to the bottom of this mess."

She said. "Really? Please—you wouldn't—"

"I wouldn't." I showed her several different kinds of

identification from my wallet, license, picture, even a fingerprint, and when I finished she was convinced. She blinked those startling blue eyes at me and said, "How awful. I'm so sorry. Can you ever forgive me?"

"Yes. Yes, indeed. Right now, I forgive you."

"You don't. You can't." For the first time since I'd seen her, she wasn't looking furious or shocked, and for the moment at least she seemed even to have forgotten about the money they'd lost. I had, I suppose, spoken with almost frantic eagerness, and now she lowered her head slightly and blinked dark lashes once, and her red lips curved ever so slightly in a soft smile. At that moment I could have forgiven her if she'd been cutting my throat with a hack saw. She said again, "You can't."

"Oh, yes, I can. Forget it. Could have happened to anybody."

She laughed softly, then her face sobered as she apparently remembered why I was here. I remembered, too, and started asking questions. Ten minutes later we were all sitting on the porch eating picnic sandwiches and drinking beer, and I had most of the story. Mr. Elmlund— a widower, and Janet's father—had run the store here for more than ten years, paid for it, saved $24,000. He was looking for a larger place and had been talking about this to a customer one day, a well-dressed man, smooth-talking, very tall, graying at the temples. The guy's name was William Klein, but he was also apparently my own Frank Harrison. It seemed Harrison was a real-estate broker and had casually mentioned that he'd let Mr. Elmlund know if he ran across anything that looked good.

Mr. Elmlund sipped his beer and kept talking. Elmlund said to me, "He seemed like a very nice man, friendly. Then when he come in and told me about this place it sounded good. He said this woman was selling the store because her husband had died not long ago. She was selling the store and everything and going back East, wasn't really much interested in making a lot of money out of it. She was rich, had a million dollars or more. She just wanted to get away fast, he said, and would sell for sixty-thousand cash. Well, I told him that was too much, but he asked me to look at it—that was Folsom's Market—maybe we could work a deal, he said. So the next Sunday we went there; I didn't think it would hurt none to look."

"Sunday? Was the store open?"

"No, it was closed, but he had a key. That seemed right because he was—he said he was agent for it. Well, it was just like I'd always wanted, a nice store. Nice market there, and plenty of room, good location—" He let the words trail off.

The rest of it was more of the same. The old con play; give the mark a glimpse of something he wants bad, then make him think he can have it for little or nothing, tighten the screws. A good con-man can tie up a mark so tight that normal reasoning powers go out the window. And getting a key which would open the store wouldn't have been any more trouble than getting the one which opened my office.

Last Sunday, a week after they'd looked over the store, Harrison had come to Elmlund all excited, saying the widow was anxious to sell and was going to advertise the store for sale in the local papers. If Elmlund wanted the place at a bargain price he'd have to act fast. Thursday—today, now—the ads would appear and the news would be all over town; right then only the widow, Harrison, and Elmlund himself knew about it. So went Harrison's story. After some more talk Harrison had asked how much cash Elmlund could scrape together. When Harrison learned $24,000 was tops, why naturally that was just enough cash—plus the deed to Elmlund's old store—to maybe swing a fast deal. All con-men are actors, expert at making their lines up as they go along, and Harrison must have made up the bit about throwing the deed in merely to make Elmlund think he was paying a more legitimate price; no well-played mark would think of wondering why a widow getting rid of one store so she could blow would take another as part payment.

Janet broke in, looking at me. "That was when Dad thought about having the transaction investigated. He talked to me about it and decided to see you, have you look into it. You see, he thought the sale was still secret, and you could check on it before the ads came out in the papers. And—he just couldn't believe it. He intended originally to invest only about ten thousand above what we'd get out of our store, but, well, it seemed like such a wonderful chance for him, for us. We were both a little suspicious, though."

"Uh-huh." I could see why Elmlund might want the deal checked, and I could even understand why he'd decided to see me instead of somebody else. The last six months I'd been mixed up in a couple cases that got splashed all over the newspapers, and my name was familiar to most of Los Angeles. But another bit puzzled me.

I said, "Janet, this morning in Pete's"—she made a face—"who was the man who charged in and yelled at you? Just as you were leaving."

"Man? I didn't see any man. I—lost my head." She smiled slightly. "I guess you know. And after—afterwards, I got scared and ran, just wanted to get away. I thought maybe I'd killed somebody."

"I thought maybe you had, myself."

She said. "I was almost crazy. Dad had just told me what had happened, and I was furious. And you'd told Dad everything was fine, that the transaction was on the level—I mean *he* had, that other Shell Scott—you know."

155

"Yeah. What about that?" I turned to Mr. Elmlund. "When did you see this egg in my office?" I already knew, but I wanted to be sure.

"At nine-thirty on Monday morning, this last Monday. I went in right at nine-thirty, there in the Hamilton Building, and talked to him. He said he'd investigate it for me. Then yesterday morning he came out to the store here and said it was all right. It cost me fifty dollars."

"Sure. That made the con more realistic. You'd have thought it was funny if you weren't soaked a little for the job."

He shrugged and said, "Then right after I talked yesterday to the detective—that one—he drove me and Janet from here to the real estate office, the Angelus Realty. Said he was going by there. Well, I stopped at the bank—those ads were supposed to come out in the papers today, you know—and got the money. Then at that office I gave him the money and signed all the papers and things and—that was all. I wasn't supposed to go to the store till tomorrow, but I couldn't wait."

Janet told me where the "real estate office" was, on Twelfth Street, but I knew that info was no help now. She said that this morning, before she'd come charging in at me, she'd first gone to the Angelus Realtors—probably planning to shoot holes in Harrison, though she didn't say so. But the place had been locked and she'd then come to the Hamilton Building. She remembered the sign "Angelus Realtors" had still been painted on the door, but I knew, sign or no sign, that office would be empty.

I looked at Janet. "This guy I was talking about, the one in Pete's bar this A.M., was about five-ten, stocky; I suppose you'd say he was damned good looking. Black hair, even features."

"That sounds like Bob Foster. Cleft chin and brown eyes?"

"That's him. Did you meet him before or after this deal came up?"

"Bob? Why, you can't think he—"

"I can and do. I'm just wondering which way it was; did he set up the con, or did he come in afterwards."

"Why, I met Bob a month before the realtor showed up. Bob and I went out several times."

"Then dear Bob told him to come around, I imagine. I suppose Bob knew your father was thinking about a new store."

"Yes, but—"

"And after you and your father talked about hiring me to make sure the deal was square, did Bob happen to learn about it?"

"Why—he was here when we discussed it. He—" She stopped, eyes widening. "I'd forgotten it until now, but *Bob* suggested that Dad engage an investigator. When we told him we couldn't believe it, that there just had to be something wrong or dishonest about the sale for the price to be so low, *he* suggested we hire a detective to investigate the man and all the rest of it." She paused again. "He even suggested your name, asked us if we'd heard of you or met you. We hadn't met you, but of course we'd read about you in the papers, and told Bob so. He said he knew you, that you were capable and thoroughly honest— and he—made the appointment with you for nine-thirty Monday."

"Good old Bob," I said. "That made it perfect. That would get rid of the last of your doubts. Janet, Bob Foster is probably no more his right name than Harrison is a real estate dealer. The guy I know as Harrison, you know as Klein; his girl friend calls him John, and his real name is probably Willie Zilch. And I'm not getting these answers by voodoo. Harrison, Foster, and the guy who said he was

Shell Scott all stay at the same hotel. They're a team, with so many fake names they sound like a community.''

"But Bob—I thought he was interested in me. He was always nice."

"Yeah, pleasant. So you saw him a few times, and then he learned your dad was ripe for a swindle. He tipped Harrison, the inside-man, and they set up the play. The detective angle just tied it tighter. It was easy enough. A phone call to me to get me out of the office, another guy bleaches his hair, walks in, and waits for your dad to show, then kills a couple days and reports all's well.''

It was quiet for a minute, then I said, "The thing I don't get is how he happened to show up at Pete's right after you did?''

Mr. Elmlund answered that one. "He and Jan were going on a picnic today. When I told her about—about losing my money she ran to the car and drove away. Right after, Bob come in and asked for Janet. I told him what happened. Said she mentioned going to see that Klein and you. Now I think of it, he got a funny look and run off to his car.''

"I hate to say it, Janet," I said, "but Bob was probably less interested in the picnic—under the circumstances— than in finding out if everything was still under control.''

I thought a minute. The white-haired egg had probably been planted outside waiting for me to leave; when I did, he went up to the office. Bob must have showed up and checked with Hazel, reached Pete's just as Janet started spraying bullets around, chased her but couldn't find her or else knew he'd better tip Whitey fast. So he'd charged to the office just in time to sap me. Something jarred my thoughts there. It bothered me but I couldn't figure out what it was.

I said, "Have you been to the police yet?"

Janet said, "No. We've been so—upset. We haven't done anything since I got back home."

"I'll take care of it, then." I got up. "That's about it, I guess. I'll try running the men down, but it's not likely they'll be easily found. I'll do what I can."

Janet had been sitting quietly, looking at me. Now she got up, took my hand, and pulled me after her into the front room of the house. Inside, she put a hand on my arm and said softly, "You know how sorry I am about this morning. I was a little crazy for a while there. But I want to thank you for coming out, saying you'll help."

"I'll be helping myself, too, Janet."

"I get sick when I think I might actually have shot you." She looked at the raw spot on my chin. "Did I—shoot you there?"

I grinned at her. "It might have been a piece of glass. I landed in some."

"Just a minute." She went away and came back with a bit of gauze and a piece of tape. She pressed it gently against the "wound," as she called it, her fingers cool and soft against my cheek. Her touch sent a tingle over my skin, a slight shiver between my shoulder blades. Then she stretched up and gently pressed her lips against my cheek.

"That better?"

It's funny; some women can leap into your lap, practically strangle you, mash their mouth all over you, kiss you with their lips and tongues and bodies, and leave you cold—I'm talking about *you* of course. But just the gentle touch of this gal's lips on my cheek turned my spine to spaghetti. That was the fastest fever I ever got; a thermometer in my mouth would have popped open and spouted mercury every which way.

I said, "Get your .22. I'm about to shoot myself full of holes."

She laughed softly, her arms going around my neck, then she started to pull herself up but my head was already on its way down, and when her lips met mine it was a new kind of shock. The blonde back there in the hotel room had been fairly enjoyable, but Janet had more sex and fire and hunger in just her lips than the blonde had in her entire stark body. When Jan's hands slid from my neck and she stepped back I automatically moved toward her, but she put a hand on my chest, smiling, glanced toward the porch, then took my arm and led me outside again.

When my breathing was reasonably normal I said, "Mr. Elmlund, I'm leaving now but if I get any news at all, I'll hurry back—I mean, ha, come back."

Janet chuckled. "Hurry's all right," she said.

Mr. Elmlund said, "Mr. Scott, if you can get our money again I'll pay you anything—half of it—"

"Forget that part. I don't want any money. If I should miraculously get it back, it's all yours."

He looked puzzled. "Why? Why should you help me?"

I said, "Actually, Mr. Elmlund, this is just as important to me. I don't like guys using my name to swindle people; I could get a very nasty reputation that way. Not to mention my dislike for being conned myself and getting hit over the head. For all I know there are guys named Shell Scott all over town, conning people, maybe shooting people. The con worked so well for these guys once, they'll probably try the same angles again—or would have if I hadn't walked in—on—" I stopped. That same idea jarred my thoughts as it had before when I'd been thinking about the guy in my office. It was so simple I should have had it long ago. But now a chill ran down my spine and I leaned toward Mr. Elmlund.

"You weren't supposed to see me—the detective—this morning, were you?"

"Why, no. Everything was finished, he already give me his report."

I didn't hear the rest of what he said. I was wondering why the hell Harrison had called me again, why Whitey had needed my office again, if not for Mr. Elmlund.

I swung toward Janet. "Where's your phone? Quick."

She blinked at me, then turned and went into the house. I followed, right on her heels.

"Show me. Hurry."

She pointed out the phone on a table and I grabbed it, dialed the Hamilton Building. There was just a chance—but it was already after noon.

Hazel came on. "This is Shell. Anyone looking for me?"

"Hi, Shell. How's your hangover—"

"This is important, hell with the hangover. Anybody there right after I took off?"

Her voice got brisk. "One man, about fifty, named Carl Strossmin. Said he had an appointment for nine-thirty."

"He say what about?"

"No. I took his name and address. Thity-six, twenty-two Gramercy. Said he'd phone back; he hasn't called."

"Anything else?"

"That's all."

"Thanks." I hung up. I said aloud, "I'll be damned. They've got another mark."

Jan said, "What?" but I was running for the door. I leaped into the Cad, gunned the motor, and swung around in a U-turn. It was clear enough. Somewhere the boys had landed another sucker, and the "investigation" by Shell Scott had worked so well once that they must have used the gimmick again. They would still be around, but if they made this score they'd almost surely be off for Chicago, or Buenos Aires, or no telling where.

* * *

Carl Strossmin—I remembered hearing about him. He'd made a lot of money, most of it in deals barely this side of the law; he'd be the perfect mark because he was always looking for the best of it. Where Elmlund had thought he was merely getting an amazing piece of good fortune, Strossmin might well think he was throwing the blocks to somebody else. I didn't much like what I'd heard about Strossmin, but I liked not at all what I knew of Foster and Whitey and Harrison.

When I spotted the number I wanted on Gramercy I slammed on the brakes, jumped out, and ran up to the front door of 3622. I rang the bell and banged on the door until a middle-aged woman looked out at me, frowning.

"Say," she said. "What is the matter with you?"

"Mrs. Strossmin?"

"Yes."

"Your husband here?"

Her eyes narrowed. "No. Why? What do you want him for?"

I groaned. "He isn't closing any business deal, is he?"

Her eyes were slits now. "What are you interested for?" She looked me up and down. "They told us there were other people interested. You—"

"Lady, listen. He isn't buying a store, or an old locomotive or anything, is he?"

She pressed her lips together. "I don't think I'd better say anything till he gets back."

"That's fine," I said. "That's great. Because the nice businessmen are crooks. They're confidence men, thieves, they're wanted by police of seventy counties. Kiss your cabbage good-bye, lady—or else start telling me about it fast."

Her lips weren't pressed together anymore. They peeled apart like a couple of liver chunks. "Crooks?" she groaned. *"Crooks?"*

"Crooks, gyps, robbers, murderers. Lady, they're dishonest."

She let out a wavering scream and threw her hands in the air. "Crooks!" she wailed. "I told him they were crooks. Oh, I told the old fool, you can bet—!" She fainted.

I swore nastily, jerked the screen door open, and picked her up, then carried her to a couch. Finally she came out of it and blinked at me. She opened her mouth.

I said, "If you say 'crooks' once again I'll bat you. Now where the hell did your husband go?"

She started babbling, not one word understandable. But finally she got to her feet and started tottering around. "I wrote it down," she said. "I wrote it down. I wrote—"

"What did you write down?"

"Where he was going. The address." She threw up her hands. "Forty-one thousand dollars! Crooks! Forty-one—"

"Listen," I said. "He have that much money on him?"

"No. He had to go to the bank."

"What bank?" By the time she answered I'd already spotted the phone and was dialing. A bank clerk told me that Carl Strossmin had drawn $41,000 out of his account only half an hour ago. He'd been very excited, but he'd made no mention of what he wanted the money for. I hung up. I knew why Carl hadn't mentioned anything about it: it was a secret.

Mrs. Strossmin was still puttering around, pulling out drawers, and occasionally throwing her hands up into the air and screeching. Gradually I got her story and, with what I already knew, put the pieces together. Her husband's appointment with "Shell Scott" had been made two days ago by real estate dealer "Harrison" himself, here in Strossmin's home. After suggesting that since Strossmin seemed a bit undecided he might feel safer if he engaged a "completely honest" detective, Harrison had dialed a number, chatted a bit, and handed Strossmin the phone. Finally an appointment had been made for nine-thirty this A.M. Strossmin had been talking, of course, to Whitey who most likely was in a phone booth or bar.

Harrison probably wouldn't have suggested me *by name* to Strossmin, expecting the mark to accept his, the real-tor's suggestion, except for one thing, which was itself important to the con: my reputation in L.A. A lot of people here believe I'm crazy, others think I'm stupid, and many, particularly old maids, are sure I'm a fiendish lecher; but there's never been any question about my being honest. This phase of the con was based on making Stross-min—and Elmlund before him—think he was really talk-ing to me when he met Whitey, the Shell Scott of the con, in my office. However, when I popped back into the office and messed up that play this morning, the boys had to change their plans fast.

At eleven-thirty, about the time I was driving to Elm-lund's, Whitey had come here to Strossmin's home, apol-ogized for not being in his office when Strossmin had arrived this A.M., and said he'd come here to spare Stross-min another trip downtown. After learning what Strossmin wanted investigated, Whitey had pretended surprise and declared solemnly that this was a strange coincidence in-deed, because Strossmin was the second man to ask for the identical investigation. Oh, yes, he'd already investi-gated—for this other eager buyer—and told him that the deal was on the level. No doubt about it, this was the opportunity of the century—and time, sad to say, was ter-ribly short. Apparently, said Whitey, negotiations were going on with dozens of other people—and so on, until Strossmin had been in a frenzy of impatience.

Finally Mrs. Strossmin found her slip of paper and thrust it at me. An address was scribbled on it: Apex Realtors,

4870 Normandie Avenue. I grabbed the paper and ran to the Cad.

Apex Realtors was, logically enough, no more than an ordinary house with a sign in the window: Apex Realtors. When I reached it and parked, a small, well-dressed man with a thick mustache was just climbing into a new Buick at the curb. I ran from the Cad to his Buick and stopped him just as he started the engine.

"Mr. Strossmin?"

He was just like his wife. His eyes narrowed. "Yes."

I took a deep breath and blurted it out, "Did you just buy Folsom's Market?"

He grinned. "Beat you, didn't I? You're too late—"

"Shut up. You bought nothing but a headache. How many men inside there?"

About ready to flip, I yanked out my gun and pointed it at him. *"How many men in there?"*

I thought for a minute he was going to faint, too, but he managed to gasp, "Three."

I said, "You wait here," then turned and ran up to the house. The door was partly ajar, and I hit it and charged inside, the gun in my right hand. There wasn't anybody in sight, but another door straight ahead of me had a sign, "Office," on it. As I went through the door a car motor growled into life behind the house. I ran for the back, found a door standing wide open, and jumped through it just as a sky-blue Oldsmobile sedan parked in the alley took off fast. I barely got a glimpse of it, but I knew who was in it. The three con-men were powdering now that they had all the dough they were after. There was a chance they'd seen me, but it wasn't likely. Probably they'd grabbed the dough and left by the back way as soon as Strossmin stepped through the front door.

I race out front again and sprinted for the Cad, yelling to Strossmin, "Call the police!" He sat there, probably

165

feeling pleased at the coup he'd just put over. He'd call the cops, next week, maybe. I ripped the Cad into gear and roared to the corner, took a right, and stepped on the gas. I had to slow at the next intersection, looked both directions and caught a flash of blue two blocks away on my right, swung in after them, and pushed the accelerator to the floorboards. I was gaining on them rapidly, and now I had a few seconds to try figuring out how to stop them. Up close I could see the Olds sedan, and the figures of three men inside it, two in the front seat and one in back. Con-men don't usually carry guns, but these guys operated a little differently from most con-men. In the first place they usually make the mark think he's in on a crooked deal, and in the second they almost always try to cool the mark out, allay his suspicions so he doesn't know, at least for a long time, that he's been taken. The boys ahead of me had broken both those rules, and there was a good chance they'd also broken the rule about guns.

But I was less than half a block behind them now and they apparently hadn't tumbled. They must figure they were in the clear, so I had surprise on my side. Well, I'd surprise them.

We were a long way from downtown here, but still in the residential section. I caught up with their car, pulled out on their left and slightly ahead, then as we reached an intersection I swung to my right, cutting them off just as I heard one of the men in the blue Olds yell loudly.

The driver did the instinctive thing, jerked his steering wheel to the right, and they went clear up over the curb and stalled on a green lawn before a small house. I was out of my Cad and running toward them, the Colt in my fist, before their car stopped moving twenty feet from me. And one of them *did* have a gun.

They sure as hell knew who I was by now, and I heard the gun crack. A slug snapped past me as I dived for the lawn, skidded a yard. Doors swung open on both sides of the blue Olds. Black-haired Pretty Boy jumped from the back and started running away from me, lugging a briefcase.

I got to my knees, and yelled, "Stop! Hold it or you get it, Foster."

He swung around, crouching, and light gleamed on the metal of a gun in his hand. He fired once at me and missed, and I didn't hold back any longer. I snapped the first shot from my .38, but I aimed the next two times, and he sagged slowly to his knees, then fell forward on his face.

Gray-haired Harrison was a few steps from the car, standing frozen, staring at Foster's body, but Whitey was fifty feet beyond him running like mad. I took out after him, but as I went by Harrison I let him have the full weight of my .38 on the back of his skull. I didn't even look back; he'd keep for a while.

I jammed my gun into its holster and sprinted down the sidewalk, Whitey half a block ahead but losing ground. He wasn't in very good shape, apparently, and after a single block he was damn near staggering. He heard my feet splatting on the pavement behind him and for a moment he held his few yards' advantage, then he slowed again. He must have known I had him, because he stopped and whirled around to face me, ready to go down fighting.

He went down, all right, but not fighting. When he stopped I had been less than ten feet from him, traveling like a fiend, and he spun around just in time to connect his face with my right fist. I must have started the blow from six feet away, just as he began turning, and what with my speed from running, and the force of the blow itself, my fist must have been traveling fifty miles an hour.

It was awful what I did to him. I caught only a flashing glimpse of his face as he swung around, lips peeled back and hands coming up, and then my knuckles landed squarely on his mouth and his lips really peeled back and he started going the same direction I was going and almost as fast. I ran several steps past him before I could stop, but when I turned around he was practically behind me and there was a thin streak of blood for two yards on the sidewalk. He was all crumpled up, out cold, and for a minute I thought he was out for good. But I felt for his heartbeat and found it.

So I squatted by him and waited. Before he came out of it, a little crowd gathered: half a dozen kids and some housewives, one young guy about thirty who came running from half a block away. I told him to call the cops and he phoned. Whitey was still out when the guy came back and said a car was on its way.

Finally Whitey stirred, moaned. I looked around and said to the women, "Get the kids out of here. And maybe you better not stick around yourselves."

The women frowned, shifted uneasily, but they shooed the kids away. Whitey shook his head. Finally he was able to sit up. His face wasn't pretty at all. I grabbed his coat and pulled him close to me.

I said, "Shell Scott, huh? I hear you're a tough baby. Get up, friend."

I stood up and watched him while he got his feet under him. It took him a while, and all the time he didn't say a word. I suppose the decent thing would have been to let him get all the way up, but I didn't wait. When he was halfway up I balled my left fist and slammed it under his chin. It straightened him just enough so I could set myself solidly, and get him good with my right fist. It landed where I wanted it to, on his nose, and he left us for a while longer. He fell onto the grass on his back, and perhaps he had looked a bit like me at one time, but he didn't anymore.

The guy who had called the cops helped me carry

Whitey back to the blue Oldsmobile. We dumped him and Harrison inside and I climbed in back with them—and with the briefcase—while he went out to the curb and waited for a prowl car. I got busy. When I finished, these three boys had very little money in their wallets and none was in the briefcase. It added up to $67,500. There was Elmlund's $24,000, I figured, plus Strossmin's $41,000, plus my $2,500. I lit a cigarette and waited for the cops.

It was two P.M. before I got away. Both cops in the patrol car were men I knew well; Borden and Lane. Lane and I especially were good friends. I gave my story and my angles to Lane, and finally he went along with what I wanted.

I finished it with, "This Strossmin is still so wound up by these guys he'll probably figure it out about next week, but when he does, he should have a good witness. No reason why Elmlund can't be left out of it."

Lane shook his head and rubbed a heavy chin where bristles were already sprouting. "Well . . . if this Strossmin doesn't come through in court, we'll need Elmlund."

"You'll get him. Besides, I'll be in court, remember. Enjoying myself."

He nodded. "O.K., Shell."

I handed him the briefcase with $41,000 inside it, told him I'd come to headquarters later, and took off. I'd given Lane the address where I'd left Strossmin, as well as his home address, but Strossmin hadn't waited. I drove to his house.

I could hear them going at it hammer and tongs. Mrs. Strossmin didn't even stop when I rang the bell, but finally her husband opened the door. He just stood there glowering at me. "Well?" he said.

"I just wanted to let you know, Mr. Strossmin, that the police have caught the men who tricked you."

169

I was going on, but he said, "Trick me? Nobody tricked me. *You're* trying to trick me."

"Look, mister, I just want you to know your money's safe. The cops have it. My name is Shell Scott—"

"Ha!" he said. "It is, hey? No, it's not, that's not your name, can't fool me. You're a crook, that's what you are."

His wife was in the door.

She screeched in his ear, "What did I say? Old fool, I warned you."

"Mattie," he said. "If you don't sit down and shut up—"

I tried some more, but he just wouldn't believe me. A glowing vision could have appeared in the sky crying, "You been tricked, Strossmin!" and the guy wouldn't have believed it. There are marks like him, who beg to be taken.

So finally I said, "Well, you win."

"What?"

"You win. Nothing I can do about it now. Store's yours." I put on a hangdog look. He cackled.

I said, "You can take over the place today, you know. Well, good-bye—and the better man won."

"Today?"

"Yep. Folsom's Market, isn't it?"

"Yes, yes."

"Well, you go right down there. Ask for Mr. Gordon."

"Mr. Gordon?"

"Yep." I shook his hand. He cackled, and Mrs. Strossmin screeched at him, and he told her to shut up and I left. They were still going at it as I drove away to the Elmlunds.

Mr. Elmlund didn't quite know what to do when I dropped the big packet of bills on his table and said the hoods were in the clink. He stared at the money for a long time. When finally he did speak it was just, "I don't know what to say."

Jan came out onto the porch and I told them what happened and I thought they were going to crack up for a while, and then I thought they were going to float off over the trees, but finally Mr. Elmlund said, "I must pay you, Mr. Scott. I must."

I said, "No. Besides I got paid."

Jan was leaning against the side of the door, smiling at me. She'd changed clothes and was wearing a smooth, clinging print dress now, and the way she looked I really should have had on dark glasses. She looked happy, wonderful, and her light blue eyes were half-lidded, her gaze on my mouth.

"No," she said. "You haven't been paid."

Her tongue traced a smooth, gleaming line over her lower lip, and I remembered her fingers on my cheek, her lips against my skin.

"You haven't been paid, Shell."

I had a hunch she was right.

Dust to Dust

•

Marcia Muller

Marcia Muller is a rarity among mystery writers in that she has been able to establish and successfully develop three different series characters: Sharon McCone, a bold, intuitive San Francisco private investigator (Games to Keep the Dark Away, There's Nothing to Be Afraid Of, Eye of the Storm); Elena Oliverez, a Chicana museum curator and amateur sleuth based in Santa Barbara (The Tree of Death, Legend of the Slain Soldiers); and Joanna Stark, a partner in an art security firm whose cases take her from California all over the globe (The Cavalier in White, There Hangs the Knife). In "Dust to Dust," she demonstrates an equally sure hand with the nonseries tale of eerie mystery and quiet horror.

The dust was particularly bad on Monday, July sixth. It rose from the second floor where the demolition was going on and hung in the dry air of the photo lab. The trouble was, it didn't stay suspended. It settled on the Formica counter tops, in the stainless-steel sink, on the plastic I'd covered the enlarger with. And worst of all, it settled on the negatives drying in the supposedly airtight cabinet.

The second time I checked the negatives I gave up. They'd have to be soaked for hours to get the dust out of the emulsion. And when I rehung them they'd only be coated with the stuff again.

I turned off the orange safelight and went into the studio. A thick film of powder covered everything there, too. I'd had the foresight to put my cameras away, but somehow the dust crept into the cupboards, through the leather cases, and onto the lenses themselves. The restoration project was turning into a nightmare, and it had barely begun.

I crossed the studio to the Victorian's big front windows. The city of Phoenix sprawled before me, skyscrapers shimmering in the heat. Camelback Mountain rose out of the flat land to the right, and the oasis of Encanto Park beckoned at the left. I could drive over there and sit under a tree by the water. I could rent a paddlewheel boat. Anything to escape the dry grit-laden heat.

But I had to work on the photos for the book.

And I couldn't work on them because I couldn't get the negatives to come out clear.

I leaned my forehead against the window frame, biting back my frustration.

"Jane!" My name echoed faintly from below. "Jane! Come down here!"

It was Roy, the workman I'd hired to demolish the rabbit warren of cubicles that had been constructed when the Victorian was turned into a rooming house in the thirties. The last time he'd shouted for me like that was because he'd discovered a stained-glass window preserved intact between two false walls. My spirits lifting, I hurried down the winding stairs.

The second floor was a wasteland heaped with debris. Walls leaned at crazy angles. Piles of smashed plaster blocked the hall. Rough beams and lath were exposed. The air was even worse down there—full of powder which caught in my nostrils and covered my clothing whenever I brushed against anything.

I called back to Roy, but his answering shout came from further below, in the front hall.

I descended the stairs into the gloom, keeping to the

wall side because the bannister was missing. Roy stood, crowbar in hand, at the rear of the stairway. He was a tall, thin man with a pockmarked face and curly black hair, a drifter who had wandered into town willing to work cheap so long as no questions were asked about his past. Roy, along with his mongrel dog, now lived in his truck in my driveway. In spite of his odd appearance and stealthy comings and goings, I felt safer having him around while living in a half-demolished house.

Now he pushed up the goggles he wore to keep the plaster out of his eyes and waved the crowbar toward the stairs.

"Jane, I've really found something this time." His voice trembled. Roy had a genuine enthusiasm for old houses, and this house in particular.

I hurried down the hall and looked under the stairs. The plaster-and-lath had been partially ripped off and tossed onto the floor. Behind it, I could see only darkness. The odor of dry rot wafted out of the opening.

Dammit, now there was debris in the downstairs hall, too. "I thought I told you to finish the second floor before you started here."

"But take a look."

"I am. I see a mess."

"No, here. Take the flashlight. Look."

I took it and shone it through the hole. It illuminated gold-patterned wallpaper and wood paneling. My irritation vanished. "What is it, do you suppose?"

"I think it's what they call a 'cozy.' A place where they hung coats and ladies left their outside boots when they came calling." He shouldered past me. "Let's get a better look."

I backed off and watched as he tugged at the wall with the crowbar, the muscles in his back and arms straining. In minutes, he had ripped a larger section off. It crashed to the floor, and when the dust cleared I shone the light once more.

It was a paneled nook with a bench and ornate brass hooks on the wall. "I think you're right—it's a cozy."

Roy attacked the wall once more and soon the opening was clear. He stepped inside, the leg of his jeans catching on a nail. "It's big enough for three people." His voice echoed in the empty space.

"Why do you think they sealed it up?" I asked.

"Fire regulations, when they converted to a rooming house. They . . . what's this?"

I leaned forward.

Roy turned, his hand outstretched. I looked at the object resting on his palm and recoiled.

"God!"

"Take it easy." He stepped out of the cozy. "It's only a dead bird."

It was small, probably a sparrow, and like the stained-glass window Roy had found the past week, perfectly preserved.

"Ugh!" I said. "How did it get in there?"

Roy stared at the small body in fascination. "It's probably been there since the wall was constructed. Died of hunger, or lack of air."

I shivered. "But it's not rotted."

"In this dry climate? It's like mummification. You could preserve a body for decades."

"Put it down. It's probably diseased."

He shrugged. "I doubt it." But he stepped back into the cozy and placed it on the bench. Then he motioned for the flashlight. "The wallpaper's in good shape. And the wood looks like golden oak. And . . . hello."

"Now what?"

He bent over and picked something up. "It's a comb, a mother-of-pearl comb like ladies wore in their hair." He held it out. The comb had long teeth to sweep up heavy tresses on a woman's head.

"This place never ceases to amaze me." I took it and brushed off the plaster dust. Plaster . . . "Roy, this wall couldn't have been put up in the thirties."

"Well, the building permit shows the house was converted then."

"But the rest of the false walls are fireproof sheetrock, like regulations required. This one is plaster-and-lath. This cozy has been sealed off longer than that. Maybe since ladies wore this kind of comb."

"Maybe." His eyes lit up. "We've found an eighty-year-old bird mummy."

"I guess so." The comb fascinated me, as the bird had Roy. I stared at it.

"You should get shots of this for your book," Roy said.

"What?"

"Your book."

I shook my head, disoriented. Of course—the book. It was defraying the cost of the renovation, a photo essay on restoring one of Phoenix's grand old ladies.

"You haven't forgotten the book?" Roy's tone was mocking.

I shook my head again. "Roy, why did you break down this wall? When I told you to finish upstairs first?"

"Look, if you're pissed off about the mess . . ."

"No, I'm curious. Why?"

Now he looked confused. "I . . ."

"Yes?"

"I don't know."

"Don't know?"

He frowned, his pockmarked face twisting in concentration. "I really *don't* know. I had gone to the kitchen for a beer and I came through here and . . . I don't know."

I watched him thoughtfully, clutching the mother-of-pearl comb. "Okay," I finally said, "just don't start on a new area again without checking with me."

"Sorry. I'll clean up this mess."

"Not yet. Let me get some photos first." Still holding the comb, I went up to the studio to get a camera.

In the week that followed, Roy attacked the second floor with a vengeance and it began to take on its original floorplan. He made other discoveries—nothing as spectacular as the cozy, but interesting—old newspapers, coffee cans of a brand not sold in decades, a dirty pair of baby booties. I photographed each faithfully and assured my publisher that the work was going well.

It wasn't, though. As Roy worked, the dust increased and my frustration with the book project—not to mention the commercial jobs that were my bread and butter—deepened. The house, fortunately, was paid for, purchased with a bequest from my aunt, the only member of my family who didn't think it dreadful for a girl from Fairmont, West Virginia, to run off and become a photographer in a big western city. The money from the book, however, was what would make the house habitable, and the first part of the advance had already been eaten up. The only way I was going to squeeze more cash out of the publisher was to show him some progress, and so far I had made none of that.

Friday morning I told Roy to take the day off. Maybe I could get some work done if he wasn't raising clouds of dust. I spent the morning in the lab developing the rolls I'd shot that week, then went into the studio and looked over what prints I had ready to show to the publisher.

The exterior shots, taken before the demolition had begun, were fine. They showed a three-story structure with square bay windows and rough peeling paint. The fanlight over the front door had been broken and replaced with plywood, and much of the gingerbread trim was missing. All in all, she was a bedraggled old lady, but she would again be beautiful—if I could finish the damned book.

The early interior shots were not bad either. In fact, they evoked a nice sense of gloomy neglect. And the renovation of this floor, the attic, into studio and lab was well documented. It was with the second floor that my problems began.

At first the dust had been slight, and I hadn't noticed it on the negatives. As a result the prints were marred with white specks. In a couple of cases the dust had scratched the negatives while I'd handled them and the fine lines showed up in the pictures. Touching them up would be painstaking work, but it could be done.

But now the dust had become more active, taken over. I was forced to soak and resoak the negatives. A few rolls of film had proven unsalvageable after repeated soakings. And, in losing them, I was losing documentation of a very important part of the renovation.

I went to the window and looked down at the driveway where Roy was sunning himself on the grass beside his truck. The mongrel dog lay next to a tire in the shade of the vehicle. Roy reached under there for one of his ever-present beers, swigged at it and set it back down.

How, I wondered, did he stand the heat? He took to it like a native, seemingly oblivious to the sun's glare. But then, maybe Roy *was* a native of the Sun Belt. What did I know of him, really?

Only that he was a tireless worker and his knowledge of old houses was invaluable to me. He unerringly sensed which were the original walls and which were false, what should be torn down and what should remain. He could tell whether a fixture was the real thing or merely a good copy. I could not have managed without him.

I shrugged off thoughts of my handyman and lifted my

hair from my shoulders. It was wheat colored, heavy, and, right now, uncomfortable. I pulled it on top of my head, looked around and spotted the mother-of-pearl comb we'd found in the cozy. It was small, designed to be worn as half of a pair on one side of the head. I secured the hair on my left with it, then pinned up the right side with one of the clips I used to hang negatives. Then I went into the darkroom.

The negatives were dry. I took one strip out of the cabinet and held it to the light. It seemed relatively clear. Perhaps, as long as the house wasn't disturbed, the dust ceased its silent takeover. I removed the other strips. Dammit, some were still spotty, especially those of the cozy and the objects we'd discovered in it. Those could be reshot, however. I decided to go ahead and make contact prints of the lot.

I cut the negatives into strips of six frames each, then inserted them in plastic holders. Shutting the door and turning on the safelight, I removed photographic paper from the small refrigerator, placed it and the negative holders under glass in the enlarger, and set my timer. Nine seconds at f/8 would do nicely.

When the first sheet of paper was exposed, I slipped it into the developer tray and watched, fascinated as I had been since the first time I'd done this, for the images to emerge. Yes, nine seconds had been right. I went to the enlarger and exposed the other negatives.

I moved the contact sheets along, developer to stop bath to fixer, then put them into the washing tray. Now I could open the door to the darkroom and let some air in. Even though Roy had insulated up here, it was still hot and close when I was working in the lab. I pinned my hair more securely on my head and took the contact sheets to the print dryer.

I scanned the sheets eagerly as they came off the roller.

Most of the negatives had printed clearly and some of the shots were quite good. I should be able to assemble a decent selection for my editor with very little trouble. Relieved, I reached for the final sheet.

There were the pictures I had shot the day we'd discovered the cozy. They were different from the others. And different from past dust-damaged rolls. I picked up my magnifying loupe and took the sheet out into the light.

Somehow the dust had gotten to this set of negatives. Rather than leaving speckles, though, it had drifted like a sandstorm. It clustered in iridescent patches, as if an object had caught the light in a strange way. The effect was eerie; perhaps I could put it to use.

I circled the oddest-looking frames and went back into the darkroom, shutting the door securely. I selected the negative that corresponded to one circled on the sheet, routinely sprayed it with canned air for surface dirt, and inserted it into the holder of the enlarger. Adjusting the height, I shone the light down through the negative, positioning the image within the paper guides.

Yes, I had something extremely odd here.

Quickly I snapped off the light, set the timer, and slipped a piece of unexposed paper into the guides. The light came on again, the timer whirred, and then all was silent and dark. I slid the paper into the developer tray and waited.

The image was of the cozy with the bird mummy resting on the bench. That would have been good enough, but the effect of the dust made it spectacular. Above the dead bird rose a white-gray shape, a second bird in flight, spiraling upward.

Like a ghost. The ghost of a trapped bird, finally freed. I shivered.

Could I use something like this in the book? It was perfect. But what if my editor asked how I'd done it? Pho-

tography was not only art but science. You strove for images that evoked certain emotions. But you had dammed
well better know how you got those images.

Don't worry about that now, I told myself. See what
else is here.

I replaced the bird negative with another one and exposed it. The image emerged slowly in the developing
tray: first the carved arch of the cozy, then the plaster-and-
lath heaped on the floor, finally the shimmering figure of
a man.

I leaned over the tray. Roy? A double exposure perhaps?
It looked like Roy, yet it didn't. And I hadn't taken any
pictures of him anyway. No, this was another effect created by the dust, a mere outline of a tall man in what
appeared to be an old-fashioned frock coat.

The ghost of a man? That was silly. I didn't believe in
such things. Not in *my* house.

Still, the photos had a wonderful eeriness. I could in-
clude them in the book, as a novelty chapter. I could write
a little explanation about the dust.

And while on the subject of dust, wasn't it rising again?
Had Roy begun work, even though I'd told him not to?

I crossed the studio to the window and looked down.
No, he was still there by the truck, although he was now
dappled by the shade of a nearby tree. The sun had moved;
it was getting on toward midafternoon.

Back in the darkroom I continued to print from the dust-
damaged group of negatives. Maybe I was becoming fan-
ciful, or maybe the chemicals were getting to me after
being cooped up in here all day, but I was seeing stranger
and stranger images. One looked like a woman in a long,
full-skirted dress, standing in the entrance to the cozy. In
another the man was reaching out—maybe trying to catch
the bird that had invaded his home?

Was it his home? Who were these people? What were they doing in my negatives?

As I worked the heat increased. I became aware of the dust which, with or without Roy's help, had again taken up its stealthy activity. It had a life all its own, as demonstrated by these photos. I began to worry that it would damage the prints before I could put them on the dryer.

The gritty air became suffocating. The clip that held my hair on the right side came loose and a lock hung hot and heavy against my neck. I put one last print on the dryer and went into the studio.

Dust lay on every surface again. What had caused it to rise? I went to the window and looked down. Roy was sitting on the bed of the truck with the mongrel, drinking another beer. Well, if he hadn't done anything, I was truly stumped. Was I going to be plagued by dust throughout the restoration, whether work was going on or not?

I began to pace the studio, repinning my hair and securing the mother-of-pearl comb as I went. The eerie images had me more disturbed than I was willing to admit. And this dust . . . dammit, this *dust*!

Anger flaring, I headed down the stairs. I'd get to the bottom of this. There had to be a perfectly natural cause, and if I had to turn the house upside down I'd find it.

The air on the second floor was choking, but the dust seemed to rise from the first. I charged down the next flight of stairs, unheedful for the first time since I'd lived here of the missing bannister. The dust seemed thickest by the cozy. Maybe opening the wall had created a draft. I hurried back there.

A current of air, cooler than that in the hall, emanated from the cozy. I stepped inside and felt around with my hand. It came from a crack in the bench. A crack? I knelt to examine it. No, it wasn't a crack. It looked like the seat of the bench was designed to be lifted. Of course it was—

there were hidden hinges which we'd missed when we first discovered it.

I grasped the edge of the bench and pulled. It was stuck. I tugged harder. Still it didn't give. Feeling along the seat, I found the nails that held it shut.

This called for Roy's strength. I went to the front door and called him. "Bring your crowbar. We're about to make another discovery."

He stood up in the bed of the truck and rummaged through his tools, then came toward me, crowbar in hand. "What now?"

"The cozy. That bench in there has a seat that raises. Some sort of woodbox, maybe."

Roy stopped inside the front door. "Now that you mention it, I think you're right. It's not a woodbox, though. In the old days, ladies would change into house shoes from outdoor shoes when they came calling. The bench was to store them in."

"Well, it's going to be my woodbox. And I think it's what's making the dust move around so much. There's a draft coming from it." I led him back to the cozy. "How come you know so much about old houses anyway?"

He shrugged. "When you've torn up as many as I have, you learn fast. I've always had an affinity for Victorians. What do you want me to do here?"

"It's nailed shut. Pry it open."

"I might wreck the wood."

"Pry gently."

"I'll try."

I stepped back and let him at the bench. He worked carefully, loosening each nail with the point of the bar. It seemed to take a long time. Finally he turned.

"There. All the nails are out."

"Then open it."

"No, it's your discovery. You do it." He stepped back.

183

The draft was stronger now. I went up to the bench, then hesitated.

"Go on," Roy said. His voice shook with excitement.

My palms were sweaty. Grit stuck to them. I reached out and lifted the seat.

My sight was blurred by a duststorm like those on the negatives. Then it cleared. I leaned forward. Recoiled. A scream rose in my throat, but it came out a croak.

It was the lady of my photographs.

She lay on her back inside the bench. She wore a long, full-skirted dress of some beaded material. Her hands were crossed on her breasts. Like the bird mummy, she was perfectly preserved—even to the heavy wheat-colored hair, with the mother-of-pearl comb holding it up on the left side.

I put my hand to *my* wheat-colored hair. To *my* mother-of-pearl comb. Then, shaken, I turned to Roy.

He had raised the arm that held the crowbar—just like the man had had his hand raised in the last print, the one I'd forgotten to remove from the dryer. Roy's work shirt billowed out, resembling an old-fashioned frock coat. The look in his eyes was eerie.

And the dust was rising again . . .

All the Bagworms on the Block

•

Francis M. Nevins, Jr.

There have been few series about con-men in mystery fiction. The most recent and successful details the exploits of Milo Turner, a very resourceful rogue who is sometimes forced to play detective in order to extricate himself from tricky situations. His creator, Edgar-winning critic (for his nonfiction book on Ellery Queen, Royal Bloodline*) and fictioneer, Francis M. Nevins, Jr., has written several short stories and two novels,* The 120-Hour Clock *and* The Ninety Million Dollar Mouse, *about Turner to date. Both are in top form in "All the Bagworms on the Block"—a scam story, a fair-play detective story, and a nostalgic look at Western films, all rolled into one.*

I put the book back on the steel shelf, three feet from the body, and listened. The storage room was empty except for the dead man and me; no sound but my own thundering heartbeat. I heard footsteps along some unseen corridor, maybe heading this way, I couldn't be sure. I knew I hadn't killed the man, and the reference book had confirmed my theory as to who had, but it still wouldn't do to be found in that film-storage vault with a fresh corpse.

So I ran. Swiftly and silently as I could, like a poor imitation of an Indian. Back through the storage room and along the corridor to the loading-dock exit. Luck stayed with me. I met no one. I took out a handkerchief to avoid leaving prints, twisted back the lock, flung the door open, and leaped down to the Thirteenth Street sidewalk. Then I made myself slow down to a brisk walk and put as much distance between myself and the offices of KBMO-TV as my legs would allow.

West half a mile, then south to Olive where I caught a Bi-State bus that took me into the thick of the St. Louis business district where I could lose myself. Then I got off and walked aimlessly, wherever the crowds were. By now both the local cops and the Feds must be hunting me. I needed quiet time to sort out the mess.

So I turned in at Stadium Cinema II, a couple of blocks north of Busch Stadium, and bought two hours of peace. The matinee attraction was one of those trendy older-woman younger-man romances, just the kind of film I could ignore completely as I leaned back in the well-up-holstered theater chair and sent my thoughts returning to where it had all begun . . .

On that soft and quiet Los Angeles evening ten days after John West's funeral, despite smog and inflation and the energy crunch, I was at peace. The profits from my last adventure guaranteed three more months of ease, and I had nothing in mind but relaxation when my annunciator bloop-bleeped and a familiar if not totally welcome voice emerged from the machine's innards. "It's Louie. Just heard you were in town. Okay if I come up?" Without great enthusiasm I consented and crossed the living room of my hideaway apartment to lower the volume on the TV, which happened to be tuned to an old John West movie.

Of course, half of the stations in the world were running West pictures that evening, and had been since a brain tumor had finally toppled the old oak two weeks before. The dozens of Westerns he'd starred in during his salad years, the war pictures, the macho action flicks—every station that could scrounge a West package from a distributor was blitzing the airwaves with the big rangy body, the king-of-the-hill walk, the drawl that had made John West a symbol of America for the world. So it wasn't really unusual that the booms and bangs of West's Korean War epic *The Beaches of Inchon* were providing background noise as Louie sat on my couch, downing a double jolt of my bourbon and trying to sell me his latest scheme.

Lou the Q—a short wiry-bodied lummox with arms as long as a monkey's and a face to match—had knocked around the fringes of scamdom for a dozen years under five dozen names. Rumor was that he'd been born Louis Quackenbush, which would explain his nickname. In Dallas he'd worked as Uthas Haggerson, in Minneapolis as J. Rudolph Klug; but no matter where he operated or what name he used, his scams had the same nasty habit of falling apart on him. He'd been slammed only once, however, and that time luck was his cellmate.

During the year he'd served at the Federal pen in Lexington, Kentucky, under the name of Harold O'Flynn, the cops never caught on that he was wanted in three other states under three other aliases. Since his release six months ago he'd been out of circulation, which wasn't surprising since most of us in the life considered him a jinx and wouldn't work with him. I had never pulled a job with him but I'd found him to be one of those dullards who inspire brightness in others, and a few of my past nifties had been conjured up during casual chats with him. Louie knew I owed him for those inspirations. That was why he was sprawled on my couch now; pitching an inspiration of his own.

"The guy in the cell next to me, he was a film pirate. One of those people who make duplicate prints or cassettes of movies and sell 'em to collectors. He was serving a year for criminal copyright infringement and I was bored in the slam so he said he'd teach me copyright law. Everybody else in the place was reading constitutional law and prisoners' rights stuff, I read copyright. Wild, huh?''

''Untamed,'' I murmured, sipping Early Times and wondering where this meandering monologue would end.

''And I watched a lotta shoot-'em-ups on the tube.'' Louie pointed vaguely across the room toward the flickers of colored light from my set. ''He was my favorite—John West as The Rio Kid. God, I musta seen those Rio Kid flicks twenty times apiece when I was a boy. Did you know his real name was Adrian Jonathan Westmoreland and he was born in Mount Clemens, Michigan?'' He scooped up last week's *Time* from the coffee table, the one with West's craggy face on the cover, and thumbed through the magazine for the lead story.

''Listen, Milo,'' he demanded, and began to read aloud from the obituary survey of the great Hollywood he-man's career. '' 'For most of the 1930s he was confined on the open ranges of the low-budget Western film, starring in some two dozen quickly lensed oaters as The Rio Kid, a border adventurer who was the hero of countless pulp magazine yarns by a long-forgotten hack named J. F. Carewe. In later years an embittered and impoverished Carewe made a sort of retirement hobby out of telling interviewers how the movies had softened and sanitized his authentic roughneck creation. Savants of horse opera agree that the films resembled Carewe's stories only in that the name Rio Kid was used for the hero, but they rank these pictures, which gave West his first crack at stardom, as among the finest series Westerns ever made. The studio went bankrupt in 1949 and the Rio Kid movies eventually fell into the public domain when no one bothered to renew the copyrights.' ''

Louie rolled the magazine into a cylinder and aimed it

at the TV. "Get it, Milo? All the Rio Kid movies are in public domain. You know what that means?"

"It means anyone can use the films as they please without paying any permissions or royalties," I hazarded.

Louie grinned like a monkey who's found an especially tasty banana. "Not quite. There's a catch I learned from that film pirate. A couple of cases say that if a public domain work is based on another work that's still in copyright, you infringe the other work if you use the public domain work. You see the plan now?"

"Vaguely," I told him. "Did J. F. Carewe renew the copyrights on his pulp stories?"

"You betcha. Like clockwork. And when he died in 1956, a lonely old widower with everything he wrote long out of print and forgotten, he left a very simple will. All his property including literary rights went to his only child, a daughter named Carolyn Carewe who's now a spinster in her seventies, living in a retirement home in northern California."

I raised my hand to halt the flow of data. "Okay, time out. Your idea is for us to contact this old lady, buy the rights to the Rio Kid stories as cheap as we can, then threaten to sue every station that runs those old movies unless they pay our price?"

"On the button, man," Louie nodded, and took a long swallow of bourbon. "You wanna be my partner or you wanna not?"

The more I tossed it around my brain pan the better I liked it, not least because technically it was legal. No wonder Louie had come to me: he needed a partner, and most confidence people wouldn't touch one of his scams with a mile-long pole. But this gem, if polished properly, had magnificent possibilities.

I answered his question with a definite maybe and watched him lurch hazily to my apartment door.

* * *

The next day I spent at the UCLA Law Library, checking out Louie's copyright theory in assorted treatises and journals, then reading the relevant judicial opinions as printed in the National Reporter System. By 6:00 P.M. I decided that the Kentucky film pirate had known his onions. The top legal scholars seemed to think the whole notion was silly—after all, if there are hidden patches of copyright in public domain works, the basic concept and rationale of the public domain is destroyed—but just as one can make bread using an off-brand of yeast, I proposed to make bread using this quirk in the law. I called Louie late that evening and closed a deal with him.

Step Two took a few days and required the services of a lawyer. I needed to form a corporation to hold legal title to the rights we were going to buy from Carolyn Carewe. In due course Western Properties, Inc. was registered with the California Secretary of State. Its president's and vice-president's names were listed as John J. Terwilliger and August Lunt, since my rightful name and Louie's were too well known in certain official circles.

Step Three took no more than a phone call to Jock Schultz, the disembodied Dublin brogue that runs our profession's human supermarket. "That's the job description, Jocko. A woman who can persuade an old spinster to sign over some worthless literary rights her father left her. A woman who can talk convincingly about old Western novels and movies if she has to. Know anyone who can do it?"

"Call ye back in an hour," he promised. And true to his word, he had my lady for me in exactly 52 minutes. ". . . and ye get a bonus, too, me bucko, in that she is a quintessential Ten. Her name is Becca Benbow. Tall, twenty-eight, form divine. She partnered with Fats Adamo last year in the Disco Cola thing."

"Speak no more," I told the Jock. "That's all the recommendation she needs. Can you set up a meet for me?"

He could and did, and that Friday evening I met her plane at L.A. International. She was honey-skinned and slender, with rich brown hair falling loosely below her shoulders. I felt like bending my knee and kissing her hand, for this lady was royalty in more than just looks.

Inside word had it that without her, Disco Cola would have been the world's fattest turkey instead of the superscam of the age. We found a dark corner in a quiet airport lounge, and as I unveiled the proposal to her she nodded and said "Uh-huh," her eyes glowing with the pure joy of the caper. "Equal split?" she asked at the end of my pitch.

I took a moment to ask myself if I could bulldoze Louie into accepting another partner, then nodded. "I wouldn't dream of offering you less," I replied, proud of my non-sexist approach to sharing the spoils. "Take a room at an airport hotel and catch PSA's first flight to San Francisco in the morning. Get cards printed up identifying you as, let's call you Roberta Ross, and your title will be Chief of the Purchasing Department, Western Properties, Inc. Then you rent a car and drive north to the retirement home where Carolyn Carewe lives. After you've signed her up, give me a call here and let me know how much I have to put in the corporate bank account to cover your check. The Rio Kid stories have been out of print for thirty years, so the price shouldn't be steep."

"And meanwhile what will you be doing?" Becca poked the ice in her Scotch-and-soda with a plastic swizzle stick.

"Research," I said. "Pinpointing our first target."

For the next two days and evenings I sat in the Reading Room of the Los Angeles Public Library, hunched over the back files of numerous out-of-town newspapers, skimming the TV sections with my eyes keen for any station that ran old Westerns and the Rio Kid pictures in particular. On the second evening I went over my accumulated list and chose St. Louis, Missouri. Home of the Gateway Arch, the baseball and football Cardinals, the Anheuser-Busch Brewery, and, more to the point, the home of KBMO-TV, Channel 39, which, according to the *Post-Dispatch* and *Globe-Democrat* listings, broadcast an old horse opera every weeknight from 10:00 to 11:00 P.M.

I had some qualms about returning to the city where four years ago one of my juciest scams had blown apart, leaving me with a pile of cash and the solution to an old murder case. But I was so excited over this new ploy—which, if it worked, could be replayed in city after city all over the land—that I told the voice of caution to be quiet.

Late that night back in my apartment, I was relaxing with a glass of white wine when the phone rang. Becca, my ESP told me, and when I lifted the receiver and cautiously helloed, sure enough it was she. "Got her!" she crowed. "And dirt cheap, too. The poor bird's so grateful anyone still cares about her father's silly old stories she practically donated them to us." After we settled the financial details I gave her the next set of instructions. "Relax tomorrow and fly back in the evening. I'll pick you up at LAX. We'll get the transfers recorded with the Copyright Office. Then we pack our bags."

"Going where?" For a second I thought she was almost too eager to know. "A place with some good shopping centers?"

"Maybe," I said coyly.

No sooner had we broken connections than I fingered the touchtones myself, punching out Louie's local number. I caught him comparatively dry and reported his newfound partner's success. Then I gave him his travel orders.

"So it's meet me in St. Louie, Louie, heh?" he muttered. "Okay, I'll fly out tomorrow and start softening up the strike zone."

"And without liquid assistance," I warned sternly. "Have a smooth flight."

Then I settled back and killed the next day rereading books on the history of the Western film until Becca called me to pick her up at the airport.

We drove out to Tarzana for a delightful Japanese dinner at a place called Mon's, and over tempura and teriyaki I brought her up to date. ". . . He's in St. Louis by now, getting things ready for our arrival after we finish our paperwork."

Becca's lovely dark eyes clouded with hints of worry. "I'm frankly not crazy about this Louie with all his names." She sipped sake from a delicate white bowl. "He's a drunk and a jinx and he could mess things up royally."

"Granted. But, my sweet, he created this scam and we can't very well freeze him out at this stage. On the other hand, after we test-market the idea in St. Louis, I may want to buy out his share in the company and work the rest of the country just with you." I dazzled her with my most suggestive smile. "In fact, I'm quivering with delight over the prospect."

It was Sunday evening when a dour Lou the Q met us near the luggage carousels at Lambert–St. Louis International Airport. He lit up with momentary pleasure when he met his new partner, but something was clearly amiss with him and I couldn't tell whether it was sour stomach, shot nerves, or a hitch in the plans. He drove us in a rented car to our downtown headquarters at Stouffer's Riverfront Inn, less than a mile from KBMO's studios and offering fine views of the muddy Mississippi. Once unpacked and settled in, the three of us convened in my suite for drinks and a briefing. Louie's highball, carefully prepared by myself, was 99 percent mixer and ice.

"I got us a lawyer," the Q reported. "His name's Napoleon Jimson and he's young, mean, and black. He took a copyright course in law school, so he knows the game. And he's been involved in a lawsuit to take away Channel 39's operating license and give it to some black coalition, so he knows our pigeons."

"Sounds like a winner," I murmured, and Becca nodded solemn concurrence. "Tell us about the people who run the station."

"The place is a zoo." Before I could stop him Louie poured himself a too-generous slug of Early Times over rocks and shook the glass in his hairy paw to cool the booze down. "The station's owned by Blair Communications Company. That's a subsidiary of Blairco, the big conglomerate. The son of the president of Blairco is the station manager. Bradford Lockwood Blair the Second. The assistant station manager is a prune named Jerome McKenna who used to run the shop himself before Blair bought the station and put in his kid as head cheese. The program director is a guy named David Wilkes. He's been with the station about a year. The word is that he and the head of advertising and promotion, a fantastic blonde named Susan Otis, are the ones who persuaded young Blair to run those old cowboy pictures. I've also heard gossip that Otis and McKenna were a combo until Wilkes took her away from him."

"With all those undercurrents of emotion it's a wonder the station manages to broadcast anything," Becca remarked, strolling to the window with her drink to look at the lights twinkling on the river.

"Our office is all rented and ready," Louie went on after a long pull at his glass. "It's on the tenth floor of the

Paul Brown Building over on Olive. An easy walk from here and from there to KBMO."

"Louie would have been a great White House advance man if he hadn't chosen another line," I told Becca.

She turned from the window and smiled at Louie's simian facade. "Teach me not to go by appearances. Milo, if the game starts tomorrow I'm turning in right now." She yawned lustily, swallowed the last of her drink, and headed for the door. "Jet lag always knocks me out. Night, guys."

A few minutes after her departure Louie got up and started to take his own leave, until I halted him with a traffic-cop arm motion. "Whoa! You don't sleep till I find out why you look like the boy whose dog just died. What haven't you told me?"

He shuffled back and forth, cracking his knuckles explosively. "I woulda told you, Milo, only I didn't wanta panic the chick."

"Ms. Benbow is a full and equal partner in this scam, you chauvinistic porker," I reproved him. "Now cough up the bad news."

"It mighta just been my imagination," he said furtively. "You can never be sure about a thing like this. But the other day, over on Twelfth a few blocks from KBMO, I saw a guy on the street that I thought I recognized."

"Who was it?"

"That's what I don't know, but I think it was someone from when I was working the South and calling myself Hal O'Flynn. It mighta been one of the Feds who got me on that rap. Milo, I swear it scared the stuffing outa me. Every damn scam I'm on, something goes haywire. It's like I'm planting trees and bushes in my yard and all the bagworms on the block pick my shrubs for their nests."

I shook him sternly by the shoulders, like a combat sergeant in a WWII flick bracing a fearful rookie before the big battle. "Come on, Louie, knock it off. You are not a jinx. You're letting your pessimism run away with you. Now go get some sleep so we can get an early start. And no more booze!"

He left, looking not the least reassured. It took me longer than usual to drop off into slumberville that night, and I couldn't help wondering if Louie's squeams were beginning to get to me.

The St. Louis headquarters of Western Properties, Inc. turned out to be a small but serviceable suite, with two side-by-side offices opening onto a reception room. Chauvinistically, we stationed Becca at the reception desk while Louie and I took the private rooms. Once we'd hung our office sign and a few framed cowboy prints and generally made ourselves at home, it was time for our first sortie against the target. This took the form of a phone call to KBMO, with me doing the honors since I was president of the company and—thanks to my Western Film Festival scam of glorious memory—knew the most about old shoot-'em-ups. I sat at my executive desk and made the pitch while Becca and Louie eavesdropped on extensions.

"May I speak to Mr. Blair, please . . . Well, if he's in conference I'll speak to Mr. McKenna . . . Good morning, sir. My name is John J. Terwilliger. I am president of Western Properties, Inc., a California corporation that owns the rights to the works of some of America's leading storytellers. Ah, have you heard of our company before?" I would have fainted from shock if McKenna had said yes, but his answer, in a decidedly prunelike voice, was that the name was new to him.

"Among the works we own," I went on, "are the original Rio Kid stories by the late J. F. Carewe." I went on with a concise statement of the copyright quirk which gave my company exclusive control over the public domain Rio Kid movies starring John West.

A series of incoherent splutters from the other end had been punctuating my harangue, but finally Mac got a grip on himself and broke in on my monologue. "Just who the hell do you think you are?"

"Your station has broadcast several hours of old Western films each week for the past nine or ten months, including the Rio Kid series. Since John West's recent death you've run a Rio Kid every weeknight. Miss Carewe could have sued you for copyright infringement at any time, and my company now stands in her shoes. Are you prepared to pay us a substantial cash settlement for prior infringements and enter into a licensing contract with us so that we will be paid royalties on all future broadcasts?"

"I'm prepared to kick you straight into hell," McKenna riposted furiously, and slammed down his phone with an eardrum-numbing clatter.

Having done likewise, though more sedately, I gave Louie and Becca thumbs-ups. "The game's underway. McKenna's bound to report the call to Blair right away. Blair will consult the station's lawyers and the lawyers will order a copyright search to confirm that we own the rights. Then he'll be in touch with us," I predicted, "hat in hand."

"So what do we do until then?" Becca asked from her perch on the receptionist's desk.

"As you please, my sweet. Shop your heart out. But you, Louie, stay thirsty till I say you can drink. Understood?"

The three of us took turns manning, or should I say personing, the Western Properties office during the next week. It was a quiet, lonely existence. I bought a Japanese miniature TV, lugged it to the office, and caught up with an abundance of game shows and old movies during my tours of duty. Becca, judging from the classy outfits she wore to her shift each day, was buying clothes by the carload. Louie spent his off-hours God knows where, but his breath and walk satisfied me that at least it wasn't in bars.

Eight days after my phone call to KBMO, just when I was beginning to believe he was going to stonewall, he called. "This is Mr. Blair," he began in a deep operatic baritone. "Bradford Lockwood Blair the Second, general manager of Channel 39. Is this Mr. Terwilliger?"

I acknowledged that it was, my adrenalin pumping.

"I want to meet with you as soon as possible," he boomed. "We have business to discuss."

"My schedule's light this afternoon, sir," I replied with a politeness that I hope disguised my elation. "How would three P.M. be, here at our office?" It never hurts to lure the enemy onto your own turf—Milo's Maxim #43.

The reception committee that awaited its guest in the office at three consisted of Napoleon Jimson for legal advice, Becca for brightening the atmosphere, and me, the handsome one in the middle, for hard bargaining. Louie had been out of touch all day, even though I'd called the hotel and left him a message, and I was afraid he was prematurely celebrating with a bottle. We expected just the head honcho, not a war party, so I was rather floored when 3:06 brought a forceful knock at the outer door, and on Becca's call to enter, a quartet of determined faces and bodies trooped in.

Three were male and the unbelievably scrumptious fourth was female. Even before the introductions, carried out sans handshakes, I'd pinned the right name to each visitor. Bradford the Two was the tall thick-chested sandyhead in his early thirties who looked like the American Siegfried in a $500 suit. The fortyish one with the dyspeptic puss and the pipe never out of his mouth was obviously the ex-station manager, Jerome McKenna. The sex fantasy had to be Susan Otis, and the third man, the one she looked at with bedroom eyes when she thought no one was watching, I rightly deduced was her current lover, program director David Wilkes. We found chairs for the quartet, passed around coffee in styrofoam cups, and began haggling.

"Surely you know those Rio Kid films have nothing in common with Carewe's stories except the name," pruneface McKenna insisted as he refilled his pipe with cherry-flavored tobacco.

"And that is totally irrelevant to my client's position," thundered Napoleon Jimson. "Read the cases I cited. Personally I think the company should demand that those disgusting Rio Kid films be banned from the air." John West had not been known for sympathizing with civil rights causes, and Jimson seemed to be enjoying the prospect of symbolically getting even. "Although my client will not go so far, when this matter is settled I may file another petition with the FCC to take away your license not only for discriminatory hiring and promotion practices but also for broadcasting racist movies."

A born diplomat, that lawyer of ours.

Suddenly David Wilkes, an obvious John West fan, lunged to his feet with his face rage-pale and took two steps in Jimson's direction. Bradford the Two flung an arm around his program director and tried to sit him down again. "Easy, Dave, we can handle it." And Wilkes roared, "That guy is pulling the same trick he tried in that other FCC thing," which in turn launched Jimson to his feet like a black torpedo aimed at Wilkes so that before mayhem erupted I had to fling an arm around my legal adviser. Just a nice friendly negotiating session. Blair finally sent Wilkes back to the station and I sent Jimson back to his office and an atmosphere of relative calm was restored.

"That outburst of Jimson's was a farce," Blair orated in his full-throated baritone. "He knows KBMO has the best equal employment opportunity figures of any station in the area. Blacks, women, ex-convicts, the handicapped—we've hired them all and we're proud of them all. Look, Terwilliger, we don't want protracted litigation over a bunch of old cowboy movies. Suppose the station pays you five thousand and you give us a release from all past claims and a license for unlimited future use of the Rio Kid package and any other public domain films based on literary works you now or may hereafter own?"

I set down my styrofoam cup and pinned the bronze god with a businessman's stare. "Five thousand's fine for settling past claims, but we'll want three thousand a year to license future broadcasts." In my fantasies I looked ahead to the time when stations in a hundred or more cities would be shelling out that amount to our corporation, and I tried to suppress a beatific smile.

McKenna unmouthed his pipe and aimed the stem at Blair. "Western Theater is pulling in the ratings now, Brad, but without the Rio Kid it could become a disaster."

"Figure a seven percent drop in total advertising revenues without them," Susan Otis chimed in. I attributed the worried look in her smoky blue eyes not to her prediction but to concern about Wilkes.

As the trio conferred I could almost see their brain-wheels grinding. How much in legal fees would it cost the station if we sued for copyright infringement? Would a settlement keep Jimson from filing another petition with the FCC? Blair and Otis and McKenna huddled and conversed in whispers while Becca and I played pokerface. When the huddle broke up, Blair rose and approached our corner.

"Your terms are acceptable," he said, as gravely as Lee at Appomattox. Then he smiled at Becca, who had said not a word throughout the session, as if to thank her for breaking the impasse, and maybe—if I wasn't misreading his look—to suggest that he'd like to thank her in a more private and intimate way. "Of course, we'll have to consult again with our law firm in Washington before we sign anything. Look, why don't we meet at the station, say Friday at three P.M., and have a signing ceremony? Bring your standard contract and have all your officers present. Meanwhile I'll have Dave make a list of all the Westerns in our vault, so we can add a rider to the agreement covering any other public domain pictures based on prior literary matter. I don't want to go through this with you people again."

It all seemed so absurdly easy, I thought, now that it was over. We engaged in a round of handshaking as we parted and I noticed that young Siegfried seemed to hang on to Becca's dainty digits longer than the occasion called for. When they were gone we hugged each other in an ecstasy of glee. "We did it!" I crowed. "Easy Street from now on. Let's find a bar and toast the victory."

We made it a quick one, then headed back to the office to call Jimson and report success. He agreed to join us at KBMO's offices at 3:00 P.M. Friday for the signing.

It wasn't until we were locking up that a sobering thought penetrated my buoyant mood. "Becca," I said as we waited in the corridor for a down elevator, "why did Blair want all of us for this signing ceremony Friday? As president of Western Properties I'm the only one whose signature's needed."

"I can't see any harm in it," she said brightly. "Maybe he wants to turn it into a media event." Then she bit down on her underlip as if she had thought of an even tougher question.

"Hey, Milo," she asked me worriedly, "what ever happened to our wonderful partner Louie?"

* * *

At exactly 5:14 the next morning by the traveling clock on my bedside table, her question was answered. I was jolted awake from lovely dreams by a loud tapping at the door, a frenzied tattoo that would have turned my nerves raw in two minutes. I cursed, kicked off blankets, and approached the door stealthily, knowing all too well who and what was on the other side.

"Let me in!" came Louie's unmistakable croak. Afraid his drumbeat would awaken everyone on my floor, I unbolted and dodged back as he lurched in.

"I don't have to ask where you've been," I said, sniffing his breath. "The meeting with Blair turned out to be a success, but we were lucky and your getting blotto could have blown the whole scam. I'll never work with you again."

"You only think you know where I've been," Louie muttered darkly. "Sure, I had some drinks this afternoon, maybe this evening. In fact, I was in the bar downstairs around eleven tonight. But I'll prove to you I wasn't drunk! You know who I saw sneaking out of the hotel about eleven thirty? Your little partner, that's who. So drunky Louie got suspicious and tailed her. She cabbed out to a luxury high-rise condominium in the Central West End and took the private elevator to the penthouse." He stopped for breath, eyed the unopened bourbon bottle on my dresser top longingly. "Now guess who lives in that penthouse?"

Given the sexy signals I'd witnessed during the afternoon's bargaining session, I hardly needed to guess. "Young Beefcake. Bradford Lockwood Blair the Second," I replied knowingly, a display that left Louie's mouth agape.

"She stayed till half an hour ago," Louie went on when he'd recovered. "I followed her back here just now. Oh,

God, why did I set up this scam? It's like the others, bag-worms all over it.''

"Calm down," I told him. "Look, so they get together. They're young, single, and healthy. Why go puritan all of a sudden?"

"The thing's coming apart," he mourned. "I feel it coming apart." He didn't stop prophesying doom until I'd fed him three shots of bourbon and put him to sleep stretched across a pair of armchairs. But his paranoia had infected me, and I spent the tail of the night wide-awake.

A little before 11:00 A.M. I rang her room, one floor below mine, and from the weariness in her hello I gathered I'd awakened her. "Four hours to our date at KBMO," I said. "Rise and shine. We have a problem I have to talk over with you in a hurry. See you in half a minute."

I left Louie snoring on his armchairs, locked the room door behind me, slipped down the firestairs, and tapped gently at her door. She opened, wearing an ankle-length caftan that concealed none of her attributes. "Okay, prin-cess," I said once inside. "Level with Uncle Milo. Why did you spend five hours at Blair's condo last night?"

A corner of her lovely mouth began to twitch. "Oh, that," she laughed softly. "Well, you must have noticed at the meeting yesterday how he was sort of sending me signals. And you must admit he's a gorgeous hunk of man, besides being the son of a multimillionaire. He, ah, called me late last night and invited me over."

"You were seen," I told her without explaining by whom, and gave her my businessman's stare. "Never again, kid. Understand? You've been in the life long enough to know it was a rotten idea. In a tender moment you might have let something slip that would have shot the scam to pieces."

Her deep brown eyes glazed over with a cat-full-ofcream look. "Milo, he is by far the best I've ever met," she said softly. "Oh, if there were only some way I could marry him I'd chuck the life and be happy ever after."

"Yeah," I said. "Until his old man had your background checked. Remember what I said—never again."

On that happy note a chastened Becca, a sullen Louie, and an increasingly apprehensive Milo picked up Napoleon Jimson at his Broadway office after lunch and made our way to the studios of KBMO-TV and our appointment with destiny.

It was a one-story tan-brick building a block west of Twelfth Boulevard, with a transmitting tower poking into the sky in its back yard. The receptionist deposited us in a parquet-floored waiting room where we sat in soft chairs and listened to the noisy electric wall clock. The hands showed 3:00. No one came to greet us. I picked up a discarded *Globe-Democrat* from a lamp table and read about how the secretaries in all the federal offices in St. Louis were staging a massive demonstration that afternoon, protesting having to make coffee for the men. The next most exciting story dealt with the annual meeting of the Mortgage Bankers Association, which was to open that evening at the Cervantes Convention Center. Obviously a slow day for news.

The clock's hands reached 3:10, and still we sat. I began to feel a return of the squeams.

At 3:12 Jerome McKenna poked his pruneface and pipestem into the room. "Sorry for the delay," he said. "Dave's still working on that list of other public domain Westerns and Brad's in conference with somebody. Okay if we make it 3:20?" He didn't wait for answers or comments but ducked out again. Louie resumed his symphony for cracked knuckles, Jimson rose and stalked the room like a black tiger, and I started asking myself some unnerving questions. What was going on in this joint? Why was Blair with parties unknown when he should have been with us? Why had he insisted on all four of us attending this soirée? Why had Becca so unprofessionally spent most of last night with him? *Milo, Milo*, the voice of common sense reassured me. *Relax, man! This operation happens to be legal.*

And then, at 3:16 by the wall clock, I realized that on one hypothesis the deal was blatantly illegal, and my spine suddenly felt like an icicle in August.

That was when Louie jumped up and said he had to visit the men's room and walked out. Leaving three of us. Two minutes later Becca smiled, said something about locating a coffee machine, and walked out. Leaving two of us. At 3:23 Louie came back and as if on signal Jimson stormed out into the hallway, saying he would find Blair and demand that we be seen.

I had better do a spot of exploring myself, I decided. "Sit," I instructed a hand-wringing Louie, and went out to the hallway and very gingerly began walking. The place was a maze of corridors and cubbyholes. I followed what looked like a major artery, past a locked double door that seemed to lead out to a loading dock. Past a closed door marked *DAVID WILKES PROGRAM DIRECTOR*, with the johns right across the hall from Wilkes's cubicle. The corridor ended at a half-open door labeled *FILM STORAGE*, but I could see another half-open door at the room's far end, so I started to walk through. I felt like a soldier behind enemy lines.

The film-storage room was crammed library-style with high steel shelves that bulged with cardboard cartons, each holding a 16-millimeter film print. The vault was stone-quiet, the narrow aisles between the shelves were empty.

Except the last one.

I threw a glance down that aisle. There was a man in

shirt-sleeves lying on his side on the floor. He didn't look as if he were taking a nap. I tiptoed over and bent down to inspect the face. It was David Wilkes. The vacant stare of his eyes told me he was dead. A long sharp knife, the kind used as a letter opener, lay on the linoleum six inches from the body, the blade reddish-brown and sticky half-way to the hilt.

A ballpoint pen was clutched in Wilkes's right hand and a pile of white $8\frac{1}{2} \times 5\frac{1}{2}$ halfsheets lay scattered around the body. I remembered McKenna's remark that David hadn't finished inventorying the Westerns—which suggested that pruneface had seen Wilkes bare minutes before the murder, or perhaps that he'd killed the program director himself—and looked down at the halfsheets again, forty or so in all. Ten or twelve looked blank. On each of the others that I could read without moving them, the title of a single horse opera was printed in sloppy block capitals. The one on which Wilkes's pen rested read MARSHAL OF LARAMIE. I noticed SMOKEY SMITH and WHERE TRAILS END on others nearby.

My thoughts, however, were not on old movies but new suspects. At first glance the likeliest candidate was McKenna, who had lost Susan Otis to the deceased. But it might also have been Ms. Otis herself—lovers do quarrel—or Bradford the Two, who might have wanted Susan for himself or might have blamed Wilkes, initiator of the idea for Western Theater, for the debacle with my company.

Then I glanced down again at the halfsheet directly underneath Wilkes's pen. And suddenly I didn't have to speculate further, because I knew.

By pure luck I found verification only a few feet away. One of the steel shelves in that aisle was being used as a sort of film-book reference library. I almost gasped with glee when I noticed among the twenty-odd titles Adams and Rainey's *Shoot-em-Ups*, a comprehensive listing of the casts and credits of every talking Western film ever made in the United States. With sweaty hands I thumbed through the alphabetical index of titles at the back of the book.

Marshal of Heldorado, Marshal of Laredo, Marshal of Mesa City—I was right. There was no such film as *Marshal of Laramie*.

Like an outlaw being chased by one of those marshals, I ran. Back through the storage room, along the corridor to the loading dock, out and away, until I'd lost myself in the cavernous darkness of Stadium Cinema II where I spent the rest of the afternoon.

When the show let out I did the only sensible thing left to me. I bought a cheap suitcase at Woolworth's, filled it with copies of the evening *Post-Dispatch*, cabbed back to Stouffer's Riverfront Inn, and—with the help of one of the paper identities I always carry for emergencies—checked in all over again where the cops would least expect to find me.

"And how long do you intend to stay, Mr. Rhodes?" the clerk inquired as she completed the registration card.

"Just for the meeting of the Mortgage Bankers Association," I said, taking the room key.

The weekend papers carried enough of the story to confirm my deductions all the way. The cops had Jimson and were investigating his role in the scam, but I was confident he could prove we had scammed him, too. They didn't have Louie, who according to the KBMO receptionist had exited the waiting room and walked unopposed out the front door within a minute after I'd left on my own excursion. And of course they had Becca. But, as I explained Sunday morning over the lobby phone to the disembodied voice of Jock Schultz half a continent away, she didn't really count.

"Remember the ex-CIA spook I used to tap a phone on that scam I ran here four years ago? I had him bug the St. Louis FBI office Friday night. It cost me a pile but confirmed my suspicions all the way. Becca's not one of us. She's a sort of free-lance bounty hunter, working under a deal that pays her so many thousand for each major operator she can hang a Federal rap on."

"Bounty hunter," Jock repeated thoughtfully. "Appropriate character in a Western film scam, wouldn't you say?"

"I suspected something like that at the TV station Friday when I asked myself how our plan could possibly be illegal. That was how I realized that if Becca had never gotten Carolyn Carewe to sign over the rights to the Rio Kid stories—say, if Becca had forged the old lady's name—well, all she'd need to do later would be to testify at our trial that the forgery was part of our scam, and Louie and I would never be able to convince a jury it was she who did it. They'd nail us for copyright fraud, wire fraud, conspiracy, and God knows what else.

"As soon as we hit St. Louis she contacted Blair, told him what was up, and they worked out the charade to lure us all to KBMO where the FBI would arrest us as soon as we'd signed the contract. That's why she visited Blair's condo Thursday night—strategy, not sex. If that Federal secretaries' demonstration hadn't made the agents late for their date to collar us at the station, Louie and I would be in the slammer this minute. Thank heaven for militant feminism!" I declaimed piously.

"So *that's* how the Feds got Fats Adamo for mail fraud so soon after the disco Cola scam," the Jock sighed. "Milo, me buck, I feel devilish guilty that I recommended the lady to ye and I'll make it up when the heat is lowered. Now what about this Wilkes murder?"

"A mere bagatelle," I replied modestly. "I solved it

thirty seconds after I found the body. You see, all it took was the tying together of five facts. One: Louie got out of the Federal pen six months ago. Two: Wilkes joined KBMO about a year ago. Three: The station has a liberal policy about hiring blacks, women, *and ex-convicts*. Four: Before Becca and I flew here, Louie thought he saw someone he knew from when he was in the South and calling himself Hal O'Flynn—an encounter that took place on Twelfth Boulevard, a few blocks from KBMO. Five: At no time before our Friday visit to the station had Wilkes set eyes on Louie in this city. During the bargaining session which Wilkes attended, Louie was off somewhere getting plastered.

"It's easy enough to reconstruct what happened Friday afternoon. On his way to the john Louie had to pass Wilkes's office just as I did. It was both their misfortunes that this time Wilkes did see Louie and recognized him as a fellow Lexington alumnus. Now remember, Blair was the only one at KBMO who knew about Becca's trap for us. It's obvious from what McKenna told us in that waiting room that he didn't know, and it's clear Wilkes didn't know or he wouldn't have gone on inventorying those Westerns as if they really mattered. So, Wilkes recognized Louie and apparently inveigled him into the film-storage room for a quiet chat.

"Louie was already nervous as a cat. Meeting a fellow con in that station was the last straw. He panicked, saw the paper knife they kept in the storage room to open cardboard film containers, and used it. Then he went to the john to wash the blood off his hands. But as soon as he left the men's room he got his directions confused, wandered back into the storage room—and found that Wilkes had not died instantly but had been able, after Louie left for the john, to begin to write on a black halfsheet the only one of Louie's many names he knew his murderer by, HAL OFLYNN, with the apostrophe being omitted for obvious reasons of haste. He'd gotten as far as the L of the last name when he died.

"I give Louie credit for quick thinking under pressure. He had only seconds to act. If he'd tried to flush the half-sheet down the toilet he might have been interrupted at any moment. So instead he took Wilkes's pen and simply added enough block capitals to each end of the dying message so that it would look just like the name of another Western—*MARSHAL OF LARAMIE*!''

"He was a prophet in one respect at least," the Jock pointed out. "The scam had bagworms all over it."

"A drunk, a jinx, a prophet, and for one split second a genius," I said. "I hope the poor schnook gets away."

Six months later—long after I had slipped out of St. Louis, sworn off John West movies, and retired to lick my wounds in solitude—I happened to pick up a copy of *Persons* in a New Orleans dentist's office. My eye was caught by a photo spread of a newlywed couple. The man was tall, thick-chested, sandy-haired, and resembled an American Siegfried. His bride was tall, in her late twenties, of form divine, smiling and radiant in white lace.

Son of a gun, I said to myself. She chucked the life and landed Young Beefcake after all.

Sniff

•

Donald E. Westlake

The marvel of Donald E. Westlake is his amazing versatility. With equal facility he has written light comedy, pure farce, private-eye stories, police procedurals, straight suspense, caper novels, mainstream fiction, science fiction, and non-fiction under his own name and pseudonyms; mysteries of penetrating psychological insight under the name Tucker Coe; and, as by Richard Stark, a series of antihero stories about a thief named Parker that are the ne plus ultra in contemporary hardboiled fiction. "Sniff" is Westlake in one of his lighter moods — the sort he used to create such novels as The Fugitive Pigeon, The Busy Body, *and his 1967 Edgar winner,* God Save the Mark.

Albert felt the sniffles first on Monday, which was Post Office Day, but he didn't worry about it. In his experience, the sniffles came and went with the changing of the seasons, never serious enough to need a call on the family doctor; how should he have known that *these* sniffles were the harbinger of more than spring? There was no reason to think that this time . . .

Well. Monday, at any rate, was Post Office Day, as every Monday had been for well over a year now. Sniffles or no sniffles, Albert went through his normal Post Office Day routine just the same as ever. That is, at five minutes before noon he took a business-size large envelope from the top left drawer of his desk, placed it in the typewriter, and addressed it to himself, thusly:

Albert White
c/o General Delivery
Monequois, N. Y.

Then, after looking around cautiously to be absolutely certain Mr. Clement was nowhere in sight, he put a return address in the upper left hand corner, like so:

After five days return to:
Bob Harrington
Monequois Herald-Statesman
Monequois, N. Y.

Finally, taking the envelope from the typewriter, Albert affixed a stamp to it from his middle desk drawer and tucked the still-empty envelope in the inside pocket of his jacket. (It was one of his small but intense and very secret pleasures that Mr. Clement himself, all unknowing, was supplying the stamps to keep the system in operation.)

Typing the two addresses on the envelope had taken most of the final five minutes till noon, and putting his desk in order consumed the last several seconds, so that at exactly twelve o'clock Albert could stand, turn to the right, walk to the door, and leave the office for lunch, closing behind himself the door on which was painted the legend JASON CLEMENT, Attorney-at-Law.

His first stop, this and every Monday lunchtime, was in the Post Office, where he claimed the bulky white envelope waiting for him in General Delivery. "Here we are, Mr. White!" cried Tom the Postal Clerk, as usual. "The weekly scandal!"

Albert and Tom the Postal Clerk had come to know one another fairly well in the course of the last fifteen months, what with Albert dropping in every Monday for his General Delivery letter. In order to allay any suspicion that might have entered Tom the Postal Clerk's mind, Albert had early on explained that Bob Harrington, the well-known crusading reporter on the Monequois newspaper, had employed Albert as a sort of legman to check out leads and tips and confidential information that had been sent in by the newspaper's readers. "It's a part-time job," Albert had explained, "in addition to my regular work for Mr. Clement, and it's very hush-hush. That's why Bob sends me the material care of General Delivery. And why we make believe we don't even know one another."

Tom the Postal Clerk had grinned and winked and cried, "Mum's the word!"

But later on Tom the Postal Clerk apparently did some thinking, because one Monday he said to Albert, "Why is it you let this stuff sit around here so long? Almost a week, most times."

"I'm supposed to pick up mail on Monday," Albert answered, "no matter when Bob may send it out to me. If I were to come in here every day of the year, it might cause suspicion."

"Oh, yeah," said Tom the Postal Clerk, and nodded wisely. But then he said, "You know, you don't want to miss. You see this up here in the corner, this 'After five days return to—' Well, that means exactly what it says. If you don't pick one of these up in the five days, well, that's it."

Albert said, "Would you really send it back?"

"Well, we'd have to," said Tom the Postal Clerk. "That's the regulations, Mr. White."

"I'm glad," said Albert. "I know Bob wouldn't want information like this sitting around too long. If I ever let a letter stay more than five days, you go ahead and *send* it back. Bob and I will both thank you."

213

"Check," said Tom the Postal Clerk.

"And you won't ever give one of these letters to somebody who *says* he's from me."

"Definitely not, Mr. White. It's you or nobody."

"I mean, even if you got a phone call from somebody who said he was me and he was sending a friend to pick up the letter in my place."

Tom the Postal Clerk winked and said, "I know what you're getting at, Mr. White. I know what you mean. And don't you worry. The U.S. Mails won't let you down. No one will ever get delivery on any of these letters but you or Mr. Harrington, and that's guaranteed."

"I'm glad to hear that," Albert said, and meant every word of it.

In the months since then, Tom the Postal Clerk had had no more questions, and life had gone along sunnily. Of course, it was necessary these days for Albert to read Bob Harrington's column in the *Herald-Statesman*, since from time to time Tom the Postal Clerk would mention one of the incredible scandals Bob Harrington was incessantly digging up and would want to know if Albert had had anything to do with that particular case. In most instances, Albert said no, explaining that the majority of leads he was given turned out to be worthless. When he did from time to time admit that yes, such-and-such a ruined reputation or exposed misdeed had been a part of his undercover work for Bob Harrington, Tom the Postal Clerk beamed like a quiz show winner. (Tom the Postal Clerk was obviously a born conspirator who had never—till now—found an outlet for his natural bent.)

Today, however, Tom the Postal Clerk had nothing undercover to talk about. Instead, he looked closely at Albert and said, "You got a cold, Mr. White?"

"It's just the sniffles," Albert said.

"You look sort of rheumy around the eyes."

"It's nothing," Albert said. "Just the sniffles."

"It's the season for it," said Tom the Postal Clerk.

Albert agreed it was the season for it, left the Post Office, and went to City Hall Luncheonette, where he told Sally the Waitress, "I think the roast beef today."

(Albert's wife, Elizabeth, would gladly have made a lunch for him, and Albert would gladly have eaten it, except that Mr. Clement did not believe that law clerks—even forty-year-old law clerks with steel-rim glasses and receding hairlines and expanding waistlines—should sit at their desks in their offices and eat sandwiches from a paper bag. Therefore, the daily noontime walk to City Hall Luncheonette, which served food that was adequate without being as scrumptious as the menu claimed.)

While Sally the Waitress went off to order the roast beef, Albert walked back to the men's room to wash up and also to continue the normal routine of Post Office Day. He took from his right side jacket pocket the letter which Tom the Postal Clerk had just given him, carefully ripped it open, and took from it the bulky wad of documents it contained. This package went into the fresh envelope he had just typed before leaving the office. He sealed the new envelope and returned it to his inner jacket pocket, then ripped the old envelope into very small pieces and flushed the pieces down the toilet. He then washed his hands, went out to sit at his normal table, and ate a passable lunch of peas, french fries, rye bread, coffee, and roast beef.

He had first stumbled across the originals of these documents eight years ago, one day when Mr. Clement was detained in court and Albert had required to know a certain fact which was on a certain piece of paper. With no ulterior motive he had searched Mr. Clement's desk, had noticed that one drawer seemed somewhat shorter than the others, had taken it out to look behind it, had seen the green metal box back there, had given in to curiosity, and within the green metal box had learned that Mr. Clement was very very rich and had become so by grossly dishonest means.

Mr. Clement was an old man, a bony white-haired firebrand who still struck awe in those who met him. And not always merely awe; he carried a cane with a silver knob, and had been known to flail away with it at persons who had been ungracious or rude to him in streets, buses, stores, or wherever he happened to be. His law business leaned heavily to estates and the affairs of small local corporations. The documents in the green metal box proved that Mr. Clement had stolen widely and viciously from these estates and corporations, had salted most of the money away in bank accounts under false names, and was now a millionaire several times over.

A confusing medley of thoughts had run through Albert's mind on finding these documents. First, he was stunned and disappointed to learn of Mr. Clement's perfidy; although the old man's irascibility had kept Albert from every really liking him, he *had* respected and admired him, and now he was learning his respect and admiration had been misplaced. Second, he was terrified at the thought of what Mr. Clement would do if he learned of Albert's discovery; surely these documents limned a man ruthless enough to stop at nothing if he thought exposure were near. And third—amazing himself—he thought of blackmail.

In those first kaleidoscopic moments, Albert White found himself yearning for things the existence of which he had hardly ever before noticed. Acapulco. Beautiful women. White dinner jackets. Sports cars. Highballs. Penthouses. Wouldn't Mr. Clement pay for all these things, in order to keep Albert's mouth shut?

Of course he would. If there were no *better* way to shut

Albert's mouth. The thought of potential better ways made Albert shudder.

Still, he *wanted* all those things. Ease and luxury. Travel. Adventure. Sinning expensively. All that jazz.

At intervals over the next few months, Albert snuck documents out of the green metal box and had them photostated. He continued until he had enough evidence to put Mr. Clement behind bars until the twenty-second century. He hid this evidence in the garage behind the little house he shared with his wife Elizabeth, and for the next four years he didn't do a thing.

He needed a plan. He needed some way to arrange things so that the evidence would go to the authorities if anything happened to him, and also so that he could convince Mr. Clement that he had the evidence and the authorities would get it, and also so that Mr. Clement couldn't get his hands on it himself. A tall order. For four years Albert had no way to fill it.

But then he read a short story by a writer named Richard Hardwick, outlining the method Albert eventually came to use, with the documents mailed to himself c/o General Delivery and a crusading reporter for the return address. Albert promptly initiated the scheme himself, pruned his evidential documents down to manageable proportions, sent them circulating through the postal system, and saw that everything worked just as Hardwick had said it would.

Now, all that was left was to approach Mr. Clement, detail the evidence and the precautions, arrange satisfactory terms, and sit back to enjoy evermore a life of luxury.

Uh-huh.

The same day Albert dropped the envelope into the mailbox for the very first time he also went to beard Mr. Clement in his den; that is, in his inner office. Albert knocked at the door before entering, as he had been taught years and years ago when he'd first obtained this employment, stepped inside, and said, "Mr. Clement?"

Mr. Clement raised his bony face, glared at Albert with his stony eyes, and said, "Yes, Albert? What is it?"

Albert said, "Those Duckworth leases. Do you want them this afternoon?"

"Naturally I want them this afternoon. I told you yesterday I would want them this afternoon."

"Yes, sir," said Albert, and retreated.

Back at his desk, he sat and blinked in some confusion at the far wall. He had opened his mouth, back there in Mr. Clement's office, with the full intention of saying, "Mr. Clement, I know all," and it had been with baffled consternation that he had heard himself say instead, "Those Duckworth leases." Besides the fact that he hadn't intended to say "Those Duckworth leases" at all, there was the additional fact that he had already known Mr. Clement would want the Duckworth leases this afternoon. Not only a wrong question, but a useless question as well.

"I was afraid of him, that's all," Albert told himself. "And there's no reason to be afraid. I do have the goods on him, and he doesn't dare touch me."

Later that same day, Albert tried again. It was, as a matter of fact, when he brought the Duckworth leases in. He placed them on the desk, stood around a few seconds, then coughed hesitantly and said, "Mr. Clement?"

Mr. Clement glowered. "What is it this time?"

"I'm not feeling too well, Mr. Clement. I'd like to take the rest of the afternoon off, please."

"Have you typed the Wilcox papers?"

"No, sir, not yet."

"Type them up, and then you can go."

"Yes, sir. Thank you."

A saddened Albert left Mr. Clement's office, knowing he had failed again and knowing also there was no point in his trying any more today; he'd only go on failing. So he merely typed the Wilcox papers, tidied his desk, and went home an hour early, explaining to Elizabeth that he'd felt a bit queasy at the office, which was perfectly true.

In the fifteen months that followed, Albert made frequent attempts to inform Mr. Clement that he was in the process of being blackmailed, but somehow or other when he opened his mouth it was always some other sentence that came out. Sometimes, at night, he practiced in front of a mirror, outlining the situation and his demands with admirable clarity and brevity. Other times, he wrote the speeches out and set himself to memorize them, but the prepared speeches were always too verbose and unwieldy.

It was clear enough in his mind what he intended to say. He would tell about his discovery and of the General Delivery scheme. He would explain his desire to travel, explain how he intended to remail the evidence every week to a new location—Cannes, Palm Beach, Victoria Falls— and point out that he would require a large and steady income to enable him to pick the evidence up each time within the five day deadline. He would say that, although he thought Elizabeth was perhaps too much of a homebody to fully enjoy the sort of life Albert intended leading from now on, he did still feel a certain fondness for her and would prefer to be able to think that she was being suitably provided for by Mr. Clement in his absence.

He *would* say all that. Some day. All hope, he believed, was not yet lost. The day would come when his courage was sufficiently high or his desire for the good life sufficiently strong, and on that day he would *do* it. The day, however, had not yet come.

In the meantime, the mailing and re-mailing of the blackmail letter had become a normal part of Albert's weekly routine, integrated into his orderly life as though there were nothing strange about it at all. Every Monday, on his way to lunch, he picked up the letter at General Delivery. Every Monday, in the washroom of the City Hall Luncheonette, he transferred the documents to the fresh envelope and flushed the used envelope away. Every Monday, on the way back to work from lunch, he dropped the letter into a handy mailbox. (The letter would reach Tom the Postal Clerk on Tuesday. Wednesday would be day number one, Thursday number two, Friday three, Saturday four, Sunday no number, and Monday five, the end of the old cycle and beginning of the new.)

This particular Monday was no different from any other, except of course for the sniffles. Sally the Waitress commented on that, saying, as she delivered the roast beef, "You look like you're coming down with something, Mr. White."

"Just the sniffles," said Albert.

"Probably one of those twenty-four-hour bugs that's going around," she said.

Albert agreed with her diagnosis, ate his lunch, paid for it and left his usual tip, and walked on back to the office, making two stops on the way. The first was at the handy mailbox, where he dropped the evidence for another round-trip through the postal system, and the second was at the Bizy Korner Stationery, where he bought a pocket packet of tissues for his sniffles.

He would have preferred to think that Sally the Waitress was right about the length of time these sniffles would be with him—the "twenty-four-hour bug" she had mentioned—but he rather doubted it. From past experience he knew that the sniffles lasted him approximately three days; he could look forward to runny nose and rheumy eyes until about Thursday, when it would surely begin to clear up.

Except that it didn't. Monday went by, uneventful after the remailing of the documents, Tuesday and Wednesday followed, and Thursday dawned clogged and stuffy, both in the outside world and in the interior of Albert's head. Albert wore his raincoat and rubbers, carried his umbrella, and snuffled his way through Thursday, going through an entire box of tissues in the office.

And Friday was even worse. Elizabeth, the kind of woman who looks most natural when wearing an apron and holding an apple pie, took one look at Albert on Friday morning and said, "Don't you even bother to get up. I'll call Mr. Clement and tell him you're too sick to go to work today."

And Albert was. He was too sick to go to work, too sick even to protest at having to stay in bed, and so utterly miserably sick that he even forgot all about the letter ticking away in General Delivery.

He remained just as sick, and just as oblivious, all through the weekend, spending most of his time in uneasy dozing, rising to a seated position now and then in order to down some chicken broth or tea and toast and then reclining at once to sleep some more.

About eleven o'clock Sunday night, Albert awoke from a sound sleep with a vision of that envelope clear in his mind. It was as though he had dreamed it; the envelope, clean and clear, sitting fat and solitary in a pigeonhole, and a hand reaching out to take it, a hand that belonged to Bob Harrington, crusading reporter.

"Good Heavens!" cried Albert. Elizabeth was sleeping in the guest bed while Albert was sick, and so didn't hear him. "I'd better be well tomorrow," he said aloud, laid his head back on the pillow, and stayed awake quite a while thinking about it.

But he wasn't well on the morrow. He was awakened Monday morning by the sound of rain beating on the bedroom window. He sat up, knew at once that he was as dizzy and weak as ever, and felt a real panic begin to slide

221

over him like a blanket of fire. But he fought it down, if not quite out; he had, at all costs, to remain calm.

When Elizabeth came in, to ask him what he wanted for breakfast, Albert said, "I've got to make a phone call."

"Who do you want me to call, dear?"

"No," said Albert firmly. "*I* have to make the call."

"Dear, I'll be glad to—"

Albert was seldom waspish, but when the mood was on him he could be insufferable. "What would make you happy," he now said, the sardonic ring in his voice muffled a bit by the blockage in his nose, "is of not the slightest interest to me. *I* must make a phone call, and all I ask of *you* is that you help me get to the living room."

Elizabeth protested, thinking to be kindly, but eventually she saw Albert was not going to be reasonable and so she agreed. He was weak as a kitten, and leaned heavily on her as they made their way down the stairs to the first floor and into the living room. Albert sagged into the chair beside the phone and sat there panting a few minutes, done in by the exertion. Elizabeth meantime went to the kitchen to prepare, as she put it, "a nice poached egg."

"A nice poached egg," Albert muttered. He felt vile, he felt vicious. He had never been physically weaker in his life, and yet he had never felt before such violent desires to wreck furniture, shout, create havoc, beat people up. If only Mr. Clement had been here now, Albert would have told him what was what in jig time. He'd never *been* so mean.

Nor so weak. He could barely lift the phone book, and turning the pages was a real chore. Then, of course, he looked it up in the wrong place first; under 'P' for 'Post Office.' Finding the number eventually in one of the sub-headings under 'US GOVT,' Albert dialed it and said to the person who answered, "Let me talk to Tom, please."

"Tom who?"

"How do I know? Tom!"

"Mister, we got three Toms here. You wand Tom Sky-lozowsky, you want—"

"Tom!" cried Albert. "At the General Delivery window!"

"Oh, you mean Tom Kennebunk. Hold on a minute."

Albert held on three minutes. At intervals he said, "Hello?" but received no answer. He thought of hanging up and dialing again, but he could hear voices in the background, which meant the receiver was still off the hook at the other end, which probably meant if he broke the connection and dialed again he'd get a busy signal.

His impatience was ultimately rewarded by the sound of Tom the Postal Clerk's voice saying, "Hello? You want me?"

"Hello there, Tom," said Albert, striving for joviality. "It's me, Mr. White. Albert White, you know."

"Oh, yeah! How are ya, Mr. White?"

"Well, that's just it, Tom, I'm not very good. As a matter of fact, I've been sick in bed all weekend, and—"

"Gee, that's too bad, Mr. White. That's what you were coming down with last week, I bet."

"Yes, it is. I was—"

"I knew it when I saw you. You remember? I said how you looked awful rheumy around the eyes, remember?"

"Well, you were right, Tom," said Albert, keeping a tight lid on his impatience. "But what I'm calling you about," he said, rushing on before Tom the Postal Clerk could produce any more medical reminiscences, "is the letter you've got for me."

"Let's see," said Tom the Postal Clerk. "Hold on." And before Albert could stop him he'd klunked the phone down on a table somewhere and gone away.

As Albert sat in impotent rage, waiting for Tom the Chipper Moron to return, Elizabeth appeared with a

223

steaming cup of tea, saying, "Drink this, dear. It'll help keep your strength up." She set it on the phone table and then just stood there, hands folded over her apron. Hesitantly, she said, "This must be awfully important."

It occurred to Albert then that sooner or later he was going to have to explain all this to Elizabeth. What the explanation would be he had as yet no idea; he only hoped it would occur to him before he had to use it. In the meantime, a somewhat more pleasant attitude on his part might serve as an adequate substitute.

He fixed his features into an approximation of a smile, looked up, and said, "Well, you know, it's business. Something I had to get done today. How's the poached egg coming?"

"Be ready in just a minute," she said, and went on back to the kitchen.

Tom the Postal Clerk returned a minute later, saying, "Yep, you've got a letter, Mr. White. From You-know-who."

"Tom," said Albert, "now, listen carefully. I'm sick today, but I hope to be better by tomorrow. Hold on to that letter. Don't send it to Bob Harrington."

"Just a sec, Mr. White."

"Tom—!"

But he was gone again.

Elizabeth came in and pantomimed that the poached egg was ready. Albert nodded and made his smile face and waved his hand for Elizabeth to go away, and Tom the Postal Clerk came back once more, saying, "Say, there, Mr. White, we've had this letter since last Tuesday."

Elizabeth was still standing there. Albert said into the phone, "I'll be up and around in just a day or two." He waved violently for Elizabeth to go away.

"You better call Mr. Harrington," suggested Tom the

Postal Clerk. "Tell him to send it out again as soon as it comes back."

"Tom, *hold* it for me!"

"I can't do that, Mr. White. You remember, we talked about that once. You said yourself we should definitely send it back if you didn't pick it up in the five days."

"But I'm sick!" cried Albert.

Elizabeth persisted in standing there, looking concerned for Albert's well-being when in point of obvious fact she was crazy to know what this phone call was all about.

Tom the Postal Clerk, with infuriating calm, said, "Mr. White, if you're sick you shouldn't be doing any under-cover work anyway. Except under the bedcovers, eh? Ha-ha."

"Tom, you *know* me! You can recognize my voice, can't you?"

"Well, sure, Mr. White."

"The letter's addressed to *me*, isn't it?"

"Mr. White, postal regulations say—"

"Oh, *damn* postal regulations!"

Elizabeth looked shocked. The silence of Tom the Post-al Clerk sounded shocked. Albert himself was a little shocked. He said,

"I'm sorry, Tom, I didn't mean that, I'm a little upset and being sick and all—"

"It isn't the end of the world, Mr. White," Tom the Postal Clerk said, now obviously trying to help. "Mr. Harrington isn't going to fire you or anything, not if you're sick."

Albert, with a new idea created by Elizabeth's unending presence directly in front of him, said "Tom, listen. Tom, I'm going to send my wife down to get the letter." It meant telling Elizabeth the truth, or at least an abridged version of the truth; but it could no longer be helped. "I'll have her bring identification from me, my driver's license or a note to you or something, and—"

"It just can't be done, Mr. White. Don't you remember, you told me that yourself, I should never give one of these letters to anybody but you in person, no matter what phone calls I got or anything like that."

Albert did remember that, damn it. But this was different! He said, "Tom, please. You don't understand."

"Mr. White, now, you made me give you my word—"

"Oh, shut *up*!" cried Albert finally admitting to himself that he wasn't going to get anywhere, and slammed the phone into its cradle.

Elizabeth said, "Albert, what is this? I've never seen you act this way, not in all your life."

"Don't bother me now," said Albert grimly. "Just don't bother me now."

He leafed through the phone book again, found the number of the *Monequois Herald-Statesman*, dialed it, and asked to speak to Bob Harrington.

The switchboard girl said, "One moment, puh-leez."

In that moment, Albert visualized how the conversation would go. He would tell a crusading reporter that a letter he had never mailed was going to be returned to him and would he please not open it? This, to a crusading reporter! Ask someone like Bob Harrington not to open a letter which has come to him via the most unusual and mysterious of methods; it would be like throwing a raw steak into a lion's cage and asking the lion please not to eat it.

Before the moment was up, Albert had cradled the receiver.

He shook his head sadly, back and forth. "I don't know what to do," he said "I just don't know what to do."

Elizabeth said, "Shall I call Dr. Francis?"

Dr. Francis had been called on Friday, had prescribed over the phone, and had himself called the pharmacy to tell them what to deliver to the White household. It had been said, with some justice, that Dr. Francis wouldn't make a house call if the patient were his own wife. But Albert, suddenly aflame with a new idea, cried, "Yes! Call him! Tell him to get over here right away, it's an emergency! In the meantime," he added, more quietly, "I'll eat my poached egg."

Dr. Francis arrived about two that afternoon, shucked out of his sopping raincoat—it was the worst rainstorm of the spring season thus far—and said, in a disgruntled manner, "All right, let's see this emergency."

Albert had remained on the first floor, reclining on the living room sofa and covered with blankets. Now he propped himself up and called, "Me, Doctor! In here!"

Dr. Francis came in and said, "You're a virus, aren't you? I prescribed for you last Friday."

"Doctor," said Albert urgently, "I absolutely have to go the Post Office today. It's vital, a matter of life and death. I want you to give me something, a shot, whatever it is you do, something that will keep me going just long enough to get to the post office."

Dr. Francis frowned and said, "What's this?"

"I *have* to get there."

"You've been watching those TV spy thrillers," Dr. Francis told him. "There's no such thing as what you want. When you're sick, you're sick. Take the medicine I prescribed, stay in bed, you might be on your feet by the end of the week."

"But I've got to go there today!"

"Send your wife."

"Yaaaaahhhhh!"

It was nothing but fury and frustration that kept Albert moving then. He came up off the sofa in a flurry of blankets, staggered out to the front hall, dragged his topcoat from the closet and put it on over his pajamas, slammed

227

a hat on his head—he was wearing slipper socks on his feet—and headed for the front door. Elizabeth and Dr. Francis were both shouting things at him, but he didn't hear a word they said.

Two steps from his front door, Albert's slipper socks skidded on the wet pavement, his feet went out from under him, down he went in a flailing of arms and legs, and that's how he broke his collarbone.

Elizabeth and Dr. Francis carried him up to his bed. And there, after Dr. Francis taped him, he stayed, silent and grouchy and mad at the world.

He was still there Wednesday afternoon, when Elizabeth came in, an odd expression on her face, and said, ''Some men are here to see you, dear.''

He knew who they were. ''I don't want to see them,'' he said. And then, in a burst of irritation, ''I don't want to see anybody! Don't you realize I've lost my job?''

The Reason Why

·

Edward Gorman

*Iowan Edward Gorman is in the front rank of new writers
who have been producing quality mystery fiction since the
early 1980s. Three of his five novels—New, Improved
Murder, Murder Straight Up, and Murder in the Wings—
feature ex-cop, amateur actor, and part-time private eye
Jack Dwyer, a man who is as compassionate (and sometimes
critical) an observer of the human condition as he is an
effective sleuth. "The Reason Why," an original story, is
Gorman and Dwyer at their best—a tale of bittersweet nostalgia that is ultimately quite moving.*

"**I**'m scared."

"This was your idea, Karen."

"You scared?"

"No."

"You bastard."

"Because I'm not scared I'm a bastard?"

"You not being scared means you don't believe me."

"Well."

"See. I knew it."

"What?"

"Just the way you said 'Well.' You bastard."

I sighed and looked out at the big red brick building
that sprawled over a quarter mile of spring grass turned
silver by a fat June moon. Twenty-five years ago a 1950

Ford fastback had sat in the adjacent parking lot. Mine for two summers of grocery store work.

We were sitting in her car, a Volvo she'd cadged from her last marriage settlement, number four if you're interested, and sharing a pint of bourbon the way we used to in high school when we'd been more than friends but never quite lovers.

The occasion tonight was our twenty-fifth class reunion. But there was another occasion, too. In our senior year a boy named Michael Brandon had jumped off a steep clay cliff called Pierce Point to his death on the winding river road below. Suicide. That, anyway, had been the official version.

A month ago Karen Lane (she had gone back to her maiden name these days, the Karen Lane-Cummings-Todd-Browne-LeMay getting a tad too long) had called to see if I wanted to go to dinner and I said yes, if I could bring Donna along, but then Donna surprised me by saying she didn't care to go along, that by now we should be at the point in our relationship where we trusted each other ("God, Dwyer, I don't even look at other men, not for very long anyway, you know?"), and Karen and I had had dinner and she'd had many drinks, enough that I saw she had a problem, and then she'd told me about something that had troubled her for a long time . . .

In senior year she'd gone to a party and gotten sick on wine and stumbled out to somebody's backyard to throw up and it was there she'd overheard the three boys talking. They were earnestly discussing what had happened to Michael Brandon the previous week and they were even more earnestly discussing what would happen to them if "anybody ever really found out the truth."

"It's bothered me all these years," she'd said over dinner a month earlier. "They murdered him and they got away with it."

"Why didn't you tell the police?"

"I didn't think they'd believe me."

"Why not?"

She shrugged and put her lovely little face down, dark hair covering her features. Whenever she put her face down that way it meant that she didn't want to tell you a lie so she'd just as soon talk about something else.

"Why not, Karen?"

"Because of where we came from. The Highlands."

The Highlands is an area that used to ring the iron foundries and factories of this city. Way before pollution became a fashionable concern, you could stand on your front porch and see a peculiarly beautiful orange haze on the sky every dusk. The Highlands had bars where men lost ears, eyes, and fingers in just garden-variety fights, and streets where nobody sane ever walked after dark, not even cops unless they were in pairs. But it wasn't the physical violence you remembered so much as the emotional violence of poverty. You get tired of hearing your mother scream because there isn't enough money for food and hearing your father scream back because there's nothing he can do about it. Nothing.

Karen Lane and I had come from the Highlands, but we were smarter and, in her case, better looking than most of the people from the area, so when we went to Wilson High School—one of those nightmare conglomerates that shoves the poorest kids in a city in with the richest—we didn't do badly for ourselves. By senior year we found ourselves hanging out with the sons and daughters of bankers and doctors and city officials and lawyers and riding around in new Impala convertibles and attending an occasional party where you saw an actual maid. But wherever we went, we'd manage for at least a few minutes to get away from our dates and talk to each other. What we were doing, of course, was trying to comfort ourselves. We shared terri-

231

ble and confusing feelings—pride that we were acceptable to those we saw as glamorous, shame that we felt disgrace for being from the Highlands and having fathers who worked in factories and mothers who went to Mass as often as nuns and brothers and sisters who were doomed to punching the clock and yelling at ragged kids in the cold factory dusk. (You never realize what a toll such shame takes till you see your father's waxen face there in the years-later casket.)

That was the big secret we shared, of course, Karen and I, that we were going to get out, leave the place once and for all. And her brown eyes never sparkled more Christmas-morning bright than at those moments when it all was ahead of us, money, sex, endless thrills, immortality. She had the kind of clean good looks brought out best by a blue cardigan with a line of white button-down shirt at the top and a brown suede car coat over her slender shoulders and moderately tight jeans displaying her quietly artful ass. Nothing splashy about her. She had the sort of face that snuck up on you. You had the impression you were talking to a pretty but in no way spectacular girl, and then all of a sudden you saw how the eyes burned with sad humor and how wry the mouth got at certain times and how absolutely perfect that straight little nose was and how the freckles enhanced rather than detracted from her beauty and by then of course you were hopelessly entangled. Hopelessly.

This wasn't just my opinion, either. I mentioned four divorce settlements. True facts. Karen was one of those prizes that powerful and rich men like to collect with the understanding that it's only something you hold in trust, like a yachting cup. So, in her time, she'd been an ornament for a professional football player (her college beau), an orthodontist ("I think he used to have sexual fantasies about Barry Goldwater"), the owner of a large commuter airline ("I slept with half his pilots; it was kind of a company benefit"), and a sixty-nine-year-old millionaire who was dying of heart disease ("He used to have me sit next to his bedside and just hold his hand—the weird thing was that of all of them, I loved him, I really did—and his eyes would be closed and then every once in a while tears would start streaming down his cheeks as if he was remembering something that really filled him with remorse; he was really a sweetie, but then cancer got him before the heart disease and I never did find out what he regretted so much, I mean if it was about his son or his wife or what"), and now she was comfortably fixed for the rest of her life and if the crow's feet were a little more pronounced around eyes and mouth and if the slenderness was just a trifle too slender (she weighed, at five-three, maybe ninety pounds and kept a variety of diet books in her big sunny kitchen), she was a damn good-looking woman nonetheless, the world's absurdity catalogued and evaluated in a gaze that managed to be both weary and impish, with a laugh that was knowing without being cynical.

So now she wanted to play detective.

I had some more bourbon from the pint—it burned beautifully—and said, "If I had your money, you know what I'd do?"

"Buy yourself a new shirt?"

"You don't like my shirt?"

"I didn't know you had this thing about Hawaii."

"If I had your money, I'd just forget about all this."

"I thought cops were sworn to uphold the right and the true."

"I'm an ex-cop."

"You wear a uniform."

"That's for the American Security Agency."

She sighed. "So I shouldn't have sent the letters?"

"No."

"Well, if they're guilty, they'll show up at Pierce Point tonight."

"Not necessarily."

"Why?"

"Maybe they'll know it's a trap. And not do anything." She nodded to the school. "You hear that?"

"What?"

"The song."

It was Bobby Vinton's "Roses Are Red."

"I remember one party when we both hated our dates and we ended up dancing to that over and over again. Somebody's basement. You remember?"

"Sort of, I guess," I said.

"Good. Let's go in the gym and then we can dance to it again."

Donna, my lady friend, was out of town attending an advertising convention. I hoped she wasn't going to dance with anybody else because it would sure make me mad.

I started to open the door and she said, "I want to ask you a question."

"What?" I sensed what it was going to be so I kept my eyes on the parking lot.

"Turn around and look at me."

I turned around and looked at her. "Okay."

"Since the time we had dinner a month or so ago I've started receiving brochures from Alcoholics Anonymous in the mail. If you were having them sent to me, would you be honest enough to tell me?"

"Yes, I would."

"Are you having them sent to me?"

"Yes, I am."

"You think I'm a lush?"

"Don't you?"

"I asked you first."

So we went into the gym and danced.

* * *

Crepe of red and white, the school colors, draped the ceiling; the stage was a cave of white light on which stood four balding fat guys with spit curls and shimmery gold lamé dinner jackets (could these be the illegitmate sons of Bill Haley?) playing guitars, drum, and saxophone; on the dance floor couples who'd lost hair, teeth, jaw lines, courage, and energy (everything, it seemed, but weight) danced to lame cover versions of "Breaking Up Is Hard To Do" and "Sheila," "Runaround Sue" and "Running Scared" (tonight's lead singer sensibly not even trying Roy Orbison's beautiful falsetto) and then, while I got Karen and myself some no-alcohol punch, they broke into a medley of dance tunes—everything from "Locomotion" to "The Peppermint Twist"—and the place went a little crazy, and I went right along with it.

"Come on," I said.

"Great."

We went out there and we burned ass. We'd both agreed not to dress up for the occasion so we were ready for this. I wore the Hawaiian shirt she found so despicable plus a blue blazer, white socks and cordovan penny-loafers. She wore a salmon-colored Merikani shirt belted at the waist and tan cotton fatigue pants and, sweet Christ, she was so adorable half the guys in the place did the kind of double-takes usually reserved for somebody outrageous or famous.

Over the blasting music, I shouted, "Everybody's watching you!"

She shouted right back, "I know! Isn't it wonderful?"

The medley went twenty minutes and could easily have been confused with an aerobics session. By the end I was sopping and wishing I was carrying ten or fifteen pounds less and sometimes feeling guilty because I was having too much fun (I just hoped Donna, probably having too much fun, too, was feeling equally guilty), and then finally it ended and mate fell into the arms of mate, hanging on to stave off sheer collapse.

Then the head Bill Haley clone said, "Okay, now we're going to do a ballad medley," so then we got everybody from Johnny Mathis to Connie Francis and we couldn't resist that, so I moved her around the floor with clumsy pleasure and she moved me right back with equally clumsy pleasure. "You know something?" I said.

"We're both shitty dancers?"

"Right."

But we kept on, of course, laughing and whirling a few times, and then coming tighter together and just holding each other silently for a time, two human beings getting older and scared about getting older, remembering some things and trying to forget others and trying to make sense of an existence that ultimately made sense to nobody, and then she said, "There's one of them."

I didn't have to ask her what "them" referred to. Until now she'd refused to identify any of the three people she'd sent the letters to.

At first I didn't recognize him. He had almost white hair and a tan so dark it looked fake. He wore a black dinner jacket with a lacy shirt and a black bow tie. He didn't seem to have put on a pound in the quarter century since I'd last seen him.

"Ted Forester?"

"Forester," she said. "He's president of the same savings and loan his father was president of."

"Who are the other two?"

"Why don't we get some punch?"

"The kiddie kind?"

"You could really make me mad with all this lecturing about alcoholism."

"If you're not really a lush then you won't mind getting the kiddie kind."

"My friend, Sigmund Fraud."

We had a couple of pink punches and caught our respective breaths and squinted in the gloom at name tags to see who we were saying hello to and realized all the terrible things you realize at high school reunions, namely that people who thought they were better than you still think that way, and that all the sad little people you feared for—the ones with blackheads and low IQs and lame left legs and walleyes and lisps and every other sort of unfair infirmity people get stuck with—generally turned out to be deserving of your fear, for there was a sadness in their eyes tonight that spoke of failures of every sort, and you wanted to go up and say something to them (I wanted to go up to nervous Karl Carberry, who used to twitch—his whole body twitched—and throw my arm around him and tell him what a neat guy he was, tell him there was no reason whatsoever for his twitching, grant him peace and self-esteem and at least a modicum of hope; if he needed a woman, get him a woman, too), but of course you didn't do that, you didn't go up, you just made edgy jokes and nodded a lot and drifted on to the next piece of human carnage.

"There's number two," Karen whispered.

This one I remembered. And despised. The six-three blond movie-star looks had grown only slightly older. His blue dinner jacket just seemed to enhance his air of malicious superiority. Larry Price. His wife Sally was still perfect, too, though you could see in the lacquered blond hair and maybe a hint of face lift that she'd had to work at it a little harder. A year out of high school, at a bar that took teenage IDs checked by a guy who must have been legally blind, I'd gotten drunk and told Larry that he was essentially an asshole for beating up a friend of mine who hadn't had a chance against him. I had the street boy's secret belief that I could take anybody whose father was a surgeon and whose house included a swimming pool. I had hatred, bitterness, and rage going, right? Well, Larry and I went out into the parking lot, ringed by a lot of drunken spectators, and before I got off a single punch, Larry hit me with a shot that stood me straight up, giving him a great opportunity to hit me again. He hit me three times before I found his face and sent him a shot hard enough to push him back for a time. Before we could go at it again, the guy who checked IDs got himself between us. He was madder than either Larry or me. He ended the fight by taking us both by the ears (he must have trained with nuns) and dragging us out to the curb and telling neither of us to come back.

"You remember the night you fought him?"

"Yeah."

"You could have taken him, Dwyer. Those three punches he got in were just lucky."

"Yeah, that was my impression, too. Lucky."

She laughed. "I was afraid he was going to kill you."

I was going to say something smart, but then a new group of people came up and we gushed through a little social dance of nostalgia and lies and self-justifications. We talked success (at high school reunions, everybody sounds like Amway representatives at a pep rally) and the old days (nobody seems to remember all the kids who got treated like shit for reasons they had no control over) and didn't so-and-so look great (usually this meant they'd managed to keep their toupees on straight) and introducing new spouses (we all had to explain what happened to our original mates; I said mine had been eaten by alligators in the Amazon, but nobody seemed to find that especially believeable) and in the midst of all this, Karen tugged my sleeve and said, "There's the third one."

Him I recognized, too. David Haskins. He didn't look any happier than he ever had. Parent trouble was always the explanation you got for his grief back in high school. His parents had been rich, truly so, his father an importer of some kind, and their arguments so violent that they were as eagerly discussed as who was or who was not pregnant. Apparently David's parents weren't getting along any better today because although the features of his face were open and friendly enough, there was still the sense of some terrible secret stooping his shoulders and keeping his smiles to furtive wretched imitations. He was a paunchy balding little man who might have been a church usher with a sour stomach.

"The Duke of Earl" started up then and there was no way we were going to let that pass so we got out on the floor; but by now, of course, we both watched the three people she'd sent letters to. Her instructions had been to meet the anonymous letter writer at nine-thirty at Pierce Point. If they were going to be there on time, they'd be leaving soon.

"You think they're going to go?"

"I doubt it, Karen."

"You still don't believe that's what I heard them say that night?"

"It was a long time ago and you were drunk."

"It's a good thing I like you because otherwise you'd be a distinct pain in the ass."

Which is when I saw all three of them go stand under one of the glowing red EXIT signs and open a fire door that led to the parking lot.

"They're going!" she said.

"Maybe they're just having a cigarette."

"You know better, Dwyer. You know better."

Her car was in the lot on the opposite side of the gym.

"Well, it's worth a drive even if they don't show up. Pierce Point should be nice tonight."

She squeezed against me and said, "Thanks, Dwyer. Really."

So we went and got her Volvo and went out to Pierce Point where twenty-five years ago a shy kid named Michael Brandon had fallen or been pushed to his death.

Apparently we were about to find out which.

The river road wound along a high wall of clay cliffs on the left and a wide expanse of water on the right. The spring night was impossibly beautiful, one of those moments so rich with sweet odor and even sweeter sight you wanted to take your clothes off and run around in some kind of crazed animal circles out of sheer joy.

"You still like jazz," she said, nodding to the radio.

"I hope you didn't mind my turning the station."

"I'm kind of into Country."

"I didn't get the impression you were listening."

She looked over at me. "Actually, I wasn't. I was thinking about you sending me all those AA pamphlets."

"It was arrogant and presumptuous and I apologize."

"No, it wasn't. It was sweet and I appreciate it."

The rest of the ride, I leaned my head back and smelled flowers and grass and river water and watched moonglow through the elms and oaks and birches of this new spring. There was a Dakota Staton song, "Street of Dreams," and I wondered as always where she was and what she was doing, she'd been so fine, maybe the most underappreciated jazz singer of the entire fifties.

Then we were going up a long, twisting gravel road. We pulled up next to a big park pavillion and got out and stood in the wet grass, and she came over and slid her arm around my waist and sort of hugged me in a half-serious way. "This is all probably crazy, isn't it?"

I sort of hugged her back in a half-serious way. "Yeah, but it's a nice night for a walk so what the hell."

"You ready?"

"Yep."

"Let's go then."

So we went up the hill to the Point itself, and first we looked out at the far side of the river where white birches glowed in the gloom and where beyond you could see the horseshoe shape of the city lights. Then we looked down, straight down the drop of two hundred feet, to the road where Michael Brandon had died.

When I heard the car starting up the road to the east, I said, "Let's get in those bushes over there."

A thick line of shrubs and second-growth timber would give us a place to hide, to watch them.

By the time we were in place, ducked down behind a wide elm and a mulberry bush, a new yellow Mercedes sedan swung into sight and stopped several yards from the edge of the Point.

A car radio played loud in the night. A Top 40 song. Three men got out. Dignified Forester, matinee-idol Price, anxiety-tight Haskins.

Forester leaned back into the car and snapped the radio off. But he left the headlights on. Forester and Price each had cans of beer. Haskins bit his nails.

They looked around in the gloom. The headlights made the darkness beyond seem much darker and the grass in its illumination much greener. Price said harshly, "I told you this was just some goddamn prank. Nobody knows squat."

"He's right, he's probably right," Haskins said to Forester. Obviously he was hoping that was the case.

Forester said, "If somebody didn't know something, we would never have gotten those letters."

She moved then and I hadn't expected her to move at

241

all. I'd been under the impression we would just sit there and listen and let them ramble and maybe in so doing reveal something useful.

But she had other ideas.

She pushed through the undergrowth and stumbled a little and got to her feet again and then walked right up to them.

"Karen!" Haskins said.

"So you did kill Michael," she said.

Price moved toward her abruptly, his hand raised. He was drunk and apparently hitting women was something he did without much trouble.

Then I stepped out from our hiding place and said, "Put your hand down, Price."

Forester said, "Dwyer."

"So," Price said, lowering his hand, "I was right, wasn't I?" He was speaking to Forester.

Forester shook his silver head. He seemed genuinely saddened. "Yes, Price, for once your cynicism is justified."

Price said, "Well, you two aren't getting a goddamned penny, do you know that?"

He lunged toward me, still a bully. But I was ready for him, wanted it. I also had the advantage of being sober. When he was two steps away, I hit him just once and very hard in his solar plexus. He backed away, eyes startled, and then he turned abruptly away.

We all stood looking at one another, pretending not to hear the sounds of violent vomiting on the other side of the splendid new Mercedes.

Forester said, "When I saw you there, Karen, I wondered if you could do it alone."

"Do what?"

"What?" Forester said. "What? Let's at least stop the games. You two want money."

"Christ," I said to Karen, who looked perplexed, "they think we're trying to shake them down."

"Shake them down?"

"Blackmail them."

"Exactly," Forester said.

Price had come back around. He was wiping his mouth with the back of his hand. In his other hand he carried a silver-plated .45, the sort of weapon professional gamblers favor.

Haskins said, "Larry, Jesus, what is that?"

"What does it look like?"

"Larry, that's how people get killed." Haskins sounded like Price's mother.

Price's eyes were on me. "Yeah, it would be terrible if Dwyer here got killed, wouldn't it?" He waved the gun at me. I didn't really think he'd shoot, but I sure was afraid he'd trip and the damn thing would go off accidentally. "You've been waiting since senior year to do that to me, haven't you, Dwyer?"

I shrugged. "I guess so, yeah."

"Well, why don't I give Forester here the gun and then you and I can try it again."

"Fine with me."

He handed Forester the .45. Forester took it all right, but what he did was toss it somewhere into the gloom surrounding the car. "Larry, if you don't straighten up here, I'll fight you myself. Do you understand me?" Forester had a certain dignity and when he spoke, his voice carried an easy authority. "There will be no more fighting, do you both understand that?"

"I agree with Ted," Karen said.

Forester, like a teacher tired of naughty children, decided to get on with the real business. "You wrote those letters, Dwyer?"

"No."

"No?"

"No. Karen wrote them."

A curious glance was exchanged by Forester and Karen. "I guess I should have known that," Forester said.

"Jesus, Ted," Karen said, "I'm not trying to blackmail you, no matter what you think."

"Then just what exactly are you trying to do?"

She shook her lovely little head. I sensed she regretted ever writing the letters, stirring it all up again. "I just want the truth to come out about what really happened to Michael Brandon that night."

"The truth," Price said. "Isn't that goddamn touching?"

"Shut up, Larry," Haskins said.

Forester said, "You know what happened to Michael Brandon?"

"I've got a good idea," Karen said. "I overheard you three talking at a party one night."

"What did we say?"

"What?"

"What did you overhear us say?"

Karen said, "You said that you hoped nobody looked into what really happened to Michael that night."

A smile touched Forester's lips. "So on that basis you concluded that we murdered him?"

"There wasn't much else to conclude."

Price said, weaving still, leaning on the fender for support, "I don't goddamn believe this."

Forester nodded to me. "Dwyer, I'd like to have a talk with Price and Haskins here, if you don't mind. Just a few minutes." He pointed to the darkness beyond the car. "We'll walk over there. You know we won't try to get away because you'll have our car. All right?"

I looked at Karen.

She shrugged.

They left, back into the gloom, voices receding and fading into the sounds of crickets and a barn owl and a distant roaring train.

"You think they're up to something?"

"I don't know," I said.

We stood with our shoes getting soaked and looked at the green green grass in the headlights.

"What do you think they're doing?" Karen asked.

"Deciding what they want to tell us."

"You're used to this kind of thing, aren't you?"

"I guess."

"It's sort of sad, isn't it?"

"Yeah. It is."

"Except for you getting the chance to punch out Larry Price after all these years."

"Christ, you really think I'm that petty?"

"I know you are. I know you are."

Then we both turned to look back to where they were. There'd been a cry and Forester shouted, "You hit him again, Larry, and I'll break your goddamn jaw." They were arguing about something and it had turned vicious.

I leaned back against the car. She leaned back against me. "You think we'll ever go to bed?"

"I'd sure like to, Karen, but I can't."

"Donna?"

"Yeah. I'm really trying to learn how to be faithful."

"That been a problem?"

"It cost me a marriage."

"Maybe I'll learn how someday, too."

Then they were back. Somebody, presumably Forester, had torn Price's nice lacy shirt into shreds. Haskins looked miserable.

Forester said, "I'm going to tell you what happened that night."

I nodded.

"I've got some beer in the back seat. Would either of you like one?"

Karen said, "Yes, we would."

So he went and got a six pack of Michelob and we all had a beer and just before he started talking he and Karen shared another one of those peculiar glances and then he said, "The four of us—myself, Price, Haskins, and Michael Brandon—had done something we were very ashamed of."

"Afraid of," Haskins said.

"Afraid that, if it came out, our lives would be ruined. Forever," Forester said.

Price said, "Just say it, Forester." He glared at me. "We raped a girl, the four of us."

"Brandon spent two months afterward seeing the girl, bringing her flowers, apologizing to her over and over again, telling her how sorry we were, that we'd been drunk and it wasn't like us to do that and—" Forester sighed, put his eyes to the ground. "In fact we had been drunk; in fact it wasn't like us to do such a thing—"

Haskins said, "It really wasn't. It really wasn't."

For a time there was just the barn owl and the crickets again, no talk, and then gently I said, "What happened to Brandon that night?"

"We were out as we usually were, drinking beer, talking about it, afraid the girl would finally turn us into the police, still trying to figure out why we'd ever done such a thing—"

The hatred was gone from Price's eyes. For the first time the matinee idol looked as melancholy as his friends. "No matter what you think of me, Dwyer, I don't rape women. But that night—" He shrugged, looked away.

"Brandon," I said. "You were going to tell me about Brandon."

"We came up here, had a case of beer or something,

246

and talked about it some more, and that night,'' Forester said, ''that night Brandon just snapped. He couldn't handle how ashamed he was or how afraid he was of being turned in. Right in the middle of talking—''

Haskins took over. ''Right in the middle, he just got up and ran out to the Point.'' He indicated the cliff behind us. ''And before we could stop him, he jumped.''

''Jesus,'' Price said, ''I can't forget his screaming on the way down. I can't ever forget it.''

I looked at Karen. ''So what she heard you three talking about outside the party that night was not that you'd killed Brandon but that you were afraid a serious investigation into his suicide might turn up the rape?''

Forester said, ''Exactly.'' He stared at Karen. ''We didn't kill Michael, Karen. We loved him. He was our friend.''

But by then, completely without warning, she had started to cry and then she began literally sobbing, her entire body shaking with some grief I could neither understand nor assuage.

I nodded to Forester to get back in his car and leave. They stood and watched us a moment and then they got into the Mercedes and went away, taking the burden of years and guilt with them.

This time I drove. I went far out the river road, miles out, where you pick up the piney hills and the deer standing by the side of the road.

From the glove compartment she took a pint of J&B, and I knew better than to try and stop her.

I said, ''You were the girl they raped, weren't you?''

''Yes.''

''Why didn't you tell the police?''

She smiled at me. ''The police weren't exactly going to

believe a girl from the Highlands about the sons of rich men.''

I sighed. She was right.

"Then Michael started coming around to see me. I can't say I ever forgave him, but I started to feel sorry for him. His fear—'' She shook her head, looked out the window. She said, almost to herself, "But I had to write those letters, get them there tonight, know for sure if they killed him.'' She paused. "You believe them?''

"That they didn't kill him?''

"Right.''

"Yes, I believe them.''

"So do I.''

Then she went back to staring out the window, her small face childlike there in silhouette against the moonsilver river. "Can I ask you a question, Dwyer?''

"Sure.''

"You think we're ever going to get out of the Highlands?''

"No," I said, and drove on faster in her fine new expensive car. "No, I don't.''

Hit-and-Run

•

Susan Dunlap

In just four novels—Karma, As a Favor, Not Exactly a Brahmin, Too Close to the Edge—Susan Dunlap's Berkeley-based Jill Smith has joined Lillian O'Donnell's Nora Mulcahaney and Dorothy Uhnak's Christy Opara as mystery fiction's most prominent policewomen sleuths. (Dunlap also writes a much different series about an amateur detective, meter-reader Vejay Haskell, the most recent of which is The Last Annual Slugfest.) "Hit-and-Run" is Jill Smith's first recorded short case—a low-key but intense story about a traffic accident on one of Berkeley's football Saturdays.

It was four-fifteen Saturday afternoon—a football Saturday at the University of California. For the moment, there was nothing in the streets leading from Memorial Stadium but rain. Sensible Berkeleyans were home, students and alumni were huddled in the stands under sheets of clear plastic, like pieces of expensive lawn furniture, as the Cal Bears and their opponents marched toward the final gun. Then the seventy-five thousand six hundred sixty-two fans would charge gleefully or trudge morosely to their cars and create a near-gridlock all over the city of Berkeley. Then only a fool, or a tourist, would consider driving across town. Then even in a black-and-white—with the pulsers on, and the siren blaring—I wouldn't be able to get to the station.

The conference beat officer Connie Pereira and I had

249

attended—*Indications of the Pattern Behavior of the Cyclical Killer in California*—had let out at three-thirty. We'd figured we just had time to turn in the black-and-white, pick up our own cars, and get home. On the way home, I planned to stop for a pizza. That would be pushing it. But, once I got the pizza in my car, I would be going against traffic. Now, I figured, I could make good time because University Avenue would still be empty.

When the squeal came, I knew I had figured wrong. It was a hit-and-run. I hadn't handled one of those since long before I'd been assigned to Homicide. But this part of University Avenue was Pereira's beat. I looked at her questioningly; she wasn't on beat now; she could let the squeal go. But she was already reaching for the mike.

I switched on the pulser lights and the siren, and stepped on the gas. The street was deserted. The incident was two blocks ahead, below San Pablo Avenue, on University. There wasn't a car, truck, or bicycle in sight. As I crossed the intersection, I could see a man lying on his back in the street, his herringbone suit already matted with blood. Bent over him was a blond man in a white shirt and jeans.

Leaving Pereira waiting for the dispatcher's reply, I got out of the car and ran toward the two men. The blond man was breathing heavily but regularly, rhythmically pressing on the injured man's chest and blowing into his mouth. He was getting no response. I had seen enough bodies, both dead and dying, in my four years on the force to suspect that this one was on the way out. I doubted the C.P.R. was doing any good. But, once started, it couldn't be stopped until the medics arrived. And despite the lack of reaction, the blond looked like he knew what he was doing.

From across the sidewalk, the pungent smell of brown curry floated from a small, dingy storefront called the Benares Cafe, mixing with the sharp odor of the victim's urine. I turned away, took a last breath of fresh air, and knelt down by the injured man.

The blonde leaned over the victim's mouth, blew breath in, then lifted back.

"Did you see the car that hit him?" I asked.

He was pressing on the victim's chest. He waited till he forced air into his mouth again and came up. "A glimpse."

"Where were you then?"

Again he waited, timing his reply with his rising. "Walking on University, a block down." He blew into the mouth again. "He didn't stop. Barely slowed down."

"What kind of car?" I asked, timing my question to his rhythm.

"Big. Silver, with a big, shiny grill."

"What make?"

"Don't know."

"Can you describe the driver?"

"No."

"Man or woman?"

"Don't know."

"Did you see any passengers?"

"No."

"Is there anything else you can tell me about the car?"

He went through an entire cycle of breathing and pressing before he said, "No."

"Thanks."

Now I looked more closely at the victim. I could see the short, gray-streaked brown hair, and the still-dark mustache. I could see the thick eyebrows and the eyes so filled with blood that it might not have been possible to detect the eye color if I hadn't already known it. I took a long look to make sure. But there was no question. Under the blood were the dark brown eyes of Graham Latham.

Behind me, the door of the black-and-white opened,

letting out a burst of staccato calls from the dispatcher, then slammed shut. "Ambulance and back-up on the way, Jill," Pereira said as she came up beside me. "It wasn't easy getting anyone off Traffic on a football day."

I stood up and moved away from the body with relief. The blond man continued his work. In spite of the rain, I could see the sweat coming through his shirt.

I relayed his account of the crime, such as it was, to Pereira, then asked her, "Have you ever heard of Graham Latham?"

"Nope. Should I?"

"Maybe not. It's just ironic. When I was first on beat, I handled a hit-and-run. Only that time Latham was the driver. The victim, Katherine Hillman, was left just like he is. She lived—until last week, anyway. I saw her name in the obits. She was one of the guinea pigs they were trying a new electronic pain device on—a last resort for people with chronic untreatable pain."

Pereira nodded.

"I remember her at the trial," I said. "The pain wasn't so bad then. She could still shift around in her wheelchair and get some relief, and she had a boyfriend who helped her. But at the end it must have been bad." I looked over at the body in the street. "From the looks of Graham Latham, he'll be lucky if he can sit up in a wheelchair like she could."

"Be a hard choice," Pereira said, turning back to the black-and-white. She took the red blinkers out of the trunk, then hurried back along the empty street to put them in place.

Despite the cold rain, the sidewalks here weren't entirely empty. On the corner across University, I could see a pair of long pale female legs, shivering under stockings and black satin shorts that almost covered the curve of her buttocks—almost but not quite. Above those shorts, a thick red jacket suggested that, from the waist up, it was winter. The wearer—young, very blond, with wings of multicolored eye makeup visible from across the street—stood partially concealed behind the building, looking toward Latham's body as if trying to decide whether it could be scooped up, and the cops cleared off, before the free-spending alumni rambled out of Memorial Stadium and drove down University Avenue.

On the sidewalk in front of the Benares Cafe, one of Berkeley's streetpeople—a man with long, tangled, rain-soaked hair that rested on a threadbare poncho, the outermost of three or four ragged layers of clothing—clutched a brown paper bag. Behind him, a tiny woman in a *sari* peered through the cafe window. In a doorway, a man and a woman leaned against a wall, seemingly oblivious to the activity in the street.

Between the Benares Cafe and the occupied doorway was a storefront with boxes piled in the window and the name "Harris" faded on the sign above. There was no indication of what Harris offered to the public. Across the street a mom-and-pop store occupied the corner. Next to it was the Evangelical People's Church—a storefront no larger than the mom-and-pop. Here in Berkeley, there had been more gurus over the years than in most states of India, but splinter Christian groups were rare; Berkeleyans liked their religion a bit more exotic. The rest of the block was taken up by a ramshackle hotel.

I looked back at Graham Latham, still lying unmoving in his herringbone suit. It was a good suit. Latham was an architect in San Francisco, a partner in a firm that had done a stylish low-income housing project for the city. He lived high in the hills above Berkeley. The brown Mercedes parked at the curb had to be his. Graham Latham wasn't a man who should be found on the same block as the brown-bag clutcher behind him.

I walked toward the streetperson. I was surprised he'd stuck around. He wasn't one who would view the police as protectors.

I identified myself and took his name—John Eskins. "Tell me what you saw of the accident."

"Nothing."

"You were here when we arrived." I let the accusation hang.

"Khan, across the street"—he pointed to the store— "he saw it. He called you guys. Didn't have to; he just did. He said to tell you."

"Okay, but you stick around."

He shrugged.

I glanced toward Pereira. She nodded. In the distance the shriek of the ambulance siren cut through the air. On the ground the blond man was still working on Latham. His sleeves had bunched at the armpits revealing part of a tattoo—"ay" over a heart. In the rain, it looked as if the red of the letters would drip into the heart.

The ambulance screeched to a stop. Two medics jumped out.

The first came up behind the blond man. Putting a hand on his arm, he said, "Okay. We'll take over now."

The blond man didn't break his rhythm.

"It's okay," the medic said, louder. "You can stop now. You're covered."

Still he counted and pressed on Latham's chest, counted and breathed into Latham's unresponsive mouth.

The medic grabbed both arms and yanked him up. Before the blond was standing upright, the other medic was in his place.

"He'll die! Don't let him die! He can't die!" The man struggled to free himself. His hair flapped against his eyebrows; his shirt was soaked. There was blood—Latham's blood—on his face. The rain washed it down, leaving orange lines on his cheeks. "He can't die. It's not fair. You've got to save him!"

"He's getting the best care around," Pereira said.

The blond man leaned toward the action, but the medic pulled him back. Behind us, cars, limited now to one lane, drove slowly, their engines straining in first gear, headlights brightening the back of the ambulance like colorless blinkers. The rain dripped down my hair, under the collar of my jacket, collecting there in a soggy pool.

Turning to me, Pereira shrugged. I nodded. We'd both seen Good Samaritans like him, people who get so involved they can't let go.

I turned toward the store across the street. "Witness called from there. You want me to check it out?"

She nodded. It was her beat, her case. I was just doing her a favor.

I walked across University. The store was typical—a small display of apples, bananas, onions, potatoes, two wrinkled green peppers in front, and the rest of the space taken with rows of cans and boxes, a surprising number of them red, clamoring for the shoppers' notice and failing in their sameness. The shelves climbed high. There were packages of Bisquick, curry, and Garam Masala that the woman in the Benares Cafe wouldn't have been able to reach. In the back was a cooler for milk and cheese, and behind the counter by the door, the one-man bottles of vodka and bourbon—and a small, dark man, presumably Khan.

"I'm Detective Smith," I said, extending my shield. "You called us about the accident?"

"Yes," he said. "I am Farib Khan. I am owning this store. This is why I cannot leave to come to you, you see." He gestured at the empty premises.

I nodded. "But you saw the accident?"

"Yes, yes." He wagged his head side to side in that

255

disconcerting Indian indication of the affirmative. "Mr. Latham—"

"You know him?"

"He is being my customer for a year now. Six days a week."

"Monday through Saturday?"

"Yes, yes. He is stopping on his drive from San Francisco."

"Does he work on Saturdays?" It wasn't the schedule I would have expected of a well-off architect.

"He teaches a class. After his class, he is eating lunch and driving home, you see. And stopping here."

I thought of Graham Latham in his expensive suit, driving his Mercedes. I recalled why he had hit a woman four years ago. It wasn't for curry powder that Graham Latham would be patronizing this ill-stocked store. "Did he buy liquor every day?"

"Yes, yes." Turning behind him, he took a pint bottle of vodka from the shelf. "He is buying this."

So Graham Latham hadn't changed. I didn't know why I would have assumed otherwise. "Did he open it before he left?"

"He is not a bum, not like those who come here not to buy, but to watch, to steal. Mr. Latham is a gentleman. For him, I am putting the bottle in the bag, to take home."

"Then you watched him leave? You saw the accident?"

Again the wagging of his head. "I am seeing, but it is no accident. Mr. Latham, he walks across the street, toward his big car. He is not a healthy man." Khan glanced significantly at the bottle. "So I watch. I am fearing the fall in the street, yes? But he walks straight. Then a car turns the corner, comes at him. Mr. Latham jumps back. He is fast then, you see. The car turns, comes at him. He cannot escape. He is hit. The car speeds off."

"You mean the driver was trying to hit Latham?"

"Yes, yes."

Involuntarily I glanced back to the street. Latham's body was gone now. The witnesses, John Eskin and the C.P.R. man, were standing with Pereira. A back-up unit had arrived. One of the men was checking the brown Mercedes.

Turning back to Khan, I said. "What did the car look like?"

He shrugged. "Old, middle-sized."

"Can you be more specific?"

He half-closed his eyes, trying. Finally, he said, "The day is gray, raining. The car is not new, not one I see in the ads. It is light-colored. Gray? Blue?"

"What about the driver?"

Again, he shrugged.

"Man or woman?"

It was a moment before he said, "All I am seeing is red—a sweater? Yes? A jacket?"

It took only a few more questions to discover that I had learned everything Farib Khan knew. By the time I crossed the street to the scene, Pereira had finished with the witnesses, and one of the back-up men was questioning the couple leaning in the doorway. The witnesses had seen nothing. John Eskins had been in the back of the store at the moment Latham had been hit, and the woman in the Benares Cafe—Pomilla Patel—hadn't seen anything until she heard the car hit him. And the man who stopped to give C.P.R.—Randall Sellinek—hadn't even seen the vehicle drive off. Or so they said.

They stood, a little apart from each other, as if each found the remaining two unsuitable company. Certainly they were three who would never come together in any other circumstances. John Eskins clutched his brown bag, jerking his eyes warily. Pomilla Patel glanced at him in disgust, as if he alone were responsible for the decay of the neighborhood. And Randall Sellinek just stood, letting the cold rain fall on his shirt and run down his bare arms.

I took Pereira aside and relayed what Khan had told me.

She grabbed one back-up man, telling him to call in for more help. "If it's a possible homicide we'll have to scour the area. We'll need to question everyone on this block and the ones on either side. We'll need someone to check the cars and the garbage. Get as many men as you can."

He raised an eyebrow. We all knew how many that would be.

To me, Pereira said, "You want to take Eskins or Sellinek down to the station for statements?"

I hesitated. "No. . . . Suppose we let them leave and keep an eye on them. We have the manpower."

"Are you serious, Jill? It's hardly regulations."

"I'll take responsibility."

Still, she looked uncomfortable. But she'd assisted on too many of my cases over the years to doubt me completely. "Well, okay. It's on your head." She moved toward the witnesses. "That's all, folks. Thanks for your cooperation."

Eskins seemed stunned, but not about to question his good fortune. He moved west, walking quickly, but unsteadily, toward the seedy dwellings near the bay. I shook my head. Pereira nodded to one of the back-up men, and he turned to follow Eskins.

Sellinek gave a final look at the scene of his futile effort and began walking east, toward San Pablo Avenue and the better neighborhoods beyond. He didn't seemed surprised, like Eskins, but then he hadn't the same type of contact with us. I watched him cross the street, then followed. The blocks were short. He came to San Pablo Avenue, waited for the light, then crossed. I had to run to make the light.

On the far side of University Avenue the traffic was

picking up. Horns were beeping. The football game was over. The first of the revelers had made it this far. I glanced back the several blocks to the scene, wondering if the hooker had decided to wait us out. But I was too far away to tell.

Sellinek crossed another street, then another. The rain beat down on his white shirt. His blond hair clung to his head. He walked on, never turning to look back.

I let him go five blocks, just to be sure, then caught up with him. "Mr. Sellinek. You remember me, one of the police officers. I'll need to ask you a few more questions."

"Me? Listen, I just stopped to help that man. I didn't want him to die. I wanted him to live."

"I believe you. You knocked yourself out trying to save him. But that still leaves the question of why? Why were you in this neighborhood at all?"

"Just passing through."

"On foot?"

"Yeah, on foot."

"In the rain, wearing just a shirt?"

"So?"

"Tell me again why you decided to give him C.P.R."

"I saw the car hit him. It was new and silver. It had a big, shiny grill. Why are you standing here badgering me? Why aren't you out looking for that car?"

"Because it doesn't exist."

"I *saw* it."

"When?"

"When it hit him."

"But you didn't notice passengers. You couldn't describe the driver."

"The car was too far away. I was back at the corner, behind it. I told you that."

"You didn't look at it when it passed you?"

"No. I was caught up in my own thoughts. I wasn't going to cross the street. There was no reason to look at the traffic. Then the car hit him. He was dying when I got to him—I couldn't let him die."

"I believe that. You didn't intend for him to have something as easy as death."

"What?"

"There wasn't any silver car or shiny grill, Mr. Sellinek." He started to protest, but I held up a hand. "You said you were behind the car and didn't notice it until it hit Latham. You couldn't possibly have seen what kind if grill it had. *You're* the one who ran Latham down."

He didn't say anything. He just stood, letting the rain drip down his face.

"We'll check the area," I said. "We'll find the car you used—maybe not your own car, maybe hot-wired, but there'll be prints. You couldn't have had time to clean them all off. We'll find your red sweater, too. When you planned to run Latham down, you never thought you'd have to stop and try to save his life, did you? And once you realized you had to go back to him, you took the sweater off because you were afraid someone might have seen it. Isn't that the way it happened, Mr. Sellinek?"

He still didn't say anything.

I looked at the tattoo on his arm. All of it was visible now—the full name above the heart. It said, "Kay."

"You were Kay Hillman's boyfriend, weren't you? That's why you ran Latham down—because she died last week and you wanted revenge."

His whole body began to shake. "Latham was drunk when he hit Kay. But he got a smart lawyer, he lied in court, he got off with a suspended sentence. What he did to Kay . . . it was just an inconvenience to him. It didn't even change his habits. He still drank when he was driving. He still stopped six days a week at the same store to pick up liquor. Sooner or later he would have run down someone else. It was just a matter of time.

"I wanted revenge, sure. But it wasn't because Kay died. It was for those four years she *lived* after he hit her. She couldn't sit without pain; she couldn't lie down. The pills didn't help. Nothing did. The pain just got worse, month after month." He closed his eyes, squeezing back tears. "I didn't want Latham to die. I wanted him to suffer like Kay did."

Now it was my turn not to say anything.

Sellinek swallowed heavily. "It's not fair," he said. "None of it is fair."

He was right. None of it was fair at all.

The Anderson Boy

·

Joseph Hansen

Joseph Hansen's series of novels about homosexual insurance investigator Dave Brandstetter—among them, Death Claims, Gravedigger, Skinflick, *and* The Little Boy Laughed—*have earned him a deserved reputation as one of mystery fiction's most accomplished stylists. "The Anderson Boy," one of his rare short stories, is a considerable departure in content, dealing not with the gay community but with a past crime and its present-day impact on an academic and his wife. Its richly evocative prose, however, is vintage Hansen.*

Prothero, fastening the pegs of his car coat, pushed out through the heavy doors of the Liberal Arts Building, and saw the Anderson boy. The boy loped along in an army surplus jacket and army surplus combat boots, a satchel of books on his back. His hair, as white and shaggy as when he was five, blew in the cold wind.

He was a long way off. Crowds of students hurried along the paths under the naked trees between lawns brown and patched with last week's snow. But Prothero picked out the Anderson boy at once and with sickening certainty.

Prothero almost ran for his car. When he reached it, in the gray-cement vastness of Parking Building B, his hands shook so that he couldn't at first fit the key into the door. Seated inside, he shuddered. His sheepskin collar was icy with sweat crystals. He shut his eyes, gripped the wheel, leaned his head against it.

The Anderson Boy

This was not possible. The trip to promote his book—those staring airport waiting rooms, this plane at midnight, that at four A.M., snatches of sleep in this and that hotel room, this bookseller luncheon, that radio call-in program, dawns for the *Today Show* and *Good Morning America*, yawns for Johnny Carson. Los Angeles in ninety-degree heat, Denver in snow, Chicago in wind, New York in rain; pills to make him sleep, pills to wake him up; martinis, wine, and Scotch poured down him like water. Three weeks of it had been too much. His nerves were frayed. He was seeing things. The very worst things.

He drove off campus. By the shopping center, he halted for a red light. He thought about his lecture. It had gone well, which was surprising, tired as he was. But he'd been happy to be back where he belonged, earning an honest living, doing what he loved. Promotion tours? Never again. His publisher was pleased. The book was selling well. But Donald Prothero was a wreck.

The Anderson boy loped across in front of him. He shut his eyes, drew a deep breath, opened his eyes, and looked again. He was still sure. Yet how could it be? It was thirteen years since he'd last seen him, and more than a thousand miles from here. On that night, the boy had been a pale little figure in pajamas, standing wide-eyed in the dark breezeway outside the sliding glass wall of his bedroom, hugging a stuffed toy kangaroo. Prothero, in his panicked flight, naked, clutching his clothes, had almost run him over.

The boy had to have recognized him. Prothero was always around. He'd taught the boy to catch a ball, to name birds, lizards, cacti, to swim in the bright-blue pool just beyond that breezeway. Prothero had given him the toy kangaroo. He should have stopped. Instead, he'd kept running. He was only eighteen. Nothing bad had ever happened to him. Sick and sweating, he'd driven far into the desert. On some lost, moonlit road, half overgrown by chaparral, he'd jerked into his clothes, hating his body.

He'd known what he had to do—go to the sheriff. He'd started the car again, but he couldn't make himself do it. He couldn't accept what had happened. Things like that took place in cheap books and bad movies, or they happened to sleazy people on the TV news. Not to people like the Andersons. Not to people like him. It could wreck his whole life. He went home. To his room. As always. But he couldn't sleep. All he could do was vomit. His father, bathrobe, hair rumpled, peered at him in the dusky hall when Prothero came out of the bathroom for the third time.

"Have you been drinking?"

"You know better than that."

"Shall we call the doctor?"

"No, I'm all right now."

But he would never be all right again. Next morning, when he stripped to shower, he nearly fainted. His skin was caked with dried blood. He nearly scalded himself, washing it off. He trembled and felt weak, dressing, but he dressed neat and fresh as always. He kissed his mother and sat on his stool at the breakfast bar, smiling as always. He was a boy who smiled. He'd been senior class president in high school, captain of the basketball team, editor of the yearbook. These things had been handed him, and he'd accepted them without question. As he'd accepted scholarships to University for the coming fall. As he'd accepted his role as Jean Anderson's lover.

His mother set orange juice in front of him, and his mug with his initial on it, filled with creamy coffee. He knew what she would do next. He wanted to shout at her not to do it. He didn't shout. They would think he was crazy. She snapped on the little red-shelled TV set that hung where she could watch it as she cooked at the burner-deck, where his father and he could watch it while they ate. He wanted to get off the stool and go hide. But they would ask questions. He stayed.

And there on the screen, in black and white, was the Anderson house with its rock roof and handsome paintings, its glass slide doors, the pool with outdoor furniture beside it, the white rail fence. There in some ugly office sat the Anderson boy in his pajamas on a molded plastic chair under a bulletin board tacked with papers. The toy kangaroo lay on a floor of vinyl tile among cigarette butts. A pimply faced deputy bent over the boy, trying to get him to drink from a striped wax paper cup. The boy didn't cry. He didn't even blink. He sat still and stared at nothing. There were dim, tilted pictures, for a few seconds, of a bedroom, dark blothes on crumpled sheets, dark blotches on pale carpeting. Bodies strapped down under the blankets were wheeled on gurneys to an ambulance whose rear doors gaped. The sheriff's face filled the screen—thick, wrinkled eyelids, nose with big pores, cracked lips. He spoke. Then a cartoon tiger ate cereal from a spoon.

"People shouldn't isolate themselves miles from town." Prothero's father buttered toast. "Husband away traveling half the time. Wife and child alone. Asking for trouble."

"He came home," Prothero's mother set plates of scrambled eggs and bacon on the counter. "It didn't help."

"All sorts of maniacs running loose these days," Prothero's father said. "Evidently no motive. They'll probably never find who did it."

His father went to his office. His mother went to a meeting of the Episcopal Church altar guild. He drove to the sheriff's station. He parked on a side street, but he couldn't get out of the car. He sat and stared at the flat-roofed, sand-colored building with the flagpole in front. He ran the radio. At noon, it said the sheriff had ruled out the possibility of an intruder. The gun had belonged to Anderson. His were the only fingerprints on it. Plainly, there had been a quarrel and Anderson had shot first his wife and then himself. The Anderson boy appeared to be in a state of shock and had said nothing. A grandmother had flown in from San Diego to look after him. Prothero went home to the empty house and cried.

Now, at the intersection, he watched from his car as the boy pushed through glass doors into McDonald's. He had to be mistaken. This wasn't rational. Horns blared behind him. The light had turned green. He pressed the throttle. The engine coughed and died. Damn. He twisted the key, the engine started, the car bucked ahead half its length and quit again. The light turned orange. On the third try, he made it across the intersection, but the cars he'd kept from crossing honked angrily after him.

The Anderson boy? What made him think that? He'd known a runty little kid. This boy was over six feet tall. A towhead, yes, but how uncommon was that? He swung the car into the street that would take him home beneath an over-arch of bare tree limbs. The boy looked like his father—but that skull shape, those big long bones, were simply North European characteristics. Millions of people shared those. The odds were out of the question. It was his nerves. It couldn't be the Anderson boy.

He went from the garage straight to the den, shed the car coat, and poured himself a drink. He gulped down half of it and shivered. The den was cold and smelled shut up. He hadn't come into it yesterday when he got home from the airport. The curtains were drawn. He touched a switch that opened them. Outside, dead leaves stuck to flagging. Winter-brown lawn with neat plantings of birches sloped to a little stream. Woods were gray beyond the stream.

"Ah," Barbara said, "it is you."

"Who else would it be?" He didn't turn to her.

"How did the lecture go?"

"Who built the footbridge?" he said.

"The nicest boy," she said. "A friend of yours from California. Wayne Anderson. Do you remember him?"

"I was going to build it," he said.

"I thought it would be a pleasant surprise for you when you got home. I was saving it." She stepped around stacks of books on the floor and touched him. "You all right?"

"It would have been good therapy for me. Outdoors. Physical labor. Sense of accomplishment."

"He said you'd been so nice to him when he was a little boy. When he saw the lumber piled up down there, and I told him what you had in mind, he said he'd like to do it. And he meant it. He was very quick and handy. Came faithfully every day for a whole week. He's an absolute darling."

Prothero finished his drink. "How much did you have to pay him?"

"He wouldn't let me pay him," she said. "So I fed him. That seemed acceptable. He eats with gusto."

Flakes of snow began to fall. Prothero said, "It's hard to believe."

"He saw you on television in San Diego, but it was tape, and when he phoned the station, you'd gone. He thought you'd come back here. He got on a plane that night." She laughed. "Isn't it wonderful how these children just leap a thousand miles on impulse? Could we even have imagined it at his age? He got our address from Administration and came here without even stopping to unpack. Not that he brought much luggage. A duffel bag is all."

"You didn't invite him to stay."

"I thought of it," she said.

He worked the switch to close the curtains. He didn't want to see the bridge. It was dim in the den and she switched on the desk lamp. He was pouring more whiskey into his glass. He said, "I didn't ask you about Cora last night. How's she doing?"

"It's a miracle. You'd never know she'd had a stroke." He

knew from her voice that she was watching him and worried. His hands shook. He spilled whiskey. "You're not all right," she said. "I've never seen you so pale. Don, don't let them talk you into any more book peddling. Please?"

"Is he coming here again?"

"Yes. This afternoon." She frowned. "What's wrong? Don't you want to see him? He's very keen to see you. I'd say he worships you—exactly as if he were still five years old."

"They don't mature evenly," Prothero said.

"He hasn't forgotten a thing," she said.

In thickly falling snow, the Anderson boy jumped up and down on the little bridge and showed his teeth. He was still in the floppy army surplus jacket. The clumsy army surplus boots thudded on the planks. He took hold of the raw two-by-fours that were the railings of the bridge and tried to shake them with his big, clean hands. They didn't shake. Clumps of snow drifted under the bridge on the cold snow surface of the stream. Prothero stood on the bank, hands pushed into the pockets of the car coat. His ears were cold.

"It would hold a car." The Anderson boy came off the bridge. "If it was that wide. Not a nail in it. Only bolts and screws. No props in the streambed to wash out. Cantilevered."

Prothero nodded. "Good job," he said. "Your major will be engineering, then, right?"

"No." Half a head taller than Prothero, and very strong, the boy took Prothero's arm as if Prothero were old and frail, or as if he were a woman, and walked him back up the slope. "No, my grandfather's a contractor. I started working for him summers when I was fourteen. I got my growth early." He stopped on the flags and pawed at his hair to get the snow out of it. His hair was so white it looked as if he were shedding.

"So you learned carpentry by doing?" Prothero reached for the latch of the sliding door to the den.

But the Anderson boy's arm was longer. He rolled the door back and with a hand between Prothero's shoulder blades pushed the man inside ahead of him. "It's like breathing or walking to me." He shut the door and helped Prothero off with his coat. "And just about as interesting." He took the coat to the bathroom off the den. He knew right where it was. Prothero watched him shed his own jacket there and hang both coats over the bathtub to drip. He sat on the edge of the tub to take off his boots. "I wouldn't do it for a living."

"What about coffee?" Barbara came into the den. Prothero thought she looked younger. Maybe it was the new way she'd had her hair done. "It will be half an hour till dinner."

"I'll have coffee." The Anderson boy set his boots in the tub. He came out in a very white sweater and very white gym socks. His blue jeans were damp from the snow. He lifted bottles off the liquor cabinet and waved them at Barbara while he looked at Prothero with eyes clear as water, empty of intent as water. "Don will have a stiff drink."

"I'll have coffee," Prothero said, "thanks."

The Anderson boy raised his eyebrows, shrugged, and set the bottles down. Barbara went away. The Anderson boy dropped into Prothero's leather easy chair, stretched out his long legs, clasped his hands behind his head, and said, "No, my major will be psychology."

"That's a contrast," Prothero said. "Why?"

"I had a strange childhood," the Anderson boy said. "My parents were murdered when I was five. But you knew that, right?"

Prothero knelt to set a match to crumpled newspaper and kindling in the fireplace. "Yes," he said.

"I didn't. Not till I was sixteen. My grandparents always claimed they'd been killed in a highway accident. Finally they thought I was old enough to be told what really happened. They were murdered. Somebody broke in at night. Into their bedroom. I was there—in the house, I mean. I must have heard it. Shouts. Screams. Gunshots. Only I blacked it all out.''

"They said you went into shock." The kindling flared up. Prothero reached for a log and dropped it. His fingers had no strength. The Anderson boy jumped out of the chair, picked up the log, laid it on the fire. Sparks went up the chimney. He rattled the fire screen into place and brushed his hands.

"I stayed in shock," he said. "I couldn't remember it even after they told me. They showed me snapshots—the house, my parents, myself. It still didn't mean anything. It was as if it was somebody else, not me."

"You wouldn't even talk." Prothero wanted not to have said that. He went to the liquor cabinet and poured himself a stiff drink. "It was on television. On the radio."

"Oh," Barbara said, coming in with mugs of coffee.

"I told you, didn't I?" the Anderson boy asked her.

"He's going to be a psychologist," Prothero said.

"I should think so," Barbara said, and took one of the mugs back to the kitchen with her.

The Anderson boy clutched the other one in both hands and blew steam off it. He was in the easy chair again. "I didn't utter a sound for weeks. Then they took me to a swim school. I was afraid of the water. I screamed. They had to call a doctor with a needle to make me stop."

Prothero blurted, "You could swim. I taught you."

The Anderson boy frowned. Cautiously he tried the coffee. He sucked in air with it, making a noise. He said, "Hey, that's true. Yeah, I remember now."

Prothero felt hollow. He drank. "Just like that?"

"Really. The pool—one of those little oval-shape ones. How the sun beat down out there—it made you squint." He closed his eyes. "I can see you. What were you then—seventeen? Bright-red swim trunks, no?"

Jean had given them to him. He'd been wearing floppy Hawaiian ones. The red ones were tight and skimpy. They'd made him shy but she teased him into wearing them. He felt her trembling hands on him now, peeling them off him in that glass-walled bedroom where the sun stung speckled through the loose weave of the curtains, and her son napped across the breezeway. Prothero finished his drink.

The Anderson boy said, "And there was a big striped beach ball. Yeah." He opened his eyes. "It's really fantastic, man. I mean, I can feel myself bobbing around in that water. I can taste the chlorine. And I won't go near a pool. They scare me to death."

"Every pool has chlorine and a beach ball." Prothero poured more whiskey on ice cubes that hadn't even begun to melt. "My trunks had to be some color."

"No, I swear, I remember. And that's why I came. When I saw you on TV, it began to happen. I began to remember—the house, the desert, my parents."

"The shouts?" Prothero asked numbly. "The screams? The gunshots?"

"Not that." The Anderson boy set down his mug. "I've read enough to know I'll probably never remember that." He pushed out of the chair and went to stand at the window. The light had gone murky. Only the snow fell white. "You can help me with the rest but you can't help me with that." He turned with a wan smile. "I mean, you weren't there. Were you?"

A shiny red moped stood under the thrust of the roof above the front door. With the sunlight on the snow, it made the house look like a scene on Christmas morning. When the motor that let down the garage door stopped whining, Prothero heard the whine of a power saw from inside the house.

271

The saw was missing from its hangers on the garage wall. He went indoors and smelled sawdust.

The Anderson boy was working in the den. He wasn't wearing a shirt. Barbara was watching him from the hall doorway. She smiled at Prothero. The noise of the saw was loud and she mouthed words to him and went off, probably to the kitchen. The Anderson boy switched off the saw, laid it on the carpet, rubbed a hand along the end of the eight-inch board he'd cut, and carried it to the paneled wall where pictures had hung this morning. He leaned it there with others of its kind and turned back and saw Prothero and smiled.

"Don't you ever have classes?" Prothero asked.

"I didn't get here in time to register," the Anderson boy said. "I'm auditing a little. I'll enroll for fall." He nudged one of the stacks of books on the floor. He was barefoot. "You need more shelves."

"I work in here, you know." The pictures were piled on the desk. He lifted one and laid it down. "I have lectures to prepare, papers to read, critiques to write."

"And books?" the Anderson boy said.

"No," Prothero said, "no more books."

"It was your book that led me to you," the Anderson boy said. "I owe a lot to that book."

Prothero looked at a photo of himself on a horse.

"I won't get in your way," the Anderson boy said. "I'll only be here when you're not." He looked over Prothero's shoulder. "Hey, you took me riding once, held me in front of you on the saddle. Remember?"

Barbara called something from the kitchen.

"That's lunch," the Anderson boy said, and flapped into his shirt. "Come on. Grilled ham-and-cheese on Swedish rye." He went down the hall on his big clean bare feet. He called back over his shoulder, "Guess whose favorite that is."

* * *

In the dark, Prothero said, "I'm sorry."

"You're still exhausted from that wretched tour." Barbara kissed him tenderly, stroked his face. "It's all right, darling. Don't brood. You need rest, that's all." She slipped out of bed and in the snow-lit room there was the ghostly flutter of a white nightgown. She came to him and laid folded pajamas in his hands. They were soft and smelled of some laundry product. "Sleep and don't worry. Worry's the worst thing for it."

He sat up and got into the pajamas. Buttoning them, he stared at the vague shape of the window. He was listening for the sound of the moped. It seemed always to be arriving or departing. The bed moved as Barbara slipped into it again. He lay down beside her softness and warmth and stared up into the darkness.

She said, "It's what all the magazine articles say."

"Who paid for the shelving?" he asked.

"You did," she said. "Naturally."

He said, "It's you I'm worried about."

"I'll be all right," she said. "I'll be fine."

The sound of the moped woke him. The red numerals of the clock read 5:18. It would be the man delivering the newspaper. He went back to sleep. But when he went out in his robe and pajamas to pick up the newspaper, he walked to the garage door. The moped had sheltered there, the new one, the Anderson boy's—the marks of the tire treads were crisp in the snow. There were the tracks of boots. He followed them along the side of the house. At the corner he stopped. He was terribly cold. The tracks went out to and came back from one of the clumps of birches on the lawn. Prothero went there, snow leaking into his slippers, numbing his feet. The snow was trampled under the birches. He stood on the trampled snow and looked at the house. Up there was the bedroom window.

* * *

In the new University Medical Center, he spent three hours naked in a paper garment that kept slipping off one shoulder and did nothing to keep from him the cold of the plastic chairs on which he spent so much of the time waiting. They were the same chairs in all the shiny rooms, bright-colored, ruthlessly cheerful, hard and sterile like the walls, counters, cabinets, tables.

Needles fed from the veins in his arms. He urinated into rows of bottles. A bald man sat in front of him on a stool and handled his genitals while he gazed out the wide and staring tenth-floor window at the city under snow. The paper of his garment whispered to and mated with the paper on the examination table while his rectum was probed with indifferent ferocity. The X-ray table was high and hard, a steel catafalque. He feared the blocky baby-blue machine above it would snap the thick armatures that held it and drop it on him. The nurse need not have asked him to lie rigid. When he breathed in at her request, the sterilized air hissed at his clenched teeth. They told him there was nothing wrong with him.

"Do you remember the rattlesnake?" the Anderson boy asked. He had cut channels in the uprights and fitted the shelves into them. The workmanship was neat. Horizontals and verticals were perfect. He was staining the shelves dark walnut to match the others already in the den. The stain had a peculiar smell. Prothero thought it was hateful. The big blond boy squatted to tilt up the can of stain and soak the rag he was using. "We were always out there taking hikes, weren't we? And one day there was this little fat snake."

"Sidewinder," Prothero said. "I thought you weren't going to be here when I was here."

"Sorry," the Anderson boy said. "I loused up the timing on this. Can't stop it in the middle. I'll be as fast about it as

I can." He stood up and made the white of the raw fir plank vanish in darkness. "If you want to work, let me finish this half and I'll clear out."

"I was trying to teach you the names of the wildflowers. It would have been February. That's when they come out. Sidewinders don't grow big."

"It's a rattlesnake, though. Poisonous. I mean, you let me handle a nonpoisonous snake once. I can still feel how dry it was. Yellow and brown."

"Boyle's king snake." Prothero took off his coat.

"You remember what you did?" the Anderson boy said.

"About the sidewinder?" Prothero poured a drink.

"Caught it. Pinned it down with a forked stick back of its head. It was mad. It thrashed around. I can shut my eyes and see that. Like a film."

"I didn't want it sliding around with you out there. You could stumble on it again. If I'd been alone or with grownups I'd have just waited for it to go away."

The Anderson boy knelt again to soak the rag. "You had me empty your knapsack. You got it behind the head with your fist and dropped it in the sack. We took it to the little desert museum in town."

"There was nothing else to do," Prothero said.

"You could have killed it," the Anderson boy said.

"I can't kill anything," Prothero said.

"That's no longer accepted," the Anderson boy said. "Anybody can kill. We know that now. It just depends on the circumstances."

Kessler was on the university faculty, but he had a private practice. His office, in a new one-story medical center built around an atrium, smelled of leather. It was paneled in dark woods. A Monet hung on one wall. Outside a window of diamond-shaped panes, pine branches held snow. From beyond a broad, glossy desk, Kessler studied Prothero with large, pained eyes in the face of a starved child.

"Has it ever happened to you before? I don't mean isolated instances—every man has those—I mean for prolonged periods, months, years."

"From the summer I turned eighteen until nearly the end of my senior year in college."

Kessler's eyebrows moved. "Those are normally the years of permanent erection. What happened?"

"I was having a crazy affair with, well, an older woman. In my home town. Older? What am I saying? She was probably about the age I am now."

"Married?" Kessler asked.

"Her husband traveled all the time."

"Except that once, when you thought he was traveling, he wasn't—right?"

"He caught us," Prothero said. "In bed together."

"Did you have a lot of girls before her?"

"None. Sexually, you mean? None."

There were *netsuke* on the desk, little ivory carvings of deer, monkeys, dwarfish humans. Prothero thought that if it were his desk he'd be fingering them while he listened, while he talked. Kessler sat still. He said:

"Then she did the seducing, right?"

"We were on a charity fund-raising committee." Prothero made a face. "I mean, I was a token member, the high school's fair-haired boy. The rest were adults. She kept arranging for her and me to work together."

"And after her husband caught you, you were impotent?"

"For a long while I didn't know it. I didn't care. I didn't want to think about sex." He smiled thinly. "To put it in today's parlance—I was turned off."

"Did the man beat you? Did he beat her?"

Prothero asked, "Why has it started again?"

"It's never happened in your married life?"

276

Prothero shook his head.

"How did you come to marry your wife? Let me guess—she was the seducer, right?"

"That's quite a word," Prothero said.

"Never mind the word," Kessler said. "You know what I mean. The aggressor, sexually. She took the initiative, she made the advances." His smile reminded Prothero of the high suicide rate among psychiatrists. Kessler said, "What do you want from me?"

"Yes," Prothero said. "She was the seducer."

"Has she lost interest in you sexually?"

"There's nothing to be interested in," Prothero said.

"Do you get letters from the woman?"

"What woman? Oh. No. No, she's—she's dead."

"On this book promotion tour of yours," Kessler said, "did you see the man somewhere?"

Prothero said, "I wonder if I could have a drink."

"Certainly." Kessler opened a cabinet under the Monet. Bottles glinted. He poured fingers of whiskey into squat glasses and handed one to Prothero. "Been drinking more than usual over this?"

Prothero nodded and swallowed the whiskey. It was expensive and strong. He thought that in a minute it would make him stop trembling. "They had a child," he said, "a little boy. I liked him. We spent a lot of time together. Lately, he saw me on television. And now he's here."

Kessler didn't drink. He held his glass. "What's your sexual drive like?" he asked. "How often do you and your wife have sexual relations?"

"Four times a week, five." Prothero stood up, looking at the cabinet. "Did."

"Help yourself," Kessler said. "How old is he?"

The trembling hadn't stopped. The bottle neck rattled on the glass. "Eighteen, I suppose. With his father away most of the time, he took to me."

"Does he look like his father?"

"It's not just that." Prothero drank. "He keeps hanging around. He's always at the house." He told Kessler about the footbridge, about the bookshelves. "But there's more. Now he comes at night on that damn motor bike and stands in the dark, staring up at our bedroom. While we're asleep."

"Maybe he's homosexual," Kessler said.

"No." Prothero poured whiskey into his glass again.

"How can you be sure?" Kessler gently took the bottle from him, capped it, set it back in place, and closed the cabinet. "It fits a common pattern."

"He's too easy with women—Barbara, anyway, my wife." Prothero stared gloomily into his whiskey. "Like it was her he'd known forever. They've even developed private jokes."

"Why not just tell him to go away?" Kessler asked.

"How can I?" Prothero swallowed the third drink. "What excuse can I give? I mean, he keeps doing me these kindnesses." Kessler didn't answer. He waited. Prothero felt his face grow hot. "Well, hell, I told him to keep out from under my feet. So what happens? He's there all the time I'm not. He's got changes of clothes in my closet. His shaving stuff is there. My bathroom stinks of his deodorant."

Kessler said, "Are they sleeping together?"

"Barbara and that child?"

"Why so appalled?" Kessler said mildly. "Weren't you a child when you slept with his mother?"

Prothero stood up.

"Don't go away mad," Kessler said. "You're going to get a bill for this visit, so you may as well listen to me. You're afraid of this boy. Now, why? Because he looks like his father—right? So what happened in that bedroom?"

"That was a long time ago," Prothero read his watch.

"Not so long ago it can't still make you impotent," Kessler said. "Thirty years old, perfect health, better than average sexual drive. It wasn't a beating, was it? It was something worse.''

"It was embarrassing," Prothero said. "It was comic. Isn't that what those scenes always are? Funny?"

"You tell me," Kessler said.

Prothero set down the glass. "I have to go," he said.

When he stepped into the courtyard with its big Japanese pine, the Anderson boy was walking ahead of him out to the street. Prothero ran after him, caught his shoulder, turned him. "What are you doing here? Following me?"

The boy blinked, started to smile, then didn't. "I dropped a paper off on Dr. Lawrence. I've been sitting in on his lectures. He said he'd like to read what I've written about my case—the memory loss."

Prothero drew breath. "Do you want a cup of coffee?"

"Why would you think I was following you?" The Anderson boy frowned at the hollow square of offices, the doors lettered with the names of specialists. "Are you feeling okay?"

"Nothing serious." Prothero smiled and clapped the boy's shoulder. "Come on. Coffee will warm us up."

"I have to get home. My grandparents will be phoning from California." He eyed the icy street. "I sure do miss that sunshine." His red moped was at the curb. He straddled it. Prothero couldn't seem to move. The boy called, "The shelves are finished. I'm going to lay down insulation in your attic next." He began to move off, rowing with his feet in clumsy boots. "You're losing expensive heat, wasting energy." The moped sputtered. If Prothero had been able to answer, he wouldn't have been heard. The Anderson boy lifted a goodbye hand, and the little machine wobbled off with him.

* * *

Prothero ran to his car and followed. The boy drove to the edge of town away from the campus and turned in at an old motel, blue paint flaking off white stucco. Prothero circled the block and drove into an abandoned filling station opposite. The boy was awkwardly pushing the moped into a unit of the motel. The door closed. On it was the number nine. Prothero checked his watch and waited. It grew cold in the car, but it was past noon. The boy liked his meals. He would come out in search of food. He did. He drove off on the moped.

The woman behind the motel office counter was heavy-breasted, middle-aged, wore rimless glasses, and reminded Prothero of his own mother. He showed the woman his university I.D. and said that an emergency had arisen: he needed to get from Wayne Anderson's room telephone numbers for his family on the West Coast. The woman got a key and moved to come with him. But a gray, rumple-faced man in a gray, rumpled suit arrived, wanting a room, and she put into Prothero's hand the key to unit nine.

It needed new wallpaper, carpet, and curtains, but the boy kept it neat. Except for the desk. The desk was strewn with notebook pages, scrawled with loose handwriting in ball-point pen, with typewritten pages, with Xerox copies of newspaper clippings.

Dry-mouthed, he went through the clippings. They all reported the shootings and the aftermath of the shootings. The Anderson boy's mother had lain naked in the bed. The man had lain clothed on the floor beside the bed, gun in his hand. Both shot dead. The child had wandered dazedly in and out of the desert house in sleepers, clutching a stuffed toy kangaroo and unable to speak. Prothero shivered and pushed the clippings into a manila envelope on which the boy had printed CLIPPINGS. He picked up the notebook pages and tried to read. It wasn't clear to him what the boy had tried to do here. Events were broken down under headings with numbers and letters. It looked intricate and mad.

Prothero tried the typewritten pages. Neater, easier to read, they still seemed to go over and over the same obsessive points. No page was complete. These must be drafts of the pages the boy had taken to Dr. Lawrence. A red plastic wastebasket overflowed with crumpled pages. He took some of these out, flattened them, tried to read them, looking again and again at his watch. For an instant, the room darkened. He looked in alarm at the window. The woman from the motel office passed. Not the boy. Prothero would hear the moped. Anyway, he had plenty of time. But the crumpled pages told him nothing. He pushed them back into the wastebasket. Then he noticed the page sticking out of the typewriter. It read:

Don Prothero seems to have been a good friend to me, even though he was much older. My interviews with him have revealed that we spent much time together. He taught me to swim, though I afterward forgot how. He took me on nature walks in the desert, which I also had forgotten until meeting him again. He bought me gifts. The shock of my parents' death made me forget what I witnessed that night—if I witnessed anything. But why didn't Don come to see me or try to help me when he learned what had happened? He admits he didn't. And this isn't consistent with his previous behavior. My grandmother says he didn't attend the funeral. A friendship between a small boy and a teenage boy is uncommon. Perhaps there never was such a friendship. Maybe it wasn't me Don came to see at all. Maybe he came—

Prothero turned the typewriter platen, but the rest of the page was blank. He laid the key with a clatter on the motel office counter, muttered thanks to the woman, and fled. His hands shook and were slippery with sweat as he drove. He had a lecture at two. How he would manage to deliver it, he didn't know, but he drove to the campus. Habit got him there. Habit would get him through the lecture.

* * *

Barbara's car was in the garage. He parked beside it, closed the garage, went into the den, poured a drink, and called her name. He wondered at the stillness of the house. Snow began to fall outside. "Barbara?" He searched for her downstairs. Nowhere. She was never away at this hour. She would have left a note. In the kitchen. Why, when she was gone, did the kitchen always seem the emptiest of rooms? He peered at the cross-stitched flowers of the bulletin board by the kitchen door. There was no note. He frowned. He used the yellow kitchen wall-phone. Cora answered, sounding perky.

He said, "Are you all right? Is Barbara there?"

"I'm fine. No—did she say she was coming here?"

"I thought there might have been an emergency."

"No emergency, Don. Every day, in every way, I'm—"

"I wonder where the hell she is," he said and hung up. Of course she wouldn't have been at her mother's. Her car was still here, and Cora wouldn't have picked her up—Cora no longer drove.

Had Barbara been taken ill herself? He ran up the stairs. She wasn't in the bathroom. She wasn't in the bedroom. What was in the bedroom was a toy kangaroo. The bedclothes were neatly folded back and the toy kangaroo sat propped against a pillow, looking at him with empty glass eyes. Its gray cloth was soiled and faded, its stitching had come loose, one of the eyes hung by a thread. But it was the same one. He would know it anywhere. As he had known the boy.

He set the drink on the dresser and rolled open the closet. It echoed hollowly. Her clothes were gone. A set of matched luggage she had bought for their trip to Europe two years ago had stood on the shelf above. It didn't stand there now. Involuntarily, he sat on the bed. "But it wasn't my fault," he said. He fumbled with the bedside phone, whimpering, "It wasn't my fault, it wasn't my fault." From directory assistance he got the number of the motel. He had to dial twice before he got it right.

The motherly woman said, "He checked out. When I told him you'd been here, going through his papers, he packed up, paid his bill, asked where the nearest place was he could rent a car, and cleared right off."

"Car?" Prothero felt stupid. "What about his moped?"

"He asked me to hold it. He'll arrange for a college friend to sell it for him—some boy. Goldberg?"

"Where's the nearest place to rent a car?"

"Econo. On Locust Street. It's only two blocks."

The directory-assistance operator didn't answer this time. Prothero ran down to the den. He used the phone book. The snow fell thicker outside the glass doors. He longed for it to cover the footbridge. Econo Car Rentals was slow in answering, too. And when at last a dim female voice came on, he could not get it to tell him what he wanted to know.

"This is the college calling, don't you understand? He wasn't supposed to leave. His family is going to be very upset. There's been a little confusion, that's all. He can't be allowed to go off this way. Now, please—"

A man spoke. "What's this about Wayne Anderson?"

"He's just a student," Prothero said. "Do you realize he'll take that car clear out to California?"

"That information goes on the form. Routinely," the man said. "Are you a relative of this Wayne Anderson?"

"Ah," Prothero said, "you did rent him a car, then?"

"I never said that. I can't give out that kind of information. On the phone? What kind of company policy would that be?"

"If this turns out to be a kidnapping," Prothero said recklessly, "your company policy is going to get you into a lot of trouble. Now—what kind of car was it? What's the license number?"

"If it's a kidnapping," the man said, "the people to call are the police." His mouth left the phone. In an echoing room, he said to somebody. "It's some stupid college-kid joker. Hang it up." And the phone hummed in Prothero's hand.

He was backing the car down the driveway when Helen Moore's new blue Subaru hatchback pulled into the driveway next door. He stopped and honked. She stopped, too. The door of her garage opened. She didn't drive in. She got out of the car, wearing boots and a Russian fur hat. Before she closed the door behind her, Prothero glimpsed supermarket sacks on the seat. With a gloved hand, she held the dark fur collar of her coat closed at the throat. The door of her garage closed again. She came toward the snow-covered hedge. Snowflakes were on her lashes. "Something wrong?"

"I'm missing one wife. Any suggestions?"

"Are you serious?" She tilted her head, worry lines between her brows. "You are, Don, dear—she left for the airport." Helen struggled to read her wristwatch, muffled in a fur coat cuff, the fur lining of a glove. "Oh, when? An hour ago? You mean you didn't know? What have we here? Scandal in academe?"

Prothero felt his face redden. "No, no, of course not. I forgot, that's all. Wayne Anderson came for her, right?"

"Yes. Brought her luggage out, put it in the trunk. Nice boy, that."

Prothero felt sick. "Did you talk with Barbara?"

"She looked preoccupied. She was already in the car." She winced upward. "Can they really fly in this weather?"

"There'll be a delay," Prothero said. "So maybe I can catch them. She's taking this trip for me. There are things I forgot to tell her. Did you notice the car?"

"Japanese. Like mine. Darling, I'm freezing." She hurried back to the Subaru and opened the door. "Only not blue, of course—I've got an exclusive on blue.'' Her voice came back to him, cheerful as a child's at play in the falling snow. ''White. White as a bridal gown.'' She got into the car and slammed the door. Her garage yawned again, and she drove inside.

Defroster and windshield wipers were no match for the snow. The snowplows hadn't got out here yet. He hadn't put on chains, and the car kept slurring. So did others. Not many. Few drivers had been foolhardy enough to venture out of town. Those who had must have had life-or-death reasons. But life and death were no match for the snow, either. Their cars rested at angles in ditches, nosed in, backed in. The snow was so dense in its falling that it made blurs of the drivers' bundled shapes. They moved about their stranded machines like discoverers from some future ice age come upon the wreckage of our own.

A giant eighteen-wheeler loomed through the whiteness. Prothero was on the wrong side of the road. He hadn't realized this. The truck came directly at him. He twisted the wheel, slammed down on the brake pedal. The car spun out of control—but also out of the path of the truck. He ended up, joltingly, against the trunk of a winter-stripped tree. He tried for a while to make the car back up, but the wheels only spun.

He turned off the engine and leaned on the horn. Its sound was frail in the falling snow. He doubted anyone would hear it up on the empty road. And if the crews didn't find him before dark they would stop searching. By morning, when they came out again, he might be frozen to death. There was a heater in the car, but it wouldn't run forever. He left the car, waded up to the road. He saw nothing—not the road itself, now, let alone a car, a human being. He shouted, but the thickly falling snow seemed to swallow up the sound. It was too far to try to walk back to town. Too cold. No visibility. He returned to the car. If he froze to death, did he care?

They found him before dark and delivered him, though not his car, back home. For a long time he sat dumbly in the den, staring at his reflection in the glass doors. Night fell. The doors became black mirrors. He switched on the desk lamp, reached for the telephone, drew his hand back. He couldn't call the police. Not now, any more than on that desert night twelve years ago. He got up and poured himself a drink. And remembered Goldberg. He got Goldberg's telephone number from Admissions, rang it, left a message. He sat drinking, waiting for Goldberg to call. *Barbara*, he kept thinking, *Barbara*.

He heard the Anderson boy's moped. He had been asleep and the sound confused him. He got up stiffly and stumbled to the front door. The snow had stopped falling. The crystalline look of the night made him think it must be late. He read his watch. Eleven. He'd slept, all right. Even the snowplow passing hadn't wakened him. The street, in its spaced circles of lamplight, was cleared. He switched on the front door lamp. Goldberg came wading up the walk in a bulky windbreaker with a fake-fur hood, his round, steel-rimmed glasses frosted over. He took them off when he stepped into the house. He had a round, innocent, freckled face. Prothero shut the door.

"Why didn't you phone?" he said.

The boy cast him a wretched purblind look and shook his head. "I couldn't tell you like that."

"Where is Anderson? Where did he tell you to send the money when you sold his moped?"

"Home. San Diego," Goldberg said. "Is that whiskey? Could I have some, please? I'm frozen stiff."

"Here." Prothero thrust out the glass. Goldberg pulled off a tattered driving glove and took the glass. His teeth chattered on the rim. Prothero said, "What was his reason for leaving? Did he tell you?"

Miserably, Goldberg nodded. He gulped the whiskey, shut his eyes, shuddered. "Oh, God," he said softly, and rubbed the fragile-looking spectacles awkwardly on a jacket sleeve, and hooked them in place. He looked at the door, the floor, the staircase—everywhere but at Prothero. Then he gulped the rest of the whiskey and blurted, "He ran off with your wife. Didn't he? I laughed when he said it, but it's true, isn't it? That's why you phoned me."

Prothero said, "My wife is in Mankato. Celebrating the birthday of an ancient aunt. I called you because I'm worried about Anderson."

"Oh, wow. What a relief." Goldberg's face cleared of its worry and guilt. "I knew he was a flake. I mean—I'm sorry, sir, but I mean, a little weird, right? I was a wimp to believe him. Forgive me?"

"Anything's possible," Prothero said.

"He really sold me." Goldberg set the empty whiskey glass on one of a pair of little gilt Venetian chairs beside the door. "See, I said if he did it I'd have to tell you. And he said I didn't need to bother—you'd already know." Goldberg pushed the freckled fat hand into its glove again. His child's face pursed in puzzlement. "That was kinky enough, but then he said something really spacey, okay? He said you wouldn't do anything about it. You wouldn't dare. What did he mean by that?"

"Some complicated private fantasy. Don't worry about it." Prothero opened the door, laid a hand on the boy's shoulder. "As you say, he's a little weird. Disturbed. And my wife's been kind to him."

"Right. He had a traumatic childhood. His parents were murdered. He told you, right?" Goldberg stepped out onto the snowy doorstep. "He said he liked coming here." Halfway down the path, Goldberg turned back. "You know, I read your book. It helped me. I mean, this is a killer world. Sometimes you don't think there's any future for it. Your book made me feel better." And he trudged bulkily away through the snow toward the moped that twinkled dimly in the lamplight at the curb.

Prothero shut the door and the telephone rang. He ran for the den, snatched up the receiver, shouted hello. For a moment, the sounds from the other end of the wire made no sense. Had some drunk at a party dialed a wrong number? No. He recognized Barbara's voice.

"Don't come!" she shouted. "Don't come, Don!"

And the Anderson boy's voice. "Apple Creek," he said. "You know where that is? The Restwell Motel." Prothero knew where Apple Creek was. West and south, maybe a hundred miles—surely no more. Why had he stopped there? The snow? But the roads would have been cleared by now. "We'll expect you in two hours."

"Let her go, Wayne. She had nothing to do with it."

She didn't sound all right. In the background, she was screaming. Most of her words got lost. But some Prothero was able to make out. "He's got a gun! Don't come, Don! He'll kill you if you come!"

"I'll be there, Wayne," Prothero said. "We'll talk. You've got it wrong. I'll explain everything. Don't hurt Barbara. She was always good to you."

"Not the way my mother was good to you."

Prothero felt cold. "You keep your hands off her."

"We're going to bed now, Don," the Anderson boy said. "But it's all right. You just knock when you get here. Room eighteen. We won't be sleeping."

"Don't do this!" Prothero shouted. "It was an accident, Wayne—I didn't kill them! I was only a kid!"

But the Anderson boy had hung up.

* * *

288

The keys to Barbara's car ordinarily hung from a cup hook on the underside of a kitchen cupboard, but they weren't there now. He ran upstairs. He was the professor, but she was the absentminded one in the family. She sometimes locked the keys inside her car—so she kept an extra set of keys. He fumbled through drawers with shaking hands, tossing flimsy garments out onto the floor in his panic.

He found the keys, started out of the bedroom, and saw the tattered toy kangaroo staring at him from the bed with its lopsided glass eyes that had seen everything. He snatched it up and flung it into a corner. He ran to it and drew back his foot to kick it. Instead, he dropped to his knees, picked it up, and hugged it hard against his chest and began to cry, inconsolably. *Dear God, dear God!*

Blind with tears, he stumbled from the room, down the stairs, blundered into his warm coat, burst into the garage. When he backed down the drive, the car hard to control in the snow, twice wheeling stupidly backward into the hedge, the kangaroo lay facedown on the seat beside him.

He passed the town square where the old courthouse loomed up dark beyond its tall, reaching, leafless trees, the cannon on the snow-covered lawn hunching like some shadow beast in a child's nightmare. No—the building wasn't entirely dark. Lights shone beyond windows at a corner where narrow stone steps went up to glass-paned doors gold-lettered POLICE. He halted the car at the night-empty intersection and stared long at those doors—as he had sat in his car, staring at the sunny desert police station on that long-ago morning. *I was only a kid!* He gave a shudder, wiped his nose on his sleeve, and drove on.

The little towns were out there in the frozen night that curved over the snowy miles and miles of sleeping prairie, curved like a black ice dome in which the stars were frozen. Only the neon embroidery on their margins showed that the towns were there. At their hearts they were darkly asleep, except for here and there a streetlight, now and then a traffic signal winking orange. He had never felt so lonely in his life. He drove fast. The reflector signs bearing the names of the little lost towns went past in flickers too brief to read.

But there was no mistaking Apple Creek, no mistaking that this was the place he had headed for in the icy night, the end of his errand, the end of Don Prothero, the end so long postponed. The Restwell Motel stretched along the side of the highway behind a neat white rail fence and snow-covered shrubs, the eaves of its snow-heaped roof outlined in red neon tubing.

And on its blacktop drive, not parked neatly on the bias in the painted slots provided by the management but jammed in at random angles, stood cars with official seals on their doors and amber lights that winked and swiveled on their rooftops. Uniformed men in bulky leather coats, crash helmets, stetsons, and boots stood around, guns on their thighs in holsters, rifles in their gloved hands.

Prothero left his car and ran toward the men. The one he chose to speak to had a paunch. His face was red under a ten-gallon hat. He was holding brown sheepskin gauntlets over his ears. He lowered them when he saw Prothero, but his expression was not welcoming.

Prothero asked, "What's happening here?"

"You want a room? Ask in the office." The officer pointed at a far-off door, red neon spelling out OFFICE. But at that instant a clutch of officers on the far side of the bunched cars moved apart and Prothero saw another door, the door they all seemed interested in. Without needing to, he read the numbers on the door. 18.

"My wife's in there!" he said.

The heavy man had turned away, hands to his cold ears again. But the brown wool hadn't deafened him. He turned back, saying, "What!" It was not a question.

"Barbara Prothero." He dug out his wallet to show identification cards. "I'm Donald Prothero."

"Hasenbein!" It was a name. The bulky man shouted it. "Hasenbein!" And Hasenbein separated himself from the other officers. He was at least twenty years younger than the bulky man. "This here's Lieutenant Hasenbein. You better tell him. He's in charge."

Hasenbein, blue-eyed, rosy-cheeked, looked too young to be in charge of anything. Prothero told him what seemed safe to tell. "He became a friend. He's disturbed."

"You better believe it," Hasenbein said. He dug from a jacket pocket a small black-and-white tube, uncapped it, rubbed it on his mouth like lipstick. "See that broken window?" He capped the tube and pushed it back into the pocket. "He fired a gun through that window." Hasenbein studied him. "Why did he stop here? Why did he telephone you? What does he want? Money?"

"There's something wrong with his mind," Prothero said. "He's got it into his head that I harmed him. He's trying to avenge himself. He phoned to tell me to come here. No, he doesn't want money. I don't know what he wants. To kill me, I guess. What brought you here?"

"The manager. He came out to turn off the signs. The switch box is down at this end. And he heard this woman screaming in unit eighteen—your wife, right? He banged on the window and told them to quiet down or he'd call the sheriff. And the kid shot at him. Luckily, he missed."

Prothero's knees gave. Hasenbein steadied him. "Is my wife all right?"

"There was only the one shot."

"There are so many of you," Prothero said. "Can't you go in there and get her out?" He waved his arms. "What's the good of standing around like this?"

"It's a question of nobody getting hurt needlessly."

"Needlessly! He could be doing anything in there—he

could be doing anything to her!'' Hasenbein didn't respond. He was too young. He was in way over his head.

Prothero ran forward between the cars. ''Barbara!'' he shouted. ''Barbara? It's Don. I'm here! Wayne? Wayne!'' Two officers jumped him, held his arms. He struggled, shouting at the broken window, ''Let her go, now! I'll come in and we'll talk—I said I'd come, and I came!''

No light showed beyond the broken window, but in the eerie, darting beams of the amber lights atop the patrol cars Prothero saw for a moment what he took to be a face peering out. The Anderson boy said, ''Tell them to let you go.'' Prothero looked at the officers holding him. They didn't loosen their grip on his arms. Hasenbein appeared. He twitched the corners of his boyish mouth in what was meant for a reassuring smile and turned away.

''Anderson?'' he shouted, ''we can't do that! We can't let him come in there—we can't take a chance on what will happen to him! Why don't you calm down now, and just toss that gun out here and come out the door nice and quiet with your hands in the air? We're not going to hurt you—that's a promise! It's a cold night, Anderson, let's get this over with!''

''Where's Barbara?'' Prothero shouted. ''What have you done with her? If you've hurt her, I'll kill you!''

''Sure!'' the Anderson boy shouted. Now his face was plain to see at the window. Prothero wondered why nobody shot him. ''You killed my father and my mother, why not me? Why not finish off the whole family? Why didn't you kill *me* that night? Then there wouldn't have been any witnesses!''

''I didn't kill them!'' Prothero gave his body a sudden twist. It surprised the men holding him. It surprised him, too. He fell forward. The cold blacktop stung his hands. He scrambled to his feet and lunged at the broken window. He put his hands on the window frame and leaned into the dark room.

"Your father came in from the breezeway—he was supposed to be out of town." Prothero heard his own voice as if it were someone else's voice. He had cut his hands on the splinters of glass in the window frame and could feel the warm blood. "He had a gun, and he stood there in the doorway and shot at us." Prothero wondered why the boy didn't shoot him now. He wondered what had happened to the officers. But the words kept coming.

"It was dark, but he knew where to shoot. I heard the bullet hit her. I've heard it in my nightmares for years. I rolled off the bed. He came at me, and I kicked him. He bent over and I tried to get past him, but he grabbed me. I fought to get away and the gun went off. You hear me, Wayne? He had the gun—not me. He shot himself! His blood got all over me, but I didn't kill him, I didn't kill him, I—"

"All right, sir." Hasenbein spoke almost tenderly. He took Prothero gently and turned him. He frowned at Prothero's hands and swung toward the officers standing by the cars, the vapor of their breath gold in the flickering lights. "We need a first-aid kit here." Hasenbein bent slightly toward the window. 'Okay, Thomas—you can bring him out now."

"My wife," Prothero said. "Where's my wife?"

"Down at the substation where it's warm," Hasenbein said. "She's all right."

A frail-looking officer with a mustache brought a white metal box with a red cross pasted to it. He knelt on the drive and opened the box.

Carefully, he took Prothero's bleeding hands. Prothero scarcely noticed. He stared at the door of unit 18. It opened and a police officer stepped out, followed by the Anderson boy in his shapeless army fatigues and combat boots. He was handcuffed. Under his arm, a worn manila envelope trailed untidy strips of Xeroxed newspaper clippings. He looked peacefully at Prothero.

"What did you do to Barbara?" Prothero said.

"Nothing. You put her through this—not me. You could have told me any time." With his big, clean, carpenter's hands made awkward by the manacles, he gestured at the officers and cars. "Look at all the trouble you caused."

About the Editors

MARTIN GREENBERG has compiled over two hundred anthologies, including nine in Fawcett's Best of the West series. He is a noted scholar and teaches at the University of Wisconsin in Green Bay.

BILL PRONZINI, in addition to collaborating with Martin Greenberg on several anthologies, is an award-winning mystery writer, the author of many novels and short stories. He lives in Sonoma, California.